CW00833280

The Witch and the Devourer of Souls

ISBN: 978-1-947578-48-7

Ink Smith Publishing
P.O. Box 361
Lakehurst, NJ 08733

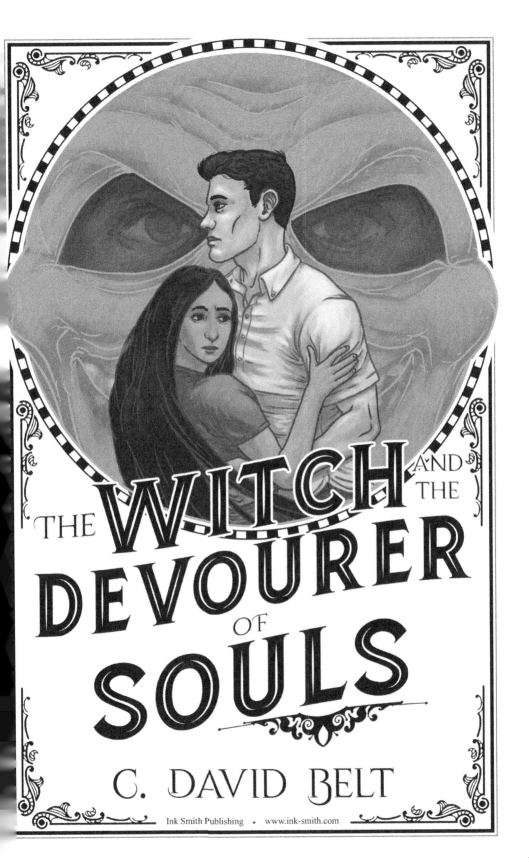

THE WITCH AND THE DEVOURER OF SOULS

C. DAVID BELT

Ink Smith Publishing • www.ink-smith.com

For Cindy,
who still has the Power to bewitch me.

For Bram Stoker,
who started me down this path at the tender age of nine.

I sometimes think we must be all mad and that we shall wake to sanity in strait-waistcoats.

Bram Stoker
Dracula

I must not fear. Fear is the mind-killer. Fear is the little-death that brings total obliteration.

Frank Herbert
Dune

Things need not have happened to be true. Tales and dreams are the shadow-truths that will endure when mere facts are dust and ashes, and forgot.

Neil Gaiman
Dream Country

Author Note

I have a confession to make. A huge confession. Let me work up my courage, take a few deep breaths, calm my trembling hands.

Okay.

<long-loud-sigh>

Here goes…

I *love* Jane Austen's "Pride and Prejudice."

There. I said it. Now all the world knows (or at least those few who actually *read* this Author's Note).

Okay, now before you take away my man-card, hear me out.

I enjoy a good, well-written horror tale, but I also enjoy a good love story. And as anyone who is familiar with my work can attest, I firmly and enthusiastically believe the two need not be mutually exclusive.

While I *do* love "Pride and Prejudice," it ends (in my not-so-humble-opinion, and with a small—very small—apology to Miss Austen) far too early in the story. I want a sequel! And not from a modern writer—I want to know from Miss Jane herself. I want to know how the Darcy's kept their romance alive! I want to know how they survived the horrors and vicissitudes of the Napoleonic Wars!

Romance doesn't end with the first kiss or even at the altar.

At least it shouldn't.

In the early 1980's, shortly after Cindy and I had completed our separate church missions (hers in Spain and mine in South Korea and Los Angeles, Korean-speaking) and early in our married life together, while I was finishing my degree at Brigham Young University (where I took exactly *zero* English and/or creative writing classes—which may be painfully obvious), I discovered a TV show called *Hart to Hart*. This little gem related the adventures of a married couple who solved mysteries together. What drew me to the show was the chemistry between the husband and wife. The two characters obviously loved each other and were devoted to each other. There was no "romantic tension." There was just romance. (All the tension came from outside—from the villains and the adventure—it was never about "will they or won't they.")

And it was exciting! And it never got old. At least not to me.

In *The Witch of White Lady Hollow*, when last we met the intrepid and courageous (and short) Tabitha Moonshadow, she had just met Josh Kilmore. And although we *knew* the two of them would or *should* end up together, that didn't happen in that first book—we merely had the *potential* for love and romance. All we had was a handshake (literally) and a spark. And a mutual penchant for watching old, scary movies.

In writing the sequel, I *could* have picked up the story right there and have related all the details of the courtship and the wedding—not too many details about the wedding, since it takes place in a temple, but I digress—but I didn't tell that part of the tale. I *skipped* all that. (Oh, the horror! <sounds-of-fanning-myself> I think I may faint. Quick! The smelling salts!) No, I jumped ahead in their lives—to when they were starving married students with a baby at BYU. I mean, so many of us can relate to similar scenarios, right? It wasn't that the courtship and the wedding weren't important—they absolutely were. Courtship is exciting and it's new, and the wedding is (or should be) glorious and beautiful and sacred. But courtship must not end at marriage. Courtship is a grand, life-long adventure.

But sometimes, the grand adventure is mired in the mundane and in the everyday problems of life. Tabitha and Josh have classes, homework, low-paying jobs, a barely running, high-mileage car, bills, nearly empty cupboards, dishes to wash, floors to sweep, laundry to do, and a baby to feed and clean and nurture. ("Whatever you do, don't you dare wake the baby!") Romance can get lost in all of that. All too frequently, it does.

So, I wanted to tell a story about two people who have to deal with all of that crap (literally—remember, there are dirty diapers to change) and somehow still find time for romance and love and rejoicing in what brought them together in the first place. In short, I wanted to tell a story of passionate, tender, married romance… with the Power and a supernatural serial-killer thrown into the mix.

I mean, we can all relate to that, right?

C. David Belt

Provo, Utah: 1982

The scent of prey filled his nostrils—sweet, delicious, and intoxicating. She was close. So very close. The crisp night air carried her essence to him, pulling at him, tugging at him. Inviting him.

He closed his eyes, just for a moment—mustn't lose sight of the prey—not that he'd been able to get a real look at her, but he needed to commit her unique fragrance to memory. *Each of them has their own woman-scent*, he thought. And he could still smell her fear as if the darkness frightened her.

Good.

Sweet, delicious fear.

He opened his eyes. She was still there, a dozen yards ahead, walking hand-in-hand with a man who stood at least a head taller.

But the man's presence didn't bother him. Prey almost always had an escort, a protector. And it was not as if he intended to take her at that very moment.

Oh, no. Not now. Fix her in my mind. For later. Not tonight.

After all, he still had a sumptuous meal waiting for him. In the Pit. *Finish her first before moving on to the ultimate feast.*

He closed his eyes once more, drawing in her scent. But try as he might, he couldn't quite affix her in his mind. It was as if her essence was so strong; her fear so all-consuming, that it overwhelmed his superhuman senses.

His breathing and pulse quickened, palms damp with sweat. *I could feast on her for weeks. Months! I might never have to feed again.*

The pair of them—the prey and the man—turned and vanished around the corner of the building.

He didn't panic, though. They're just heading to the parking lot.

She's not escaping. She's not.

Can't let this one escape. No, not this one. Not this prize.

11

He hastened his step, still following her delightful scent. But it was not her scent alone that drew him in—he could feel her. Feel her like no other before. The blood pounded in his ears.

Just need to get the license plate. He could find her through that, as he had some of the others. *Just get the license plate,* he urged himself.

He shuddered in a near paroxysm of ecstatic anticipation. *But I will have her. Claim her as mine. My Prize. God's gift to me and me alone. Consume her—*

But suddenly, she was gone.

"No!" he said under his breath. *Not now!*

In a panic, legs trembling, he rounded the corner. The parking lot was still quite full, a few cars making their way toward the exit. He stared at each moving car briefly, but intently. But the prey was not in any of the departing vehicles.

Where is she? Where did she go?

He spun around in circles, desperately trying to find her. But she was nowhere. He couldn't smell her. He couldn't feel her.

He ignored the other women in the parking lot. On any other night, half of them might have made suitable targets, but after he had been so close to her, the rest seemed inadequate.

Where is she? She didn't just fly away.

With a bestial snarl, he wheeled and stomped away, toward his own car, parked back on the street.

Go straight to the Pit. Consume the one I've already got.

He'd been planning to make that one last a day or two more. But not anymore, his rage was burning inside him and only a full meal would even begin to sate him.

Reaching his own car, he jammed the keys into the ignition and started the engine. His fingers curled around the steering wheel, knuckles turning white as he drove off. He screeched around the next corner and pounded his fist against the steering wheel, roaring with rage.

It's as if she just flew away!

Tabitha Moonshadow Kilmore clung tightly to her husband as the two of them flew through the night sky, high above the lights of Provo, Utah. Tabitha reveled in the sheer ecstasy of the Power flowing from her and into Josh.

She imagined a hypothetical observer on the ground catching the two of them silhouetted against the ghostly full moon—an observer possessing high-powered binoculars, gazing in wonder at what appeared to be a couple slowly dancing in the air. The man was tall in comparison to the woman—perhaps a head taller—and her feet dangled much higher than his. The woman wore a long skirt—as she always did—and her waist-length, coal-black hair billowed on the light breeze. Their hands—his left and her right—were clasped together. Her left arm reached around his neck. His right arm encircled her waist, holding her close, pressing her body against his.

Nobody's watching, she thought. *And if they are, I really don't care.* She tilted her head back and gazed at her husband. She gave him a smile.

Josh bent his head and kissed her, and the tingle of the Power made Tabitha quiver as it coursed from her lips to his. He smiled at her. "Better?"

She nodded and laid her head on his shoulder. "Much better."

"Do you want me to turn you around, so you can see?"

Tabitha considered his suggestion for a moment, and then shook her head. "No. This is what I needed." She tightened her arm about his neck, snuggling closer. "This."

He sighed and lifted a hand to stroke her hair. "Me too."

"I'm sorry I suggested it."

Josh chuckled. "Flying? Or the movie?"

Tabitha lifted her head and nipped playfully at his ear. "The movie, you goof." Then she kissed the lobe she'd bitten.

He laughed. "Careful, Sweetheart. If you distract me too much, we could fall."

The Power, of course, came from Tabitha, but she couldn't wield it directly. No woman could, though all possessed it to some degree. Only a man could channel her Power. And only a very few men possessed that talent.

In her lifetime, Tabitha had met only five men who could channel her Power. And one of them held her in his arms.

She shook her head, grinning at Josh. "You won't drop us." However, the image of Joseph, their five-month-old son, popped into her head. "But I'll save the frisky stuff for when we're safely on the ground." She winked at him.

One side of his mouth raised in a lopsided grin that—had she been standing on the ground—would have made her knees wobble. "That a promise?" he asked.

She bit her lower lip and raised an eyebrow. "Well, you'll just have to wait 'til we get home and see."

He suddenly shivered, despite the fact that the channeled Power kept them both warm. "That's it. We're heading back!"

She squeezed him again, shaking her head. "Just a little longer. Besides, we need to wait 'til the parking lot clears out. Otherwise, someone might see us."

He nodded. "Just a little longer."

As far as they knew, nobody in Utah knew anything about the Power or channeling. Nobody knew Tabitha was a witch either, perhaps the most powerful in the world. And nobody knew Joshua Kilmore was her warlock. They had agreed to keep it that way.

Josh could do nothing without *her*, and she could do virtually nothing without *him*—not with the Power, anyway. But together? Together, they were magnificent.

Josh sighed. "I'm sorry about the movie too. With a title like Ghost Story and that cast of great old-time actors… I mean, Fred Astaire in a horror movie! Who'd have thought?"

She shrugged. "It sounded promising. And it *was* scary, but it was also"—she grimaced—"gross. At least it wasn't just a slasher film. That's not horror. They just don't make 'em like they used to."

"Yeah. Give me *Bride of Frankenstein* or *The Blob* any day. Or any night."

Tabitha wrinkled her nose in disgust. "The Blob? Okay, now we are getting desperate!"

Josh gritted his teeth. "Desperate enough to take a chance on an R-rated movie." He shook his head. "Should-a known better. Oh, well. Live and learn."

"I'm still holding out hope someday *somebody* will make a good modern horror flick."

"You and me both." He kissed her again, and the Power surged through their lips once more. He rubbed the tip of his nose lightly against hers, sending tingles where their noses touched. "I love you, my beautiful witch."

She gave him a wicked grin. "My sexy warlock."

He spun them around a couple times as if they really were waltzing across the night sky. Tabitha laughed with delight.

"Ready to go home?" Josh asked. "Or back to the car at least? We've both got homework, and it's gotta be getting close to time to feed the baby."

At the mention of feeding Joseph, Tabitha was suddenly very much aware of the need to do just that. "I hope he'll wake up enough to eat." *I hate that darn breast-pump.*

Soon they were circling above the small parking lot behind the theater, scanning the area, making sure the coast was clear. Exactly two cars remained—one, a small, dark sedan of some sort, and the other, their aged, yellow VW Bug. No one appeared to be approaching from any direction. Even for a Friday night in downtown Provo, West Center Street looked dead.

Josh and Tabitha alighted in a dark corner of the lot, still holding hands. Once safely on the ground, the flow of the Power ceased. Tabitha experienced a small pang of loss.

Josh squeezed her hand. "Never gets old."

"No, it doesn't"—Tabitha shivered—"but now I'm freezing." Without the Power flowing, the September night no longer felt crisp. It felt downright wintry.

"Sorry, sweetie." Josh let go of her hand and rushed to open the passenger-side door for her. Like Josh's uncle—who also happened to be Tabitha's stepdad—Josh Kilmore had been raised with the manners of a southern gentleman. But unlike his uncle, Josh had no trace of a southern accent. In fact, at least to Tabitha's ears, he sounded vaguely Scottish—a trait he'd picked up during his two-year missionary service in Scotland.

Tabitha followed him around the car, but halted when she heard her husband mutter a very Scottish epithet.

"Bollocks!" Josh had stopped and then squatted beside the right rear tire. He shook his head.

"Flat tire?" Tabitha could clearly see the deflated rubber, even in the shadows.

"Yeah," he growled as he stood. "I'll get the jack and the spare." He went to the front of the Volkswagen where the trunk was.

Tabitha gathered her long skirt and knelt on the cold asphalt. She stared at the flat. "Why don't we try the Power?"

"To change the tire?" Josh leaned around the open trunk.

Tabitha shrugged. "Why not? It should be simple enough. It's just moving stuff around."

He nodded slowly. Then he grinned. "Yeah. Why not?" He pulled the spare from the trunk. "And it'd be a lot safer than using that rusty, old jack."

She gave him a wink, extending her hand. "Not to mention, it'd *feel* really nice." *And warm. Warm is good.*

Josh took her hand and knelt beside her. And the Power flowed, thrilling her, exciting her. Warming her. Warming them both.

Tabitha watched in joy as the back of the car lifted a few inches off the ground. One by one, each tire lug-nut spun off and settled in front of Josh's knees. Then off came the flat tire. The spare was on in moments and the lug-nuts spun and tightened into place. Then the yellow Bug settled once more to the ground.

And, as if by magic, the spare tire held, remaining inflated—mostly. It was a little low.

"Try to inflate it," Tabitha suggested.

The Power ceased flowing. Josh turned to her, his eyes scrunched in doubt. "How?"

Tabitha shrugged. "Depress the tire valve and force air into it."

"But I can't see the air."

Tabitha nodded. "I saw Magnus do it. And Joey. And even Daddy… your uncle Mike. *I* can't do it, obviously—not by myself—but you have to *imagine* the air going in."

He scratched his head with his free hand. "If I mess it up, I'll just let the air out of the tire, and then we'll be in *real* trouble." He paused. "I might even blow it up."

Tabitha's shoulders slumped. "You're right." Then it hit her. "Practice on—"

"—the flat tire!" he said, grinning. "Great minds think alike, I guess!"

She winked, raised one eyebrow, and favored him with a toothy grin. "And don't you forget it." She gave him a quick kiss. "Give it a try. It's cold."

He nodded, then turned his attention to the flat.

The Power pulsed through Tabitha and into Josh. Tabitha could feel it, but nothing seemed to be happening with the flat tire.

Then she heard the hiss of air.

And the tire began to inflate. In a few moments, the formerly flat tire remained round and plump. The Power ceased, but not the hiss of air.

"Deflating again," Josh said. "I'll get it patched tomorrow."

Tabitha squeezed his hand. "But you did it! Now do the new one."

Josh chuckled and shook his head. "Sweetie, nothing about that tire could ever be called new."

One Power-filled minute later, the tire on the car was full. Or mostly full. Josh said, "I don't want to over-inflate it. I'll check the pressure tomorrow when I get the other tire fixed."

Tabitha nodded, sighing as the Power ceased flowing. "That was a lot more fun than using that stupid jack. Everything's more fun with the Power."

Josh kissed her quickly. "Everything's more fun *together*. Besides, there's stuff you can do without me." Josh let go of her hand, stood, and picked up the still-hissing tire. "Be right back." He carried the flat tire around to the front of the car and the open trunk.

Stuff I can do without you? Tabitha thought as she rose to her feet. *Yeah, two things. One I can't control and one I can barely control.* She smoothed her long, blue skirt.

Two things. One triggered by anger, the other fueled by it—or just by me getting really, really upset. And neither of them pleasant.

Josh slammed the trunk closed.

And that's when Tabitha saw the man. Coming up behind Josh.

"Josh! Behind you!"

Josh whirled.

The stranger hesitated. "Hey, man." He raised both hands, palms outward as if in a placating gesture. "Easy. No harm done."

Josh raised his fists. "Back off." His voice was low and almost steady. Almost. Josh was no fighter. "Leave us alone."

The man shook his head. He was tall, muscular—like a football player, but he was also a youth. He wore a Provo High School Bulldogs letterman's jacket. "You changed that tire pretty damn quick. You work in the Indy 500 or something? Race car driver?" He gestured toward the VW. "That Herbie the Love Bug?" His laughter sounded loud and cruel.

Tabitha heard answering laughter from behind her. She spun about.

Two more young thugs sauntered toward her, coming from the direction of the parked sedan. One of the doors on the dark car sat open. The newcomers wore letterman's jackets as well. One of them carried what looked like a liquor bottle. The other, a long, thin knife.

Tabitha backed up. *If I can only get to Josh, get hold of his hand...* "Go away!"

She looked back at Josh, but the stranger had managed to get between Josh and Tabitha. She heard a soft swish and a click. She saw a knife in that stranger's hand as well.

Josh was forced to take a step back. "Leave us alone!"

She turned her attention back to the two men approaching her.

"Hey, pretty thing," said the one with the bottle. "Wanna have some fun?"

Rage and fear welled in her, roiling in her gut. She trembled and felt as if she might throw up. "Leave us alone."

The man approaching her, knife in hand, chuckled. "Come on, girl. You know you wanna party with us."

"Go away!" she snarled. "You don't know who you're messing with." She swallowed hard. "Go away. G-go away… or I'll hurt you." *I don't want to do this. But I will.*

Her palms became slick with sweat. She clenched her fists. Blood roared in her ears. Pushing aside her terror, she tried to focus all her rage on the knife in front of her. *Keep it small. Just his hand.* "You play football, boy? Try playing football without—"

"Boy?" The kid in front of her stopped, snarling like a rabid dog. "Boy? I'll show you 'boy!'" His hands—knife and all—went toward his pants, fumbling with his belt buckle.

NO! If I hit him there, I'll kill him!

"Do it!" Josh yelled. "Now!"

"Shut up!" hissed the man behind her.

What do I do? How can I—

WHAM!

The door of the sedan slammed closed.

Everyone jumped, including Tabitha. *Rage. Made the door slam.*

As startled and frightened as she was, she still had her rage. She needed the rage. She focused on the car, on where she thought the gas tank would be.

Now! Tabitha let all her rage loose with a BOOM!

The sedan's gas tank exploded in an orange fireball. Heat washed across her skin, as the wind caught the fire.

All other sounds ceased. She could still feel the blood pounding in her ears, but

17

she couldn't hear it. It felt as if cotton had been shoved into her ears.

The two assailants in front of her were sprawled on the asphalt, knocked to the ground by the blast. One of the thugs had his pants tangled around his knees. The knife lay harmless, and the liquor bottle smashed. Somehow, the stench of the spilled whiskey overpowered the smell of burning gasoline and oil. Tabitha swallowed down bile.

Even though she'd anticipated the blast, had braced for it, Tabitha swayed where she stood. She turned unsteadily toward Josh and his attacker.

The thug was on his knees. Josh kicked toward the boy's knife hand, and the weapon flew away. Josh drove an uppercut into the kid's jaw. The boy's head snapped up and back, blood and teeth flying.

In an eerie silence, Josh grabbed Tabitha's arm, opened the passenger door, and pushed her in.

Tabitha barely had the presence of mind to gather her long skirt before Josh slammed the door closed. He rushed around to the other side and got in, fumbling in his pocket for his keys.

Tabitha opened her purse and snatched her own keys. "Take mine!" she said, still unable to hear her own voice.

Josh complied, jamming the keys in. He pumped the gas twice, stomped on the clutch, and turned the key. Tabitha felt rather than heard the starter motor turn.

Don't flood! Please don't flood! she begged the engine.

The engine jerked, then died.

No!

Josh tried again, but the engine refused to come to life.

Tabitha glanced out the back window and saw the two boys she'd knocked down with her blast getting to their feet. They lurched toward the car, one of them pulling up his jeans.

She grabbed Josh's hand even as he turned the key once more. The car remained as dead as if it were no more than a metal heap in a junkyard. Josh turned toward her, and she shouted, "Get us out of here!"

That time she heard her own voice. Just barely. Josh nodded and squeezed her hand. And the Power flowed.

The VW Bug lifted off the ground, floating in the air, a dozen feet above the parking lot. The car rotated in place and then shot toward the street.

Tabitha looked out the back window and caught a glimpse of two upturned faces. They stared wide-eyed and open-mouthed at the flying car. The third boy—the one Josh had decked—still lay where he'd fallen.

Then the VW was in the street—or twenty feet above it—and whizzing around the back corner of the theatre and into the night.

"They saw us," Josh said, his voice bleak. "They saw." He kept one hand on the steering wheel—which he turned back and forth as if he were steering the car on the road and not flying it—and held onto her hand with the other.

Tabitha squeezed his hand, her body shaking with the rush of adrenaline, even as the Power tingled pleasurably. "Doesn't matter. We're safe." She trembled. "And Joseph still has a mom and dad." As she pictured her baby's face, she felt herself leaking into her nursing pads. "Let's go get him, please. Hurry."

Josh nodded. "We're safe. You're safe." He let go of the steering wheel—but not her hand—and dashed away a tear that spilled from his eye. He shivered. "I don't know what I'd have done if they'd hurt…" He gritted his teeth and growled. "I'd have killed them! I'd have—"

"My mom told me once," Tabitha said, trying to smother her own rage, "'You don't want that on your conscience.'" *But I could have killed them. And not have blinked an eye. Not if they'd hurt my husband.*

Or if someone hurt my son. I wouldn't hesitate.

But I did. I hesitated back there. They could've hurt Josh.

"We're safe." *Next time… Please, Heavenly Father, don't let there be a next time!*

"But what if they tell somebody?" Josh thumped the steering wheel with his fist. "What if they tell someone what they saw?"

Tabitha shook her head. "Who'd believe them? A flying Volkswagen?"

"Speaking of which… I'd better take us higher or land someplace. Or there'll be a *lot* of reports of flying Volkswagens."

Tabitha hugged her chest with her free arm. "Just take us straight to Mikey's house. If we don't get there soon, I'll be leaking everywhere."

Josh gave her a mischievous grin. "More worried about someone seeing your soaked blouse than a flying car, huh?"

She pursed her lips and glared at him in annoyance. "Just get us there."

"Why don't you just change your nursing pads?"

Her glare morphed into a look of exasperation. "How? I can't do it with one hand."

He gave her a lascivious wink. "I could do it with the Power."

She actually considered it for a moment, picturing it in her mind. "Just… Just fly. I need to see my baby."

Josh set car down, a half block away from the babysitter's home, on a tree-lined street in south Provo. A few houses in each direction were completely dark, the risk of being seen slight. So few people in the college town felt the need to keep an outside light on. Even the lights of the streetlamps were shaded by the trees. Josh let go of Tabitha's hand, and the tingling, warm pleasure of the Power winked out as if a switch had been flipped.

Tabitha groaned and pointed down the street with her now empty hand. "Mikey's place is over there."

"I know. But this seemed like a dark spot, and"—he stepped on the clutch and turned the key—"and I wanted to try"—the engine sputtered to life, and he grinned—"to start the car."

Tabitha nodded, holding both arms across her chest. "Just hurry."

Josh drove to the curb in front of an older house, but left the engine running. "You wait here. I'll get him."

Tabitha opened her mouth to object, but then nodded. "I'll change my pads."

Josh grinned. He seemed as if he were about to make some suggestive comment, then appeared to think better of it. "Lock the doors. Be right back." Then he was gone, nearly sprinting up the walk to the well-lit porch of Mikey and J.L. Montrose.

Tabitha pulled a plastic sandwich bag from her coat pocket and dug out one of the dry nursing pads from inside. She closed her eyes and pictured the sedan burning in the movie theater parking lot. A wave of nausea washed over her like a river of sewage. It had been a long time since she'd created one of her imprecise blasts with the Power— the only thing she could consciously do on her own. Without Josh.

I could've killed them, she thought.

I would have killed them, and not have regretted it.

But the explosion… I didn't mean for it to be so big.

I could've killed Josh and myself.

Then Joseph would be all alone.

The darkness seemed to close in around her like black fog, seeping into her bones. She shivered, and not with the night's chill.

All alone.

I need to see my baby.

"Hurry up, Josh. Please hurry."

Hell was black—black and cold.

And it stank of urine and feces.

All her life, Marisol had been taught by *los padres santos* and by her mama that *el Infierno* was a bottomless pit with a lake of endless fire into which the wicked were cast, where, if she was a bad little *niña*, she would burn forever and ever. *El Diablo*, she had been told, had horns and a tail, and dressed all in red. She had also been told that the Devil was always there in Hell to laugh at the wicked and lash them with his whip. But her mama and the holy fathers had been wrong. Nothing was as Marisol had been told. Hell was black as coal dust and cold as a desert night in winter. And the Devil, who was not *always* there, came and went as he pleased, had a skull for a head, wore solid black, and sounded like a *gringo*.

Marisol had been very bad—she knew that. She had not listened to her mama. If Marisol had listened, she wouldn't be in Hell.

But all I did was kiss a boy! That was not so bad, was it? Only a kiss. She had repeated this, pleaded it many times, defending herself to the darkness and all the unheeding saints. She'd even pleaded her case to the Devil, but *el Diablo* didn't seem to understand Spanish, and Marisol's English was not so good. *A kiss is not a sin. Not even if it is before I am fifteen.*

I know I should not have snuck out to meet Miquel… even if he is seventeen and I am only thirteen, but… It was only a kiss!

Not a sin! I am not a puta—not a whore. I am not!

Only a kiss!

But no one listened to Marisol.

Not even the Devil.

Hell was not bottomless either. No, Hell had a floor—hard, cold, and rough as concrete. Marisol's wrists and ankles were bound behind her back—bound by cold iron shackles secured by padlocks. Under the shackles, her flesh was torn and crusted with dried blood. The shackles were attached by very short chains to some heavy iron mass behind her. Marisol had felt the unseen shape, exploring it with numb fingers. But though she was certain the cold thing was some type of machinery; she could not identify it. In fact, the chain was so short, she could barely move. She couldn't turn over, not even to relieve the constant ache in the left side of her body where it rested against the floor of the pit. All she could do was lie there, the sound of her rasping breaths and pounding heart her only companions, on the cold floor—waiting for the Devil to return once again.

Her neck was bound by a band of cold iron, like a dog's collar—also secured with a padlock. The collar had its own chain, but the other end of that chain was attached to nothing, simply left on the floor, like the end of a leash.

Marisol's thin body shivered violently as she sobbed. She wept, but no tears came. She had no more water to make tears. Her blue jeans stank of urine and feces. Fettered as she was, she'd had no choice but to relieve herself into her pants. But even that humiliation had ceased as her body had nothing left to expel.

She had prayed—so many times she had prayed—to *la Virgen Bendita*. Marisol pleaded for deliverance, but no deliverance came.

Because I'm in Hell. Because I've been bad. The Blessed Virgin does not listen to whores. My prayers can go nowhere.

"Mama!" Her voice came out as a croak, and fresh cracks opened in her dry lips. *I'm sorry, Mama!*

Marisol's throat and mouth felt dry as the desert sand of her native Mexico. She couldn't remember the last time she'd tasted water. In fact, she couldn't remember what water tasted like. She was so thirsty, she would gladly have lapped up her own urine, but what had pooled under her hip and thigh had dried up long ago. Only the stench remained.

Please, Santa Maria! Please tell Mama I'm sorry. Tell Mama—

Metal clanking against metal stilled her pleas. The Devil had returned.

As if the earth above the pit had opened like a door, light—unbearably bright—smote down from above. She squeezed her eyelids tight against the daggers of light. A strangled scream ripped itself painfully through her parched throat and past her sandpaper tongue and cracked lips.

She heard the sound of the Devil's ladder being lowered into the pit. Then she heard him descending, one rung at a time.

Horror froze the air in her lungs. She couldn't breathe. She could barely think. *No! Please!*

But as terrified as she was, another powerful need seared through her damned soul, ripping itself past her fear. "*Agua*," she croaked, "*por favor*." Then remembering that the Devil hadn't seemed to understand Spanish, Marisol whispered, "Water... please." She opened her eyes to the merest slits and saw him as he turned from the ladder and toward her.

The Devil laughed, and the horrific sound filled the pit. As he laughed, the skull face did not move. The bony jaw did not move. The Devil said something in English, but Marisol caught only "water" and "no."

The Devil squatted in front of her and tilted his hooded, hornless head.

The light didn't feel as bright now. Marisol opened her eyes. "Please. Water."

The Devil reached forward and gripped the chain that ran to her neck. Marisol couldn't see eyes in that skull face, but she had the distinct impression that the Devil was sizing her up. A tiger deciding if the mouse it had caught was worth eating. The Devil drew back his shoulders, loudly sucking in a deep breath.

Don't eat me! Don't eat me! Don't eat—

The Devil howled.

And Marisol screamed.

Her thirst didn't matter anymore. The agony in her throat didn't matter. Only the terror.

She screamed again. And again. And again.

The Devil now gripped the chain with both hands. "Yessss!" He threw back his head. "Ah! Yesss! YESSS!"

Marisol screamed again, but not as loudly. She could feel it. Her soul, her life, being ripped from her body. It drained from her, through the iron collar, into the chain.

Into him.

Buh-BOOM! Buh-BOOM!

Her heart thundered painfully in her chest. She could not catch her breath. All she could do was scream.

Buh-BOOM! Buh-BOOM! Buh-BOOM!

But they grew less and less frequent, quieter. She grew less and less. Her sense of self, of everything that was Marisol—slipped away through the collar.

Buh-BOOM! Buh-BOOM! Buh-BOOM! BUH-BOOM!

Her overtaxed heart exploded.

The draining ceased.

For Marisol, everything stopped.

Mama, forgive me.

Breathing hard and sweating as if he'd just staggered across the finish line of a marathon, he released his death grip on the chain. He shuddered as he grasped at the fading ecstasy of his feast. *Too quick. Over too quick.*

He stared down at the soulless husk on the concrete.

Damn you. He stood and drew back his black hood. He removed the full-head Halloween mask, tossing the latex skull up and over the side of the Pit. *Damn you to hell.* He gave the corpse a viscous kick and was rewarded with the sound of cracking ribs. Then he grunted in disgust.

Not you, girl. Damn the one who got away tonight. But I'll get that bitch. I'll get her.

"Not enough." He snarled and kicked the husk once more. *There should have been more! So much more.* "What did you do, you little wetback bitch? Give yourself a heart attack? Is that what you did? Rob me of my reward? It was so good—*you* were so good. Sweet fear. But…"

Never long enough.

"You robbed me." He sighed, then dug into his pocket. He pulled out a key. He knelt and opened the padlocks at the corpse's neck, wrists, and ankles. Then he pocketed the key once more. As he unfastened the shackles and the collar, he said, "Yes, you have robbed me. And will a man—or a girl—rob God?" He shook his head. "Okay, *not* God, but *a* god… Will a girl rob a god? Yet you have robbed me. Even this whole…" He giggled.

"I could've feasted on you for a week. But then"—he sighed again—"but then, I would've had to give you some of that *agua* you wanted, huh?" He nodded as a grin spread across his face. "Could've sprayed you down with the hose." He chuckled. "Let you lick it up." Then he shook his head and growled. "Could've lasted a week. Bitch!"

He shrugged. "No, that's not fair. Forgive me." A titter escaped him. "Forgive me? Forgive? Like that's gonna happen. You can't forgive anyone. You don't even have a soul! I ate it! Well, most of it, anyway." He chuckled, but the mirth quickly changed to anger. "A week!" *But… not your fault, though. Not really.*

It was hers. She made me so angry!

He began stripping the husk, tossing the clothes into a corner. He'd burn them later—after he pulled up the ladder. As he removed the filthy blouse, he discovered a small wooden crucifix bound about the corpse's neck by a braided string. He gripped the cross, then yanked hard. The string snapped. He opened his fist and examined the wooden trinket. "Not much, is it? Hardly any proof you ever existed." He shrugged and stuffed the memento into his pants pocket. "But don't you worry, girl—you are part of *me* now." He resumed stripping the last of the husk's clothing. "I just granted you immortality."

He wrinkled his nose as he worked. "You stink, you know that? I mean, you reek, *señorita*! Now, I gotta clean out the darn pit."

He looked at the drain in the center of the floor. "Get the hose down here and wash the whole flippin' thing."

He hoisted the corpse onto his shoulder, which definitely weighed less than when he'd carried it down three days before. Then he stood and made for the ladder. "Let's look on the bright side. Even if you have robbed *me*, even if I didn't get *my* entire feast, there is some left of you, girl. Meat and bones"—he giggled—"and byproducts for Ozzie and Harriet and their brood to feast on, at least. So, let's get you to them. Whaddaya say?" He laughed aloud. "You say nothing!"

A savage grin spread across his face as he ascended. "Yeah, clean up the Pit. Get it ready for my Prize. I think you're right, señorita. I think I'll put some water down here. Maybe a mattress. Or at least a blanket. Can't have her dying on me, can I? Not until I have devoured every last morsel of her soul."

Because I will have you. God sent you to me. God wants me to find you. And then I will truly feast.

24

"What beast was't, then, that made you break this enterprise to me?" As she stood on the ancient stage, Tabitha fixed her gaze on the director where he sat in the front row of the decrepit theatre of the old Brigham Young Academy building. She could see the man well enough—this was not a fully lit theatrical production in front of an audience shrouded in the anonymity of darkness. This was an audition. But even clad in her customary full-length skirt and blouse, Tabitha had transformed herself. At that moment, she was no longer Tabitha Katherine Moonshadow Kilmore. She was Lady Macbeth. And the director—a spectacled, gray-haired man she'd never heard of and to whom she'd introduced herself only moments before—had, in her mind, become her craven and shrinking husband, Macbeth, Thane of Cawdor, foretold by witchcraft to one day be crowned King of the Scots. But that could happen only after the murder of King Duncan.

And at that moment, Lady Macbeth despised her husband, for he had not as yet carried out the agreed-upon regicide that would make Macbeth king and Lady Macbeth queen. "When you durst do it, then you were a man; and, to be more than what you were, you would be so much more the man. Nor time nor place did then adhere, and yet you would make both." She paused, tilted her head back and looked down her nose at him with a sneer of contempt. "They have made themselves, and that their fitness now does unmake you."

She paused, cradling an imaginary baby in her arms. "I have given suck, and know how tender 'tis to love the babe that milks me." She smiled lovingly down at the phantom in her arms—and for the briefest instant, she pictured Joseph gazing up at her as she nursed him. She loved him with all the tenderness and devotion of a mother for her child. And he loved her, utterly dependent on her for life and nourishment. "I would," she continued, "while it was smiling in my face"—her tender smile vanished, her expression transformed to the coldness of contempt born of unbridled ambition— "have pluck'd my nipple from his boneless gums"—she lifted the fictional infant in both hands, allowing the conflicting emotions roiling within her—maternal love, lust for power, predatory dispassion, and horror—to chase each other across her face before her countenance locked into cold-blooded resolve—"and dash'd the brains out"—she swung her unseen babe against an imaginary castle wall—"had I so sworn as you have done to this."

She trembled, breathing hard, forcing down the unbidden images of Joseph—her own child—from her mind. *Not Joseph. Lady Macbeth's child.*

She swallowed hard, dashing away the tears leaking from her eyes. Then she looked down at the director and forced a smile, nodding her head toward him. "Thank you," she said, signaling the end of her audition piece.

The director raised both hands and clapped slowly, deliberately, and loudly. "Bravo!"

He didn't do that for the other girls. She nodded again and repeated, "Thank you." Tabitha waited anxiously on the stage. *If he says, "Thank you," I'll be done.* Coming from a director, such a response would be tantamount to "Don't call us—we'll call you." At least "Bravo!" was encouraging.

"Tell me, Miss Kilmore." He paused and glanced down at her audition sheet, then looked back up at her with a smile. "*Mrs.* Kilmore, and wouldn't *that* last name be interesting on the playbill, why did you pick that particular speech? You are auditioning for the part of Lucy, right?"

Tabitha nodded, smiling sheepishly, even as her heart sank. "True confession? I only heard about this audition this morning. I thought about doing something light and sweet—perhaps from *My Fair Lady*—but thought that might be *too* light. So, I went to the other extreme." She shrugged.

Please, please, please! I really want to be in this show.

He shook his head, laughing softly. "The other extreme. Yeah. You know, I saw you as Lady Macbeth at BYU. You were brilliant. Scary. I mean, truly frightening."

He saw my performance? Tabitha's nervousness eased a bit. "Thank you." She curtsied.

He looked down at the audition sheet again. "I see you actually played Eliza Doolittle in *My Fair Lady* in high school."

She nodded at the memory—a time filled with triumph, discovery, and horror— and suppressed a shudder. She smiled at him. "One of my favorite roles."

"I wish I could've seen you in that. And Guinevere."

"Yes. Another favorite."

"In high school?" He squinted up at her.

Oh, no! He thinks I'm lying. "Yes."

"How could a high school afford to do those shows? I mean, forgive me, but the royalties alone would be…"

Tabitha nodded quickly. "Astronomical, yes. But we—the theatre program— received a rather large donation… from an anonymous source."

From Magnus. To trap me. To keep me there. So he could steal my Power.

And it worked. Magnus almost had me.

"I see." He cocked his head and gave her a quizzical look. "You know, this isn't a musical, right? This is the 1927 stage play."

"*Dracula* by Deane and Balderston." Tabitha nodded. "Yes. I've never seen the show, but I've read the script. At the BYU Library."

The director appeared taken aback by that. "You've read it?"

Tabitha shrugged and grinned sheepishly. "I just love old horror movies. When I heard about this production, I just knew I had to be a part of it."

He smiled at her, and Tabitha had the distinct impression that she might've found a kindred spirit.

"Ah," he said, "I see." He glanced down at her audition sheet again, then up at her. He pursed his lips and shook his head. "Mrs. Kilmore… Tabitha… May I call you Tabitha?"

Tabitha nodded, with a tight-lipped smile that did not reach her eyes. "Certainly." *Here it comes. At least I won't have to wait to see the cast list without my name on it.*

"Tabitha"—he frowned and paused for an eternal second—"to be perfectly honest, I think you'd be utterly wasted as Lucy Seward… or as Miss Wells the maid. Any one of the actresses who auditioned ahead of you could play those roles."

Tabitha nodded, attempting to make her disappointment appear as gracious as possible. *I would've taken the part of the maid if it got me into this show.* She curtsied again. "Thank you." She turned to walk off the stage.

"Mrs. Kilmore! Tabitha! "

She froze, then turned back to the director. "Yes?"

"As I said, your talent would be wasted in those roles. Would you consider… the role of Renfield?"

Tabitha blinked. *Renfield?* "The madman?"

"Yes." He stood and raised a placating hand. "You'd be able to play him… I mean *her* as female. I think you'd be brilliant as Renfield. What do you think?"

A grin blossomed on Tabitha's face. "Are you offering me the part?"

He nodded enthusiastically. "Yes, I am."

Tabitha curtsied and nodded her head. "Then I accept!"

"Whoo-hoo!" The cheer came from the very back of the dilapidated theatre. There stood her husband, Josh, holding their infant son in his arms.

Tabitha froze, dreading a scream from little Joseph. She saw a tiny fist jerking, but Josh quickly turned away, presumably in the act of inserting a pacifier into the baby's mouth. She watched as Josh hurried out the door.

"Brought your own cheering section, I see?"

Tabitha turned her attention back to the director. And her grin came back. "Yep."

"Well, the official cast list will be posted on Monday, but you've got the part of Renfield."

"Cool!" *I get to be in* Dracula*!* "Very cool." She took one deep breath to compose herself. Then she mussed her hair with both hands, took on a crazed expression, threw back her head, and howled with insane laughter. "The blood is the life!" She cackled again, crouched, and tilted her head to the side. "The blood is the life! The blood is the LIFE!"

The director had taken a step back, a look of shock—and even fear—on his face. Then his countenance split in a wide, toothy grin. "You're gonna be great! Rehearsals start Tuesday night at seven." He paused, obvious concern narrowing his eyes. "You have a baby. Is that going to be a problem?"

"No," Tabitha replied, perhaps a little too quickly. "My husband and I have a system worked out. And in a pinch, we have a great… and reliable babysitter."

He chuckled, obviously relieved. "Okay. I was gonna offer to have my teenage daughter babysit." He ran a hand through his gray hair. "Guess she's off the hook."

Wow. He must really want me! She favored him with a wink. "You bet. She's off the hook."

"Great." He stepped to the edge of the stage, extending his hand. "I'm Trevor Andersen, by the way."

Tabitha took the proffered hand and shook it, only slightly annoyed that she barely had to bend down to reach it. As an actress, her short stature frequently worked against her. "Very pleased to meet you, Trevor Andersen By-The-Way."

He grinned up at her and her joke. "I'm so glad we get to work together!" He cupped a hand to his mouth and stage-whispered, "I'm a horror movie fan, myself. Try to never miss one." He released her hand. "Have you seen *Ghost Story*?"

Tabitha twitched, then grimaced, her cheeks suddenly flushing. "Yeah. We saw it last night. It was… not as good as we'd hoped."

He grimaced as well and shook his head. "Me too. Last night. And I agree with you. It could've… *should've* been better. So much potential. Such a great cast too." He looked away embarrassed. "Ruined by gratuitous…"

Ruined by gratuitous nudity. "Yeah."

"Well," he said, grinning once more, "that particular thing won't be an issue in our production. Of course." His cheeks reddened, and he ran a hand through his hair again. "Stupid thing to say. You'll find out, I say a lot of stupid things. Anyway, welcome aboard!"

Tabitha nodded, grinning like the lunatic she'd be playing. "See you Tuesday night!" Then she added, "Trevor."

"Tuesday night. Oh, and, Tabitha, if it's not too much to ask…"

"Yes?"

"Please, don't cut your hair. I think long, black hair…" He pointed at her tousled locks. "Disheveled, long, black hair will work great on our Renfield."

She winked. "Wouldn't dream of it!"

With that, she hurried off the stage. As she passed the director, she waved quickly. Then all her attention was on the handsome man waiting at the back of the theatre— the man and the baby in his arms. Josh—her own personal cheering section—beamed and opened one arm to embrace her. "Hey! Congratulations!"

Tabitha threw her arms around his neck, taking care not to disturb the baby. "I got it!" The instant her skin came into contact with his, she felt the Power flowing.

"Well, you got something, alright! But Renfield? Who'd-a thought?"

"Yeah! Surprised the heck out of me. But I read that in the original 1924 production,

28

Quincy P. Morris was played by a woman—probably because there weren't enough male actors. World War I, you know."

"Well, whoever *she* was, she wasn't half the actress you are."

"Well," she said, lifting one eyebrow. "You're prejudiced."

"You bet I am! Doesn't mean I'm not right."

He bent his head to kiss her, and she lifted herself onto her toes. But even standing on tiptoes, she wasn't tall enough to reach, and he, holding the baby, couldn't bend quite far enough. She felt tingling pleasure surge as she was lifted by the Power until her face was level with his. With Josh's arm around her waist, to anyone who might happen to be looking, it *might* seem as if Josh were simply hoisting her up with his stout muscles.

Their lips met, and they shared a short, but passionate, Power-tingling kiss.

Tabitha was the first to pull back. "Better put me down before someone sees."

He grinned. "Spoilsport." Nevertheless, he allowed her to settle back to her feet.

Josh had never—not since he'd discovered that he could channel her Power—never once used her Power without her permission or against her wishes. A little, spontaneous, joyfully lifting didn't count—in fact she welcomed it. Once establishing the connection, he could, of course, have violated their unspoken contract, and if he ever did, there was nothing—almost nothing—Tabitha could do to stop him. Him or any channeler. But Tabitha trusted Josh with her Power. And he had never broken that trust.

Tabitha pulled out of his one-armed embrace, instantly mourning the cessation of the Power, and focused on her little son. "Hello, handsome." She smiled at the baby.

Joseph, mouth full of pacifier, beamed up at her. He reached for her with two chubby little hands.

Tabitha gently pulled her baby from his daddy's arm. "You were such a good boy! You were so quiet during Mommy's scary, loud audition, weren't you?" She rocked Joseph and cooed. "Yes, you were!"

The baby gurgled happily, patting her cheek.

Josh put his arm around her waist once more. "Yes, he was. He was a good little man. Didn't even freak out when you went into that creepy Renfield laugh. Scared the living snot outta me, though."

Tabitha gave him a wicked smile. "Scared the director too."

"Really? Cool." He glanced at his watch. "We need to go. We've got a few minutes to spare, but not enough time to go home first." He grabbed an old-fashioned broom from where it stood, propped against the wall. "If we leave soon, though, you can drive me straight to work, and I won't be late." He made as if to hand the broomstick to Tabitha, then pulled it back. "I'll carry it. You've got your hands full. If that's okay..."

"Sure." Tabitha's habit was to carry the antique broom to every audition, to every rehearsal, to every performance. She always kept it backstage, but White Lettie's broom had become a sort of talisman, a good luck charm. In fact, if Tabitha had to be separated from Josh, from her warlock, she preferred to keep the heavy broom for emergencies. She shifted Joseph to her right arm, then took Josh's hand in hers. She sighed happily as the she felt the tingle of the Power once more. *Spooky old building. Perfect venue for this show.* "Hey, Jo-o-osh! Guess what?"

He grinned. "You get to be in *Dracula*?"

"Yeah! I get to be in *Dracula*! It opens on the twenty-ninth! Friday before Halloween!"

He squeezed her hand. "Best Halloween ever! Getting to see my wife in *Dracula*."

She squeezed back, but heard him grunt as if in pain. "What's wrong?"

He shrugged, sighed, then lifted their clasped hands. "Still hurts."

Tabitha stopped and stared at Josh's hand. Bruises darkened his knuckles. "I'm sorry." *Why didn't I see it before? Too busy freaking out about this audition, I guess.* "From last night?"

He nodded. "Lucky, I didn't break my hand."

"Did you put ice on it? Oh, honey! I would've put ice on it for you!"

He shrugged again. "Last night, the adrenaline... and what came after..." He sighed happily at the memory. "It only started really hurting this morning. You were so worried about J.L.'s message... about the audition... I didn't want to bother you with it. I did ice it today."

"Oh, sweetie, I'm so sorry."

He shook his head and squeezed her hand again. "Don't worry about it. Not broken, just bruised."

She tried to pull her hand from his, but he stopped her.

"Just don't let go," he said. "That's all I need."

"Try using the Power... to reduce the swelling."

He shook his head. "I don't know how to do that."

"Just imagine it. Concentrate. Please."

"Later. Right now—"

"Congratulations, Tabitha!" The voice had come from behind them.

Josh and Tabitha wheeled around, carefully keeping their hands locked, carefully keeping the Power flowing and ready—especially after the events of the previous night.

A tall, thin man waved as he approached. Silhouetted against the light coming through the theatre door, Tabitha didn't recognize him at first. But as he entered the hallway, the light from the windows illuminated his salt-and-pepper hair and a pair of sparkling brown eyes set in a gaunt, familiar face.

Tabitha smiled. "Dr. Thorpe! What are you doing here?"

The older man stopped in front of them, grinning, showing a mouthful of yellowing teeth. "You must be the lucky man Tabitha's always raving about—her Air Force ROTC cadet." He extended a hand. "I'm Eli Thorpe."

Josh extricated his hand from Tabitha's, and the Power ceased. He took the older man's hand and somehow managed to keep from grimacing during the handshake. "Josh Kilmore. Pleased to meet you, sir. You're Tabitha's sponsor at the Y, her theatre mentor."

Dr. Thorpe grinned, bowing his head slightly. "I do have that honor." He gripped

Tabitha by both shoulders. "Renfield! Now that's really something. When I saw you walk in with your customary broom"—he gestured toward the broom in Josh's hand—"I thought you'd be a shoo-in for Lucy. But Renfield! Congratulations." He stepped back, took Tabitha's hand, bent, and kissed it.

Tabitha barely managed to suppress a shudder. Dr. Thorpe was always a little "handsy"—never inappropriate... not exactly—just a bit more familiar than Tabitha preferred. But she always chalked it up as a "theatre thing."

The older man released Tabitha's hand and turned his gaunt, beaming countenance on Josh. "I directed her in"—he dropped his voice dramatically—"the Scottish play."

Josh blinked. "The Scottish play?" Then his eyes widened in understanding. "Oh, you mean Macb—"

"Tut-tut, young man!" Dr. Thorpe held up an interrupting finger. "We never mention the name of that play *anywhere* near a stage." He winked. "Unless we're performing it, of course. Bad luck, you know."

Josh nodded. "So I've heard. Sorry."

"It's okay," Tabitha said, gingerly taking hold of her husband's hand once more—and feeling the pleasant tingle of the Power. "No harm done."

The theatre professor winked. "Absolutely! No harm done."

"But Dr. Thorpe," Tabitha said, "what are you doing here?"

The tall man stood even taller. "We will be performing together, my dear."

"We? You?" Tabitha couldn't help but grin at the thought. "You're in the show?"

He bowed. "I have the honor of playing the title role."

Josh gasped. "You're 'Dracula?'"

Dr. Thorpe nodded, grinning. "I was asked to perform the role long before the auditions."

Well, if anybody looked the part... "That's really cool, professor!"

The lean face smiled warmly. "In this context—but never on campus—you must call me Eli. We are to be castmates, after all."

That's going to be awkward. But she nodded anyway. "It'll be fun working together, Eli."

Josh squeezed her hand—a little harder than was comfortable for her and probably painful for him.

Are you jealous, honey?

"It's been a pleasure to meet you, sir," Josh said. "But we have to go. I'm gonna be late for work."

"See you in class, Tabitha," said the older man.

"See you Monday," she replied. "And Tuesday night!"

As soon as the little family had safely exited the building, Josh said, "Is that what they call typecasting? Your Dr. Thorpe looks like a vampire!"

Tabitha didn't even try to suppress a giggle. "He's a great teacher, and I'm sure he's a great actor."

"He sure seems to like you."

Tabitha detected the tension in Josh's voice. "It's okay," she said. "He's just a theatre guy. You know—emotions always over the top?"

"Guess so."

"You know, honey, if you're jealous…"

He chuckled softly. "Not jealous. Not really. Not of that old guy."

She gave him a wicked grin as he lifted their clasped hands. "You can always kiss my hand too."

He pulled her hand to his lips and kissed it. "It's just… the way he called you 'my dear.'"

"Yeah." She grimaced. "You know, Magnus used to call me that. I guess, Dr. Thorpe just doesn't creep me out the way he did." *But there are times when…*

Dr. Thorpe… Eli is nothing like Magnus.

"If you say so."

"He's nothing like Magnus. He's not going to murder all my friends or torture my mom. He would never try to kill her just to possess me and my Power."

Josh grunted. "Tabitha, sweetie, my hand."

"Sorry!" Tabitha eased her death-grip on Josh's injured hand. But she did not let go. "I'm so sorry."

"It's okay." He lifted her hand and kissed it once more. "Sorry I brought it up."

"You didn't. I did." She pulled his hand to her lips and gently kissed each of his bruised knuckles in turn. "See? Kissed it all better."

He grinned. "Yep. All better."

Joseph gurgled, drawing Tabitha's attention.

She smiled at her son. "Oh, do you want kisses too, handsome?"

Joseph spit out his pacifier and gave his mother a toothless grin guaranteed to melt any mother's heart.

But as she bent to kiss her only child's smiling face, Lady Macbeth's impassioned words came unbidden to her mind. *I would, while it was smiling in my face, have pluck'd my nipple from his boneless gums, and dash'd the brains out…*

"I didn't mean it. Honestly. Mommy didn't mean it." Tabitha gazed down at her little child as she nursed him. A tear fell from her eye and splashed on Joseph's forehead. His little body jerked, and his tiny face looked worried.

Tabitha brushed the tear away from his eye. "I'm sorry, handsome. That wasn't me. And I wasn't talking about you."

But that's not entirely true, is it? I became Lady Macbeth. I was her, and she was me. But when I played her before, you, my little man, hadn't even been born. I didn't know what it was to be a mother—a mommy.

To contemplate the murder of my own sweet baby.

"Mommy loves you, Joseph. You know that, don't you?"

For his part, Joseph seemed at peace. His blue eyes, so like his daddy's, slowly closed. His sucking became sporadic.

Then he jerked again, his eyes flying open.

Softly, Tabitha began to sing the lullaby from *Dumbo*. "Baby mine, don't you cry." Joseph's eyes drifted slowly closed once more.

"Baby mine…"

Before the end of the verse, the baby was asleep. Tabitha continued to sing as she covered herself. By the end of the second verse, she had transferred her precious bundle to the playpen at the other end of their apartment living room.

"I love you, my handsome little man," she whispered. She gazed lovingly upon her child as he slept. *I will always, always be your mommy. And I would never kill you.*

"I would die for you."

Like my mom almost did for me. I love you, Mom.

She patted the pocket of her skirt. Through the fabric, she wrapped her fingers around a flat, circular object. A hard object. A comforting object.

It was an old iron washer that had once been part of a railroad track. It was a memento of a heroic incident in her maternal grandfather's life. Her grandfather had given the flat, iron circle with the square hole in the center to his daughter, Molly, Tabitha's mother. And Molly had passed it down to Tabitha.

At that moment, Tabitha longed to feel her mother's embrace, to bask in her mother's love. Tabitha knew how to do just that. As long as she possessed that iron object—which had last belonged to Molly—she could feel her mother's love at any time.

Just for a moment.

She went to the door and double-checked the lock.

Then she sat on the sofa, next to Joseph's playpen. Once she was settled and comfortable, she reached into her pocket and closed her fingers around the iron.

The world went white, and Tabitha slipped into a memory, seeing a cherished moment through the eyes of the last woman to own the iron.

"Mommy loves you," she said, gazing down at the four-month-old baby girl in her arms. "Do you know that, Tabitha, my sweet little girl? Mommy loves you."

The baby, Tabitha, smiled toothlessly at Molly. The child burped, and spit-up leaked from the tiny lips.

Molly wiped at her daughter's mouth with a cotton cloth. "There. Hope that's the last of that. Time for your nap, little Tabby-Cat." She sang softly, "Have you ever seen the seagulls…"

It was one of Molly's favorite lullabies. As originally performed by Sean Connery in Darby O'Gill and the Little People, it hadn't been intended as a lullaby. But "My Darlin' Irish Girl," sung soft and slow, usually had the desired effect. And the song seemed to capture the wonder Molly felt every time she gazed at her only child, her precious gift from God.

By the time Molly finished the song, Tabitha's eyes were closed, and her tiny chest rose and fell in the steady rhythm of slumber.

"You are my dear, dear, darlin' one," Molly whispered. She bent her head and

kissed the baby's cheek. "So perfect. So precious." She grinned mischievously at the sleeping child. "Especially when you're fast asleep."

Gingerly she stood and placed her only child in the cradle. "You're safe with me, little one. I would die for you."

Tabitha let go of the iron, and the vision ceased. But the glow of her mother's love still lingered in her heart and on her lips. She gazed tenderly on her son. "I would die for you," she whispered.

Tabitha sighed as she turned her eyes from her baby to the small dinette table. Atop the table, sat her typewriter. The avocado-green IBM Selectric beckoned. No, not the typewriter—the stack of handwritten papers beside it were calling her.

Tabitha gave her pocket a final pat—from the outside, so she didn't touch the iron. Then she rose from the sofa and walked toward the table and the typewriter and turned on the light, then sat in front of the machine and flipped the power switch. "Time to pay the rent." She examined the term paper at the top of the stack. The title, written in tight, left-slanted cursive read, "Monkey and Bananas: Problem-Solving in Artificial Intelligence." *Josh cleans toilets for a living, and I type up other peoples' boring term papers.* She inserted a blank sheet into the machine, hit the carriage return a few times. She calculated the correct number of spaces needed to center the title, then counted as she tapped the spacebar. *Sometimes, I think maybe Josh has the better job.*

With her fingers poised above the keys, she glanced toward the playpen. *At least I get to stay at home with my baby.* Then she focused on the paper and began to type.

Monkey and Bananas

She backspaced to the beginning of the title and typed "Monkey and Bananas" again over the top of the original to darken it.

The phone rang.

Tabitha jumped up and scrambled for the phone in the bedroom. *Don't wake the baby! Don't wake the baby!* She got to the thunderously loud telephone on the third ring. Lifting the receiver, she said, "Hello?"

"Hi, Tabby-Cat!"

Tabitha held her breath, listening with dread for a cry coming from the other room. Silence.

She exhaled in a massive sigh of relief.

"Tabitha? Are you there?"

Tabitha quietly closed the bedroom door before answering. "Hi, Mom. You know, I meant to call you."

"Oh really? What about?"

Tabitha grinned. "Well… I auditioned for a show today."

"Already? I thought you're still doing *Fiddler on the Roof.*"

"That closed last week."

"Don't you think you need a break once in a while?"

34

"Mom, I have to do at least three more shows in order to graduate."

"But, Tabby-Cat. That's so soon. Are you still trying to finish in just three years?"

Tabitha rolled her eyes. "Mom, we've been over this. If I don't finish next spring when Josh is done, he'll have to delay going on active duty. You just don't do that. He could lose his pilot slot."

"But your scholarship…"

"Dr. Thorpe talked the university into covering the spring and summer terms too, as long as I keep my grades up."

"How *are* your grades?"

"A's." *So far.* "Can't afford to do any less. You know that."

"Yes, I do. Although a single B wouldn't kill you." The phone was silent for a moment, then Molly asked, "How's my grandson?"

Tabitha chuckled. She lowered her voice to a stage-whisper. "Sleeping."

"Oh! Did I wake him?"

Tabitha paused, listening once more for sounds from the living room. "Nope. You tried, though."

"I did not!"

Tabitha's face split in a wicked grin. *Mom, you're too easy!* "Just kidding. He's fine, by the way. Joseph. Fine."

"Oh, good."

"So, I had an audition today."

"How'd it go?"

"Mom, it's *Dracula*."

"*Dracula*? A play?"

"Yes, Mom. A play."

"Neat! How'd it go?"

"Well, there were only two female roles. Lucy and a maid."

"Oh. So, when do they post the cast list?"

"Monday. But, Mom, I already know. I didn't get either of those parts."

"Oh, Tabby-Cat! I'm sorry."

"The director… He said I'd be wasted in those parts."

"So, he didn't even cast you? What a shame! Well, his loss."

Tabitha paused, savoring the moment. "So, he cast me as Renfield!"

"Renfield? The guy who eats flies and spiders?"

"Yep! Although, I'll be playing it as female. It's going to be really cool!"

"Wow! That's wonderful, sweetie! Congratulations!"

Tabitha imagined her mother bouncing up and down at the other end of the line, because Tabitha herself was doing the same. "*Dracula*, Mom! We open just before Halloween!"

"Oh, how fun! Let me tell Mike!"

"Not 'Mike,' Mom. Daddy." *He's my daddy now. Not like…*

But Molly was no longer listening, and Tabitha could hear her talking to Mike Kilmore—who was both Tabitha's stepfather and Josh's uncle—in the background.

Tabitha heard her mom squealing with delight. Then her daddy was on the phone.

"Congratulations, honey!" he said with his Missouri accent. "I'm so proud of y'all!" He chuckled. "I can just see you playin' that ol' lunatic. You'll do great. But... y'all sure you're not disappointed you don't get to play a vampire?"

"Nope! Not in the slightest. Renfield is a much juicier role."

"Well, if y'all're happy, then I'm happy."

"We're *both* happy!" yelled Molly in the background.

"That's great, honey," Mike said. "The twenty-ninth, you say?"

"Yep. Right before Halloween. It's gonna be really cool!"

"Well now," he said, "that's too da— uh, too dang bad. I wish we could see it. I sure as he— sure as *heck* wish the timing were better. Doggone-it!"

"What do you mean?"

"Well, that's the reason... one of the reasons we called. We're coming out for a quick visit."

"You are? When?"

"In three weeks. I'll be attending a law enforcement conference in Salt Lake City. Be there all week. Your mom is gonna fly out and join me that Friday, and we can visit y'all on Saturday. Then fly home Sunday."

"That'd be cool!" Tabitha was bouncing up and down again. "We can go flying! You, me, and Mom!"

He chuckled. "That'd be swell, honey. What about Josh?"

"You know it doesn't work that way. Only one channeler at a time."

"Well now, ain't I the lucky fella! My two best gals." Tabitha imagined Mike winking at her mom. "But just one man at a time. Josh'll just have to sit this one out."

Tabitha grinned. "Well, someone's gotta take care of the baby!"

"How's my nephew-slash-son-in-law doin'?"

"He's at work."

"Cleanin' commodes, huh?"

"Yeah." *With a bruised hand.*

Should I tell Daddy about last night? No. It's long-distance. And even if I did, there's nothing he can do about it. "He's doing fine. He's busy. We're both so busy."

"Sure y'all can spare us a Saturday?"

"Well, I'll probably have rehearsal. But you can visit with Josh and Joseph during the morning. Josh can either swap shifts and get the afternoon off from work, or you can just hang out with me and your grandson. Then we can go flying that night, while Josh babysits."

"Sounds like a plan. We'll take y'all out to dinner to make it up to my favorite nephew. I want you to pick out the best, most expensive restaurant in Provo, ya hear?"

"How does French cuisine sound? There's this great place called La France on University Ave."

"Sounds good to me. Hey, Molly? How does French cuisine sound to you?"

"Heavenly," came her mother's distant reply. "Now let me talk to her!"

Mike chuckled. "Your mom's got some news of her own. Well, it isn't just all her news, but… Here she is."

"Tabby-Cat!" Molly said, once more in possession of the phone.

Tabitha grinned. "Seriously, Mom! Am I ever going to outgrow that silly nickname?"

"Not if I can help it! You'll always be my little Tabby-Cat."

And you'll always be my mom. My mom who sacrificed, who laid her life on the line when Magnus… "What's your news? Daddy told me you're coming—"

"Sweetie, you're gonna be a *sister*."

Tabitha blinked. "A sister? But I don't… You're pregnant? At your age?"

"Oh, come on! I'm only forty. I'll be forty-one when I have the baby. And everything's okay. We've had all the tests and… Honey, be happy for us. Please?"

"Oh, Mom! I am happy for you. I was just surprised, that's all."

"Well, if it's any consolation, it was a surprise to us too. We'd been trying, but we'd given up. But now…"

"How far along are you?" *I'm going to have a baby brother. Or sister.*

"Twenty weeks."

"Twenty w— Five months? And you're just now telling me?"

"We wanted to be sure everything was okay. Didn't want to get our hopes up. As you so graciously pointed out, I am older. The risks are higher and—"

"Congratulations, Mom. And Daddy. I'm happy for you!"

"Thanks, Tabby-Cat. You know, with Mike being your stepdad—"

"My *daddy*," Tabitha corrected. "He's my one-and-only daddy. The only one that matters, anyway. I've been sealed to him."

"Yes, sweetie. You're right. Well, with him being both your daddy and your uncle-by-marriage, that will make your brother or sister also your cousin."

Tabitha laughed softly. "Well, when you put it that way, it sounds just gross! Like a bunch of inbred hillbillies."

Molly chuckled. "Well, it's all your fault you went and married Mike's nephew."

"Oh, my fault, is it? And who was it that told Josh to date me? Hm? Your husband! But"—she sighed—"I'm so glad he did. Mom, I'm so happy. Exhausted and frazzled, but happy. And I'm so happy for you. For both of you. But you gotta admit, it makes for one weird family tree!"

"Yep! That's the Moonshadow's and the Kilmore's!"

"Sounds like the Hatfield's and the McCoy's!" Tabitha wagged a finger that, of course, her mom couldn't see. "See? I told you. Hillbillies!"

"No, honey. More like the witches and the warlocks. Well, you're the only witch in the family. I'm just the witch's mother, you know. But maybe, if it's a girl, with your stepdad's genes, maybe your sister will have the Power too."

Tabitha wasn't so sure she liked that idea. *Another woman with the Power. Or rather, a lot of the Power.* "Mom, you have the Power too. All women do."

"Yes, honey, but most of us just possess a trickle. Mike can barely pick up spilled popcorn with me. It's not like… when you were here." She paused. "So, you are being discreet, aren't you? Nobody else knows, right?"

You had to ask, didn't you, Mom? "Well, we were. But last night, there was an incident."

"An incident? Oh, Tabby-Cat. What happened?"

"Better put Daddy on the phone too. I'll tell you all about it."

Tabitha heard her mom say, "Mike? You better listen in."

Then she heard her daddy say, "Okay, honey. We're here. Tell us what's going on." When Mike was acting in his official capacity as a sheriff's detective, he was all cop. The folksy accent disappeared. "And don't leave anything out."

And so, Tabitha told her parents about the incident in the theatre parking lot—about the three drunken teenagers, about the car Tabitha had blown up, and how Josh and Tabitha had made their escape in a flying VW Beetle.

When she finished, there was silence on the other end of the line. Tabitha imagined Mike and Molly sharing the telephone handset and giving each other meaningful, concerned looks. But, as Tabitha knew, her mom couldn't handle long silences. So, Molly spoke first. "It sounds like you did what you had to do. It's not like those creeps are going to report what they saw, not after they tried to…"

"No," Mike said, "not to the police they won't. But you've got a perp with a broken jaw. He'll be going to the hospital. They probably won't talk to the cops, but they'll talk to someone. It'll get out. They won't be believed, most likely. But I wouldn't go flying around in a yellow car any time soon. If ever again."

Tabitha groaned in exasperation. "We weren't planning on it that time either! We were just trying to escape!"

"Calm down, Tabby-Cat," her mother said. "Mike's just trying to help."

"I know." *I shouldn't have told them.*

"Listen," her stepdad said, "I've got an old buddy out there who works in the Provo Police Department. We were missionaries together in Korea. Not companions—we were just in the same apartment in Chun-Ho Dong. We talk from time to time. I'll give him a call and feel out the situation."

Tabitha begun to protest, but Mike continued. "We'll just catch up. Compare cases, you know. If I hear anything to be concerned about, I'll let you know." He paused. When he started speaking again, the Missouri charm had returned. "Don't y'all worry, honey. I won't mention you or Josh. Trust me."

"Okay," Tabitha said. "I trust you." However, Tabitha could not suppress a tremor of unease.

An hour later, just as Tabitha was covering up a typo with White-Out on the paper she was typing, the phone rang again.

With a glance at the playpen and its precious occupant, Tabitha scrambled for the phone once more. When she answered, her daddy said, "Honey, I want you to talk to the police—to my friend. His name's Lieutenant Daniel Folau. He's a good—"

"Daddy! I trusted you!"

"And, honey, I didn't tell him anything. Nothing."

"Then why should I talk to him?"

"Because he needs your help."

That brought Tabitha up short. "My help?"

"Uh-huh. He's investigating a number of missing-persons cases. All of them women."

Oh, no. "How am I supposed to help with that?" But Tabitha knew the answer even before Mike answered.

"At least three of the missing women," he said, "left behind objects made of iron. Iron, honey. And my friend, Danny Folau, is completely stumped. He's got no leads. He needs your help. He needs a witch."

5

"He wants you to *what*?" On the phone, Josh sounded both angry and shocked.

"He wants me to help the police." Tabitha cradled Joseph in one arm and held the phone in her free hand.

For his part, Joseph was fussing, having been awakened by the phone ringing once too often. He sucked anxiously at his pacifier—his binky, as Tabitha called it. Wide awake, perhaps he sensed his mother's anxiety and worry as well.

"I get that," Josh said, "but how did Uncle Mike explain it to the police?"

"He told them I was a psychic. And that's"—*a lie*—"close enough to the truth. The thing I can do with iron—"

"The thing you can do with iron that leaves you completely defenseless. Yeah. You can't even use your blasts."

"But if you're here…"

"If you can't touch the Power when you touch iron, then I can't channel it!"

"Honey, there's more to being a man than channeling." But she regretted the words as soon as they'd left her lips.

There was silence on the other end of the line.

"Josh," she began, "I'm sorry. That didn't come out right. It's just, if you're here when he comes, then—"

"Someone's coming there? A policeman?"

"Yes. A Detective Folau. Daddy told him I had a baby at home and—"

"When's he coming?"

"Any moment. I tried to call earlier. I would have come to get you."

"I understand. Not your fault. Bollocks! I called as soon as I got your message. Maybe I can get a ride home with someone. I'll be there as soon as I can."

"Maybe I can call Mikey. Maybe she can come over. To be with me—"

"Then Mikey would find out about the Power."

Tabitha grimaced, and Joseph began to cry. "Mommy's sorry. It's okay." She put the binky back in his mouth.

"Is he okay?" Josh asked.

"He's just upset, because I'm upset." She bounced her baby gently. "Baby mine," she sang softly, "don't you cry."

As Tabitha sang and smiled at him, Joseph's fussing eased.

She sang a few more lines of the song, then said into the phone. "There. That's calmed him down. So, maybe I won't call Mikey."

Josh was silent. "No. Go ahead and call Mikey. I trust her."

"Okay. I won't tell her about the Power, maybe just the iron thing. I'll hang up and call right now. If you can get a ride home, call me. Otherwise…"

"Otherwise, you'll pick me up at the normal time?" There was a note of pleading in his voice.

He thinks I'm mad at him. "Of course! Don't worry, honey. I'll be okay. We'll be okay." *I hope.*

"Yeah. We'll be okay." He paused. "I love you."

"I love you too. See you soon."

"I'll try." Then the line clicked, and Tabitha was all alone. All alone with her baby.

Dear Heavenly Father, please help me. Please help Mikey to understand… and not ask too many questions. In the name of Jesus Christ. Amen.

She dialed the Montrose's' number.

"Hello?" It was J.L.'s voice.

"Hi, J.L.," Tabitha said quickly. "It's Tabitha. Is Mikey there?"

"Tabitha! Hey, how'd it go this morning?"

In spite of her worries, Tabitha smiled. "I got the part of Renfield."

"The spies and fliders… I mean, flies and spiders guy?"

Tabitha chuckled at the slip-up. *I've made that mistake myself.* "Yeah. I'll be playing him as female, but… I really need to talk to Mikey. It's important."

"Sure." J.L. spoke loudly, "Mikey! Tabitha's on the phone." He paused. "She's coming."

"Cool. Uh, thanks for letting me know about the audition."

"No problem. As soon as I saw the notice in the paper, I thought of you. I mean, it's not Hodel, and I don't have time to be in it with you, playing opposite you again, but that's pretty neat, you getting to play Renfield and all. Uh, here she is."

"Tabitha?" Mikey sounded like her normal cheery, too-perfect self. "You got into *Dracula*?"

"Yes. Mikey, listen. Can you come over here? Right away? I need a *huge* favor."

"Come over? Just a sec."

Tabitha heard the phone being muffled, then a few quick, muted exchanges between Mikey and her husband. Then she was back. "Sure. I'll be there in five."

"Thanks a ton," Tabitha said.

"What's up?" J.L. was back on the line. "Everything okay?"

"Yeah. I think so. I just have someone… *a man* coming over, and with Josh at work, I thought maybe…"

"…maybe you needed company. Female company. I get it. She's already out the door." He sighed dramatically. "Leaving me with the kids. Again!"

Tabitha chuckled. "Well, after Fiddler, it's your dang turn, Perchik."

He laughed. "Suppose you're right, Hodel! Good times. I miss it already."

"Me too."

"We had great chemistry, didn't we?"

And there it was again. The uncomfortable suspicion that J.L. had developed feelings for her during the course of the show. It was no uncommon thing for actors and actresses to develop feelings for the person who played their romantic interest, especially if they got along, especially if they were friends offstage as well. She forced a small laugh. "It worked in the show. And it was fun! But now we're back to the real world!"

"Yep. Real world." He paused, and the silence became uncomfortable as it lengthened. "Hey, congrats on Renfield."

"Thanks."

Joseph jerked, drew in a deep breath, and screamed.

Tabitha had never been so grateful for a baby's scream in her life. "Gotta go! Thanks again!"

"I'll lend you my wife anytime, you know that. Babysitter, confidant."

Tabitha put the binky back in her son's mouth, but he was having none of it. "Gotta go. Seriously."

She hung up.

Just the fact that Joseph had his mother's undivided attention seemed to calm the little boy somewhat.

Better feed you while I can.

So, Tabitha nursed her son.

And waited.

Joseph was asleep again and back in his playpen before the first knock came.

Tabitha opened the door and found Mikey Montrose waiting. She was smiling, but that smile looked worried. "What's up?"

Tabitha stuck her head out the apartment door. She glanced to the stairs and to the parking lot, but saw nothing. Her view was limited by the direction her doorway faced, so she could have missed something. Her nerves were jangling like bells on a sleigh. "Come in. Quick."

Mikey Montrose was barely thirty, but with her blonde-bombshell hair, blue eyes, and hourglass figure—in spite of two babies—she looked like a model. She was dressed in jeans, t-shirt, and sneakers, but her makeup and hair were perfect. As always. Mikey always reminded Tabitha of a nineteen-fifty's sitcom wife—always dolled up, even after a day of cleaning and cooking, who always had dinner ready the instant her husband walked in the door. Mikey was perfect enough to make any mundane *mortal* wife and mother—including Tabitha—feel like a mousey drudge.

Mikey glided into the living room.

Tabitha raised a quieting finger raised to her lips. "We can talk, but…" Tabitha pointed at the playpen.

Mikey nodded in understanding, her waves of blonde hair bouncing like Farrah Fawcett's.

Tabitha led her friend to the dinette table with its typewriter and papers. They both took a seat facing each other.

"So, what's up?" Mikey asked with practiced softness that came from nearly five years of motherhood.

Tabitha opened her mouth, then shut it again. Then she steeled her resolve and plunged in. "I have a secret."

Mikey's eyes narrowed. "Go ahead. Whatever it is, you can tell me."

For a fleeting, horrible second, Tabitha thought that Mikey suspected her husband, J.L., of being overly fond of Tabitha. Or worse, Tabitha returning that affection—which, of course, Tabitha did not. "I have a… special talent."

Mikey blinked. "You're what? A superhero? A mutant?"

Tabitha chuckled nervously. *Too close to the truth.* "No. I'm like a psychic. But not exactly. I can see memories. I can *live* memories from other women. By touching something that last belonged to them. Something made of iron."

Mikey raised one skeptical eyebrow. "Oh, really?"

Tabitha growled in exasperation. "I'm serious. It started when I was seventeen. I know it sounds stupid, but—"

"It sounds incredible. And by incredible, I mean, lacking credulity, *id est*, unbelievable."

"I know what the word means, Miss Substitute Teacher."

"Sorry, but—"

"But it's the truth. And the police, a detective, is on his way here. To consult with me."

Mikey blinked. "Do you consult with the police often?"

"Never. Well, I did with my daddy back in Missouri. He's a sheriff's detective there."

"I see." She pursed her lips, then reached out and took Tabitha's hand in her own. "I'm sorry. I guess you wouldn't be telling me this if it weren't true. You're not the type."

"Not the type?"

"To lie to me. Lots of people lie to me. I guess it's 'cause I look like the stereotypical dumb blonde."

"Mikey, I need you." She squeezed her friend's hand. "I can't face this alone, and Josh isn't here."

Mikey took Tabitha's other hand and squeezed gently. "I'm here. And I believe you." Her face twisted in a grimace. "I think. So, will I get to see a demonstration? When the police come?"

Tabitha shrugged. "I don't know. Maybe. It's not like they can just carry evidence wherever they go. But, if you like, I'll give you a private demonstration some other time. It has to be something made of—"

A knock at the door. A loud knock.

43

Tabitha jumped to her feet, trying to get to the door before another loud thumping could disturb Joseph.

She opened the door to find a man with strong Polynesian features marred by a long, ragged scar running down the right side of his face. He wore a rumpled suit and a severe expression. "Mrs. Kilmore? Mrs. Tabitha Kilmore?"

Tabitha nodded. "Yes."

The man pulled his suit jacket aside, revealing a gold-looking police badge clipped to his belt. "Detective Danny Folau, ma'am. Provo Police. Your stepfather sent me."

Tabitha stepped aside. "Won't you come in?"

The detective scanned the room with wary, brown eyes. "Thank you." His eyes alighted on Mikey and then the playpen.

Tabitha gestured at her friend. "This is Mrs. Montrose. She's a friend. I didn't want to be alone when you arrived."

He gave a curt nod. "Very sensible." Then he nodded toward Mikey. "Pleased to meet you, ma'am." He did not offer to shake hands. "May I sit down?" He pointed toward the sofa.

"At the table, please," Tabitha said, pointing at the playpen.

Again, the man gave a curt nod. His sour expression didn't soften. "After you."

Tabitha turned her chair—the chair next to Mikey—to face the man.

The detective pulled back a chair and sat. "Let me get straight to it, ma'am. I have no stomach for fakes. And since I've never met a psychic who wasn't a fraud."

"Then why are you here?" Mikey asked.

Detective Folau's eyes flickered to Mikey, then came back to bore into Tabitha's eyes. "I'm here, because a man I trust—your stepfather—told me to trust you."

"I see," Tabitha said. "I've… never done this before. Except for my *father*." She emphasized the word. *He's my daddy. The only one that matters. I've been sealed to him in the temple of the Lord.*

The man's expression softened. A little. "I hope you don't mind if—"

"How many women are missing?" Tabitha asked.

The corner of his mouth twitched. "I can't tell you that. This is an on-going investigation."

"If you don't trust me and you aren't willing to tell me anything, how am—"

"*You're* the psychic. You tell *me*."

Tabitha shook her head. "It doesn't work that way. All I can do is see memories. Only women's memories. Do you have anything that belonged to one of the missing women? Something iron?"

He reached into his jacket and pulled out an inch-long object that looked like a huge plastic ladybug. He extended it toward Tabitha.

"That's plastic," Tabitha began. "I need—"

He turned the object over, revealing a small, metallic disk embedded in the back of the hollow plastic.

A magnet. A refrigerator magnet.

Tabitha nodded. "Okay." She turned her head toward Mikey. "Mikey, please hold onto my shoulders. In case I start to fall."

The detective rolled his eyes. "Really? It's that dramatic?"

Tabitha felt Mikey's hands grip her shoulders firmly. "I'm here," Mikey said.

"Thanks." Tabitha narrowed her eyes at the detective. "I could fall. It depends. I can't predict what happens, what I'll see, how I'll react." She took the plastic bug from his hand, exercising care to not touch the iron magnet. Not yet.

Tabitha took a deep breath. Then she very deliberately placed her thumb on the smooth iron disk.

The world went white.

She put a protective hand over her swollen belly. "Danny, can you please slow down?" She glanced at her husband in the driver's seat. Her belly tightened, and she groaned as the contraction seized her. Her fingers found her ladybug pendant as the contraction eased. She sucked in a breath and held it as another wave hit her.

Danny Folau spared her a glance. "Julie, baby. That's quicker than the last one. What are they? Two minutes?"

She breathed slowly, pursing her lips as she exhaled slowly, fighting through the pain. Two minutes. Don't scare him. "Three. Only three. Now, please slow down! The ice and snow are making the roads too slippery."

"I'm a cop, Pooh Bear. I know how to drive in—"

She saw the red pickup truck, spinning, careening toward them from the right.

She screamed. "Danny!"

The pickup slammed into her side of the car, crushing her, shoving her toward Danny.

Metal smashed into her arm, her side, and her head. She felt ribs snapping.

Something ripped into her belly.

Tabitha dropped the magnet. The agony, the pain was still there, in her head, her arm, her side. In her womb. But it was fading fast. Her hands went to her stomach in a vain attempt to shield the doomed baby that had never really been there.

She stared at Detective Folau. Danny. Her Danny. Only he was older. Harder than she remembered. And scarred.

And he was scowling at her.

No. Not my Danny. Not my husband. Not my baby.

She still felt Mikey's comforting hands on her shoulders, steadying her.

"What?" said the detective. "What did you see?"

Tabitha moistened her lips. "Your wife."

He jerked as if slapped. "My wife? You saw my wife?"

Tabitha nodded. Then shook her head. "No. I saw you. Her name was Julie. She was pregnant. In labor. Hard labor. And you were on the way to the hospital. Icy roads. Hit by a pickup."

His lips curled in a snarl. "You could've looked that up," he snapped. "How *dare* you?"

"How dare *you*?" Tabitha snapped back. "You were testing me?"

His tight-lipped scowl returned.

"You were younger," Tabitha said. "No scar. You called her Pooh Bear."

His eyes grew wide. "How did you—"

"Her contractions were two minutes apart, but she said they were only three. She wanted you to slow down."

Tears fell from his eyes. He ignored them. He bent and snatched the ladybug magnet from the floor. He stared at it for a while. Without looking at her, he said. "We were pinned. She was crushed. All I could do was hold her while she bled out. She never regained consciousness. I, uh, I never called her Pooh Bear in public. I, uh—" He wiped at his tears, then looked up at her, meeting her eyes. "I owe you an apology, ma'am."

His shoulders hunched forward, and his head bowed. A sob ripped from him.

In an instant, Tabitha was out of her chair, pulling herself free from Mikey's comforting hands. Tabitha bent and wrapped her arms around his quaking shoulders. She held him, glancing occasionally at Mikey.

Mikey stared back at her with a mixture of wonder and sadness.

Tabitha put her lips next to Danny's ear. "It wasn't your fault. And she loved you very much. I was only in her memory for a minute, but she loved you." Her own sob escaped. "With all her heart."

He grasped her arm with one trembling hand and shook as he wept.

After a minute, he released her, and she released him. She sat in front of him once more as he wiped at his tears. She took one of his big hands in both of hers. "I want to help. How many? How many women are missing?"

He nodded, swallowed, then met her gaze with red, swollen eyes. "Twelve. Twelve women. Could be more. Maybe a lot more. My gut tells me they're all dead. I think we have a serial killer on our hands."

6

"Twelve?" Tabitha stared at him aghast and trembling. "Why haven't we heard about this on the news?"

Detective Folau huffed in disgust. "Do you read *The Daily Herald*? Does anybody really?"

Tabitha shook her head. "I might read *The Daily Universe*, you know, the BYU paper, once in a while."

"We read *Herald*," Mikey said. "I don't remember anything about women disappearing. It hasn't been on KSL either."

Folau nodded. "The *Herald* has mentioned a couple of disappearances, but they were hardly front-page news. Besides, we've yet to find a single body. A corpse would be on the front page." He sighed. "And quite frankly, not everybody believes there's been any foul play. Teenagers run away. So do housewives. Even moms run off, sometimes. Right now, these are missing-persons cases, regardless of what I might personally believe."

Tabitha reached for his hand and squeezed it. "How can I help? Do you have something belonging to one of the missing women?"

He pulled his hand out of hers, then reached into the outer pocket of his jacket. He produced a rusty horseshoe. "This is from one of the early ones."

Tabitha's eyes were riveted to the object in his hand. "Mikey, please hold my shoulders." In moments, Tabitha felt her friend's hands. The grip was tighter than before.

Tabitha locked eyes with the detective. "If it has belonged to another woman since, it won't show me anything. Even if it hasn't, I may not see anything useful. I may not see the killer, or even the incident."

He extended the artifact. "Just try, ma'am."

"Before we start, do you see that broom?" She pointed at the broom where it leaned next to the doorframe. She waited until Folau nodded his head before continuing. "The broomstick itself has an iron core. I think it used to be a Japanese fighting staff." She waved a hand in dismissal. "That doesn't matter. What matters is that a long time ago, it used to belong to a woman called White Lettie. She was beaten and her son murdered by her husband. Later, she was raped. And after she gave birth to the child of that rape, she was lynched. I've seen it all. Through her eyes."

Tabitha heard Mikey gasp and felt her tremble.

Mikey asked, "Why do you carry that horrible thing around?"

"To remind me," Tabitha said, her eyes focused on Folau's, "of the evil that men can do. A-a-and women too. And because it makes a darn good weapon."

Folau turned his head away, appraising the broom, then he focused on her once more. "Are you trained in how to use it?"

Tabitha nodded. "I've had some instruction. From my dad."

He gave her the slightest of nods. "Mike. Good man."

"Yep." She turned her gaze to the iron horseshoe in his hand. The iron and unknown terrors it contained. "I saw all those things. But not every time. Sometimes, there are good memories." She thought of the iron washer in her pocket. "But violent, life-changing events... they seem to come first. I'll try."

She gritted her teeth, steeling her resolve. Then she snatched the horseshoe from his hand. The real world whitened and flashed out of existence.

She stomped her way down the sidewalk. The rain had left puddles everywhere. Normally, she enjoyed splashing in puddles, especially if she could splash some water on Jim. Normally, splashing was fun. But she wasn't in the mood.

Everything's falling apart. Everything.

They were always fighting over something. Over money. Over sex. Over what she fixed for dinner. Even over what to watch on TV. This time, it'd been over her latest failure. Another early pregnancy test that morning. Another negative result. Another failure.

It's not my fault!

But she was afraid it was her fault. Maybe her body just wasn't capable. Infertile. The word terrified her. It made her palms sweat and her legs tremble. It made her feel sick to her stomach.

So scared. What if I'm not enough?

And then there had been that hair—that long, blonde hair she'd found on his shirt. She'd been about to confront him about it, but he'd chosen that moment to mention the EPT. She was angry. So angry. But she was also afraid. Lately, she was always afraid. Of Jim leaving her. Of Jim catching some disease and passing it on to her.

There was a splash behind her.

She whirled on him. "I said leave me alone, Jim!"

But it wasn't Jim.

The man silhouetted in the light of the streetlamp was definitely not her husband. He was taller and thinner, wearing a dark, hooded jacket.

The figure hesitated, one hand hidden behind his back. Then he started toward her.

She turned and ran. She tried to scream, to call out for help, but her traitorous lungs couldn't seem to draw in enough breath. Her knees wobbled. She stumbled and barely kept her feet.

Panic gripped her. She watched the ground, terrified she was going to fall.

Her lungs burned.

She couldn't hear him, but she knew he was right behind her. She could hear only her own wheezing gasps and the thundering of her heart. She could see the corner of her street. Home and Jim were only just ahead. She forced her legs to pump harder, faster.

A blinding pain struck the side of her head.

She stumbled and fell to the grass beside the sidewalk. Her lungs were too busy sucking air in to scream. She grabbed clumps of grass, ready to heave herself to her feet.

But then he was on her, pinning her to the ground. Covering her mouth, smothering her.

A sharp pain pricked the side of her neck. A sensation of cold flooded over her. She clung to consciousness, desperate to survive.

A face loomed above her. Inhuman. White, with red and blue and yellow. And teeth.

Her panicked breathing slowed, her fingers relaxed their grip on the grass, and the world dissolved into black.

The horseshoe fell from Tabitha's hand and clanged on the linoleum. She began to sway. Hands on her shoulders held her, kept her sitting firmly upright.

She shook herself, shuddering from her toes to her head. She put one hand over Mikey's on her shoulder. She took one deep breath, then blew it out. "I'm okay." She locked eyes with Detective Folau, but she squeezed Mikey's hand again. "You can let go, Mikey. I'm okay."

Mikey eased her grip, then removed her hands from Tabitha's shoulders.

The detective gestured at the fallen bit of iron. "What was her name?"

Tabitha shook her head, hiding another full-body shudder. "I don't know."

His bloodshot eyes narrowed. "You don't know?"

Testing me again? Tabitha rubbed both her shoulders. "I see through her eyes, think her thoughts, feel what she feels. At least in that particular memory. Never current stuff. Nothing *now*. Just memories. If she doesn't hear or speak or think her own name, I don't know it. But her husband's name—at least I assume it was her husband—is Jim. They were trying to get pregnant. She thought he might be having an affair. With a blonde with long hair. She'd found a hair. They'd had a fight about a pregnancy test. A *failed* pregnancy test."

Folau's eyes softened. "What else did you see?"

Tabitha closed her eyes, recalling every possible detail. "I... *She* was out walking. After the fight with Jim. It'd been raining earlier, but it wasn't raining at that moment. A man attacked her."

"What did he look like?" said the detective. "Sound like?"

"Tall. Thin. Taller and skinnier than Jim—I remember that. Dressed all in black.

With a hood on his jacket. His face was… wrong."

"What do you mean, 'wrong?'"

Tabitha snapped her fingers. "It was a mask! A clown mask. White with red and blue and yellow around the eyes, nose, and mouth. There were teeth. On the mask."

"What? A Halloween mask?"

She shook her head. "One of those expensive rubber masks. You know, the kind that go all around?"

He frowned. "Like it had hair on it or something?"

"I didn't see any hair."

"Did he talk?"

She shook her head again. "Not a sound. He… I think he injected her with something. Sedative, maybe." She rubbed the side of her neck. "Here."

"What about his hands? What color was his skin?"

"I don't know. I don't remember seeing his hands."

Detective Folau looked away, then grunted. "Great. Tall and thin. Not much of a description."

"I'm sorry."

His right eye twitched. His scar seemed to twitch with it, like a thin snake on the side of his face. "Well, at least now I know she was abducted. She didn't just run off. It's not much, but it's something."

"I"—Tabitha swallowed—"can try again." *And see something worse.*

"Will you see something different?"

Tabitha nodded. "I never see the same memory twice." *Except for my mom's memories.* Remaining seated, Tabitha pointed at the horseshoe on the floor. "Would you pick it up for me, please? If I'm bending down when I touch it—"

"You'll fall on your face," Mikey said. Her tone was flat, devoid of emotion. She put her hands on Tabitha's shoulders once again. "Don't worry. I've got you. I won't let you fall."

In spite of the dread writhing its way through her gut, Tabitha smiled. "Thanks, Mikey."

Folau bent and retrieved the iron object. He extended it to Tabitha. "Are they… the memories… Do they come in chronological order?"

Tabitha shook her head. "No. They don't seem to. In fact, this next one might be a happy memory. Maybe she died when he stuck that needle in her neck. There might not be anymore."

"But you'll try?" he asked.

She nodded and grasped the horseshoe.

Jim smiled down at her. "Well, Mrs. Miller? Are you ready for this?"

She smiled back at him from where she lay on the soft bed. She took a deep breath, trying to calm her nerves, trying to keep the nervousness out of her voice. "Yes, Mr. Miller. I'm so ready."

She put a hand up to his naked chest and—

Tabitha dropped the horseshoe as if it were burning her. She shook herself. "Definitely a better memory." She blushed furiously. "Wedding night."

Folau blushed as well and grimaced. "Yeah. Well, try again?"

She nodded. "Oh, her last name is Miller. And she's married."

"That's right." Folau bent and scooped up the fallen horseshoe once more.

Tabitha took a deep breath, released it, and extended her hand.

She awoke to darkness and the pungent reek of urine and dung. The air stank like an open-air latrine on a hot summer's day. But there was no sun, no light, and she shivered with the cold.

She coughed and gagged on the pungent, acrid stench. She tried to bring her hand up to cover her nose, but couldn't.

She tugged, yanked at her arms—and felt the ropes biting into her wrists. Felt something tug at her neck too. A collar.

She screamed into the dark. "Help! Help me! Jim! Please!"

Her voice reverberated around her as if she were in a tight space, full of shadow. Then the shadow moved. A shape stirred, black upon black. It advanced toward her.

She screamed again, kicking out with her feet—whether to flee or to strike at the darkness, she didn't know.

But she couldn't move her feet either. Her ankles were bound as well.

Like a helpless worm on a hook, she wriggled, trying to move, to inch away from the black shape.

She heard the sound of metal dragging. Her eyes were trying to adjust to the dark. She caught the distinctive scents of rust and motor oil.

But all of that was overshadowed by her desperate need to get away from the black presence looming over her.

A light flashed on and off, briefly illuminating a face.

White and red. Blue and yellow. Our Primary colors are... Huge, insane eyes. Leering mouth, full of cartoon predator teeth.

She screamed and thrashed. "No!"

The light flashed again. The demonic clown leered down at her.

She pulled harder at her bonds, her muscles straining against their metallic strength.

She heard the metal scraping again and knew the monster was creeping closer.

Then she felt a tug on her neck, on the cold metal collar.

"Look at me!" screeched a voice, high-pitched and booming, yet muffled slightly by the rubber mask.

The light appeared and stayed on. A flashlight shining up onto the clown's face. Only on the face.

The clown laughed, but his features still did not move. Mad laughter enveloped her.

"Scream for me," said the frozen clown face with too many teeth. "Scream!"

She screamed. And she screamed.

And the clown's demonic laughter filled the small, confined space.

"Yes! Feed me! Your soul! Give it all to me!"

And even as she filled her lungs to scream again, she felt herself begin to slip away. It was as if everything that made her who she was, everything that made her Kelsie-Anne Miller was pouring into the collar, like water down a drain. Her life, her very soul siphoned out of her, draining into the collar, through the metal chain, and into the clown.

"Feed me!" he shrieked through unmoving lips and feral teeth.

She screamed—or she tried to. There wasn't enough left of her to give voice to the terror pounding in her chest. Her mouth opened and closed like a fish out of water.

"Yes!" hissed the clown. "Fear! Sweet fear." He tilted back his head and howled.

Then he bent his head toward her. "Woman's fear," he whispered, and the softness of his voice was more horrible than his screams. "The conduit for a woman's soul."

She blinked, slowly—her thundering heart slowing. An irregular thump…thump… Her chest hurt, her breaths a heavy, desperate pant.

"That's it," he whispered. "Pant like a dog, like the bitch you are." He laughed, long and slow. "You are mine. All mine. Come to me. Yes."

And she did. She went to him.

The last of Kelsie-Anne drained out of her.

The iron fell from Tabitha's limp hand for the third time.

She slumped in her chair. Someone was shaking her by the shoulders.

"Tabitha!" Mikey cried. "Tabitha!"

Mikey. Good old Mikey.

A pair of strong hands gripped hers, shaking them as well. "Mrs. Kilmore! Stay with me."

Tabitha opened her eyes.

Detective Folau was kneeling in front of her, holding both her hands. His eyes were wide, his scar livid in contrast to his pale skin. "Mrs. Kilmore?"

A shudder ripped through her. She closed her eyes again. She felt a scream clawing its way up her throat, and she clamped her lips tight. *Don't wake the baby!* Another, more violent shudder consumed her. Then she took in a deep, cleansing, calming breath.

And sat up straight once more. She turned her head in Mikey's direction, though she could only see her friend on the edge of her periphery. "Thanks. You're a lifesaver. As always."

Mikey patted her shoulders. "Are you okay?"

Tabitha took another trembling breath. "Yeah. I'm fine. That one was… bad."

"What did you see?" asked Folau. He leaned forward, his eyes narrowed and intense.

Tabitha swallowed hard. "She's dead," she said, her voice flat and lifeless.

He nodded. "I knew it!" His lips writhed as if around an unspoken curse.

"Her name was Kelsie-Anne Miller."

He nodded again, more slowly that time. "That's right. What else did you see?"

"It was dark. And it stank. Smelled like an outhouse. Maybe a farm?"

The detective nodded enthusiastically. He pulled out a notepad and a pen. He began scribbling. "A farm. That's good. Animals. Cows? Pigs? Chickens?"

Tabitha shook her head, grimacing. "How would I know? I've never spent time on a farm. I couldn't see any animals either. It reeked. That's all I know." *I'll never forget that stench.*

"Okay. What about the perp?"

Tabitha closed her eyes. So real. *It was like I died.* "In a second. There were other smells. Iron. Motor oil."

"Motor oil? Okay. But Iron? You're sure?"

Tabitha gave him a smirk of annoyance. "Trust me, Detective. I know iron."

"Okay. Back to the perp."

"He wore a mask. That clown mask I saw before. I couldn't see him, though. The mouth... lots of sharp teeth. The eyes... the mask's eyes... were insane. Like an *evil* clown. Not funny or-or sad. Evil."

"Skin color?"

She closed her eyes, forcing herself to remember. She growled in frustration. "It was dark. He was wearing black. I don't think he was wearing gloves, but... I'm sorry. Maybe on the next one." *I don't want to do a next one!*

"Can you go back in and take another look, maybe?"

Tabitha shook her head. "I told you—I can never see the same memory twice."

"Okay, yeah. You said that. What about eye color?"

"Like I said, it was dark. I couldn't see his eyes. There were just holes in the mask."

"Okay. Tall and thin, but, well, frankly, Mrs. Kilmore, from a woman's perspective, 'tall' is a relative thing." He gestured toward her with his pen. "And you're kinda..."

Tabitha nodded. "Short. I know. But don't use *my* height as your baseline. Only Kelsie-Anne's height matters."

He tapped the point of his pen against the notepad. "Good point. So, did you see the death? How she died?"

Tabitha nodded, her lips pressed tight together.

Mikey gasped. "Her death... You *experienced* it?"

Tabitha didn't look at her friend. *Don't break down! Don't cry!* Tabitha stared down at her hands; fingers clasped tightly together in her lap. "Yeah. He devoured her."

Another gasp from Mikey.

Detective Folau's eyes were wide with shock. "He *ate* her? Cannibalized her?"

Tabitha shook her head in frustration, barely holding back tears. "No. Not like that. He *drained* me. Uh, I mean, her. He sucked out— No, that's not the right word. He drew out her soul—her essence. Pulled—no—*dragged* it out of her."

Folau's eyes narrowed. "That doesn't make sense. What do you mean? You can't drag out a soul."

Tabitha shrugged, blinking her eyes furiously to keep them from leaking. *Don't lose it. Not now.* "That's what it felt like. I can only tell you what I saw, what I heard. What I felt." She put her hand around her neck. "There was a collar. An *iron* collar. With a chain attached to it. The chain was iron too. I'm sure of it. He grasped the chain"—she mimed gripping and pulling on an imaginary chain—"and he drew out her soul." She paused, glancing down. "At least, he called it her soul. He also said, 'Fear. Sweet fear. Woman's fear. The conduit for a woman's soul.'"

"Fear?" Mikey asked. "Like he's feeding on her fear?"

"So, she was afraid?" Folau asked.

Tabitha quivered, and the tears at last fell from her eyes. "She was terrified. Wouldn't you be? It was dark. She was alone. Tied up—"

"Tied up?" Folau said. "That's another detail you didn't mention."

Tabitha nodded. "Yeah. Wrists and ankles. Wrists behind her back. Oh! And there must have been a little light so she could see his shape. In the darkness. What little there was came from above."

"Most lights come from above," said the detective.

"Yes, but it was—I don't know—*way* above. I don't know how else to explain it."

Folau nodded, then made some more notes. "Okay. It's not a lot to work with, but it's a heck of a lot more than I had before." He looked up once more. "Anything else?"

Tabitha thought for a second. "He kept screaming things at me. At *her*. 'Feed me. Scream. Give me your soul.' Stuff like that."

"Okay." He scribbled some more. "That's good. He wasn't afraid of making noise. Maybe—like you said—a farm. Isolated. Out in the middle of nowhere. That's all good stuff."

Tabitha shivered. "Do you have more objects? From other victims?" *No more! Not just yet. Please.*

He chuckled mirthlessly and shook his head. "Not right now. I honestly didn't expect this to work."

"But you brought Kelsie-Anne's horseshoe."

"Yeah. I… well, your stepdad is pretty persuasive."

Tabitha smiled. Another tear rolled down her cheek. "He's pretty special." Like his nephew. She wiped at the tear, then grabbed a Kleenex from the box on the table. "And he's not my stepfather. He's my daddy. I've been sealed to him. In the temple of God."

Danny Folau nodded, and a smile stole across his face. "I understand." He flipped through the pages of his notepad. "I think that's all for now. You've been very helpful. Very helpful. Thank you." He reached forward and grasped her hand briefly. "I mean it. I'll get in touch with you later. Probably later today. I have a few more objects for you to read. Well, to touch. If that's okay, with you, Mrs. Kilmore."

Tabitha nodded, dabbing at her nose with the tissue. *More? Of course, there are more. Maybe even eleven more.* She grimaced, suppressing a groan. "You'd better call me Tabitha—" She caught herself before she could say, "Danny."

You're not my Danny. And I'm not your Julie.

Even if—for a second—I was.

He stuffed the notepad, the pen, and the horseshoe into the pockets of his rumpled jacket. "If it's all the same, ma'am—and as unusual as this… as these circumstances are—I think it's best if I keep this professional."

"Sure." *Danny*.

"I'll, uh, see myself out." He rose. He nodded to Mikey. "Mrs. Montrose."

He went to the door, put his hand on the knob, and then paused. He turned back and fixed Tabitha with his eyes. "I'm grateful, ma'am. Not just for your help, but my Julie and I… We're sealed in the temple too. What you said… It"—he swallowed, and his voice became thick, choked—"means a lot to me. I was… I *am* a lucky man."

Tabitha wiped away fresh tears. "She loved you very much. She still does. I could *feel* it."

He nodded. Then he turned and was quickly out of the door.

Tabitha slumped forward in her chair. She put her face in her hands, and she wept. She let the horror and the grief take control.

She'd seen death before. She'd seen her one-time friends slaughtered by Magnus. She'd lived through it. She'd even *died* before. White Lettie. Jeffrey Thibodeaux's mother.

But she'd never gotten used to it. And she hoped she never would.

That poor woman! Kelsie-Anne. She was so afraid.

That monster! He fed on her fear.

On my fear.

"No!" she said softly. "Not my fear. It wasn't me!"

She felt Mikey's hand on her shoulder. Then she became aware that Mikey was kneeling beside her. Tabitha turned and threw herself into Mikey's arms. Mikey hugged her while Tabitha wept and quivered.

But Mikey said nothing.

After a while—after what felt like an eternity of mourning—Mikey's silence broke through Tabitha's grief. Mikey spoke no words of comfort, made no cooing, soothing noises. Nothing.

Tabitha extricated herself from Mikey's arms. "Mikey?"

But Mikey wouldn't meet her gaze. She simply remained as she was, kneeling, staring pointedly at the floor.

"Thank you," Tabitha said, "for coming. I don't know what I'd have…"

Still not looking at Tabitha, Mikey rose to her feet. Mikey retrieved her purse. "I need to go. J.L.'s alone with the kids and who knows what kind of mischief they'll—"

"I'm sorry I scared you."

Mikey blinked. "Scared me?" She finally looked Tabitha in the eye. "Scared me?"

Tabitha shrugged. "Yeah."

Mikey's head shook almost imperceptibly from side to side. "You were the one who experienced the fear."

"But this must seem so strange to you." Tabitha extended a hand toward her friend.

Mikey took a step back and crossed her arms protectively, closing herself off from Tabitha. "Strange?" She laughed, but there was no humor in the laughter. "Yeah. You might say that."

Tabitha withdrew her outstretched hand and crossed her own arms. She felt as if a canyon had suddenly opened in the floor—a gulf between them and there was no bridge across that distance. "I'm sorry."

Her friend laughed again—bitterly that time. "Sorry? For what? For not telling me your secret? That you've got this psychic power?"

If you only knew the whole truth. "Yeah. It's just that… Well, it's not something I like to talk about."

Mikey's eyes hardened, and so did her voice. "You've been in my house. You've touched my things." She paused, then spat out, "What have you seen?"

Tabitha's eyes widened in shocked understanding. "Nothing! I—I haven't seen anything! I *avoid* iron. Like the plague. I don't *want* to know! It's not like I want to know everybody else's secrets."

"I've got nothing to hide."

"Of course not!"

"It's just everybody's entitled to privacy."

Tabitha spread her arms, palms open and exposed. "Why do you think I never told you about—"

"How can I trust you?"

Tabitha jerked back as if she'd been slapped. "Mikey! I promise, I would never… I *have* never…"

Mikey turned her face away. Tears spilled from her eyes. "Shoot." She began fishing in her purse.

Tabitha wheeled and snatched a tissue from the box. She turned back and extended the Kleenex to her friend.

Mikey's mouth twitched. She glanced up. "Thanks. Darn mascara. Won't do to show J.L. a sloppy face." She dabbed at the corners of her eyes.

Tabitha watched as Mikey retrieved a compact from her purse, opened it, and carefully examined her makeup.

"Mikey, you're my friend. I didn't—"

"Don't. Just don't." Mikey began to cover and smooth over the streaks in her foundation with face powder. All her attention was on fixing her makeup. She didn't look at Tabitha. "This is a big deal. And it's hard to take it all in. I want to believe you." She finally glanced at Tabitha. "I do. But…" She snapped the compact closed and stuffed it back into her purse. "And after you… Did you… *feel* her death? Did it feel like you yourself died?"

Tabitha nodded, not daring to say anything, afraid to set off another deluge of weeping.

Mikey managed a tight-lipped smile. "I'm sorry. You're so brave. I wish I—" Without warning, she threw her arms—purse and all—around Tabitha. Mikey held her tight, while Tabitha cautiously returned the embrace.

"Mikey, I promise I would never violate your trust."

Mikey nodded. "I know. And—and if you need me again, all you have to do is ask. But…"

Tabitha waited for her friend to continue, however Mikey said nothing more. Tabitha couldn't stand the silence. *I'm so like my mom.* "But what?"

Mikey chuckled softly. "But don't be offended if I hide all the refrigerator magnets when you come over."

7

"That's enough!" Josh growled, glaring daggers at Detective Folau.

Josh held Tabitha in his lap, one arm around her trembling shoulders as she wept. He gripped her hand tight as she held their clasped hands against her breast.

Tabitha buried her face in his shoulder, muffling her sobs.

Josh hadn't needed to see Tabitha release the cast-iron skillet when she'd ripped herself out of the latest vision. He'd known the instant her skin broke contact with the iron, because the Power had burst into him. It was as if a switch had been turned on—one moment, there was nothing, and the next he felt the pleasant lightning of that uniquely feminine strength.

Josh wasn't doing anything with the Power—though, at the moment, he was sorely tempted to use it to slam Folau against the living room wall. Or rip the man's head off.

"Get that thing away from her," he said, jerking his head toward the black skillet where it lay on the sofa. The iron was touching Tabitha's long skirt, but not her flesh. The fabric of the skirt provided just enough insulation to protect her from the object.

Folau nodded. The detective sat on a dinette chair positioned in front of the sofa, facing Josh and Tabitha. "Pardon me, ma'am." He reached forward and retrieved the heavy iron object. The detective hid the skillet in a big, leather valise on the floor next to him. The leather bag contained the other objects he'd brought, belonging to other victims.

Josh drew on more of the Power. *Oh, Sweetheart! I wish I could use the Power to take away your pain. We can do so much, but not that.* However, Josh knew that just the pleasant, tingling flow of the Power might make Tabitha feel a little better. He clung to that hope.

However, Tabitha's sobbing continued unabated.

Josh kissed the back of her head. "I'm sorry, sweetie. I'm so sorry."

Tabitha took a hitching breath, then lifted her head a little. "He w-wore a F-F-Frankenstein m-m-mask this time. Not Dr. Frankenstein—F-Frankenstein's M-Monster. He k-kept asking, 'Does this one scare you?'" She shifted in Josh's lap, turning so she could look at the detective. Tears coursed down her cheeks, and her lower lip trembled. "It d-did. It scared me." She shook her head violently, and a tear flew, splashing onto Josh's chin. "It scared *her* so much! That movie frightened her. Harry, my big b-brother— No, *her* big brother used to scare her. He used to scare Christie when she was a little girl. He'd wear a cardboard Monster mask. Cut it off the back of a cereal box. He'd hide and jump out with a roar. The Monster always scared Christie."

"So, it was her brother?" Folau asked as he wrote on his notepad.

Tabitha squeezed Josh's hand tight as she appeared to be thinking. "I don't think so. I get the idea he's dead. Yeah. She thought it was Harry's ghost."

Folau grimaced, and Josh was certain he could hear the man grinding his teeth.

He's upset, Josh thought. *Thought he might've had a suspect.*

For one savage moment, Josh took perverse delight in the detective's disappointment.

Stop it. We want to catch this monster. We all do. Folau's just doing his job. But he's hurting Tabitha to do it.

"Okay," said Folau, "I'll check on the brother, Harry, just to be sure. Easy enough to find out if he's dead."

"But all those other times," Tabitha said, wiping at her tears with a wad of Kleenex she clutched in her hand, "with the other masks, she was scared then too. I mean, she was really scared, but nothing like with the Monster mask. And that time"—her voice hitched, and she appeared to be choking down yet another sob—"that time was it. That's when he consumed her. When he drained her."

"So, the other masks"—Folau consulted his notes—"clown, skull, werewolf... They didn't scare her as much?"

Tabitha shook her head. "No. She was scared, terrified, but those other times, she *tried* to be brave, to talk to him, to reason with him."

"Smart." Folau nodded. "Humanize herself. Get the perp to think of her as a person—a person of value. A person with feelings."

Josh growled low in his throat. "There's only one feeling this creep's interested in."

"Fear," both Tabitha and Folau uttered the word together.

"It was almost"—Tabitha wiped at her dripping nose—"as if he wasn't getting *enough* from her before. Like he was disappointed or frustrated those other times."

Folau tapped on the notepad with his pen. "You said he didn't grab the chain those other times. Did he grab it this time?"

Tabitha sat bolt upright on Josh's lap. She nodded vigorously. "Yes! Yes! He did. You're right! He didn't even touch it before. That must mean there's..."

"A threshold," Josh said. In spite of the warmth of the Power flowing from Tabitha, a chill rippled up his spine. *Like with the Power. Once we cross the threshold...*

"Yes!" Tabitha said, her face brightening. "A threshold! If he doesn't get her to that *level*, maybe he can't devour her."

Folau shot Josh a menacing look. "Mr. Kilmore, don't you put words in her mouth. If you persist in doing that, I'll have to ask you to leave."

Oh no, you don't! Josh bared gritted teeth. "This is *our* home. You don't get to—"

"This is a police investigation!" Folau snapped.

"Yeah. Right. A police investigation!" Josh released a mirthless laugh. "You're really going to write up a report about you bullying a woman into giving you psychic readings?"

Tabitha turned her anguished face to him. "Honey, he's not bullying—"

"Oh, yes, he is!" snapped Josh, somehow managing to keep the volume of his voice down. *Don't wake the baby!* "He keeps pushing you into *dying* over and over." He turned his fury on Folau. "You don't know what you're dealing with here."

Folau glared right back at him. "And you do, Mr. Kilmore? Are *you* the psychic? Can you do what she does?"

"What I do is—" *Keep your mouth shut. Don't say anything to put us in danger. More danger than we're already in.* "It's complicated."

"We work best together," Tabitha said. "Josh has a lot more experience with this, with me, and what I can do. And how to help me through it."

Folau shook his head and scowled. His scar seemed to darken to the color of dried blood. "I can't have the evidence tainted by—"

"Are you kidding me?" Josh wasn't even attempting to hide his contempt. "You know you can't use anything she gives you as evidence, Officer. Not in court. You'd be laughed out—"

"I'm trying to stop a serial killer!" Folau snarled. "Perhaps you don't underst—"

"Keep your voice down!" Tabitha hissed. "If you wake my baby, I swear I'll kick you out myself."

Folau shook his pen at Tabitha and then at Josh. Then the detective's mouth snapped shut with an audible clicking of teeth. He flipped back and forth through the small pages of his notepad as if he were looking for something specific.

He's not looking for anything—just trying to get control of his anger.

Then Folau lifted his eyes to meet Josh's. His calm expression was belied by the twitching of his livid scar. "I apologize," he said through clenched teeth. "It's just… Well, I haven't had a lead in months. Just a growing list of missing women. *Dead* women—if your wife's visions are true. We have no bodies, no other evidence of murder." His jaw relaxed. "I appreciate everything you're doing." He turned his gaze to Tabitha and then back to Josh. "Both of you. I mean it."

Josh took a deep breath through his nostrils, not trusting himself to reply with any measure of civility. He held the breath for a moment until he felt he had enough control to speak. "And we want to help. But I think you've pushed Tabitha too far today."

Tabitha squeezed his hand. "Josh understands what I can do better than anyone. He knows my limits. We're so much better together."

Folau's lips tightened into a straight, tense line. "Yes. I understand. But I don't want him suggesting ideas that you then *inject*, for lack of a better word, into what you've already seen."

"Okay." It was all Josh could think of to say. *Maybe he has a point.*

"You said something about a 'threshold,'" Folau said. "Like that meant something."

Josh and Tabitha exchanged a meaningful and cautionary glance. *Don't say it. It's not the same as the Power. It can't be.*

Tabitha gave Josh a tiny smile. Her eyes were wide and earnest, as if to say, *Trust me.* She cleared her throat, then turned her face to the detective. "I can't explain it—not exactly—but there are things that I… that we've experienced that make it seem as if once a woman passes a certain threshold—in this case with her *fear*"—she let the word linger in the air like some terrible secret—"that the fear becomes exponentially more powerful."

A crease furrowed the detective's brow. "I don't understand."

It was Josh's turn to clear his throat. "It's like it takes on a life of its own. As if it's virtually—"

"Unlimited," Tabitha finished. "What if the killer can feel the fear before it reaches that threshold, but it's only *after* the fear passes that level…"

"…that he can draw on it," Josh finished. "Draw on her."

Tabitha nodded. "*Feed* on her. Maybe he gets some kind of sick pleasure out of her fear *before* the threshold, but it's only *after* the threshold that he can consume her."

Folau eyed them both in turn. Then he shrugged. "Okay. I get what you're saying. I just don't believe in consuming souls."

An image popped into Josh's mind from Tabitha's audition that morning—Tabitha howling like a lunatic, *I know the secret! The blood is the life!*

He shuddered. Renfield believed he was consuming souls. Well, not souls, but lives.

Tabitha's head snapped back to him with a look of concern.

Josh gave her an almost imperceptible shake of his head.

She responded with a slight nod.

"I don't believe it either," Josh said. "He can't be devouring their souls." *But then what?*

"'There are more things in heaven and earth, Horatio…'" Tabitha said.

A corner of Folau's mouth lifted in a half smile. "'…than are dreamt of in your philosophy.' Hamlet. I know that one."

Josh forced a slight grin. *Like I needed another reason to despise you. Now you're speaking Tabitha's language.*

"Okay." Folau began flipping pages in his notepad again. "So, let's recap this, shall we?" He didn't wait for a response. "At least four masks—clown, skull, werewolf, and Frankenstein."

Frankenstein's Monster, you ignorant jerk. There's a difference.

But neither Josh nor Tabitha corrected the detective.

"Always black clothes," Folau continued. "A hooded jacket or sweatshirt. But you still haven't seen his hands. Don't know his skin color."

"Not a detail I've noticed," Tabitha said, sounding apologetic. "I'm preoccupied when I'm in there. I can't control the vision."

"She sees only what she sees," Josh said. *And she's given you a ton of information.*

Folau nodded, almost impatiently. "Sure. Still no hair color or eye color. Always a hypo needle to the neck during the abduction. You added the detail of the engine or engine block in the dungeon or wherever it is."

"The iron shackles," Tabitha said. "On the wrists and ankles."

"Oh, yeah." Folau scribbled quickly. "And the bit about the ladder. Wherever it is, he has to climb in and out."

"Like a pit," Tabitha suggested.

"Maybe," Folau replied.

"The sound of wood creaking," Josh added, "when he arrives. She mentioned that too."

Folau nodded. "Got that one. Yep." He looked up. "Did you smell anything new? Like blood?"

Tabitha closed her eyes tight, then she nodded. "With the shackles, yeah. But it was old blood. And my wrists and ankles were raw. Uh, I mean, *her* wrists and ankles."

Folau grimaced, but made a note anyway. "Okay. Still don't know what he does with the bodies."

Tabitha shivered, and Josh just knew she was picturing herself as a corpse. Josh drew a little bit more on the Power. It felt so good to him. *Please, Heavenly Father, help her feel better.*

Though her eyes were still wet with tears, Tabitha gave him a warm, affectionate smile.

Yes!

I thank Thee, Father.

"Any sounds of traffic?" Folau asked.

You already asked that one, Josh thought.

Tabitha shook her head. "But I swear I could smell a car."

"Hm." Folau gave a thoughtful nod and took down another note. He looked up. "Hot engine, you mean?"

Tabitha shook her head. "No. Not a hot engine. A cold one, maybe. Not the engine block in the pit. But from above. Does that make sense?"

"Anything else you remember?"

Tabitha shook her head. "Just the terror. The dying. I'm sorry, Danny." Tabitha's body twitched, and her face flushed. "I mean, D-Detective Folau."

Danny?

Josh noticed Folau's eyes widening. The man blinked. And then he nodded. "Thank you, *Mrs. Kilmore.*"

Josh also noticed the emphasis Folau gave the formal name. *What's going on?* Josh wasn't jealous exactly. *They only met today, right? I really don't like this guy.*

Folau put away his pen and pad. He bent and retrieved the valise from the floor. "I think that's all for now." He stood, but didn't make a move toward the door. He fixed Josh with an icy stare. "By the way, Mr. Kilmore, it's *Detective*, not Officer."

Josh blinked. *He's pissed? Because I called him Officer?* "Sorry." *I guess he doesn't like me either. Fine with me.*

Josh gently eased Tabitha out of his lap. She stood. And slowly, reluctantly, she let go of his hand. The Power's flow ceased.

Tabitha turned to check on the baby who snored softly in his playpen, oblivious to the turmoil.

Josh got to his feet. "I'll see you out, Detective." *Don't let the door hit you in the butt on the way out.*

When Josh had locked the door behind Folau, he turned and beheld his wife and son. The Madonna-like vision smote his heart. *I love you, woman.*

Tabitha sat beside the playpen, staring lovingly down at their son. "I can't believe he slept through all that."

"He's a good kid."

"Yeah."

"Honey, can I, uh, get you anything?" Josh pointed toward the kitchen. "A drink of water? Milk?"

She turned her adoring gaze on him, making his heart flutter. "Yeah. Milk, please. I'm thirsty. And hungry too. I feel so wrung out. But please"—she extended a hand toward him—"let's do it together. I need *that* more than I need food or drink."

"I know exactly what you mean." Josh grinned as he took her hand. The Power flowed deliciously from her into him. Using her strength, he caused her to float up from the sofa and into his arms.

They clung to each other like dancers—his arm around her waist, her arm around his neck, and their hands clasped. And together, reveling in the Power, they floated to the kitchen.

With a thought, Josh caused a cupboard to open, and a plastic tumbler floated toward the refrigerator. With a mental tug, the fridge door opened. He imagined the milk jug floating out while the lid unscrewed itself. And of course, the jug obeyed. The jug tipped, and milk poured into the tumbler. "I think I could've done this faster by hand."

He pirouetted Tabitha around as if she were a ballerina, while carefully keeping contact with her fingers. He knew the trick of maintaining the flow after physical separation, but that took a lot of concentration. He could do it, but he hadn't quite mastered it yet, and Josh didn't want to drop his bride.

"Sure, you could," she said as he used the Power to press her back against him. "But this is a lot more fun. And you're getting faster at it, Mr. Warlock." The glass floated into her hand. She drank half the milk, then offered the rest to him.

He took it and drained it. Then he floated the tumbler to the sink. The water turned on—as if by magic—filling the glass, then shut off. "Now if only I could figure out how to Power the dishes clean."

She reached up with her free hand and put it behind his neck, causing the Power to flow there too. "Someday, my love. Practice makes perfect. But right now, I need you to turn me around and give me a kiss."

"Your wish is my command, princess." He complied, and soon their lips were joined, and the Power flowed through that exquisite point of contact as well.

They floated into the living room and slowly rotated inches above the floor, pressed together as if in a slow, languorous waltz. Tabitha laid her head on his shoulder, and he rejoiced in the scent of her.

"You smell good. Like strawberries."

"It's my shampoo, you doof."

"Yeah." He sniffed her in. "But it smells good on you." *Everything smells good on you.*

She sighed. "Thank you. I don't think I could've gotten through that. Or through so many of those awful visions, not without you."

"I didn't do much."

She shook her head slowly. "You held me. When each one was over, you drew the Power through me. It comforted me."

"Well, you are most welcome, sweetie. You know, it feels good to me too." *But it was so hard watching you suffer.* He squeezed her tight against himself. "You're amazing, you know that? So brave. So strong."

"Not without you."

"You were brave long before I met you. Uncle Mike told me stories."

A violent shudder tore through her. "I don't want to think about that."

"Okay," he said. "Sorry."

She let out a quivering breath. "I'm sorry too. And I know what's bothering you."

Bothering me? "What? I'm so sorry you had to go through all that. It must've been…"

"Horrible. Yeah, but… that's not what I meant."

"What then?"

"I called him Danny."

And there it was again—that ugly feeling—not quite jealousy, but something bordering on distrust—foulness intruding on their tenderness, like the scent of rotting meat in a rose garden. "Yeah," was all he managed to say.

"I told you he tested me. When Mikey was here."

"Uh-huh."

"The first iron he gave me. It was from his wife. His dead wife. She died in a car crash."

Wow. "You, uh, saw through her eyes."

She nodded, her head still pressed against his shoulder. "I saw him through her eyes."

Oh, no. "And you felt what she felt." *Love. You felt love for him. Even if only for a moment.*

She nodded. "He's not a bad guy."

Josh sighed. "I know he's not. But he sure is irritating." *And now I have one more reason to dislike him.*

She chuckled. Then she lifted her face and kissed him. "I love *you*."

He grinned down at her. "Just you keep on remembering that."

"He's not you." She nipped his nose playfully.

It was his turn to chuckle. "So, what you're saying is, you only love me because I can channel, huh?"

She nipped his nose again—just as playfully, but a bit harder. "You're wicked, mister!"

He grinned. "Yep. That's me. Mr. Wicked."

She glanced in the direction of the playpen. Then she gave him an inviting wink. "Well, Mr. Wicked, the baby's still asleep…"

He was hungry. Not just hungry—starving.

And the four Snickers bars he'd snuck into the theater and gobbled down hadn't helped one bit. It wasn't chocolate, caramel, and peanuts he craved.

It was fear. Woman's fear. A particular woman's fear.

She's not here. Of course, she's not. She wouldn't come two nights in a row. Not to the same lousy picture. Why'd they have to go R-rated? R-rated movies just don't sell in Provo. It's not like it's scarier with a bit of nudity.

Please, God. Send me a new one. Tonight. Something sweet. Just a snack. That's all I'm asking for. Just a morsel to get me by. Until I find her. My Prize.

He glanced around the darkened theater. Probably no more than a dozen couples were scattered around, plus one small group of girls sitting together. *Probably roommates out on a girls' night.*

He'd come in very late, missed most of the show. But that didn't matter. He knew when the scariest parts of the movie were. He'd seen it a few times already and memorized all the scream-worthy moments.

One of the best was coming up.

Sweat moistened his palms. He tensed in anticipation. *Come on!* "Give it to me," he whispered to the darkness.

On the movie screen, all was pitch black in the old, spooky house. Suddenly, Alice Krige's face, with its creepy and unnerving closed-lipped smile appeared out of the darkness.

A few screams. He felt the fear. He tasted it. It came from all around him, from every woman present. And it was sweet.

But it was also fleeting.

Like cotton candy. Sugary, but melts on the tongue. Then it's gone. Too fast.

He cursed softly. *Not scared enough. Not strong enough. Not a one of them.*

Worthless bitches. Damn them all.

Lousy R-rated piece of crap!

He grunted in disgust, stood up, and strode quickly from the dark cinema with its flickering, ghostly light. Alice Krige's too-deep-for-a-woman voice followed him, mocking him. As he entered the lobby, he angrily hit the button on the side of his Texas Instruments digital wristwatch. The red LEDs flashed the time.

Enough time to run out to the farm. Check on Ozzie and Harriet. See if they've finished off last night's feast.

He was confident Ol' Oz and the brood would've already consumed the girl's husk. After being thwarted himself the previous night—at least partially—he'd worked out his rage on the corpse. He'd chopped it into nice, bite-sized chunks.

Definitely gone by now. In spite of his own unsated hunger, he smiled.

After all, pigs will eat anything.

8

"The soul is eternal." From under knitted brows, Bishop Torrance Smith regarded Tabitha with his intense brown eyes. He folded his dark hands on top of his desk. The noontime sunlight of that beautiful—if crisp—Sunday morning shone through a frosted window, illuminating the bishop's office in the Sunset Chapel.

Tabitha shifted in her chair, careful not to disturb Joseph as he slept in her arms. "I know that." *Maybe this was a mistake.* She was grateful the bishop had made time during Sunday school to talk to her in private. Joseph had been fussy toward the end of sacrament meeting, and that fussiness had blossomed into a full-blown, red-faced, screaming fit. So, Tabitha had taken the baby out to the mothers' lounge to feed him. After sacrament meeting, as everyone else, including Josh, was heading off to Sunday school, she'd encountered Bishop Smith in the hallway.

Acting on impulse, she'd asked for a few minutes of his time.

As the bishop studied her with a piercing gaze, Tabitha had begun to feel anxious. A small part of her felt guilty—had always felt guilty—for keeping her secret—hers and Josh's—from her ecclesiastical leaders. "It's just…" She forced herself to meet his eyes. "Well, the scriptures talk about the *destruction* of a soul, the *loss* of one's soul."

He nodded slowly, finally looking away. "That's a metaphor. It refers to damnation, the stopping of one's progress. You know, basically not making the Celestial Kingdom. The scripture says that the spirit and the body are the soul of man." Then he hastily added, "And woman." He chuckled nervously. "I have to be careful to say that now. So many sisters—and I'm not suggesting you're one of them—are *offended* by male-centric language." He looked at her with a small degree of concern.

Tabitha shook her head dismissively. "Don't worry about that, bishop. I'm very comfortable with my role as a woman, with my value as a woman in the Church." *I wasn't always, but I am now. I understand now.* "And I interpret that word to mean 'mankind,' or 'humankind,' in that case. So, I guess, by 'soul,' I mean 'spirit.' Can the spirit be destroyed?" But "destroyed" wasn't the word she really wanted to use. *Consumed would be more accurate, but it'd be harder to explain.* "Permanently, I mean?"

He blinked once, as if he were surprised by her question. "No." He paused. "Not in the sense, I *think* you mean. It cannot be erased from existence."

"The Indians—at least some of them—believed that by taking their picture you could steal their souls."

"Do *you* believe that, Sister Kilmore? Do you believe a photograph can steal someone's soul?"

Now you sound like my doctor. And not just because you are my doctor. "No. Of course not."

"Then I'm not sure what you're getting at, Sister Kilmore."

She took a deep breath, then plunged in. "Can someone steal another's soul?"

He let out a single chuckle, but it was a laugh without amusement. "You mean, like in a ghost story?"

Tabitha almost flinched at the phrase. *Shouldn't have gone to that stupid movie.* "No."

"Like a vampire? Dracula?"

Not Dracula. Like Renfield. He believed he was consuming souls. "What about the devil? Satan?"

He shook his head decisively. "Not even the devil. Satan's not more powerful than God. He can corrupt. He can tempt. But he cannot claim a soul. We're told that even the Sons of Perdition, even Cain will rule over Satan in the end."

She nodded slowly. *That's right.* "Maybe not steal, but capture? Ensnare?"

"What's bothering you, Sister Kilmore?"

"Bothering me?"

"You seemed pretty anxious to talk to me." He paused for a long time, and his eyes became unfocused, as if he was engaged in some inner debate. "Look, I'm going to be honest with you. This doesn't feel like a normal interview. I mean, I don't feel like you're here to confess some… sin or transgression. If you'll pardon the expression, I'm not getting that *vibe* from you—not like I get from some folks. But I know something's bothering you. Something you need to get off your chest. I've felt it for a long time. You *and* Brother Kilmore."

This was a mistake. I'm not telling you about the Power. It's not a sin to use the Power.

"We're fine," was all she could think of to say.

He nodded. "I know you are. But if you ever need to talk, to discuss this secret." He gave a small grin. "Don't worry. Your temple recommends aren't in danger, or anything. I just know something's off." He shook his head. "And I, quite frankly, have no idea why I'm telling you that. Except that I feel it's true. And if you decide to confide in me…" He trailed off as if waiting for Tabitha to reveal something.

Tell him something. Anything. Anything true. "We're fine." That's not something. That's nothing. "I lost someone. Yesterday. Someone close." *Four someones. Women I came to know far too well, if only for a very short time.*

"I see. I'm sorry." He leaned back in his chair. He ran a hand across the top of his close-cropped, tightly curled, black hair. Then he sat forward again, leaning on his elbows. "What can I do to help?"

She gave him a sad smile. *Such a good man.* And suddenly, tears spilled from her eyes. "I'm okay. Really."

He nudged the ever-present Kleenex box—standard equipment for any bishop's office—toward her.

"Thanks." She plucked up a tissue and dabbed at her cheeks.

"Who was it? That passed away?"

Julie. Kelsie-Anne. Susan. Christie. "A friend. She was murdered." *Except for Julie. That was just an accident. A horrible accident.*

His eyes widened. "Murdered?"

She nodded slowly. "Yes." *I can tell him that.* "Before she died, she was convinced… She felt as if someone was… devouring her soul."

"Oh. My. I'm so sorry."

Tabitha wiped her nose. "Thank you."

"And that is why you asked…"

She nodded.

"Well, it's impossible. No one can take another's soul—I mean, spirit."

"Thank you. I've taken enough of your time."

He gave her a warm smile. Dazzlingly white teeth in a handsome black face.

For one heart-stopping instant, he reminded her of Joey Parsons—her friend from high school. And she wondered, as she hadn't for a very long time, whatever had become of Joey and Beulah. Joey—one of the very few men who could channel—and Beulah, Tabitha's friend and Joey's girlfriend—the girl who had been the strongest in the Power in Blue Beech Ridge. That was before Tabitha and her mother had moved into the cottage in White Lady Hollow. Joey and Beulah had run away to escape Magnus. Together.

Tabitha had heard nothing from them since.

"Sister Kilmore?"

Tabitha blinked. *Did I miss something? Was he talking?* "What?"

Bishop Smith chuckled nervously. "I thought I'd lost you there for a second. You seemed far away."

A sad smile played at the corner of her lips. "Old memories. You reminded me of someone."

He raised an eyebrow. "Someone nice, I hope? I mean, I hope they were pleasant memories."

"Some of them." A fresh tear fell. "Some of them"—horrific—"not so nice." *So much death. Mom and Daddy almost died. And now, more death. More murder.* "But I have some fond memories of my friend." *I hope they're okay. I hope they're happy.*

But the odds against them were so great. "I really better get going. Josh is taking the baby to priesthood." She sighed. "So, I can get a break in Relief Society."

The bishop grinned. "Good man."

And suddenly, Tabitha truly felt like smiling. "Yes, he is. The best." *And not just for taking the baby for a bit.* She stood—slowly, so as not to wake Joseph. The bishop rose as well and strode to the door. He held it open for her and extended a hand.

Tabitha carefully curled a hand away from her son. "Thank you."

He took her hand, clasped it gently, but he didn't shake it at all—for which Tabitha was grateful. "My pleasure," he said. "And if you ever want to talk again"—he gave her the slightest of winks—"I'll be ready to listen."

She nodded and released his hand. She turned to go and almost collided with Jesse Levi Montrose.

"Tabitha!" he said, just as surprised as she was.

"J.L.!" Though he wasn't as tall as Josh, Mikey's husband still towered over Tabitha. And being right in front of him, she had to crane her neck to look him in the eye. During *Fiddler*, she'd gotten a stiff neck during their dance number. Every single night.

J.L. took a step back. "I, uh, didn't know you had an appointment with the bishop." "I didn't."

Bishop Smith put a hand on his executive secretary's shoulder, startling J.L. "It's okay, Brother Montrose. She didn't need one. I had a free moment, and Sister Kilmore had a quick question." He shook J.L.'s shoulder gently and smiled. "Not everyone's as time-conscious as you."

J.L. ran his fingers through his short, brown hair, chuckling nervously. "Of course! I knew you didn't have Tabitha on your schedule. I, uh, didn't mean to imply… "

That I'd come to confess some great sin? She gave him a friendly smirk. "Honestly, J.L. Letting your imagination run away with you again?" But as soon as the words escaped her lips, she regretted them.

His pale cheeks flushed to a rosy pink. "I didn't mean it like that."

Oh, no. He thinks I'm referring to… He can't still imagine I might have feelings for him, can he? That I went to talk to the bishop about that? "I know you didn't." She lowered her eyes, looking for a gap between J.L. and the bishop large enough for her and Joseph to escape through.

Her thoughts briefly returned to the last night of the show, when the two of them— she and J.L.—had stood side-by-side, waiting off-stage for their next entrance. He had whispered, "In another life… " His hand had brushed hers, lingering just a moment too long. She'd snatched her hand away. It had been just a moment, but that moment had flustered her so badly, she almost botched their dance. *Not that it takes much to make me screw up a dance routine.* However, since that night, there had remained a marked awkwardness between them.

Out of the corner of her eye, Tabitha could see Bishop Smith's eyes flickering between her and J.L. "Brother Montrose, what's up next on my schedule?"

J.L. blinked, then turned his attention to the bishop. "Let me check." He opened the slim, three-ring binder where he, as executive secretary, kept the bishop's schedule.

"If you'll excuse me," Tabitha said, grateful for the interruption, "I'm going to go sit with my husband for the rest of Sunday school. As long as the baby cooperates." She gave Bishop Smith a smile. "Thanks, Bishop!"

Then she scurried away as fast as possible.

Little Joseph did indeed cooperate, and soon Tabitha was seated next to Josh in the Relief Society room on a padded folding chair. Josh had saved her a seat, of course. He took her hand, and she felt the comforting tingle of the Power. The flow was just a trickle—not enough to distract her from listening to the last fifteen minutes of the Gospel Doctrine lesson—but just enough to establish the link between them. Just enough to assure her that, in spite of her fears and all the evils in the world, she and Josh were united. They were one.

He bent his head and whispered. "Everything okay?"

She squeezed his hand. "As of this moment, yes." A small surge of the Power set her heart fluttering. *I've got that darn dance to do in class tomorrow, and I still can't get the steps without tripping. Things are awkward with J.L. and with Mikey. I still have two papers to type tomorrow night.*

I died four times yesterday. And there's a serial killer out there. But right now, at this moment... "Couldn't be better."

Josh chuckled softly, then whispered, "Doesn't the scripture say, wo unto the liar, for she shall be thrust down to hell?"

Tabitha flashed him a wicked grin. "As I recall, it says 'he shall be thrust down to hell.' And for once, I'm very content to let the male-centric language stand *exactly* as written."

"How very convenient!" He winked. "Must be nice to always have that excuse."

"You know it. Advantage of being a woman."

The Power surged, eliciting a gasp from Tabitha.

Josh squeezed her hand. "Not the only advantage, I hope."

"Behave." Another surge. "We're supposed to be listening to the lesson. You're distracting me."

He chuckled. "I sure hope so."

She narrowed her eyes and pursed her lips in mock anger. "I'm warning you, buster. I've got an iron washer in my pocket and I'm not afraid to use it!"

"And risk a vision in the middle of Sunday school? I don't think so." He put his lips right next to her ear. "Besides, you're holding the baby, and I'm not letting go of your hand. So, I've got you."

The Power surged again. "I'll do it," she whispered back. "I will. I'll yank my hand free and—"

"A word of advice, Sweetheart. You may be a great actress. But don't ever play poker. You can't bluff worth beans."

She was sorely tempted to nip at his nose—not that she could have reached it. "I thought you said I was going to hell."

"I said you were *lying.* Okay, maybe I *did* imply you might be going to hell, but the point was you were lying." He winked. "I didn't say you were *good* at lying." He kissed the tip of her nose, sending tingles of the Power through that sensitive point.

But the pleasure was swallowed up in a sudden itching in her nose. Tabitha found herself fighting the urge to sneeze. She barely managed to avoid letting loose a violent explosion of air and spittle on Josh's cheek. Or worse, on Joseph's. Her sudden movement startled her son. Joseph's little face reddened and balled up, and he let loose with a howl.

Tabitha yanked her hand free of Josh's, and the Power ceased.

She glared at her husband as she handed the baby to him. "Your turn!"

He grinned sheepishly. "Yep. Serves me right." He grabbed the diaper bag, stood, and headed for the exit—they always sat at the back of the room for just such emergencies—leaving Tabitha alone for the last ten minutes of the Sunday school lesson.

She'd barely caught a word of the lesson before Joseph's outburst and Josh's departure. However, as she tried to listen and focus, her thoughts drifted—first to the baby and Josh, then to J.L. and Mikey, and finally, inexorably, to the fiend who was murdering women. Draining them.

He can't be consuming their souls. He can't. But that's how it felt. He drained them. It was as if he sucked their very essence, the core of their being, whatever made them unique and special, whatever made them who they were. He—

I can't keep calling the killer 'he,' without knowing it was a "he." But it felt like a man—all that hatred directed at women. But who is he?

He wears a mask, like Magnus did. Hiding who he truly is.

A coward. That's what he is. A monstrous coward.

"Malachi says in chapter three, verse eleven"—the teacher, a tall, balding, middle-aged man named Spencer Johansen, peered through bifocals at his scriptures—"'And I will *rebuke* the devourer for your sakes.' Did you catch that? The Lord will *rebuke* the devourer. Who is the devourer, brothers and sisters?"

A shudder ripped through Tabitha, shaking her from head to toe. *The Devourer.* She locked onto the name.

The teacher continued, "And what does he devour?"

Tabitha leaned forward, waiting for the teacher to validate the thoughts rushing through her head.

Souls. Women's souls. He consumed them. He made them nothing. No. Not them. Not nothing. They had names.

Kelsie-Anne. Susan. Christie.

I saw your deaths. I felt your deaths.

Heavenly Father, help Danny, Detective Folau. Help him catch the Devourer.

Stop calling him that!

But that's what he does. He devours *them.*

And in that instant, Tabitha knew the name would stick in her brain, like a thorn in a festering wound.

Please, Heavenly Father! Help Detective Folau. Help him stop the Devourer. Before he consumes another woman.

Please, rebuke the Devourer for their sakes. For my sake. Guide Detective Folau.

"The devourer," the teacher said in answer to his own question, "is the Devil himself."

Laden with the diaper bag, his son ensconced in his carry-cradle, and both sets of scriptures—he was attempting to be chivalrous, after all—Josh climbed the last flight of stairs to their apartment, looking forward to a lazy Sabbath afternoon. However, any hope of relaxation vanished the instant Josh spied the scarred detective leaning against the apartment doorpost.

Dressed in a gray suit that looked just a few artificial fibers short of threadbare, Detective Folau wore a too-casual smile that did not reach as high as his eyes.

Bollocks! Josh thought. *What's he doing here?* "Detective Folau!" Josh wasn't breathing hard, not really, but he was gripped by a sudden desire to prove he wasn't breathing hard.

Folau tipped his head in greeting. "Mr. Kilmore."

"Can we help you, Detective?" asked Tabitha as she caught up to Josh on the stairs. "Do you have another object?" Josh noted with a touch of annoyance that Tabitha wasn't breathing hard, but then again, she wasn't carrying the baby, the diaper bag, and both sets of scriptures.

"Mrs. Kilmore." Folau's eyes flickered away from Josh and over to Tabitha, but returned quickly to Josh as he reached the stair landing. "Actually, I'm here to speak to you, Mr. Kilmore."

"Me?" *What does he want me for?*

"Josh?" Tabitha came to stand beside her husband. She took the baby-laden carry-cradle from Josh and then grasped Josh's newly freed hand. His bruised hand. Her firm grip almost made Josh wince. Almost.

Josh drew just enough of her Power to let her know he was ready for trouble. "Why do you want to talk to me?"

Still brandishing that insincere smile, Folau jerked a thumb toward the door. "Can we talk inside, please?"

Josh nodded. "Hold these for a second." He handed the scripture cases to Folau, who shrugged and took them. Without breaking contact with Tabitha, Josh fished out his keys, unlocked the door, and pushed it open. "After you, Detective."

Folau raised an eyebrow. "So, I have your permission to enter your home?"

What are you? A vampire? You need permission to cross the threshold?

Tabitha nodded. "Of course, Detective. Please."

Folau detached himself from the doorpost, and sauntered in, carrying their scriptures. Josh glanced at Tabitha. She met his eyes, and he saw concern there, but no fear. Josh entered, gently pulling Tabitha behind him.

Folau had deposited the scripture cases on the dinette table and was already carrying a chair toward the sofa.

Josh almost gave into a nasty impulse to use the Power to rip the chair out of the man's hands. *Not without Tabitha's permission. Never without Tabitha's permission.*

Except in an emergency. We agreed on that long ago.

As the annoying man sat in the commandeered chair, Josh said, "Hey, I've got an idea, Detective. Why don't you make yourself comfortable? Pull up a chair or something."

Folau's smirk epitomized arrogance. "Thanks, Mr. Kilmore. Don't mind if I do. Now, if you'd take a seat"—he indicated the sofa—"I have a few questions. Mrs. Kilmore"—he pointed at the bedroom door—"if you'd be so kind as to give us a little privacy… "

Tabitha's hand trembled in Josh's. "Detective, this is our home. My home. I will be where I choose to be."

Folau's smirk faltered a bit. "It's always best if I question witnesses separately."

"Witnesses?" Josh asked. "Witnesses to what? Tabitha's visions?"

The smirk returned in full force. "Mr. Kilmore, did you know you own the only old-model, yellow Volkswagen Beetle registered in Utah County?" Folau pointed at Josh's bruised, swollen knuckles.

And Josh felt the blood in his veins turn to ice.

Folau's smirk widened, becoming a toothy, wolfish grin. "So, tell me, Mr. Kilmore—how'd you injure your hand?"

9

"Now before you answer, Mr. Kilmore"—Folau held up a hand in a halting gesture—"*Mrs.* Kilmore, would you please give us a few minutes alone?"

Still holding Joseph's carry-cradle in one hand and Josh's hand in the other, Tabitha turned to her husband. She whispered, "Hold onto it."

Josh nodded and whispered back, "As long as I can." *I can do this*, he thought. Reluctantly, he let go of her hand.

But the Power still tingled within him. *Yes!*

A small, sly grin lifted the corners of Tabitha's lips. She turned toward the detective, and her expression became icy as a glacier. But she said nothing. She and Joseph disappeared into the bedroom, Tabitha closing the door softly behind them.

Once the door was closed, Folau turned a feral smile on Josh. "Now, Mr. Kilmore, tell me about Friday night."

Josh held up a finger. "Just a moment." He concentrated, imagining forming a cone of air, like an invisible megaphone with the large end facing the detective and himself, and the other flat against the bedroom door. He felt the Power surge—surge and hold steady.

Once the cone was in place, he relegated it to the back of his mind. The cone would hold as long as he maintained the connection with Tabitha.

He smiled. "Okay, Detective. Fire away."

Folau had his notepad open, his pen ready. "Friday night, between the hours of eleven and midnight—where were you?"

Tell him the truth, but not all of it. Nothing that would betray Tabitha and her Power.

"We—Tabitha and I—went out to the movie theatre. The one on East Center Street. We didn't enjoy the show all that much. In fact, it sucked."

Folau seemed amused. "The one with Fred Astaire and John Houseman?"

"Yeah. We shouldn't have. I mean it was scary and all, but it sucked. Anyway, we decided to take the night air for a bit. We don't get out a lot. Without the baby, I mean."

75

"You went for a walk? Late at night?"

Josh nodded. *A thousand feet in the air. I think our feet were moving. A little.* "Yeah."

"Did you walk home?"

Josh lifted an eyebrow. "You know we didn't. Are you trying to trick me into lying or something?"

"Are you lying or something, Mr. Kilmore?"

Perhaps it was just the Power flowing into Josh from his wife. Perhaps it was the fact that he was finally mastering the skill of retaining the remote connection—holding onto it, as Tabitha had said. Perhaps it was the fact that he really didn't like Folau. Whatever the reason, Josh felt confident, even cocky. He knew he should be scared, but he wasn't. Not too much, at least.

He leaned forward and looked Folau in the eye. "No." *I'm not lying.*

Folau's eye twitched, and his scar twitched with it. "So, you went for a walk. Around the block?"

I'm sure we circled it at some point. "Yeah."

"Then what?"

"We went back to our car in the parking lot behind the theatre. You know the small one?"

Folau smirked. "I know the place."

"When we got back to our car—"

"The yellow Volkswagen?"

"Yep. But you already know that."

Folau's smirk hardened a bit. "Go on."

Getting irritated, Detective? "We had a flat tire. I had to put on the spare."

"Are you still driving on the spare?"

Why would that be important to him? "Tabitha took it to Discount Tire yesterday afternoon and got it fixed. While I was at work. But I bet you already know that, too."

Folau flipped back a page in his notepad. He made a mark on the page as if he were checking off a line on a checklist. "Go on. What happened after that?"

Already verified that? Okay, so he's been to Discount Tire. But when? Tabitha went on Saturday afternoon. Before she met with Folau. And they're closed on Sundays. Is he just trying to make me think he already knows everything? He can't have been to Discount Tire.

But he does know about the fight. And the explosion. And our car.

Josh's confidence nearly evaporated. He very nearly lost his hold on the Power.

Stick to the truth. Just don't tell him about the Power.

He suddenly remembered reading Captain Larry Chesley's book, "Seven Years in Hanoi," about the air force pilot's experiences as a prisoner of war. How Chesley had learned to resist his captors—and his interrogators.

Details. Distract Folau with details.

"So," Josh continued, "when I went to put the tire away—it turned out to be a nail, by the way—this big guy—he wore a Provo Bulldogs jacket and looked like a football player—came up behind me. Blonde hair cut short. He'd obviously been drinking. I could smell it on him. He had two friends with him. Same jackets. All big guys. They said they wanted to 'party' with my wife. At least two of them had knives. One had a liquor bottle." He paused, wanting to give the next words plenty of emphasis. "They were going to *rape* her."

"And how do you know that?"

"Seriously? They said they wanted to 'party' with her."

"'Party' could mean a lot of things."

"I'm not stupid, Folau. And neither are you. Quit playing dumb."

The scar twitched. "Still, you can't be certain."

Didn't like that, did you?

Why am I being so mean? That's not like me.

Because he's being a jerk. He's threatening me and my family. "And if that isn't proof enough, one man dropped his pants. How's that for certain, huh?"

"Is that when you broke the jaw of one of the kids?"

"He came at me with a knife. Their car exploded. When he was distracted, I kicked the knife away and hit the jerk. If I broke his jaw"—Josh remembered teeth flying from the kid's mouth—"good."

"And the car just happened to blow up."

Josh shrugged. "That's what I saw."

"It just spontaneously combusted. How do you explain that?"

"I don't have to explain it. It just happened."

"You're a witness. And you just confessed to committing aggravated assault. That's a Class Three felony, you know. Up to five years in prison. And the end to your Air Force career before it even begins."

An icy claw of dread seized Josh's gut. And twisted.

Hold onto the Power. Hold onto it!

He did, but he'd come perilously close to losing it. Or to lashing out.

Don't you have to read me my rights? You didn't read me my rights. You're not going to arrest me. So, what's your game? To force us to cooperate?

But we're already cooperating. You know what, Folau? I've had enough of you. I could hurt you. But I won't. Tabitha would not approve. And it's her Power. I'm just borrowing it.

Josh pictured the air twirling next to Folau's cheek, tickling with eight tiny points of pressure. The Power surged just slightly.

The detective yelped. He slapped at his own face. "What the—"

Josh kept his expression neutral as he caused the air to tickle Folau's forehead.

Folau slapped himself again. "Yah!"

"What's the matter, Detective?"

Folau frantically waved his hands over his head. "Spiders!"

"Spiders? We don't have spiders here. Not that I've seen." Josh imagined another "spider" on the man's nose.

"Gah!" Folau brushed at his nose. He jumped up from his chair.

Josh was certain he heard muted laughter coming through the bedroom door. *So, she is hearing every word. Cool.* "So, are you going to arrest me?"

Folau's wide, panicked eyes jerked as he scanned the room. He brushed at the air once more, his breathing rapid.

Don't give him a heart attack. He's so spooked. I don't have to do anything else. But Josh felt a stab of guilt—for what he'd just done to Folau, not for what they'd done to the creeps in the parking lot. *Might as well ask anyway.* "So, the would-be rapists—are they gonna be alright?"

Folau settled into his chair once more, but his eyes still darted around the room. "You broke the kid's jaw. Knocked out three teeth. Shattered another. The one who dropped his pants got serious abrasions on his privates." Folau swatted the air again—although Josh hadn't done anything. "Two of them have ruptured eardrums. And their football coach wants them to press charges."

"You're saying I did something to somebody's privates? So, now, I'm being accused of some sort of sexual attack?"

"No. Just aggravated assa—"

"Why were his pants down, Detective?"

"That's not the—"

"Because he was going to *rape* my wife. Why haven't you gone after these creeps for that? Why go after me?" Josh gave into temptation and caused an imaginary arachnid to brush Folau's ear.

Folau slapped at the air. "Are you going to file a complaint?"

"So, why haven't you arrested me?"

Attempting to slow his rapid breathing, the detective focused on Josh once more. "Tell me about the car. Your car."

"What about it? I told you I changed the tire. That was when they tried to—"

"How did you get away?"

Josh shrugged his shoulders. "In the car."

Folau grunted in obvious frustration. He flinched at nothing again. "I know that."

"So, what do you want to know?" *Did we fly away? That's it, isn't it?*

"Did you..." Folau scratched out something on his notepad with a fury that left a rip in the small page. "Never mind."

The creeps did talk about the flying car. "So, are you going to arrest me?"

Folau glared at him. Then he bowed his head and shook it, muttering something about "knuckleheads."

And suddenly, Josh understood. "This isn't the first time these kids have been in serious trouble, is it?"

Folau shook his head slowly. "I can't discuss that."

"Have they raped someone before?"

"I can't discuss that."

Josh nodded, then fixed the detective with his gaze. "You know what I think, Detective?"

Folau said nothing.

"I think these creeps are serial troublemakers. And I think they keep getting off, maybe without even a slap on the wrist. I think their crimes keep getting swept under the rug, because they're jocks, star athletes. I'll bet their rotten football coach keeps providing them with alibis." He paused. "Stop me if I'm wrong."

Folau maintained his silence.

"And I bet you're secretly glad they're off the streets and off the football field." Josh leaned forward. "And you know what, Detective? I think this whole farce—this *joke* of an interrogation—has been a thinly veiled attempt to coerce me, to coerce us into cooperating with you. Well, we're already cooperating."

Suddenly, Josh realized he was furious. "Tabitha—my wife—has already *died* for you, for your investigation. *Four times!* I don't know what else we can possibly do for you, Detective. If Tabitha wants to continue helping, then fine. I'll support her. I'll be there to hold her when she cries and trembles at night, when she wakes up *screaming*. Because that's what happened last night. But you will *never* come into our home and threaten us again. In fact, if you want our help again, you will treat my wife with the respect she so richly deserves." He paused, tamping down his anger. "Are we clear?"

Folau's lips were drawn into a tight line. His scar twitched.

But he nodded. "We're clear." He looked away for a moment, then looked Josh in the eye once more. Any vestige of arrogance had vanished. "Maybe I needed to know if… she was credible. If you were a violent man. And after I learned about the incident…" He sighed. "I owe you both an apology. Especially *you*, sir." He extended his hand. "Can we start over?"

Josh nodded slowly. Then he nodded more vigorously as he took the extended hand and shook it. "Sure." Josh sat back once more. "Now, do you still need to question Tabitha?"

Folau shook his head. "No. To be honest, this isn't even my case. I saw the report and I knew I'd seen that yellow Bug outside. Put two and two together. And I thought I'd…" He waved dismissively. "Aw, you know what I thought. Anyway, did you know those knuckleheads claimed your car flew away?" He chuckled. "Flew through the air. They must've been really drunk."

"Flew?" An amused—and relieved—grin spread across Josh's face. "Flying. Like in *The Absentminded Professor*? Flubber? That kind of thing?"

"Yeah. Pretty dang stupid, huh?" He chuckled, shaking his head. "And just so you know, in spite of what Coach Harwood wants, nobody's taking the case seriously. I mean, obviously the kids were injured, but their testimony is compromised by them being intoxicated and by the whole flying-car bit." His eyes narrowed as if he were searching Josh's face for a reaction.

Still seeing if I'll bite. "Cool."

"So, how did you blow up the car?"

"Blow up the car? Detective, I promise you, neither Tabitha nor I touched their car."

Folau nodded. "Fair enough."

"Now, going forward, no more jerking us around. Okay?"

Folau raised his right hand to the square. He extended three fingers while holding his pinky down with his thumb. "Scout's Honor."

Josh allowed the megaphonic funnel of air to dissipate. But he kept the Power flowing. "Sweetheart," he called, "you can come out anytime."

Two seconds later, Tabitha emerged. She wasn't holding the baby or the carry-cradle.

Joseph is still asleep. Good kid.

Tabitha looked at Josh, and he could detect the hint of a smile. She turned her attention to Folau. "My turn?"

Folau shook his head. "No, ma'am. I have what I need. I'm truly sorry to disturb you folks on the Sabbath." He stood. "I can't say enough just how grateful I am for your help. Both of you."

She smiled sweetly. "Anything we can do."

"Yes, ma'am. Now if you'll excuse me, I'll let myself out."

Josh followed the detective to the door and locked the door after him. Then he turned back to his wife.

She took a step toward him, but he used the Power to lift her off the floor and fly her into his arms.

Her delighted smile brightened the entire room. "You're getting better at that." She threw her arms around his neck. "You held onto it the whole time!" She kissed him. "I mean, obviously you held onto it."

"Yeah," he said. "It was nice staying connected to you. Your strength... You sustained me."

She laid her head on his shoulder. "I always will."

"I love you, Tabitha."

"I love you too." She paused. "I'm glad you guys worked things out."

Josh nodded. "Me too."

"He's a good man. We need to catch the Devourer."

Josh blinked. "Did you give the killer a nickname?"

She shrugged. "Yeah. I need a way to refer to him."

Josh nodded. "The Devourer it is."

Her face split in a wide grin. "But you, Mr. Warlock! You're absolutely wicked. Spiders!"

"Hey!" Josh matched her grin. "Maybe we should use it on trick-or-treaters this Halloween!"

She gave him a horrified look. "Don't you dare! Not with my Power! Not on those cute little kids!"

"Well, maybe just on the obnoxious teenagers. You know, the ones who don't even bother to dress up and just demand candy?"

Her grin returned. "Well, maybe. But we'll still give them candy, okay? Just freak them out a little."

"Deal!"

Her countenance fell. "No, wait. Halloween is on a Sunday this year."

"Yeah. So?"

"The kids'll be trick-or-treating on Saturday. I'll be doing the show. We're gonna miss out on all the cute costumes!"

Josh gave her a wink. "So, maybe I'll just drop some air-spiders on members of the audience. In that creepy old theatre." At her sudden look of horror, he quickly added, "Just kidding!"

Her eyes narrowed. "You better be, Mr. Warlock. You most definitely do not have my permission to terrorize the audience." The grin returned in all its wicked, witchy glory. "That's *my* job."

Here it comes. Now! Let it be now!

Suddenly, Alice Krige's pale face with its creepy, unnerving smile appeared out of the darkness of the old house.

A scream. A woman's scream. Shrill and filled with terror.

Sweet and delicious and strong. His eyes snapped in the direction of the lovely sound.

Two rows down and three seats to the right. Sitting alone.

Not as strong as her. *Not my Prize. But strong enough. For now.*

When he'd entered the movie late, the prey had been sitting with a male—a protector. But just as Alice Krige had uttered the chilling, "And you will be too. Dead and wet and cold," there'd been a whispered, heated exchange between the prey and protector. He hadn't caught a word, but it had been clear they'd been arguing, fighting. Then the protector had stomped out of the dark cinema, abandoning the prey.

He should not have left you alone, he'd thought. He doesn't care about you. He doesn't value you. Not like I do.

She'd bowed her head and wept then. She'd been afraid. Not because of the rotten movie—at least not at that moment. She was afraid of being left alone.

He let the tidal wave of fear crash over him, engulf him. *So sweet!*

He shuddered in delightful anticipation.

You will die alone.

I will consume you. Your soul will be mine. A part of me.

You will live on. In me. And we will be together. Forever. He patted the front of his jacket, over his belly, and felt the ridges of the vinyl werewolf mask hidden inside. He caressed his jacket pocket. The capped syringe snug inside was ready for her.

He was ready.

While still basking in the ecstasy of delectable, female terror, he felt a rush of gratitude.

Not the Prize, but she will do. For now.

Thank you, God! Thank you for sending me sustenance.

His unwilling fast would soon be over.

10

As Tabitha exited the Harris Fine Arts Center on the BYU campus, she spotted Josh easily. He stood out from the crowd—and not just because of his height. While there were several AFROTC cadets in their blue uniforms, striding quickly across campus, all of them heading north, he was the only one hefting a carry-cradle, a diaper bag, and a bookbag—all three somehow clutched in his left hand. His right hand, of course, needed to be free to salute at any moment.

The blue pastel baby blanket, which covered Joseph's carry-cradle to shield him from the cool September air and the Monday morning sunshine, and the diaper bag adorned with images of Winnie the Pooh and his friends contrasted wildly with Josh's dark-blue polyester uniform and his shiny, black patent-leather shoes.

As imbalanced as he was, carrying all that extra weight on one side, he to stride with a perfect, straight-backed, military bearing.

Man, he makes that look good! she thought, smiling widely.

Josh's military bearing, however, was compromised the instant he laid eyes on her.

Tabitha stood out as well, she knew, and not just because of her short stature. She was probably the only woman on campus in a full-length skirt. She rarely wore anything else, except on stage.

Josh's stoic face broke into a huge grin, and he waved with his saluting arm.

She gathered her skirt in one hand and hastened toward him. *Gotta hurry, so he can get to Lab.*

Josh quickened his pace, but slowed just long enough to return the salute of a young, green-uniformed, army ROTC cadet. As a cadet-major, most cadets saluted Josh, but he was required to acknowledge and return the salute of those of lower ranks. Once he'd returned it, he hurried toward her.

"How'd the dance go?" he asked. He bowed his head and kissed her. The tingle of the Power briefly through her lips into his instantly lifted her spirits.

She grimaced. "I squeaked out a B." She gently extricated the diaper bag from Josh's left hand. As she hung the bag's strap over her shoulder, she muttered, "And I think the instructor was being generous." She breathed a low growl. "Dang it." She took the carry-cradle with its precious cargo from Josh, leaving only his bookbag in his left hand.

He shook his head. "You worked so hard on it. I'm sure you deserved *at least* a B."

"They don't call me Stumble-Foot Tabby for nothing."

He grinned. "Nobody calls you that, but you, sweetie."

"Yeah, well, I knew when I took this class, it'd be rough."

"You're not going to lose your scholarship over a B. You only have to maintain a B-average anyway."

She resisted the sudden urge to stomp her foot. "I hate B's."

"Always the perfectionist. Makes the rest of us mere mortals feel small." His grin became positively wicked. "And for someone as short as you…"

She fixed him with a withering glare. "Ooh, you'd better watch it, buster."

He bent and kissed her again, sending a Power-fueled jolt of pleasure through her. "Gotta run. We're practicing for a parade-in-review. More marching. Yay." He snapped a quick salute to an army ROTC cadet-lieutenant-colonel. "At least the army gets to shoot stuff or go rappelling down cliffs. We get to march. Again."

"You are going to fly airplanes, mister. So, quit yer whinin'!" She smiled up at him. "I love you."

"I love you too."

She glanced at the carry-cradle. "How's he been?"

"Itching to get out. Just took care of his poopy diaper." He glanced toward the Marriott Center parking lot. "Gotta run!"

One more brief but Power-tingling kiss, and he was off, striding away at a pace that wasn't exactly a run. Tabitha watched him go for a few seconds. *I really love that man.*

Then Joseph began to fuss.

"Okay, little man. Let's get you inside. I'll try to find us a practice-room where you can play." As the baby's fussing grew in volume, she became almost uncomfortably aware that she needed to feed him as well.

So, she turned about, with a swirl of dark skirt, and hurried back into the HFAC. She headed for the nearest staircase with the intent of descending to the basement with its array of sound-proof practice-rooms.

Hope there's an empty one.

"Tabitha!"

Tabitha paused and spotted Dr. Daisy Engelhard, one of her theatre professors. Her favorite professor. Blonde, gray-eyed, and slightly stocky, Dr. Engelhard was undeviatingly cheerful.

Tabitha waved. "Dr. Daisy!" Rather than moving toward the woman, Tabitha allowed the professor to come to her. "What's up?"

Dr. Engelhard gave Tabitha the briefest of hugs. "Do you have a minute? Or ten?"

"I was just about to feed the baby." Right on cue, Joseph began to cry. "He's tired of being cooped-up." She grinned sheepishly, shifting her shoulders against her discomfort. "And I need to nurse."

Dr. Daisy gripped Tabitha's arm gently. "Let's talk in my office. You can nurse in there." The professor reached for the carry-cradle and its noisy occupant. "May I?"

Tabitha grinned and handed the carry-cradle to the older woman. "Thanks."

A couple minutes later, Tabitha was seated across from Dr. Daisy in the professor's office. The door was closed, and Tabitha was nursing Joseph under the cover of his blanket. She looked quickly at the wall covered by playbills and focused immediately on "South Pacific." *I'd never have gotten Nellie Forbush without Dr. Daisy.* She smiled gratefully at the older woman. "Thank you. Sometimes, all the practice rooms are full, and I just *hate* nursing in public."

Dr. Daisy chuckled. "I'm with you there. When I was in school here, before the HFAC even existed—back in the late Jurassic—I never could find a private place to nurse on campus."

"Well, I really appreciate it, Professor. So, why'd you want to see me?"

"Well…" Dr. Daisy placed both hands, fingers spread wide, on her cluttered desk. "I heard about *Dracula* and Renfield. Congratulations. Trevor Andersen's good to work with. We were in *Arsenic and Old Lace* together. Played opposite each other. Lo-o-ong ago."

"How'd you know about *Dracula*?"

Dr. Daisy sighed dramatically. "Well, I'd like to tell you that I knew you couldn't pass up an honest-to-goodness horror play and that I knew you'd be a shoe-in. But the truth is that Dr. Thorpe was crowing about it this morning. Couldn't resist a chance to tell me about his latest coup." She rolled her gray eyes. Then she put her hands together and drummed her fingertips against each other. She lowered her voice in a fair imitation of Dr. Thorpe's baritone. "'I'll get her yet! Ha-ha-ha!'" She shook her head, her lips twisted in a smirk. "That man is positively Machiavellian."

"But, Professor, I want this role! And he had nothing to do with it."

Dr. Daisy chuckled again, waving dismissively. "I know you want it. And it's a juicy role. Much better than the *female* roles in the show, in my opinion. Although, you would have made a wonderful Lucy, I'm sure."

Tabitha realized she was blushing. "Thanks." Accolades on stage were one thing, but in-person compliments never failed to embarrass her.

Dr. Daisy continued, "I also know Eli Thorpe had nothing to do with you getting the role. It's the unique position he'll be in—in the same cast, with the chance to *work* on you."

Tabitha was about to ask what the professor meant, but just at the moment, Joseph began to fidget. He pushed away from her.

Tabitha sighed as she covered up. "I guess he's done." *Wish you'd nursed on both sides, you little stinker.* "Is it okay if he lays on the floor? I'll put his blanket out and—"

"Oh, absolutely! Let him play! Is he crawling yet? My office isn't exactly baby-proofed."

Tabitha shook her head. "Not yet. He's rolling over. Sometimes he scoots a little. But he's sitting up." She couldn't hide the pride in her voice. "I'll just lay him on the floor with a couple of toys. Wouldn't want him falling over on this hard floor."

"Go right ahead!"

Tabitha spread the blanket and laid Joseph down, on his belly. She set his toy plastic keys and a teething ring within his reach. Soon, Joseph was happily shaking both. He quickly rolled over and waved the keys at her, grinning toothlessly—and melting his mother's heart.

"He's a beautiful baby," said the professor.

"Thanks."

"And so well behaved"—Dr. Daisy raised the pitch of her voice—"aren't you, you little cutie?"

"Most of the time." Tabitha smiled down at her son. "Most of the time. And sometimes he's got more energy than he knows what to do with. More than *I* know what to do with."

"Typical boy."

Tabitha chuckled softly. "I suppose so. And as frustrated as I get sometimes"—she smiled at her son, who was gurgling and grinning right back at her—"I wouldn't have it any other way."

The professor plucked the large duck-feather quill pen from the cylindrical holder on her desk. Tabitha had never seen an ink bottle for the pen—just the clean quill itself, unstained with ink. Dr. Daisy ran the edges of the feather between her thumb and forefinger, as Tabitha had seen the woman do many times while the older woman was thinking. Like most thespians, it seemed the professor couldn't abide her hands being idle.

One of the most difficult dilemmas for an actress—what to do with your hands?

"He has designs on you, you know."

Joseph? No. Dr. Thorpe. "What do you mean? I know he wants me to—"

Dr. Daisy lowered the pitch of her voice. "Forget all this nonsense of singing and dancing. You, my dear, should be performing the works of the Bard!"

Tabitha bit her lower lip to keep from laughing out loud. "Something like that."

"Exactly like that. I've heard him!"

Tabitha shrugged, then nodded. "Yeah." Then she frowned. "But that's nothing new."

"Did you know he wants to start a professional Shakespearean repertory company?"

Tabitha shook her head. "No."

"Well, he does. And he has his eye on you for the female lead in the company."

Tabitha blinked. "A professional company?" *Cordelia. Portia. Beatrice. Juliet. Hermia. Desdemona.* "But I can't. Josh graduates in the spring and then he'll be on active duty. Pilot training. I'll be graduating too." *If everything stays on track. If I survive next semester. Let alone this one.* "We're moving."

Dr. Daisy lifted an eyebrow. "Not if Eli Thorpe has anything to say about it."

"But I can't. I'm going with Josh. He can't delay. That's why I'm trying to finish up next semester. But even if I don't graduate…"

"You'll be going with him. I know. But just be warned. Eli will have you alone while you're doing *Dracula*. A lot. He's going to *work* on you."

"Okay. Thanks for the warning."

"More importantly, he'll have more contact with your husband. Eli will be working on him too."

Tabitha chuckled. "He won't succeed. Josh is stubborn." *Man, is he stubborn!* "And committed. *Legally* committed."

"But Eli might try to get him to defer active duty or to get you to stay behind for a season."

Tabitha opened her mouth, then shut it quickly. "I'm not tempted." *Not too much. No. Not tempted at all.* "As much as I love the stage, I love Josh more. And Joseph. We're going together. As a family. Community theatre will be good enough for me." I hope.

We'll probably end up in Columbus, Mississippi, for pilot training. Who knows what they'll have there? Might be lucky to have a movie theatre.

Stop it. Columbus is not Blue Beech Ridge.

Dr. Daisy nodded. "Good answer. I just wanted you to be forewarned. And if you need me to, I could be your sponsor—your academic advisor."

Tabitha considered the offer for several long seconds. Then she shook her head. "No. Dr. Thorpe's been good to me. He got my scholarship extended to cover spring and summer terms, and I'm grateful. I wouldn't have been able to even get close to graduating without it. We're 'starving students,' you know. We couldn't have afforded the extra tuition." *We're barely making it as it is.* "And as persuasive as Dr. Thorpe can be, well, doggonit, I'm stubborn too. And committed." Then she quickly added, "Not that I don't appreciate the offer, Professor."

Dr. Daisy set the quill back in its holder. "Just thought I'd suggest it, just in case. And at least, now you know what to expect."

"Yeah. Thanks."

Joseph was fussing again. Tabitha bent down and picked him up. "Are you still hungry, little man? Maybe you're ready to nurse on the other side." *I hope.*

"Take your time. I'm going to step out for a few minutes. Just close the door when you leave, okay?"

"Thank you, Professor. For everything."

After five minutes, Joseph had nursed again and Tabitha was relieved, she burped him and then wiped up the inevitable spit-up. Then Joseph fell fast asleep in her arms. She cautiously patted the baby's diaper and decided a diaper change was unwarranted. *That's right. Josh said he changed him.*

She sighed. *Gotta love that man.*

"You too, handsome," she said aloud as she secured Joseph in his carry-cradle. She silently counted to twenty. Joseph was still slumbering, and Tabitha sighed in relief. *As Josh would say, mission accomplished!*

Another half a minute later, and she had the carry-cradle shrouded in the blue pastel blanket and the diaper bag packed. She glanced at the clock on the office wall. Plenty of time. Eat my PB&J and study for my Old Testament test.

She closed the office door and headed down the hallway to the stairs.

"Tabitha!"

Speak of the Devil, and he shall appear.

That's not fair. Stop it.

Tabitha halted, gathered her resolve, and turned to greet the familiar, tall, lean figure. "Dr. Thorpe!"

The older man, dressed in dark slacks and a black turtleneck—which had the double-effect of making him look even taller and at least a decade out-of-style—smiled toothily, his brown eyes flashing with obvious delight. "I was hoping to run into you. Before class this afternoon, that is."

Tabitha mentally braced herself. *Forewarned is forearmed.* "What for?"

"I hope you'll forgive the liberty, but I picked up your copy of the script. For *Dracula.*"

Tabitha blinked. "Wow! That was nice of you."

Dr. Thorpe jerked a thumb up and over his shoulder and tilted his head in the same direction. "It's in my office. Are you in a hurry? Would you mind accompanying me there?"

"Sure. I mean, not at all."

The older man extended a hand toward the carry-cradle, just as Dr. Daisy had done. "May I?"

Why is everybody being so nice to me today? Do I look like I'm weak and overburdened or something? "Sure. Thanks." She handed over the carrier.

Dr. Thorpe's grin widened, showing more of his yellowing and not-so-straight teeth. "I'd say, 'Ladies first,' but I imagine you'd rather keep this precious little guy in sight as we walk."

"Smart man." She grinned. "Lead on, Professor."

He inclined his head, turned, and strode quickly along the familiar path to his office.

Once they arrived, Dr. Thorpe placed the carry-cradle on the floor next to his office's small sofa. He gestured toward the couch. "Please rest for a moment, if you can."

So, it's not just about the script. Tabitha sat.

Dr. Thorpe left the door open—as he always did when alone with a female student—and stepped behind his desk. He bent at the waist and reached down. Tabitha assumed he was rummaging in his ancient, leather briefcase. He straightened, holding up a thin, red, paperback book. Dr. Thorpe presented the book to Tabitha.

She read the title, *Dracula,* and beneath that, *The Vampire Play in Three Acts.* "Thanks!" She waved the script at him. "This will give me a big jump on memorization."

The older man chuckled softly and winked at her. "If I know you, young lady, you'll have all your lines memorized before the first rehearsal tomorrow night."

Tabitha could not suppress a grin of her own. "Maybe."

Dr. Thorpe sighed as he took his seat behind his desk. "Sadly, my ancient brain is not as youthful and robust as yours, my dear. I'll be on-book—"

Tabitha attempted to resist the sudden urge to cringe at the words, "My dear." She did not entirely succeed.

"Tabitha!" said the professor, clearly alarmed. "Whatever is the matter? Are you ill?"

Tabitha waved a dismissive hand. "It's nothing, Professor."

He shook his head as he came from behind his desk. "It is very clearly far from nothing." He stood over her and then, in an apparent effort to diminish his looming presence, sat on the edge of his desk. "Have I done something to distress you? Is it something I said?"

She shook her head, then slowly nodded. "There was a man when I was in high school. He *hurt* my mother, my daddy, even my friends. Hurt me."

The gaunt face was suddenly ashen. "Oh, my dear! I'm so, so terribly sorry."

"He used to call me"—Tabitha swallowed—"'my dear.'"

Dr. Thorpe slid off the edge of his desk and dropped to one knee. "Oh, my d— Oh, I'm so sorry. And I remind you of this monster?"

No. Not really. You are nothing like Magnus. She shook her head. "No. Only that phrase."

He began to reach for her with one hand, then snapped his hand back. "Please forgive me." He bowed his head, and his shoulders slumped.

"It's not your fault, Professor. You didn't know. How could you know?"

"And yet I have caused you pain. At the very least, discomfort." He looked up, meeting her eyes. "I shall endeavor to never use that phrase again."

Tabitha was surprised when tears leaked from her eyes. She swiped at both cheeks with her hands. "I'm sorry."

"No need to apologize, my—" He shook his head in disgust. "Clearly, this was a traumatic experience. In your past. But please"—he put a thin hand to his lips—"I am not prying. You can, of course, confide in me, if you wish, but I am not prying."

Tabitha nodded, brushing away fresh tears. "I appreciate it, Professor. You've been so kind to me. So helpful. But these past few days have been very stressful." *I died. Four times!*

"My d—" He grimaced. "If there is anything, *anything* at all that I can do?"

Tabitha extended a hand, reaching for his. He reached forward, and she clasped his hand. "You are so kind. Thank you, Professor."

He squeezed her hand warmly with his boney fingers. He smiled, then let go. He nodded wordlessly, then rose to his feet and retreated to the other side of his desk.

They both sat in silence for a few, eternal moments.

At last Tabitha said, "You wanted to speak with me, Professor?"

Dr. Thorpe glanced at the small bust of Shakespeare on his bookshelf, looking rather guilty, then he shook his head. "It can wait for another time." He cleared his throat. "Is your soliloquy ready for this afternoon?"

He was going to bring up the repertory company. She shrugged. "As ready as it will ever be. But, please, Professor, go ahead. What was it you wanted to say?"

The professor risked one more glance at the Bard. "Are you planning on auditioning for *A Midsummer Night's Dream*?"

Tabitha blinked. Then she laughed softly—so as not to wake the baby. "Sure. But Dr. Browne is directing, and he doesn't like me."

The professor seemed visibly taken aback. "Doesn't like you?"

Tabitha shrugged. "Well, he's never cast me in *anything*. Not even as window-dressing."

"Ah. I see." His toothy smile had returned. "Well, I have it on very good authority that he will not only cast you, but he will cast you as Hermia, if I'm not mistaken."

Hermia? The female lead? "Seriously?"

Dr. Thorpe chuckled. "Well, we both know he won't cast you as Hippolyta. You're a bit too short to be the Queen of the Amazons, but the part of Hermia is yours, if you want it."

"Want it?" Tabitha was almost bouncing on the couch. "Of course, I want it!"

"Good. Then audition for it. I've no doubt Dr. Browne will give you the part." He gave her a sly grin.

"Why? Do you have something to do with this?"

He folded his thin hands on top of his desk. "I may have whispered a strategic word here and there."

And I'd bet real money—if I were a betting woman—that it has something to do with your repertory company. But she wasn't about to open that particular can of worms.

"You're still doing the Hermia speech today, correct?"

"Yes." She nodded. "At your recommendation."

Suddenly, his smile was all crooked, yellowing teeth. "I just thought I'd let you know that Dr. Browne will be observing my class today."

Oh, no! So much for that. "Way to make me super nervous."

He chuckled and shook his head. "He saw your Lady Macbeth. Grudgingly, yes, but"—Dr. Thorpe leaned forward, across his desk—"he said you were brilliant."

"Wow."

He nodded. "Wow, indeed. And I know you will be brilliant again today."

Tabitha glanced at the wall clock and gasped. "I've gotta go. Old Testament Two-Oh-One."

Dr. Thorpe stood and moved toward the door. "Hurry along, Tabitha. I'll see you in class later."

"Thanks, Professor." Tabitha gathered the diaper bag and her baby and scurried out the door. She dug her peanut butter and jelly sandwich from her bookbag and wolfed it down as she rushed across campus.

Hermia! Thank you, Dr. Thorpe.

Don't think I don't know what you're up to, though. But, Hermia! Bless you, even if you are a sneaky, old goat!

We're still moving in the spring, though.

Even if it is to Columbus, Mississippi.

Tabitha felt as if she were dancing on air—even without Josh and the Power.

Her monologue had gone very well. She knew it had gone well, because Dr. Browne himself had come up to commend her after class. And then he had personally asked her to audition for *A Midsummer Night's Dream*.

She'd finished her last class of the day, and Josh had the baby for the next hour. Tabitha had an hour to kill before meeting her husband for the drive home.

I should study for my Old Testament test.

The *Dracula* script was beckoning like the siren voices of Dracula's vampire wives or Christopher Lee's velvet bass.

Stomping down a small twinge of guilt, she pulled the little, red book from her bag. She found a vacant bench in the HFAC and sat, highlighter in hand, and set about marking Renfield's lines in fluorescent greenish-yellow. She read and savored each word, emoting softly to herself, channeling her inner lunatic. "...please leave me my spider," she read in a high-British accent. "...so nice and fat... another dozen flies—"

"Mrs. Kilmore!"

Tabitha's head snapped up and toward the now familiar voice. *What's he doing here? On campus?*

Detective Danny Folau strode purposely toward her. "I'm so glad I found you!"

"How *did* you find me?"

He halted in front of her, but didn't sit down.

She was forced to crane her neck to look up at him.

He pointed toward the north. "I asked at the Smoot Building—at administration." He lifted the gold shield attached to his belt. "They told me your last class was here. So, I came right over."

Thanks bunches, BYU. However, she managed a gracious smile. "How can I help you, Detective?"

"Can we talk on the way?"

"On the way? Talk on the way where?"

His lips scowled, but an eager light burned in his eyes. "I need you to do another reading—another vision. Downtown."

Not another one! "Downtown? I—I only have an hour before I have to meet my husband."

"It won't take that long. Please, Mrs. Kilmore. I need you. But we have to move quickly."

"What's going on? What's the hurry?"

His scar and his lips twitched, but the light in his eyes intensified. "There's been another murder."

11

"Another murder?" Tabitha shuddered, but she was already stuffing the *Dracula* script into her purse.

Folau nodded. "Yes, but you need to come with me. Downtown."

"Why downtown? Why not just bring the object here? We could find a practice room."

He shook his head slightly. "It can't be moved. Please? Will you come with me?"

Tabitha bit a quivering lip. *Die again.* "Of course." She got to her feet and headed toward the southern doors of the HFAC.

"No," said Folau. "This way."

Tabitha halted a couple paces away and turned to look back at him. The detective pointed toward the north doors, visible up on the second floor. "I'm parked up by the Smoot Building."

Tabitha shook her head, not budging. "I'm not getting into a car alone with you or any other man. I'm a married woman. And I'm parked over by the ROTC building."

Folau stepped toward her, closing the distance. "Come on. I'm serious."

Tabitha folded her arms. "So am I. Besides, I told you. I have to be back here in an hour to pick up my husband and my baby. I'm not stranding them here. Josh'd have no idea where I am. He'd worry. *I'd* worry."

A handful of students had stopped and were staring at them. One male student was leaning forward as if he was about to ask if she needed help. Folau glanced around, grinding his teeth together as if he were chewing on rusty nails. "Fine. I'll meet you over there. Just hurry." He blinked. "Wait. How will I find you?" Then he rolled his eyes. "Never mind. Dang yellow Bug."

"I'll be waiting." Tabitha spun on her heel and strode rapidly toward the southern exit.

She did not look behind her to see if Folau was racing off in the other direction. Visitor Parking—where she assumed Folau's vehicle was parked—was just outside the north exit, and the ROTC building was at the far end of the western student parking lot, at the very edge of campus. But Tabitha was grim-faced with determination. *I'm going to beat him there, even if I have to run.*

By the time she reached her car, she had gathered her long skirt in one hand and dashed the length of the lot, weaving between parked cars as she went. Her heart was pounding, and she was out of breath, but she grinned savagely through gritted teeth.

Told you I'd be waiting.

She had clambered into the Volkswagen and gotten the old Bug started just as Folau pulled up beside her in an unmarked, blue sedan. His window was down, so she rolled hers down as well.

He slapped a flashing blue light atop his car. "Follow me!"

He waited for her to pull out of her parking space, then drove away.

Tabitha followed as best she could, but her little car didn't have the acceleration of Folau's vehicle. And her confidence at driving a stick shift, even with two years of experience, slowed her even further.

Man! He even drives like he's impatient.

Be fair. He's trying to catch a serial killer. Women are dying. Another one is dead.

She shivered, and a cold sweat slicked her palms.

I'm about to die again.

Wish he'd slow down a little. If I get into an accident, I could die for real.

She glanced worriedly at the fuel gauge. The needle was sitting just above the "E" line. She had only three dollars and some change in her purse—not even enough for three gallons. Her eyes flicked heavenward—or at least toward the roof of the car. "Heavenly Father, please don't let me run out of gas!"

Maybe I should have just ridden with him after all.

"No," she said aloud, rebutting herself. "It wouldn't be right. Wouldn't be proper."

Wouldn't be safe.

But I can trust Danny. She growled in angry frustration. *Stop calling him that! Folau. I can trust Folau. He's a good guy.*

A sudden thought, ugly and disturbing, ripped a gasp from her. *How do I know Folau isn't the Devourer? Under those masks, he could be anybody. Any man.*

She was certain the Devourer was a man.

As she followed the detective's car through a red light, she said aloud, "Folau's not the killer! He can't be."

Can he?

"Where's the body?" Tabitha whipped her head around, scanning the rather unremarkable residential street corner in southeastern Provo. The small brick homes were old—probably constructed before the first world war. An elderly couple stared from the concrete porch of their home at Folau and Tabitha, but there was no indication—at least so far as Tabitha could see—that she was looking at anything out of the ordinary, much less the scene of a murder.

"The body?" Folau scratched behind his ear. "With the medical examiner. Awaiting an autopsy. And a tox-screen."

"Oh. Yeah."

"Do you need to see the corpse? Would that help?"

Tabitha shook her head with a vehemence that surprised her. "No! Uh, I mean, no thanks."

"Can you get a reading from the corpse? I can arrange it."

Tabitha shivered. She'd seen death before. She'd seen murder before. *The girls of the Circle. All dead and mangled.* "No. It doesn't work that way."

"Okay. I get it." He pointed at the ground near the corner. "It's over here."

The iron object? "I don't see anything."

Folau knelt beside the concrete gutter that ran between the road and the sidewalk. "Here."

Tabitha shook her head. "I don't see—" She stared as his hand patted a two-foot-long, rectangular, dark-brown opening in the curb. "The storm drain?"

He nodded. "Yeah. It's iron. The victim—her hand was touching it when we found her."

"It doesn't work like that." Tabitha grimaced. "It has to have *belonged* to her—not just have been touched by her." She pointed at the iron of the drain. "I doubt that was *ever* owned by a woman."

"Please." He looked up at her expectantly. "Just try? I'll, uh, hold your shoulders—keep you steady."

It won't work. It'll only— She groaned. "Fine. Okay, fine." She knelt on the sidewalk.

Folau knelt beside her. He put his arm around her, gripping a shoulder in each strong hand. "Ready whenever you are."

A small part of Tabitha felt comforted by his touch—his firm, strong hands on her shoulders, his arm about her. She felt a twinge of guilt.

At least we're in public. Not alone.

She glanced at the elderly couple watching them. The man had his arm around his wife's shoulders, protecting her. Fear on their faces.

Did they see the body? They must've. Did they see the murder? The killer? Could the old man be the killer?

Stop it. Stop suspecting every male you see, Tabitha argued with herself.

She shifted her gaze to the cold, rusty iron below and in front of her knees. She took a deep, shuddering breath.

It's not going to work, and I hate touching iron.

"Mrs. Kilmore?" Folau gave her shoulders a gentle squeeze. "Are you okay?"

"Yeah. Just scared." Gingerly, she reached down. She hesitated for another second, her hand an inch away from the iron, then she pressed her skin against it.

The weakness, the dizziness—the sure knowledge that the Power was blocked, even if she couldn't feel it without Josh there to channel it—made her sway. But although the world spun a little, it didn't dissolve.

She hissed through clenched teeth and snatched her hand away as if the cold iron burned her. The debilitating weakness popped like a punctured balloon.

"Anything?" Folau asked, not removing his steadying hands.

She shook her head and let out a shuddering breath. "No. I'm sorry. But I told you it wouldn't work." *At least I didn't have to die again.*

Folau muttered a single syllable that didn't sound like English, but definitely sounded like a curse. He let go of her shoulders. "Sorry. Pardon my language." He let go of her shoulders, then stood and offered his hand to help her up.

Tabitha allowed him to assist her to her feet. She wiped her hands together, as much to brush the dirt and rust away as to banish the memory of being Powerless. "Are you sure this is connected with the killer?"

He shook his head, staring down at the unhelpful storm drain. "No, but I feel it in my gut."

"But why would he leave the body here? You've never found a body before."

He pointed at her neck. "She had a small, red mark here and a spot of blood. Like a needle had been jabbed in."

"But that's not how he"—*consumes*—"kills them. That's just how he captures me— I mean, *them*."

"I think he screwed up. Overdosed her. Or maybe, she just died of a heart attack. Won't know 'til I get the autopsy and tox-screen results. At least we should know what he's injecting them with. But when she dropped dead, I think he panicked. Left her here and ran away." He shrugged. "That's my theory, at least."

Tabitha nodded, breathing heavily. "I'm sorry I can't be of more help, Detective."

"Are you okay, Mrs. Kilmore?"

Tabitha turned her head toward him.

He was looking at her with obvious concern in his eyes.

She nodded, attempting to reign in her labored breathing. "I'm fine. I've gotta go."

"Really takes a toll on you, doesn't it? Even if there's no vision?"

She shrugged. *You have no idea. And let's keep it that way, okay?* "I'm just glad I didn't have to *die* again. I do feel sorry for her. What was her name?"

He grimaced. "No offense—you've been so much help—but I just can't discuss details of cases you're not consulting on. We haven't even been able to notify the next of kin yet. And I can't be absolutely certain—not at this point—that we're dealing with the same killer. The only thing that connects this case to what you've seen is that needle mark on the neck."

Tabitha nodded, then shook her head. "It's okay. I really don't need"—*or want*—"to know." She glanced at her watch. "Oh, crud. I gotta go!"

Folau nodded. "Thanks for trying."

Tabitha waved quickly as she headed to her car. "Bye. Good luck. Catch this guy."

She got into the Bug, started the car, and groaned at the fuel gauge. The needle was definitely *below* the "E."

There's a gas station just up Nine-Hundred East, right?

I'm gonna be so late!

Tabitha spied Josh waiting in front of the ROTC building as she pulled up. He was laden with the carry-cradle, the diaper bag, and his bookbag. He most definitely not happy.

Even before Josh reached the door, Tabitha heard her son howling.

"I'm so sorry I'm late, sweetie!" she said as he opened the passenger door. "Is he okay?"

Josh said nothing as he pulled the seat forward. He glanced at her, then set about transferring the screaming baby to his car seat in the back.

"Is Joseph okay?" she asked again when Josh got into the front passenger seat.

"Does he sound okay?"

"I'm sorry. I had to get gas."

He gave her a look of supreme irritation. "We could've gotten it on the way home. Besides, I thought you were broke."

"I had three bucks."

He nodded, then leaned over and gave her a perfunctory kiss. There was not even a momentary tingle of the Power.

"I'm sorry," she said again.

He let out a brief huff and stared forward. "Let's just go home, okay?"

Tabitha put the stick shift into first gear, then let out the clutch. "Have you tried his binky?"

Josh shook his head. "Of course, but he's not having it. He's pissed, and that's all there is to it."

Joseph wailed as if in confirmation.

"Probably picked up on my mood," Josh said with a grimace. "It's not your fault. I mean, it *is* your fault that you're late. Why'd you run off to buy gas?"

"I didn't 'run off to buy gas.'" She made a deliberate effort to stifle her own irritation. "I'm sorry you're angry, but I wasn't just being an inconsiderate jerk, you know."

He flinched. "Sorry. I'm sure you had your reasons."

Might as well get it over with. "Well, I *did* have a reason, but you're not going to like it."

He closed his eyes, and Tabitha was certain he was silently counting to ten. He let out a long, slow breath. "Okay. Shoot."

The volume and frequency of Joseph's screams began to lessen as she drove. During one of the brief lulls, she dove in. "Detective Folau came by. Looking for me."

His head snapped toward her. "Folau? Came onto campus?"

She nodded. "Yeah. There's been another murder."

She glanced at him and saw the color had drained from his face. "Wow. And you went with him?"

She nodded.

"Alone?"

"Not exactly. I drove myself."

Josh's lips twitched. "Another vision?"

"It was supposed to be. But it didn't work."

"Why didn't he just bring the object to you?"

She let out a mirthless laugh. "He couldn't. It was a storm drain cover. Iron, yeah, but it didn't belong to her—to the victim."

He stared at her in amazement. "Well, of course that's not going to work! Why'd you go?"

"I didn't know what it was!" She was no longer trying to hide the exasperation in her voice. "Not 'til I got there."

He said nothing. Even Joseph had gone silent.

"I was just trying to help." She felt tears spill from her eyes as she stopped the car at a red light.

"I know." Josh placed his hand atop hers where it rested on the gear shift.

And she felt the Power flow—sweet and tingling. Fresh tears fell, but those new tears were not as bitter.

Josh squeezed her hand. "I'm sorry."

Tabitha took her left hand off the steering wheel, and quickly wiped her tears. "Me too."

"Forgive me?"

She turned her face toward him. "Always. Forgive me?"

He smiled. "Always." He leaned over and gave her a proper, though brief, kiss, setting her lips tingling—and not only with the Power.

A honk from behind them snapped Tabitha's attention back to the road. The light had turned green. Josh let go of her hand, and the Power's flow ceased. But in a moment—Power or no Power—they were moving forward again. Together.

"We could've been together! Forever!"

Standing at the bottom of the Pit, he stomped viciously on the cheap mattress—the mattress he'd obtained for the Prize—the cushioning that would make the Prize more comfortable, make her last longer while she fed him.

He gave the mattress another stomp—right where the prey's head should be. But her head wasn't there. *She* wasn't there. "We could've been one! United. For eternity!"

He stooped and seized the empty, iron collar and its attached chain. He gripped it in one white-knuckled hand and the chain in the other. He screamed at the cold metal. Screamed as he would have at the prey—if he could have gotten the prey back to the Pit. Then he broke into a string of curses such as he rarely used, words he'd never dream of uttering in the presence of a woman.

He flopped down on the mattress. He sat and stared morosely at the collar that *should* have been around the prey's neck right at that very moment. But it wasn't around her neck. The collar was empty.

He was empty.

Instead, he put the collar around his own neck, closing the iron, but not locking it. The collar was a tight fit, but it didn't scrape or pinch. It wouldn't leave a mark.

"You should have been mine, damn you. Mine!"

He put both hands on the chain. Somehow, gripping it helped him feel closer to them—the ones he *had* taken, the woman-souls he *had* consumed.

Woman's soul is so much stronger than man's. So much stronger.

Only women can nourish me.

"Bitch!"

In his mind, he went over every detail of the failed hunt the night before—stalking the prey, following her as she walked home alone, reveling in her scent, her delicious fear, the faint sound of her sobbing wafting sweetly back to his hypersensitive ears. As he'd stalked her, he'd silently made her a vow—a sacred vow. *He abandoned you—the one who was supposed to protect you. He left you alone. But I never will. I will never leave you. And you will never leave me. You will be mine. I will claim you. I will consume you and take you into myself—just as God intended. And we will be united. One. Forever.*

Forever and ever. Hallelujah. Hallelujah.

After the movie, he'd followed her for several blocks. When he'd seen her approaching the deeper shadows of a dark and quiet spot under a burned-out streetlamp, he'd donned his mask—the werewolf—and pulled up his hood. He'd uncapped the syringe and held it ready. He'd come up behind the prey. She'd never seen him coming. And he plunged the syringe into her neck.

The prey had managed a stifled scream before the drug suppressed her breathing. Then she'd collapsed. Then she stopped breathing altogether.

I didn't give her too much! I know *I didn't! Haven't made that mistake since…*

Probably had a bad heart. Yeah. That's it. Not my fault!

In impotent fury, he pounded both fists on the mattress. "Not my fault!"

Gone. Wasted.

He tilted his head back and howled at the heavens. "I didn't waste it! I didn't waste the precious gift You sent me. It was all her. It was the bitch's fault!"

He removed the collar from his neck and cast the heavy iron aside. It clanked dully on the concrete floor and lay still. Lifeless.

So hungry. It hurts.

He bowed his head and sobbed. "Please send me another one! Please!"

But even as he said it, he knew he couldn't go hunting again. Not for a while. *Not after last night.*

He'd panicked. He'd left the husk—no, *husk* wasn't the right word—he'd left the *corpse* behind.

"They found it! They found it, and now they're looking for me!"

They'll know where she went last night. To that stupid movie. Can't go back now.

Not for a while. If I could find the Prize. One last glorious meal. A Last Supper. To fill me for eternity. I'd risk everything. If I could have her, I'd be truly immortal. We'd *be immortal. My woman-souls and I. My Prize and I.*

A fresh wave of sobbing ripped through him. He hugged himself, vainly attempting to hold in his grief. And his fear. "But I'm so hungry!"

I can't go back to the theater. I have to find another place to hunt. Haunted houses. Corn mazes. BYU campus late at night. Any number of places where women are alone and afraid.

But she *won't be there. No, she won't! The* Prize *won't be there. I must find her!*

Please, God! Help me to find her! "Lead me. Guide me. Walk be—" A giddy titter escaped his lips. He closed his eyes and remembered that night. The blessed, cursed night. The night he'd almost had her.

There was something about her—the way she walked, the taste of her fear.

"I *know* you. I'm certain I do know you." He began to laugh, low in his throat. "Yes. From somewhere… So familiar…" He just couldn't put his finger on it. "Don't you worry, my Prize, my Treasure. I'll find you. And then we shall be one."

His face split in a wide, toothy grin. He licked his lips and then his teeth.

"Together. Forever. Hallelujah."

"To hell with you and your souls! Why do you plague me about souls?" Tabitha ranted from the old stage, her hands clenched into claws, her long black hair disheveled, and her eyes alight with madness. Josh thought she was gorgeous. Scary, but absolutely beautiful. In full Renfield-mode, she whirled on the man playing Dr. John Seward, a middle-aged, slightly paunchy actor named Alex Royal. Josh knew the names of everyone in the cast, of course, because Tabitha talked about the play constantly at home. "Not their souls," she spat. "I want their *lives*! The blood is the life—"

"She is certainly in her element," said a familiar baritone voice, soft and low.

Startled, Josh, nearly jumped out of the old, wooden, theatre seat. He turned quickly and gazed, wide-eyed and panting, into the gaunt and shadowed face of Dr. Thorpe. *No wonder this guy is Dracula!* Josh thought as he struggled to calm his rapid breathing. He could do nothing about the pounding of his heart.

Sitting one row behind Josh and perched on the edge of his seat like a vulture—or a vampire—Dr. Thorpe wasn't looking at him. The old man's eyes were focused on the stage. On Tabitha.

"Yeah," Josh managed after gaining a little control over his breathing. "She's really scary."

"She's magnificent!"

"Uh, aren't you supposed to be onstage?"

Thorpe shook his head, never taking his intense, almost hungry gaze off Tabitha. "They're going to be running this scene again, well before my entrance." He chuckled softly. "Unless you count the bat that'll be fluttering outside the window. That's supposed to be me, of course. But they don't have that bit going yet."

"Run the scene again?" *You really creep me out sometimes. The way you look at Tabitha. Like you could devour her.*

Thorpe nodded. He spared a brief glance and a wink at Josh, and then his deep-set, piercing eyes were back on Tabitha. "If I know the director—and I do—he'll want more of a reaction from Harker." Thorpe pointed with a cadaverous finger at

Bjorn Carpenter, the young, handsome actor playing Johnathan Harker. The corner of Thorpe's mouth lifted in a half-smile. "Bjorn's a fine actor. But he should be visibly flinching. Under the lighting we'll be using, that little jerk of his head? It simply won't be enough. Weeks ago, at the beginning of rehearsals, when they first encountered Tabitha's Renfield, their reactions were much bigger." His smile broadened, showing his long, crooked teeth. "Because, at that time, they were truly shocked by the raw intensity of her performance."

Thorpe turned his grin on Josh. "Did you know she came to the first rehearsal, to the first read-through—just one day after receiving the script—with all her lines memorized?" He winked. "Of course, you do. She's a professional, your lovely wife. A treasure." He inclined his head toward the stage. "She was Renfield from the first moment she stepped onto that stage." Thorpe sighed like a young swain in love. "Magnificent!"

"Okay!" the director said in a booming voice from where he sat in the third row. "Let's go back to Renfield's entrance. And, Harker, I want a bigger reaction from you. A bigger flinch. More fear. More disgust. Bigger! Okay?"

Thorpe chuckled, nodding. "Good man. Trevor's doing a fine job."

"Yeah," Josh said. "Tabitha likes him. Says he's good to work with. And she doesn't say that about everybody." Then he hastened to add, "She says that about you, though."

The older man chuckled. "Kind of you to mention that. So, young Mr. Kilmore, why are you here? I thought you worked nights, though I confess I have seen you here before. You're a custodian on campus. Am I correct?"

Josh nodded. "I get Friday nights off. It's our date night. But when she's doing a show, if the director lets me in—and not all of them do—I'd rather watch her than sit at home. And sometimes, I actually do my homework, when she's not on stage." He lifted the thick, brown textbook in his lap and showed the cover to Dr. Thorpe. The title read, *Making Progress in Russian: A 2ⁿᵈ Year Course.*

"Russian, eh? Might come in useful for a soldier, I suppose. Know your enemy, and all that."

Josh shrugged. "The Russian people aren't my enemy. Just their leaders. And, of course, their military. Well, the military leaders. In any case, as one of my AFROTC instructors says, we fight as much for the freedom of the Russians—and of all Heavenly Father's children—as we do for our own."

"There it is!" Dr. Thorpe pointed at the broom lying across the seats to Josh's right. "I see you are keeper of the witch's broom tonight. I wondered where it was. Tabitha usually has it backstage. Close to hand."

Josh grinned as he patted the top of the thick and heavy broom. "She lets me hold onto it when I come to her rehearsal." He gave the professor a sly wink. "That way, I know she won't leave without me."

"A-ha! Holding the lucky talisman hostage, are you?" He grinned and wagged a boney finger at Josh. "You are nefarious, young man. But I approve absolutely!"

Josh chuckled. "Hey, I gotta have *something* to make her keep coming back!"

"I have never seen Tabitha show up for a rehearsal or a performance without it. I was worried. I thought something might be up with her or with you two."

"Nope. I'm just the designated Keeper of the Broom."

The professor nodded. "I see. Well played. What about your son? Where is little Joseph?"

"With the babysitter. Date night, you know? Even if we can't be together-together, I can still be near her, watching her doing what she loves." *And with a serial killer out there, I want to make sure she's safe.*

"Yes." Thorpe's grin had taken on an almost feral quality. "Doing what she loves."

Josh looked forward again, trying to focus on Tabitha. *Here it comes. Again.*

"You know, Josh... May I call you Josh? Off-campus, at least?"

Josh hesitated for just a moment—a pause he was certain the older man had noticed—then nodded. "Sure."

Thorpe nodded. "And you must call me Eli, off-campus."

Josh resisted the sudden urge to call the old man Eli-Off-Campus. Instead, he merely said, "Cool."

"I ran into Major Kimball on campus this week. I believe he's one of your instructors over at the ROTC building."

Instantly, Josh was on his guard. "Yes, sir."

Thorpe gave a slight shake of his head. "No need to call me sir, Josh. I'm neither in the military—not for many years—nor your professor. And as I said, we are off-campus."

"Force of habit, s— uh, Eli." *Especially when you're talking to Major Kimball. Behind my back.*

"I want you to know that I did *not* mention your name or Tabitha's. I merely posed to the major a hypothetical question."

Josh clenched his jaw. *You had no right! And whether you mentioned my name or not, the major probably knows exactly who you were talking about.*

"I asked him," Thorpe continued, sounding as if he were discussing nothing more significant than the price of rice in China, "if one of his cadets—a pilot cadet, for example—could delay the start of his active duty, his pilot training, until the end of the summer. And he assured me that such a thing was done all the time. It's common, for example, for a cadet to need the summer to finish his degree."

"Dr. Thorpe—"

"Eli. Please."

Josh turned to face the older man. "Begging your pardon, sir, but in this case, I think I need to address you as Dr. Thorpe."

Thorpe's smile, diminished, became less broad, less toothy—but it didn't vanish. He inclined his head. "Very well. I understand."

"I don't need the summer to finish my degree." Josh kept his voice even. *Not angry. Well, not that angry.* "I'm not going to ask for an educational delay."

"How about a family delay?"

What? "What do you mean?"

Dr. Thorpe's eyes seemed to focus up and to the right, as if he were musing on a perplexing conundrum—one for which he'd already found a most convenient solution. "Major Kimball told me that a cadet—or rather, a newly commissioned second lieutenant—could take the summer to, for example, allow his wife to finish *her* degree or to deal with some other family concern."

Josh opened his mouth to object. He hesitated. "You mean, your Shakespeare company." *Again.*

The old man nodded. "Just so. We'd be done by August, which is within the deferment window Major Kimball described. And you know it would mean the world to her."

It would. Dang it. It would mean the world to Tabitha. "I…"

"I know it's asking a lot, but this small delay for Tabitha's sake… I give you my word I would not press her nor invite her to stay beyond the summer. You could both— or rather, all three of you—be off to the Air Force, pilot training, and your military career on the first of August."

Man! I hate it when… When what? When he might be right? It would be an incredible opportunity for Tabitha—headlining a Shakespearean theatre company. Am I just being selfish? "I'll think about it."

Thorpe patted his shoulder. "Good man." He paused, and the smile vanished. "Pray about it too. Together. In the end, what I want is of no consequence." He waved a dismissive hand. "What matters is Tabitha."

Josh nodded. "You got that right." Then he sighed. "Okay. We'll talk about it. And we'll pray."

Dr. Thorpe's hand squeezed Josh's shoulder gently. "And I promise you that I will abide by and support your decision, whatever it may be." He glanced at the stage. "Now, I really must prepare for my entrance."

On the stage, Tabitha snarled, "You know too much to live, Van Helsing!" With a bloodcurdling shriek, she launched herself at Zechariah Mosby, the gray-haired fellow playing Van Helsing.

Josh shuddered. *That's new! I've never seen her do that before.*

Sure scared the crap outta me! A grin stole across his face. *Incredible!*

"Magnificent!" said Thorpe, rising to his feet and striding quickly away.

Josh continued to watch the rehearsal until Tabitha exited the stage. Then he sighed and opened his Russian textbook.

He stared at the Russian-language story he was supposed to be reading, but he found concentration difficult. He had no illusion that Tabitha would come out to sit with him—she'd be needed on stage again soon—but that wasn't the source of his distraction.

It would mean the world to her, and it's only three months.

I wouldn't be a student anymore, so I couldn't work on campus. I'd have to get a summer job. J.L. manages that custodial company, doesn't he? Maybe he could get me a job.

Three more months of cleaning toilets. Yay. But if it makes Tabitha happy…

"Gentlemen," said Dr. Thorpe from the stage in a strong but perfectly enunciated Slavic accent. The old man stood tall and stately, like a nobleman. Like a count. He bowed deeply to Sarah Abercrombie, the pretty blonde who was playing Lucy. "Miss Seward," Dr. Thorpe said. "How are you?"

Yep! The old guy makes a great Dracula.

Josh grinned wickedly. *Typecasting.*

"Thought that guy was never gonna leave."

At the sound of the newcomer's voice, Josh's head snapped around once more.

Perched in the same seat that Thorpe had lately occupied, sat a man in a worn suit, with a familiar, scarred face.

Folau. "What are you doing here?"

The detective smirked at him. "My job, of course. Trying to catch a serial killer."

"But it's late. And this rehearsal isn't open to the public."

Folau lifted an eyebrow. "The public, huh? Are *you* in the show?"

"I have special permission. Besides, I'm trying to keep Tabitha safe."

Folau nodded. "Yeah. Me too. Trying to keep her safe, that is. And every other woman in this town." He nodded toward the broom. "So, what's with the antique broom? I saw it at your apartment, but what's the story there?"

It seemed an innocent-enough question. But Josh knew nothing was ever innocent with the detective. "Tabitha's good luck charm. She brings it to all her rehearsals and performances," Josh said, sticking to their normal story about the broom.

"It looks like a witch's broom."

"It is. Sorta."

Folau gave him a dubious look. "What d'you mean?"

"It belonged to a woman people thought was a witch. Long time ago."

"Kind of a weird thing to carry around. Doesn't it attract attention? Unwanted attention?"

Josh shrugged. "It makes Tabitha happy." *Here's something he'll appreciate.* "Besides"—Josh grasped the broom and pushed the top of the stick toward Folau—"it's more than it appears to be. Take a look at the tip."

Folau squinted. "Why's it dark in the middle?"

"Touch it."

Folau put a finger on the end of the broom. He immediately snatched it back. "Cold!"

"It's iron. Iron-cored." Josh shook the broomstick. "This, Detective, is a cleverly disguised weapon—a Japanese *bo*-staff."

"What the..."

"Tabitha knows how to use it. She took some training." Josh didn't attempt to mute the pride in his voice. "She can break bones with this thing."

"Kill too." Folau's voice was hard. He eyed Josh. "Always more to her than meets the eye. More to *both* of you."

Josh suddenly felt uncomfortable under the detective's critical gaze. *He knows about the visions. It's not a huge leap to suspect more.* Josh set the broom back on top of the chairs.

Folau gestured at the broomstick. "What about the iron in the broom? Isn't that a problem for her?"

"She doesn't touch the iron. She's seen enough of that poor woman's life. It wasn't pretty. Short. Violent. Tragic. White Lettie—that's the original owner—was raped and lynched because people thought she was a witch."

"*Was* she a witch?" Folau's eyes narrowed.

"No. She was just a woman who was different. Albino. Mute. Lived alone in the woods. Good with healing herbs when no doctor was around."

"So, what *are* you doing here, Detective?" Josh asked, turning the conversation away from witches. "Isn't this just a bit after-hours for you?"

Folau huffed and curled one corner of his mouth, causing his scar to twist. "Crime never sleeps." He huffed again and shook his head. "Yeah. Corny. I know. But true, even in Provo. Actually, I have an object for your wife to read."

"In the middle of a rehearsal?"

"No. But after that last failure with the storm drain…" He shrugged. "Well, I didn't want to bother her without running it by you first."

"Me?"

"Yeah. The last time, even though she didn't have a vision, it seemed to drain her, to take a lot out of her. I don't want to push her too hard."

Concern for Tabitha? "I appreciate that."

"She still having nightmares?"

More concern. "Yeah. Not every night, but yeah. She's managing."

"She's a tough one."

Josh nodded. "Yep. She's seen death and murder before."

"I know. I checked up on her. Back in Missouri, wasn't it? Must've been horrible. All those girls. That guy who'd fixated on Tabitha. No wonder she's having nightmares."

And you're giving her a fresh set of 'em. "Yeah."

"I was watching from the back. She's scary." He shook his head. "Does she pull it up from inside? From what she's been through?"

"Maybe. But I don't think so. She's just a really, really good actress."

"Good, yeah. Scary-good." Folau scowled, then reached into a suitcoat pocket. "Anyway," he said, producing a small, yellow object, "I wanted to run this past you. It belonged to someone else, another missing-person case." He held up a plastic letter "H" pinched between his thumb and forefinger. He turned the letter over, exposing the back. A dark rectangle was embedded in the middle of the object. "It's a refrigerator magnet."

"I can see that. Why 'run it past' me?"

"Take it." He handed it to Josh. "Feel the magnet on the back."

Josh looked at the hollow back of the "H" and ran a finger over the magnet. "Okay. I get it. This won't work with this rubber coating. Tabitha won't be able to get a vision from this."

Folau nodded. "She's gotta be able to touch the iron directly."

Josh handed the plastic letter back to the detective. "Yeah. Rust is okay. Some rust. But not this."

"What if I were to scrape the rubber off? Expose the iron?"

Josh shook his head. "Still wouldn't work. The woman, the victim, never touched it. Never touched the actual iron inside."

Folau pocketed the "H" again. "That's what I thought."

"And that's why you wanted to run it by me first?"

Folau nodded. "I don't want to stress her out if I don't have to. If it won't do any good."

Josh couldn't help but grin. "Don't make me like you, Detective."

Folau chuckled. "Dang it. You've seen right through me." He sighed dramatically. "And I was trying so hard!"

Josh grinned. "I could tell!" Then his smile faded. "So, how's the investigation going?"

"I can't give you details of an ongoing investigation. You know that."

Josh shook his head. "I'm not asking for details. I just want to keep Tabitha safe."

"Yeah. Me too." Folau paused, then grimaced. "I can tell you this much. Our perp has been keeping a low profile lately. After the botched abduction a few weeks ago, the one you know about, with the storm drain, I think he got spooked. There's this missing-person case"—he patted his pocket—"up in Orem, but I really don't think it's related. Not my jurisdiction, but I'm keeping my ears open for similar cases in the area. I thought our guy might've roamed further afield. But I guess not."

"That's good, isn't it?"

"Yes and no. Yes, in that nobody else has been abducted and killed, that we know of. No, in that he hasn't really stopped. Serial killers don't just *stop*. They *escalate*. The longer they go between murders, between getting their *fixes*, the more they bottle up inside whatever demons are driving them, the more desperate and violent they become. He's going to strike again, and the next time, it'll be worse somehow." He grimaced and rubbed a finger along his scar as if it itched. "It also means he'll get sloppier. And that might help us."

"But it also means another victim." *It's like we're waiting for someone else to die.*

"Yep. Anyway, that's not the only reason I wanted to talk to you."

"Okay." Josh braced himself. *This can't be good.* "Shoot."

"It's *because* our killer is getting more desperate. I just want to make sure you're keeping a close eye on Tabitha. I know she's out here late at night."

Josh nodded. "I'm with her every moment I can be." He pointed at the men on the stage. "They're all keeping an eye on her too. Do you see the old guy, the tall one?"

"Dracula? The one who was talking to you?"

"Yep. He walks Tabitha to her car every night when I'm not here."

Folau nodded. "Okay. But Tall-Pale-and-Spooky up there, he might've been enough to protect her before, just by his presence alone. Now, though, with the killer getting more desperate, he might not be enough to deter the creep."

Fear ripped through Josh like a jagged knife. "Wow. I get it. Okay. I'll... I'll ask

Dr. Thorpe to have *two* men walk her to the car each night. Or maybe all the ladies can walk with him, as a group."

"That would help. Do you own a gun?"

"No."

"You might want to get one, wicked *bo*-staff or no wicked *bo*-staff. Get a gun. Have Tabitha carry it. It might not help, given the killer's M.O."

"We can't afford one."

"Mike Kilmore, your uncle, Tabitha's stepfather. He's in Utah right now, isn't he?"

"Yeah. He and Tabitha's mom are coming down to visit tomorrow."

"Good. Tell him. I bet he'd buy her one. In a heartbeat."

"O—okay. Good idea. I'll ask."

"You do that. I know you two—together—can defend yourselves." His scar twitched again.

The fear knifed even deeper. Josh opened his mouth to object, not knowing what he could say. He couldn't outright lie.

Folau looked him right in the eye. "I don't know how you did it, but I *know* you blew up that car somehow. I'm not sure I buy the whole flying-Volkswagen-thing just yet. Not yet. But there's definitely more to you two than you're letting on." He grinned, baring his white teeth. "I bet you don't even have spiders in your apartment."

Josh swallowed hard, but said nothing. Afraid or not, however, Josh met the detective's stare.

"Listen," Folau said, "I'm not asking how you did it. Not yet, anyway. All I'm asking is for you to keep your wife safe. No matter what it takes. No matter *how* you do it. She's special. I don't want anything to happen to her." His cheeks colored, and his eyes flickered away. "And I know you don't either." He focused on Josh once more. "You're one of the good guys, Kilmore. Flippin' irritating, yeah. But still one of the good guys. Because you protect her."

Josh nodded slowly. *He knows.*

"Anything you need from me," Folau said, "any way at all I can help, I will. All you have to do is ask. Just keep her safe."

"I will."

"You'll try. We both will." Folau stood. "Whatever it takes." He walked quickly away.

Josh stared after the detective until Folau had exited the theatre. Josh closed his Russian textbook, giving up any pretense of studying.

More desperate. More violent. Fear prickled at the base of Josh's skull.

On the stage, Renfield was kneeling at Lucy's feet. Tabitha's hands were upraised, pleading with Sarah. "Pray God I may never see your sweet face again"—Tabitha had chosen a cultured British accent for the role—"your soul will pay for it. You're in the power of—" Tabitha's head snapped toward the window in the unfinished set's wall. She leapt to her feet and ran to the window, screaming her lunatic scream. "The Master is at hand!"

They floated just below the black clouds. Initially, Tabitha and Josh had flown just high enough to be enshrouded in mist—inside the cold, wet darkness of the low overcast. They'd been completely hidden from mortal sight. But after a minute or so, Josh had pointed out that they might be drifting with the winds.

"I don't feel any winds," Tabitha had said. *It's not even cold,* she'd thought, *not with the Power flowing through us. Josh is getting better and better at this.*

"The air mass is actually moving pretty fast," he'd said. "We just don't feel it, because we can't see the ground and we're moving along with that air mass. And I don't want to get hit by some aircraft flying on instruments. They can't see us, and we can't see them in this soup."

"You know, Mr. Kilmore, you've become a regular *killjoy* ever since you started studying aviation. You're taking all the fun out of flying."

"All the fun?" He'd kissed her then, and she'd felt a lovely surge of the Power through every point where their skin touched.

She'd snuggled closer—or at least pulled herself tighter against him as they floated, embracing like dancers in a slow, languid waltz. "Well, not *all* the fun. Oh, well, you have a point. Even if your hair covers it." She'd grinned at the old joke, and so had he.

And so, they'd descended to just below the clouds.

Josh had been right. Tabitha had been shocked by just how far they'd drifted in so short a time. The old Academy building and the parking lot with their yellow Bug had been miles away. Josh had flown them back the way they'd come, until the car was in sight once more—even if the Bug was the apparent size of a yellow insect.

"I love you, my lovely witch," he said.

"I love you too."

"But I have to admit I'm jealous."

She tilted her head back and gave him a quizzical expression. "Why?"

He shrugged. "All these other men who get to spend time with you. Especially on Date Night."

Her jaw dropped. "But I thought—"

"I *don't* begrudge you your time in the theatre. I don't. It's just I think Thorpe's in love with you."

She stared at him agape. "You're not serious!"

He shrugged again and looked away. "Well, maybe not *romantically* in love, but… he really cares about you. Deeply. Folau does too."

Danny? "Folau?"

"Yeah."

"What makes you say that? About either of them?" She felt Josh take a deep breath and let it out slowly.

"Both of them came and chatted with me tonight. About you. You didn't see them?"

She shook her head. "I was in character. I wasn't looking out, off-stage. You know how I get."

He nodded. "Yeah, I do. Well, Thorpe came out to talk. He talked about his Shakespeare company. Again."

"I hope you told him our decision. Again."

"That's just it. It doesn't feel like it's our decision. It feels like it's my decision, or at least, that it's all about me."

She shook her head. "Oh, honey! Don't do that. It's our decision. We're moving. And that's all there is to it."

"Thorpe told me he spoke to Major Kimball."

She gasped. "He didn't!"

Josh grimaced. "Yeah, he did. He said he didn't mention either of us by name, but—"

"But Major Kimball will know *exactly* who Eli was talking about!"

"Yeah, but—"

"Don't you yeah-but me! He had no right!"

"Nope, but it's done."

"That makes me so…"

Josh kissed the tip of her nose. "It's okay. Really. It got me thinking. I could ask for a deferment for the summer."

She shook her head vehemently. "No! Don't do that."

"It'd just be for the summer. Then you could do the Shakespeare company."

"No. It'd hurt your career."

"It's called a 'family deferment.' It'd just be for the summer. Thorpe said you'd be done by the first of August. Apparently, Major Kimball said it was no big deal. Said it's done all the time."

"But we can't." *Can we?*

"Why not? You'd love it. I can get a job for the summer, maybe with J.L. I'd bet there are tons of toilets with my name on them."

No. "You'd be an Air Force officer working as a janitor. That's just not right."

"I won't be on active duty. Besides, I'd do it for you. Please, Sweetheart. What do you say? Can we at least pray about it?"

A tear spilled from her eye. She nodded. Then she kissed him. She put her lips to his ear, and though there was no one else to hear, she whispered. "I love you so much!"

"I love you too."

She laid her head on his shoulder. "I know you do. No matter what we decide—no matter what the Spirit says to do—you are willing to clean toilets, just so I can go play Cordelia." *Portia. Beatrice. Juliet. Ophelia. Desdemona.*

"Sweetheart, how could I rob the world of the best Cordelia the stage has ever known? That would be a crime against humanity."

She kissed his earlobe. "You big goof!"

"Hyuck-hyuck-hyuck!" Josh did his best imitation of the Disney character. "That's me!"

She nipped his ear playfully. Then she tilted her head back, suddenly sobering. "What did Dan— What did Folau want?"

"He said the killer hasn't been active lately."

Josh then related the gist of his conversation with the detective. "He's worried about you. He wants you to get a gun."

Tabitha grimaced. "I don't know."

"Look. Uncle Mike says you're a good shot. It might be a good idea. You're not *opposed* to guns, are you?"

Tabitha shook her head. "No. A gun saved my life, and my mom's. No. that's not true. My daddy saved our lives. He just used a gun to do it."

"So, what do you think?"

She shook her head. "Sweetie, we're broke." *We're always broke.* "We can't afford it."

"That's what I told Folau. But he suggested we ask Uncle Mike to buy you one."

"No. I don't want to do that."

He fixed her with his eyes. "I want you to be safe."

"I have my blasts."

"And you have to be angry to use them. Angry, not scared."

"I have my broom. Nobody knows it's a weapon."

Josh grimaced again. "Uh, not nobody. Folau knows. I told him."

"Why would you do that?"

"He asked about it."

"It's a good luck charm. You should've just told him that."

"I did, but I guess I wanted him to know you were protected. I'm just so proud of you. You and what you can do."

She rolled her eyes. "Next you'll be telling him about the Power."

"Uh, he already knows."

Her eyes grew wide. "What?"

"Well, he suspects something. He knows we can do *something* together."

Tabitha groaned. "Oh, great!"

"He's no dummy. He says he doesn't believe in the flying car yet. But he knows something's up."

She sighed. "Well, I suppose it's not a huge jump from me seeing visions to us doing something supernatural. I guess we'll have to be more careful around him. He knows too much about us already. I'm not going to tell him about the Power."

"It may not do any good. He's a detective. That's what he does—deduce things."

"Yeah."

"Besides," Josh said, "Folau's not the danger."

Tabitha gave him a solemn nod. "The Devourer."

"And according to Folau, the Devourer will be getting more—"

"Desperate and violent." A shudder tore through her. "Nothing could be worse than what he d-does." She buried her face in Josh's shoulder and sobbed.

Josh held her more tightly. "I'm sorry, sweetie. So sorry. I wish I could…"

He pulled a huge surge of the Power through her, eliciting a gasp of pleasure. Breathlessly, she looked at him. "Take me home. Now. Well, back to the car. Let's go to Mikey's and get Joseph. Then let's go home. I need… We need…"

He nodded. "Hold on tight."

In spite of the urgency he felt, Josh took his time during the descent. He scanned the area, but saw no one in the parking lot or in front of the Academy building. *Taking no more chances,* he thought. *Folau really got me spooked.* "The coast looks clear."

"Good," Tabitha said.

He set them down on the passenger side of the yellow Bug. Josh held onto her hand—and onto the Power—as he unlocked and opened the door for her. Then, after a last Power-tingling kiss, he released both.

Tabitha climbed into the car and pulled her skirt clear of the door. Then she glanced into the backseat.

Josh smiled. *It's still there, honey. Right where you left it.* White Lettie's broom lay on the backseat, leaning over Joseph's empty car seat.

Josh closed Tabitha's door, then scampered around the back of car. He had barely inserted his key into the lock on the driver-side door, when he heard a noise from Tabitha that he'd never heard from her, unless she was on a stage.

Tabitha was screaming.

Tabitha screamed, "No!"

She yanked on the car door handle. She shoved the door open and clambered out of the car, tripping on her long skirt. She fell to her hands and knees on the hard, cold asphalt. Lurching upright, she howled, "Look out!"

Less than fifty yards away, two figures abruptly halted on the sidewalk on the far side of the street. The closer figure was short, a young woman, bundled up against the chill of the October night.

The second figure, who'd been following about ten paces behind and, until Tabitha screamed, had been rapidly closing in on the girl, was taller and wore a dark, hooded jacket.

Both figures pivoted toward Tabitha.

The hooded figure's face caught the light of a streetlamp. It was bone-white, with black holes where the eyes should be.

Terror gripped Tabitha, freezing the air in her lungs. *Skull mask!* Even at that distance, she was certain—*The Devourer!*

The hooded figure held his right hand clenched with his thumb extended.

Syringe!

Tabitha opened her mouth to scream again, but couldn't force out another noise. Instead, she waved her arms frantically. "Be-Behind!" she wheezed. Then she found her voice. "Behind you!"

The girl wheeled around, facing her pursuer, and froze, rooted to the spot.

The skull-faced man turned toward his prey, then back toward Tabitha. He seemed to be staring at her.

The black holes where the eyes should've been drew her in, pulling at her soul.

Her knees trembled, and she tottered, nearly falling. The world around her dissolved.

She was in the pit. With him. *Kelsie-Anne. Susan. Christie.* She was them, and he was there, draining her, consuming her.

No! Not in the pit! Not chained!

I'm Tabitha! Tabitha!

She shook herself, and the memories vanished into the blackness.

Still his black-hole eyes bored into hers.

Stop him! Blast him!

Rage! I need rage! Rage!

But all she could find was fear. Terror.

A car door slammed behind her, causing her to jump. *No! Not fear! Rage!*

She glanced at the door. Then she saw Josh—he was sprawled on the asphalt as if he'd tripped while rushing toward her from around the car. She turned back to face the Devourer, the demon who haunted her nightmares.

But the hooded man had vanished into the night.

Gone!

"No!" Anger. She'd found her rage—finally—but it was fury directed at herself, at her own powerlessness.

Suddenly, Josh was at her side. He gripped her hand.

The Power flowed, but there was nowhere to direct it. There was no target.

"Where'd he go?" Josh cried.

He's gone! I let him go!

The girl, the intended victim, was running, stumbling toward them. "Help!"

Without releasing Josh's hand, Tabitha opened her arms and caught the young woman.

"H-help me!" The girl clung to her, sobbing.

"It's okay," Tabitha said, weeping hot tears of her own. *I had him! He was right there! I could have stopped him. I could have killed him. Blown him to bits. Am I really prepared to do that? Kill? Even a monster like that?*

In her pounding heart, she wasn't sure.

Josh put his free arm around both of them, encircling them in his strength. "You're safe," he said. "You're safe now."

None of us are safe. I let him get away because I was scared. Now more will die because of me.

The girl wailed, and Tabitha sobbed with her.

I let him get away!

Tabitha! What the hell is she doing there?

He crouched in the dense shadows beside an unlighted house, panting like a cornered dog. His heart thundered in his chest.

But he was hidden. He was safe.

She shouldn't be here. Rehearsal's over. She should've been long gone. Everybody was gone. Nobody was supposed to be there!

He could still see them—Tabitha, Josh, and the prey. Maddeningly close.

Almost had her!

He'd followed the girl for blocks. It had been his to plan go up to BYU campus to find prey. Any amount of woman-fear to feed his starving soul.

He would easily have found a woman walking alone. A woman walking alone at night was *always* afraid.

But before he'd even gotten close to campus, before he'd reached the foot of the ramp leading uphill to campus, he'd found a girl. Purely by chance.

A gift from God.

Fear—sweet, delicious, nourishing fear—had wafted off the prey like jasmine on a night breeze. His mouth had watered in anticipation of his first meal in weeks.

But then had come the scream.

He'd frozen, turned, and there she'd been.

Tabitha.

Tabitha Catherine Moonshadow Kilmore.

And her fear, her terror had crashed upon him like a tidal wave of warm honey, enveloping, drowning him in its raw sweetness. It almost driving him to his knees.

He'd seen Josh too, of course. He'd seen the protector scurrying and stumbling around that ridiculous car. He'd seen Josh trip and fall while rushing to Tabitha's side.

For one moment of insanity, he'd almost run toward her, ignoring Josh's presence, heedless of the danger. His need had almost driven him to cast all caution away.

He'd turned back to the prey, but he'd known the girl was lost to him. He couldn't take her—not in front of witnesses. Not with *her* watching.

The door of the Beetle slammed. Hard and loud, without anyone touching it.

Tabitha's doing. He was certain of it. He didn't know how she'd done it, but he knew in his gut it was Tabitha. Or maybe it was both of them—Tabitha and Josh together.

No, it was Tabitha. It's always Tabitha.

At the sound of the door slam, Tabitha jumped and turned her head away. He seized the moment and fled, ducking out of sight. He settled into the darkness, becoming one with the night, and watched. Josh and Tabitha coaxed the weak prey into the backseat of their Volkswagen.

Stupid, little car. The bitch will have to hold the damn broom in her lap.

They'll drive her home. Call the police from wherever the prey lives.

That's okay. I'll be long gone by then.

Just have to wait 'til they're gone. So no one will see me walking away.

He shivered, but not with the chill. Rage for the loss of his rightful prey surged through him. He felt hollow and yet still full of anger. The chosen prey wouldn't have sustained him for long, but it would have curbed his appetite while he hunted for more worthy prey.

Once the Bug's headlights had disappeared from sight, he eased from his crouch and removed his mask. He emptied the syringe onto the dirt and pulled an old, oil-stained shop rag out of his jacket pocket. Holding the rag in his gloved hands, he wiped down the mask, inside and out, to dissolve all fingerprints with the motor oil.

He wiped down the syringe as well before depositing both the mask and the syringe into a trashcan.

Let them find the damn mask and syringe.

He shoved the rag back into his jacket pocket and tucked his hood into his collar, out of sight.

A savage, predatory smile spread across his face, and a quiet cackle escaped him—a wolf's grin and a hyena's laugh. He licked his lips. He may have lost this evening's meal, but he had found something better.

I found *her. Tabitha!*

My Treasure.

14

"Look at that tooth!" Molly Moonshadow Kilmore cooed and fawned over her grandson as she bounced Joseph on her knee, keeping the baby well clear from her growing belly. She sat next to her daughter on the sofa in Tabitha and Josh's living room. Molly gave the baby a wide-eyed, exaggerated smile. "Yes! This little man is growing so fast!"

Tabitha, who had barely finished covering up after feeding her son, grimaced. "Yep. Tooth came in this morning. and he sure knows how to use it. I'm pretty sore."

Molly turned a sympathetic face toward her daughter. Molly's dark brown hair wasn't as long as Tabitha's, but it still framed her pretty face. "My poor Tabby-Cat!" There was a wistful note to Molly's voice. "I have all that to look forward to again." She gave Tabitha a knowing wink. "You were a biter too, you know."

"You're going to breastfeed this time too?"

Molly returned her attention to the baby, but she nodded. "Of course. It was out-of-fashion when I had you, but you know me—I was such a rebel. Still am."

Tabitha chuckled. "Like when you changed our last name to Moonshadow?"

"You know it!"

To think I used to resent that silly, hippy-sounding name, Tabitha thought with a sly grin. *Now, it's like this cool secret only Mom and I share.*

A secret born of the betrayal by Jerry, my biological father.

"So," Molly asked, "how was the gun range? Mike said you managed a fairly tight grouping."

Tabitha glanced at her purse, with the brand-new Beretta 92SB nine-millimeter semiautomatic handgun safely hidden inside. The firearm was a gift—a very expensive gift—from her mom and daddy. "That one has a lot less kick to it than your old Saturday Night Special. After I got used to that—and to *not* anticipating the drop whenever I pulled the trigger—it went pretty well."

"You'll have to take Josh and teach him."

Tabitha rolled her eyes. "Josh knows how to shoot, Mom. He's a Kilmore, for crying out loud."

"But he's never shot your new weapon. Mike says it's a new model. Josh needs to try it out."

"I know. I was just teasing you."

"It's too bad he couldn't go with you and Mike."

Tabitha shrugged. "He has to work 'til five. We just can't afford for him to miss a shift." She glanced at the clock. "He should be getting home in a half hour or so. Besides, it was nice having time alone with Daddy."

"And I had a nice time with my cute grandson!" Molly lifted Joseph and giggled at him.

Joseph giggled right back.

"Oh, he's gonna be a heartbreaker."

As happy as Tabitha was to have her mom take such a delight in Joseph, Tabitha felt the slightest twinge of jealousy. Joseph's smiles were usually all for her—and for Josh—and Mikey Montrose. However, she stifled the urge to reach for Joseph and take him from her mom. "He already is a heartbreaker." She smiled at the baby. "Aren't you, handsome?"

"Oh, yes, he is!" Molly cooed. "Oh, yes, he is!"

Joseph giggled and gurgled at his grandmother.

Tabitha glanced at her mother's belly. "So, how are you? How's your health? The pregnancy?"

Molly shrugged. "We're doing fine. Technically, it's high-risk, but other than the usual aches and pains and general fatigue, everything's fine. I haven't even had morning sickness in months. Everything's normal." She smiled at Tabitha. "Mike is so happy. We'd given up hope." Molly's eyes widened. "He's kicking! Wanna feel?"

"Yes!" Tabitha placed a hand on her mother's belly. She felt nothing for a second. Then Tabitha felt a definite kick. She gasped. "Oh, my heck! Hello, little one!" She beamed at her mother and then withdrew her hand.

Molly looked at her askance. "Oh, not you too!" She chuckled.

"What?"

Molly grinned and shook her head. "You've gone native."

Tabitha laughed. "What are you talking about?"

Molly rolled her eyes and said, "'Oh, my heck?' I don't think I've ever heard that outside of Utah."

Joseph laughed, and Molly turned her attention to him. "That's right, little man! Your mommy has gone full-Utahn. Next, she'll be saying 'flip,' and 'scrud,' and 'Get out of my road.' I've only been out west for one day, but I hear those silly things from everybody! Even my own daughter!"

Tabitha covered her mouth, hiding her laughter. "Everybody says stuff like that out here. I even heard Dr. Thorpe say, 'Scruddy flipper!' backstage this morning."

"Dr. Thorpe? That's your acting professor?"

Tabitha nodded, grinning widely. "Yep. Dracula himself! Surprised the heck outta me! I nearly busted a gut laughing at him. I couldn't help myself. He blushed. And apologized! It was the funniest thing!"

"They're cuss-word substitutes, aren't they? Like Mormon swearing?"

Tabitha shrugged. "Maybe. Sorta. Sometimes, I guess, it feels that way—when *some* people use 'em. But I don't think most people mean it that way. It's just local color?"

"Oh, my"—Molly gave her daughter a wink and a wicked grin—"heck!"

Tabitha giggled. "I love you, Mom."

"I love you too, Tabby-Cat."

Tabitha's eyes caught movement on her mom's swollen belly. "Do you have names picked out?"

"Well, if it's a girl, Mike wants to name her Molly." Tabitha's mother grimaced and stuck out her tongue. "I'm not sure how I feel about that. I'm leaning more toward Mary."

Tabitha's face split in a wicked grin. "I *like* Molly!"

Her mother rolled her eyes. "Oh, don't you start."

"What about a boy's name?"

Molly matched Tabitha's grin. "I was thinking, Michael."

Tabitha laughed out loud.

Joseph laughed as well.

"See?" Tabitha said. "Joseph approves."

"Mike wants Adam. You know, like in his favorite musical? *Seven Brides for Seven Brothers*?" Molly shrugged, still grinning impishly. "We'll see. When it comes to the Kilmore men, we Moonshadow women tend to get our way. They're just putty in our dainty, little hands."

Tabitha grinned. "You got that right!"

"Tabby-Cat, I do have a question."

"Sounds serious."

Molly shook her head. "Not really. Just curious."

"Okay, shoot."

"When you were pregnant, did you notice a... *change* in the Power?"

Tabitha blinked. "Not that I remember. What's going on?"

Molly's cheeks reddened. "It's just, during the pregnancy, I've noticed the Power seems to be growing stronger. I mean, not as strong as when you join us. But Mike used it to lift my cast-iron skillet the other day."

"Really? That's tremendous!"

"Well, it's a lot more than picking up spilled popcorn, but it's not flying. We tried once, just in the living room, but as much as he could pull from me, it still wasn't enough." She smiled at the memory. "It felt *so* good, though!"

Tabitha returned her grin. "Yeah, it does. But that's interesting—that it is stronger during pregnancy. Maybe, the baby is a girl, and she's really strong? No. Wait. Even if the baby *is* a girl, it wouldn't change anything. The Power wouldn't manifest until puberty. Or later."

"It didn't with you."

With me, it wasn't until that horrific summer with Jerry. "Maybe, it's hormonal?"

"Hormonal?" Molly chuckled. "Mike can tell you I've been that in spades." She sighed. "It'll probably go back to just a pleasant tingle after I deliver."

"I guess you'll have to just wait and see." Tabitha shrugged. "We just don't know enough about—"

Joseph screeched happily.

Molly performed a fair imitation of her grandson's noise. "You are so cute! Oh, yes, you are! So, is this little man coming with us to the restaurant? La France, I think you said?"

"Yeah, La France. It's the best. Josh and I have only been able to afford to go there once. And, no, we're not taking Joseph. Mikey offered to watch Joseph again tonight. She's my best friend here, other than Josh. That makes about a dozen times I owe her for babysitting. Not that she'd ever mention it."

"You trade off?"

Tabitha shrugged. "That's supposed to be the arrangement, but I feel like I'm taking advantage of her lately. She's got two darling, little girls—Stacy and Mary—and I really don't mind babysitting over there. But ever since Mikey found out about the visions, she's been skittish. I *have* been over there to babysit since, but it's less often than before. And now that I'm in *Dracula*, Mikey's been helping out more."

Tabitha laid her head on her mother's shoulder and sighed. She closed her eyes—only for a moment. But when she did, she saw *him* again. *Skull mask in a hood. Syringe in hand.* Without warning, she was suddenly on the verge of tears, tears she'd kept at bay all morning. "Mom, I'm so glad you're here."

Molly leaned her head on Tabitha's. "I'm so sorry, sweetie."

Black holes, sucking me in. "I should have stopped him. I should have blown him to bits."

"You couldn't, Tabby-Cat. You were *afraid*. Not *angry*."

"But now more women will die! Because of me!"

"Oh, sweetie!" Molly kissed the top of Tabitha's head. "That's not your fault. And you did save that girl's life. Don't forget that."

Joseph suddenly looked worried, as if he were picking up on his mother's distress.

Tabitha forced a wide smile. "It's okay, handsome. Mommy's okay."

Joseph's one-toothed smile returned.

Though Tabitha maintained her own smile, she said, "It's like Magnus all over again. Like seeing White Lettie's life and death again. I don't know if I can handle this."

"I promise you, sweetie, you can. Heavenly Father won't give you more than you can handle. You'll get through it."

"But I'm so scared. I feel so helpless."

Molly laughed softly. "Oh, Tabby-Cat! You? Helpless? You are the strongest person I know."

"Mom, you would have killed Magnus if you could've, right?"

Molly said nothing for the space of two breaths. "Yes. To protect you, I would have."

"But you told *me* not to, when I had the chance."

"I didn't want you to have to live with that."

"But *you* would have."

"I'm a mother. I'd do anything to protect my daughter."

You crawled on broken legs to protect me. "And now I'm a mother." Tabitha smiled at Joseph through her tears. "And I'd do anything to protect my baby. I just think of all those other women. Some of them were mothers. And now their babies are motherless."

"Listen to me, Tabby-Cat." Molly lifted her head and turned it toward her daughter. "Look at me."

Tabitha turned her face to meet her mom's gaze.

Molly looked her square in the eyes. "That monster is the only one responsible for his evil. You're doing everything you can to stop him."

"Not everything."

"Yes. Everything."

"Even last night"—Tabitha shook her head slowly—"I didn't see anything new. He wore gloves. I couldn't see his hands. The way he crouched. I couldn't even tell how tall he was." She shuddered. "All I know is he's real. Real. Not just a vision. Not just a nightmare. And he saw me. Mom, he's coming for me."

"You don't know that."

"Yes, I do. I can feel it. He's coming for me. He's coming to *devour* me."

Joseph was reaching for Tabitha, and Tabitha took her son from Molly. She held the baby close.

"What are you going to do?" Molly asked.

"I don't know." Tabitha let out a long, slow sigh. "But I'll tell you what I'm *not* going to do. I'm *not* going to run away."

Molly put an arm around Tabitha and hugged her. "My brave Tabby-Cat."

Tabitha shrugged, and fresh tears fell from her eyes. "I'm not brave, Mom. Not like you. Part of me wants to run. But if I do, I *know* the Devourer will come after me."

"How can you possibly know that?"

"It was the way he looked at me."

"I thought you said you couldn't see his eyes."

"I couldn't, but I *felt* them. Mom, I'm so scared."

"So scared, and yet you aren't going to run. That's what makes you so brave."

"I don't feel brave."

"That's funny," Mike Kilmore said, as he emerged from the bedroom. "I don't think I've ever met two more courageous—not to mention stunningly beautiful— ladies in my entire life." He gave them one of his dazzling smiles. "And that's sayin' somethin'!"

Tabitha returned his smile. Once upon a time, she had a starry-eyed schoolgirl crush on the chisel-jawed sheriff's lieutenant, but Mike had never had eyes for anyone except Molly. Tabitha still admired her stepfather's rugged handsomeness and masculine aura. She elbowed her mother. "He hasn't changed a bit."

Molly grinned. "Nope. He's still the same silver-tongued charmer I married."

Tabitha gazed at her mother. *When Mom's with him, she just glows. I thought it was just the pregnancy, but it's him—her love for him, and the way he absolutely adores her.*

Like the way Josh makes me feel.

Joseph gurgled happily, turning his head toward his grandfather.

One corner of Mike's grin lifted as he winked at his grandson. "Hey, pardner! Can ol' grandpa hold you?" Mike's midwestern accent, which he used almost exclusively when he was trying, consciously or unconsciously, to be charming, was at full-strength.

And whether it was the accent or the disarming grin, Joseph responded, holding his chubby hands out to his grandpa.

Mike grinned at Tabitha. "May I?"

"Oh, absolutely!"

Mike scooped up Joseph and held him aloft. Keeping his eyes on the baby, Tabitha's daddy tilted his head toward her. "Don't worry, honey. I'm not going to toss him up in the air."

Tabitha chuckled. "Probably not a good idea. He'd probably puke on you."

Mike laughed. "Baby barf. I reckon I better get used to it soon!"

"Honey," Molly said, "you were gone a long time. Everything okay?"

Mike made a buzzing noise with his lips, causing Joseph to laugh. "Y'all probably thought I was takin' a d— uh, using the facilities, I was gone so long. Nope. I was just talkin' to Danny Folau on the phone."

Molly rolled her eyes. "We know that, silly." Her smile disappeared. "What did he say?"

Tabitha's own grin vanished. "Did you learn anything?"

Her daddy's grin remained intact, but whether for her sake or Joseph's, Tabitha wasn't sure. "Scooch over, sweetie-girl. Let me sit."

Tabitha scooted over, making room for Mike. Her daddy sat, then set the baby on his knee and bounced him gently. His smile never faltered, but his tone changed completely. "Danny Folau's a good man. Good detective." All trace of Missouri twang was gone.

He's all business now. "I sense a 'but' coming."

Mike shrugged. "Not so much a 'but,' as a caution."

Tabitha waited, but said nothing.

Her mom, however, had never done particularly well with silences. "Well?"

"I didn't learn much," Mike said, "at least not that I can share—not even with you. But, Tabitha, sweetie, you told me about the time you went with him to a crime scene. How you were alone with Danny."

Tabitha nodded, then shook her head. "We weren't alone. I didn't ride with him—"

"That's good," Mike said. "Make sure you don't."

"And even once I got there, we were in public. There were witnesses."

Mike nodded, his grin never fading as he kept his eyes on Joseph. "I know. That's good, but in the future, make sure Josh is with you. Every single time. If not Josh, then someone else."

"Daddy, what are you saying?" But she knew, even before he replied.

"There's no easy way to say this." Her daddy shook his head. "Danny Folau is sweet on you."

Just like Josh said last night. "Did he say that?"

Mike shook his head slightly. "Not directly. He'd never say that. I'm not sure he knows it himself. Not consciously, anyway. But it was in a lot of little things he said—or more in the *way* he said them. And some things he *didn't* say."

"But, Daddy—"

"Now, don't get me wrong, honey. I don't think he has designs on you, and I know you haven't encouraged him, but I just don't think it's wise for you to be alone with him. Not even in public."

Molly put a hand on Tabitha's shoulder. "That's good advice, Tabby-Cat."

Tabitha fought down a sudden surge of annoyance. *Why am I angry?* "I refused to ride with him in his car." *But I already told you that.*

"And that's good," Mike reiterated. "Like I said. Just be careful."

Tabitha nodded. "I will. I am."

"And I'm glad you have the gun," Mike said. "That was a good suggestion on his part." He muttered, "Wish I'd thought of it." He flapped his lips at Joseph, making another buzzing sound. The baby giggled in response.

Then Mike continued, "But don't be too dependent on the gun."

Tabitha looked at him quizzically. "What do you mean?"

Mike's smile faltered just a bit. "With what we know about the perp's M.O, you probably won't see him coming. Your greatest safety lies in never being alone."

Tabitha gasped. "Do you think Danny, Detective Folau, is the Devourer?"

Mike shook his head. "No. But at this point, I'd suspect any male. The only man you know for sure is safe is Josh. Because Josh was with you last night when you stopped the attack."

"Josh?" Molly said. "You suspected Josh?"

"No. But as a detective, my job is to suspect everybody. At least, until I have a good reason not to."

That's awful! You can't trust anybody. "Even Folau?"

Mike shrugged again. "I don't want you alone with any man. Except Josh. You can trust Josh. And me, of course."

Tabitha shuddered, and her palms were suddenly moist. "I think he—the Devourer—he knows who I am. He knows me."

Mike nodded slowly. "Yeah. I think you're right."

Hearing her daddy say it, confirming her fear, sent a tremor through her. "You do?"

"Yep. When you yelled at him, he stared at you. He didn't run away. At least, not at first. I think you're right. He knows you. He knows who you are."

He knows me. "He's coming for me."

Joseph let out a cry, squirming on his grandfather's lap.

Mike made a goofy face at the baby. "What's the matter, little fella?" The Missouri accent was back.

Tabitha wrinkled her nose. "He needs a change."

Mike chuckled and handed the baby over to Tabitha. "He's all yours, honey."

Tabitha rose from the sofa with Joseph in her arms. As she carried the baby over to the changing table next to his playpen, she gave Mike a smirk. "I'll have you know, Daddy, Josh has *never* let me change a diaper when he's home. Not once."

Molly chuckled. "Oh, I like that! Did you hear that, Sweetheart?"

Mike shot to his feet. "Teach me how, sweetie-girl. Can't have my favorite nephew-slash-son-in-law showin' me up!"

"How strong is Mikey?" Tabitha asked. "In the Power, I mean?"

She and Josh held hands as they walked quickly back to their Volkswagen after dropping off the baby at Mikey and J.L.'s house.

The tingle of the Power surged a tiny bit as Josh glanced at her. "Not at all. No more than any other woman we've met out here. At least, the ones I've shaken hands with. Sister Smith, you know, the bishop's wife, she's a little stronger than most. Of course, nobody compares to you." He squeezed her hand, and the Power's flow increased. "By a *long* shot. Why?"

Tabitha glanced at Mike's rental car, which was parked and idling at the curb behind their yellow Bug. She waved at her mom and daddy sitting inside. "Wait 'til we get in the car."

She looked up and down the dark residential street. *He could be anywhere. Hunting me.* But she saw no one. Even so, she patted the Barretta hidden in her purse. *I've got something better than a gun.* "Hold onto the Power 'til we're safe in the car."

Josh shot her a look of worry as he reached for the VW's passenger-side door. "I'll try." He let go of her hand.

She felt the warmth and tingle of the Power continue to flow. She favored her husband with a smile as he hurriedly opened her door. "Doing great," she said as she gathered her long skirt and sat inside the car.

He grinned. "Practice makes perfect." But he scanned the darkness as if looking for danger as he closed the door.

Tabitha felt the Power continue to flow as her husband scurried around the car and got in on the driver's side. They both locked their doors. Then he leaned over, and they exchanged a quick, tingling kiss.

Then he released the Power.

Tabitha sighed wistfully. *Even without touching, we were connected, and now we're not.*

As Josh started the car, he said, "That's a good idea. Anytime we're out at night and not touching. If I'd held it last night"—he gritted his teeth—"I'd have had him!"

"It's not your fault, Sweetheart." She paused. "Any more than it is mine."

"But he got away."

"And if I had found enough rage to blast him—"

"Okay," he growled. "Neither one of us is at fault. But he's still out there."

I know.

Josh started the car rolling forward.

Tabitha twisted around and looked behind. The rental's headlights were following them.

"So," Josh said, "why'd you ask about Mikey? And the Power?"

Tabitha grimaced. "It was just the way she was acting. The way they were both acting."

"Mikey and J.L.?"

"Yeah. Didn't you feel the tension? Between them?"

Josh shifted gears as he drove. "Not especially. Sweetie, every marriage has some tension from time to time. Even us, sometimes." He shrugged. "Mikey and J.L.'re no different."

Tabitha shook her head. "Did you notice the house? How *messy* it was?"

Josh laughed softly. "Mikey's house is *never* messy." Then he paused. "Well, now that you mention it, it was a *little* messy. Was that *glitter* on the carpet?"

"Yeah. And I smelled burnt cooking."

Josh chuckled. "Like you've never burned food. Hey, if it ain't ravioli…"

The hint of a grin played on Tabitha's lips. "You too, Mr. I'm-a-pretty-decent-cook-if-I-say-so-myself."

Josh tilted his nose in the air, smiling. "I don't know what you're talking about."

Tabitha's own grin faltered. "But I've *never* smelled even a *hint* of burned food at Mikey's. She's like Betty Crocker. And her house is always perfect. Not to mention her hair and makeup. And both were *off* tonight."

Josh pursed his lips and nodded. "Yeah. I guess she was a little different tonight."

"Mikey's like Betty Crocker, Donna Reed, and Barbie, all rolled into one. Makes me sick."

"Okay. She's darn near perfect." Josh's eyes grew wide, and he glanced worriedly at Tabitha. "Not that you're not. Darn near perfect, I mean. You are…" He seemed to be floundering for the right word.

At any other time, Tabitha might've found some small amusement in letting Josh squirm as he tried to wriggle himself out of the hole he'd just dug, but she was too worried about Mikey and J.L. at that moment. "It's okay. I know what you mean."

Josh let out a relieved chuckle. "Good. I love *you*. Mikey's beautiful and all, but it feels like it's all on the outside. Like she's *too* perfect. Like it's all for show."

Tabitha shook her head. "No, that's not it. I mean, she *does* care about appearances. A lot. And not just her hair and makeup."

"So, why'd you ask about Mikey and the Power?"

Tabitha hesitated, before answering. "You remember when I first taught you about the Power? Where it comes from? Well, where I was *told* it comes from?"

"Yeah." Josh nodded slowly. "You said all women have it, to one degree or another."

"Okay, yes, but where the energy itself comes from?"

Josh cocked his head as if trying to remember. "From the emotional energy around a woman. Like she absorbs all the joy and happiness and conflict in the room. She can either radiate it back or convert it to something else."

"If Mama's happy, everybody's happy. If Mama ain't happy…"

Josh grinned slightly. "Ain't *nobody* happy."

"Well, that's pretty much how Beulah explained it to me back at White Lady Hollow."

"So, you think, what? That Mikey's not strong in the Power, so she can't absorb conflict in her marriage?"

"I think… I think Mikey tries really hard to be perfect. That's how she maintains—how she makes her marriage work. But if she can't absorb the *negative* energy all that well…"

"Then when things aren't quite perfect, when something goes wrong…"

Tabitha nodded. "Then things go *really* wrong. Does that make sense?"

"I guess so." Josh shook his head, then muttered, "Bollocks!"

"What? What is it?"

He shrugged his shoulders. "I just hate to think of people I care about going through a rough patch."

"I may be making way too much out of it. A mountain out of a molehill."

"Yeah, but like you said, Mikey's such a perfectionist. I bet she was embarrassed to have us see anything less than perfection."

Tabitha nodded. "Embarrassed? She was mortified."

"How could you tell? She wasn't blushing or anything."

"Like you could see her blush under all that makeup?"

"I guess not."

Tabitha sighed. "I could feel it. A fight or something. You may be able to detect the Power. I can't. No woman can. But feelings? It's like I'm that empath on Star Trek or something."

"Gem?"

Gem? What is he talking about? And then it hit her—"Gem? That was the name of the empath in that dumb Star Trek episode?"

Josh nodded quickly. "Yeah. Of course."

"Seriously? Is there any obscure bit of Star Trek trivia you don't know?"

He shrugged. "Sure. I can't remember the name of the actress. It was a third season episode, though, which was, of course, the worst season."

"You can't remember the actress?" Tabitha rolled her eyes. "Wow. You're really slacking off, Mister Trekkie!"

"Trekker," Josh corrected. "Maybe I am slacking off, but you're the only actress I really care about."

"Ooh, nice save." She winked at him, and he grinned in return.

"My wife—the most powerful witch in all creation—at least that we know of—

and an *empath* to boot. No secret is safe from you. Should I be afraid?"

She gave him a wicked grin. She waggled her fingers at him as if she were some mythical witch casting a hex. "Yesss! You ssshould be frrrightened out of your witssss!"

His smile faded. "So"—he lowered and softened his voice—"I'm assuming you know J.L.'s in love with you."

Tabitha felt heat in her cheeks. "Yeah. I know." She gazed at Josh's profile. "I don't—"

He shook his head. "I know you don't. You wouldn't. And I'm not accusing you of anything. But I'm just wondering, might that be the source of the tension between them?"

Tabitha bowed her head. "I hope not. He *loves* Mikey. I know he does. It's just because of *Fiddler*. It'll pass."

"Hopefully." He let out a mirthless chuckle. "That's three men. Three other men. J.L., Dr. Thorpe, and Folau. And that's just today."

Daddy even mentioned Folau.

"And that doesn't make you jealous?"

He shook his head. "Naw. I'd be jealous as heck if I thought you reciprocated their feelings."

"Well, I don't."

"I know for *sure* you don't."

"And why is that?"

He gave her a wicked grin. "Because none of *them* can channel the Power. Not even a lick."

She stared at him aghast. "You think that's why I love you so much? The Power?"

He gave her a quick wink. "Doesn't hurt."

"Oh, you're awful!" But Tabitha couldn't help grinning.

"That's me—Mr. Awful!"

"You know that's not it."

He nodded. "I know. And it's not why I love you. But seriously, you gotta admit it. We are pretty lucky."

She sighed. "Yes, we are. We are blessed."

"Just whistle while you work!" he sang and then whistled as he scrubbed the walls of the Pit. He'd purchased *real* Pine-Sol—not some lousy store-brand equivalent cleaner. The Pit smelled like an evergreen forest, with hints of roses and motor oil.

He'd already swept and mopped the floor, but try as he might, he couldn't get rid of the motor oil smell.

He'd disposed of the used twin mattress from the Deseret Industries thrift store. He could tell they'd cleaned it, but it was still stained. It didn't smell new, fresh, either.

So, he'd bought a brand new one—a nice, comfy mattress. But just a mattress—no frame or box-springs.

Can't have her reaching the pit cover.

He wasn't afraid she could lift it, heavy as it was—he had to use a winch himself—but he wanted to be safe. He wanted *her* to be safe.

Safe and sound! He giggled to himself. Then he launched into another chorus of the Disney song. "Just whistle while you work!"

He'd even bought fresh sheets, warm blankets, and a down comforter for the bed. And pillows, of course. Big, fluffy pillows. Two of them.

He'd purchased a chemical, camping toilet, and toilet paper. Charmin, of course. There was a large wash basin too, with soap. New towels and washcloths. Jugs and jugs of distilled water, and paper cups and paper plates, because glass would be foolish.

He shook his head. *No knives, forks, or spoons. Not even plastic ones.*

There was also a small table and two chairs. Admittedly, unlike the mattress, those *were* from DI, but that would allow her to sit somewhere other than on the mattress. It was also somewhere for the two of them to share a meal together.

Even if it is just fast food. At least she can eat it with her hands.

Better get some napkins and Kleenex. He laughed. *And Kotex. Can't forget the Kotex!*

And on the table sat a vase of fresh flowers, a dozen, long-stemmed, red roses. The flowers were just for practice—to see how they'd look in the room. He would, of course, need to purchase fresh flowers later.

Of course, the engine block was still there, with the iron collar and chain padlocked to it. But the chain itself was long. Even collared, she'd be able to stand and walk about one half of the Pit, but not all the way to the other end.

The shackles were gone, of course. She wouldn't need shackles. The collar and chain would be sufficient.

I want her to be happy here.

He paused in his pine-scented scouring and gazed at the mattress. *Queen-size. For when she's ready. Ready for us to be together.*

His heart beat faster in anticipation. He licked his lips.

Someday, Tabitha, my love. My Prize. My Treasure. My gift from God.

You will be mine. We will live together in love.

Then I will consume you, take you into myself, and we will truly be together forever.

"But not yet," he said aloud, shaking his head. "Not yet."

No. The play means so much to her. Let her do the play. Can't take that away from her. Let her do the play first. Then I'll take her.

"But I'm so hungry!" He began to weep. "Please, Heavenly Father! Can I not have a morsel? Just for now? Something to tide me over?"

Rage flared within him. "I'm letting her do the damn play! I'm being so damned generous!" He panted, almost hyperventilating. "Because I love her. I love her!"

He raised a fist to heaven. "Just a snack! That's all I ask! Is that so much?" He sank to his knees, the scrub brush falling from his hand and onto the concrete. He hugged himself. "How am I supposed to survive until then?"

With a sob, he lurched to his feet. He snatched up the pail of diluted Pine-Sol, went to the center of the Pit, and poured the contents down the drain in the floor. Then he grabbed the scrub brush and deposited it in the pail. He went to the ladder and climbed it, tossing pail and brush into a corner of the garage. He went to the winch and lowered the heavy wooden cover until the Pit was sealed. Then he stared at the Pit.

No. It's not a pit anymore. It's our honeymoon suite. Mine and Tabitha's.

A few minutes later, after a quick check on Ozzie, Harriet, and their brood, he was driving down the deserted, dirt road, heading back into town. He drove with the lights off, of course. He didn't need lights. He knew the way. Nobody—other than himself— ever went this way. Not anymore. And he didn't want anyone to see him, to follow him, to know where his lair was, to recognize his car.

He drove slowly, quietly—without speaking, without even thinking. Even the ache, the horrible need could not wrench a sound from his lips.

It was time to change his face—to hide his true self and wear the facade, the mask he wore in front of the world.

He saw headlights in front of him. In a panic, he pulled off the road. He shut off the engine.

And he waited.

But the lights did not move. He listened to the thundering of blood in his ears, to his own frantic breathing. But he heard no other sound.

And he waited.

But still the lights did not move.

Then he caught it. The faint scent of prey. The lovely, delicious aroma of Woman's fear. Strong fear. Not as strong as Tabitha—oh, no—but strong enough.

He laughed then. *Thank you, God! Thank you!*

He started the car, turned on the lights, and drove back onto the road.

As he approached the other car, he saw clearly that the vehicle was pulled off to the other side of the narrow, country road. A lone figure crouched by the front, driver-side wheel. The tire was unmistakably flat.

He pulled to the opposite side of the road, then rolled down his window. The woman was no more than a silhouette in the headlights. Not slender, but not heavy either.

Nice, womanly curves. Shivering too. Not dressed for the chill. He began to reach for the hood of his jacket, but stopped. *Might make me look too scary. Just have to rely on the darkness. I can at least disguise my voice. Youthful. Foreign.*

He decided on a high-pitched, Australian accent. "Need some 'elp, Miss?"

She stood, rubbing her arms as if warding off the chill. "Yes! Oh, thank you for st-stopping! I've got a flat. I don't know how to work the j-jack. It—It's a r-rental—the car, I mean. Not like my Ford back home. I'm l-lost. I took a wrong turn. Then this hap-p-pened." Her voice shook, and not entirely with cold. The fear wafted from her in sweet, fragrant waves. She gestured at the jack with a trembling hand. The jack was one of the newer, screw-type devices, not a traditional ratchet jack. "C-Can you help me?"

He smiled. "Too right! Oh, I *'ate* them bloody things. Got me a better jack in the boot 'ere. Just gimme a second to get it."

He shut off the engine and got out of the car—slowly, so as not to spook the prey. In spite of his hunger, he took his time getting to the back of his car. He opened the trunk and rummaged around. He got the jack and tire iron ready to go, but then he retrieved the hidden syringe. He ignored the latex clown mask. *Save that for later.*

He smiled, baring a mouthful of teeth. "Don't worry, Miss. I'll 'ave you fixed up in a jiffy."

Josh ripped the tiny cast-iron skillet from Tabitha's tight-clenched hand. "Tabitha!" he cried.

For a moment, she didn't respond, her body stiff as a corpse in *rigor mortis*. Her eyes flew open.

She sucked in air like a drowning woman breaking the surface of the ocean. Then she clamped her lips shut and stifled a scream. She threw her arms around him and clung to him as her body quaked with violent sobs.

He'd been holding her in his arms, on his lap, during the vision, but once the vision was over, he slipped one hand under her hair and placed it on the back of her neck. He tried to draw on the Power, but... Nothing. No tingle. No Power.

His eyes darted around in panic. *She's suffering, and I'm Powerless!*

His eyes alighted on the tiny pan still clutched in his own hand. As if it burned him, Josh dropped the object to the floor in front of the sofa. Instantly, the Power flowed from where his other hand touched Tabitha's flesh.

He wanted to channel the Power to throw Folau against the wall, but the need to comfort his wife was much stronger. "It's okay, Sweetheart," he cooed softy. "It's over."

"It's over!" Her echo came out as a choked wail of despair. "She's dead!" She drew a hitching breath. "He *devoured* her!"

Folau, sitting in a chair in front of the sofa, bent and picked up the tiny, cast-iron frying pan. The miniscule skillet was barely large enough to fry a single egg. On the bottom of the pan, Josh could see the word "UTAH" cast into the iron. The object must have come from a souvenir shop and was probably not intended to actually be used in the preparation of food. The detective put the pan back into his bag. He retrieved his notepad and pen from his jacket, then he leaned forward, staring intently at Tabitha.

Angry though he was, Josh focused on his wife. "It's okay, Sweetheart." He drew more of the Power, eliciting a gasp from Tabitha. Her sobs ceased. Her ragged breathing quieted. She pressed herself closer against Josh's chest.

Folau grimaced, and his scar twitched like a pale snake on the side of his light brown face. "Anything new?"

He's got the hots for Tabitha, Josh thought, *but he drives her like she's just some beast of burden. Just a tool to be used.* Josh said nothing aloud as he glared daggers at the man. *But Tabitha's committed to this. Giving it everything she has. As she always does. With everything.*

Tabitha nodded slowly. "S-something's ch-changed."

Folau waited a few moments, but when Tabitha didn't respond, he asked, "What's changed? You told me he wasn't wearing a mask when he abducted Mrs. Koenig. You saw that. In the first vision. But you couldn't see his face—just a vague outline. A shadow. You mentioned that Aussie accent. But you thought it might be fake, because it was pitched too high, you said. It didn't sound quite natural."

Tabitha shook her head. "No. Not just *Mrs. Koenig.* J-Janessa. Her name was *Janessa.* She was a w-widow. She had a son, Harry. He's six. Six and a half. Now, he's an o-orph-phan."

"Yes, but—"

"But what?" Tabitha snapped, turning a livid, tear-streaked face toward Folau. "This is *personal,* Danny! Janessa *mattered* to someone. She loved, and she was loved. She's not just another case file!"

Folau nodded. "I'm sorry. You're right, of course."

"H-He's white," Tabitha said. "Or at least, light-skinned."

"Lighter or darker than me?" The detective gestured toward his Polynesian face.

Tabitha paused, considering, then pressed her face back on Josh's shoulder. "At least as light as you. I couldn't see him very well. But when he came into the pit, he w-w-wasn't w-wearing gloves." Then she shook her head violently. "Or maybe they were gloves after all. I can't be sure. No. I think I saw his hands."

"Is that it?" Folau appeared annoyed. "Is that all you got?"

"That's enough!" Josh snarled, keeping his voice down to avoid waking the baby. "She just died for you, man! Again! Now, back off!"

Folau opened his mouth as if he was about to bark out a retort, but then he snapped it shut. His eyes blazed at Josh.

"Once upon a time," Josh said, regaining some control over his rage and the urge to pin Folau to the ceiling, "that would've been enough for you—that little detail. You were always asking about his skin color. Now you've got it. And it's not enough." He narrowed his eyes. "Or is it too close to home, Detective?"

Folau's head snapped back as if he'd been struck.

For a second, Josh was worried that he'd slipped up and struck out with the Power.

Folau's Adam's apple bobbed up and down as if he were choking on bile. He bowed his head. "I'm sorry. I crossed the line." He looked at Josh's wife. "Tabitha." His voice was softer, gentler. "You said that something had changed. His skin color? Is that what you meant?"

She shook her head. "No. He's furnished the pit."

Folau blinked. "Furnished? Like with furniture? A couch? A bed?"

"There's a mattress." Tabitha turned toward the detective. She reached for Josh's hand and took it. The Power flowed between them. She leaned into Josh, sharing their strength.

"A mattress?" Folau made a note on his pad.

Tabitha nodded, wiping her tears away. "Big. Queen-sized, maybe? With sheets, pillows, a-and a blanket. A small table, with two chairs. And a vase of roses." She hunched her shoulders and gritted her teeth as if in revulsion.

"Roses?" Josh asked. "Did you say roses?"

She nodded. "Roses. In a vase. Fancy—the roses, at least. The vase looked plastic."

"Why roses?" Josh asked.

Folau's eyes shifted to Josh. "It makes a twisted kind of sense." He pointed his pen at Josh. "Think about it. Before, he was all about scaring his victims. Now, he wants to make them comfortable. At least for a little while."

"But why the change?" Josh asked. "Is it because—"

Tabitha gasped. "The shackles! They're gone!" She put a hand to her neck. "The iron collar and the chain. They're still there. But the shackles are gone." She squeezed Josh's hand. "I could sit up. I mean, *Janessa* could sit up. Maybe even walk around a little. I was sitting on the bed, the mattress, when the ceiling opened."

She shut her eyes and wrinkled her brow. "I didn't stink."

"What?" Both men spoke as one.

Tabitha grimaced, then sniffed and wiped at her nose. "Every other time, I— *she* had wet herself. Many times. Usually soiled herself too."

Folau didn't look up as he wrote furiously on his notepad. "Because, maybe this time he hadn't kept her as long?"

Tabitha shook her head. "No. That doesn't make sense. The pit didn't stink of urine or feces, either. I mean, there was still the stench of animals, but that's different. There is a drain in the floor." Then she shook her head. "No, there's a *toilet*. I didn't realize what it was until just now. Small. White. Plastic-looking. Like something you take camping maybe?"

Seriously? A camping toilet? Is that a girls camp thing? Us Boy Scouts always just went in the bushes.

Folau nodded. "Okay. That goes along with the idea that he's trying to keep them comfortable. Before he kills them."

"Was she hungry?" Josh asked. "Thirsty?"

"Mr. Kilmore!" Folau snapped. "Do not put ideas in her head! I'll have to ask you to leave."

Oh, you'd like that, wouldn't you? But he has a point. Dang it. "Sorry."

Tabitha closed her eyes, took a deep breath, and let it out, shuddering as she did so. "Hungry, yes. Starving. Weak. But not thirsty. Not this time. There was water. Somewhere down there. I didn't see it, but it has to be there."

She opened her eyes, turning her face to Folau. Her voice was ice. "Josh stays. Always. Are we clear, Detective?"

Folau nodded again. "Yes, we are. Clear as crystal. But *please*, Mr. Kilmore.

No more suggestions. Eyewitness accounts—even such as these—are notoriously unreliable. Because witnesses can be very suggestible."

"Sorry," Josh repeated. *I hate it when he's right.*

"He wore the clown mask," Tabitha said. "I don't remember her being scared of it—the mask, I mean. Not especially. She kept saying, 'I didn't see your face!' She was pleading for him to let her go. Saying she couldn't identify him."

Folau made another note. "Did he speak this time? In the pit, I mean?"

Tabitha shook her head. A shiver ripped through her. She closed her eyes and sobbed. "No. Just screamed. Like before."

Josh drew more of the Power through her.

She shivered once more, but she sighed. She opened her eyes and gave Josh a weak smile. She mouthed, "Thank you." Then she turned her face back to Folau. "The rest was pretty much as before. The screaming. The terror." She stifled a sob. "He pulled it right out of her. He drained her. Everything she was. Gone. I don't know what else to tell you."

Folau nodded. He even smiled. "No. That's alright." He glanced quickly at Josh, then focused on Tabitha again. "You've done enough." He reached for his bag, then stopped. "Wonder why that jack handle didn't work? She had it out. She'd touched it."

Tabitha shook her head quickly. "You said it was a rental car. It didn't belong to her. To Janessa. She has to own it. Not just borrow—"

There was a knock at the apartment door.

Tabitha jerked, startled.

Josh and Folau jumped as well.

Folau glanced at the door. "Expecting someone?"

The knock repeated. Tabitha jumped up, rubbing at her eyes, smearing her mascara even worse. "I'll get it."

As soon as she broke the contact, the Power ceased.

"No, Sweetheart," Josh said. "Let me get it. You go dry your eyes."

She nodded and headed off to the bedroom, pausing to glance at Joseph, who was somehow still asleep in his playpen, sucking on his binky.

Josh got quickly to his feet and went to the door. He unlocked and opened the door only to find a familiar, pretty woman with a flawless chocolate complexion, lovely brown eyes, and shining, long black hair that hovered in waves right at her shoulders. Even with the fine laugh-lines around her eyes, she had the face of a fashion model. She was dressed casually in a light jacket, blue-jeans, and sneakers.

Josh could not recall ever seeing the bishop's wife dressed so casually before. "Sister Smith! To what do we owe the pleasure?"

Maddie Smith appeared startled, as if she'd been about to leave when Josh had opened the door.

"Oh, hi, Brother Kilmore!" She smiled, showing a row of pearly, white teeth in a disarming smile. She glanced past him at Folau. "I'm sorry. I didn't know you had company."

Folau stood. "That's okay." He stuffed his notepad and pen into his jacket pocket.

"I was just leaving."

Thank heavens for small miracles! Josh smiled at Maddie Smith and stepped to the side. "Please come in!"

Still hesitating, she glanced past him again. "Is Tabitha here?"

Josh nodded. "Yeah."

Sister Smith smiled with relief. "Oh, good!" She stepped inside the apartment.

Folau approached the door. He stopped in front of Josh. "Thank you. You've been very helpful. Both of you. I'm sorry it didn't go smoothly." He extended his hand.

Josh took it. He shook his head. "It's never going to go smoothly. Nature of the beast."

Folau's scar twitched. He turned to Maddie Smith and extended a hand. "Daniel Folau."

Maddie hesitated for just a second before shaking the detective's hand. "Madison Smith." She smiled. "Pleased to meet you."

"You know," the detective said as he finished the handshake, "you really shouldn't be out alone at night. It's not safe these days."

Maddie furrowed her brow. "I thank you for your concern, Mr. Fo—"

He gave her a small, tight-lipped grin. "Folau."

"Mr. Folau. But I'm fine."

Folau turned to Josh. "You'll walk her to her car?"

Josh nodded. "Of course."

Folau's scar twitched. "Good." He turned back to Maddie. "Good night, ma'am." And then he was out the door.

Josh closed the door, shutting out the Saturday night chill and thoughts of Danny Folau. He turned back to the bishop's wife. "I'll go check on Tabitha."

But at that instant, Tabitha emerged from the bedroom. Her first glance was at Joseph asleep in his playpen. Then she turned her freshly made-up eyes on Sister Smith. Her face lit up in that dazzling smile that still caused Josh's heart to flutter. However, at that moment, the smile was not directed at him. "Maddie!"

Tabitha rushed over and threw her arms around the older, taller woman. Maddie returned the hug, although it seemed to Josh with less enthusiasm.

Tabitha stepped back. "What are you doing here?" Tabitha blushed and quickly added, "I mean, you're always welcome, but it's been a while."

Hasn't been over since Maddie Smith was Tabitha's visiting teacher.

Maddie's cheeks darkened. "I tried calling, but your phone was busy."

Tabitha chuckled. "Oh! Oh, yeah. I, uh, took the phone off the hook. Sorry." She gestured toward the sofa. "Won't you sit down?"

Maddie hesitated, then nodded. "Thank you." She sat at the end of the sofa, away from the baby's playpen. Tabitha sat beside her.

Josh was about to take the chair recently vacated by Folau when Joseph let out a scream. He grimaced. "Probably needs changing. I'll do it."

As Josh scooped the baby up, he heard Maddie ask, "He changes diapers?"

"Always does!" Tabitha said. "At least when he's home. Never lets me do it."

Joseph had stopped fussing by the time Josh got him to the changing table.

"Well, I'm impressed!" Maddie said.

Josh shrugged as he set about his task. "It's no big deal. Tabitha provides the food, and I take care of the by-products." He grinned. "Seems fitting. I do clean toilets for a living."

Maddie chuckled. "Ooh, I'm gonna have to tell Torrance about that! Well, if we ever have any more kids. But I think we're done." When she said that final statement, her usually subtle Southern drawl came out unusually thick. She and Tabitha shared female giggles. "But if Torrance ever *persuades* me to consider a fifth child, I'll tell him that it'd be on the condition that he follows Brother Kilmore's example and changes all the dang diapers!" The two women exchanged another feminine laugh.

"So, what brings you here?" Tabitha asked.

As Josh wiped his son's rear end and then applied baby powder, Joseph beamed at him, displaying his single tooth. Josh smiled back. "Hey, big fella!" he whispered, even as he listened to the women behind him.

"Well, I'm in a real bind," Maddie said, the Southern accent fading back into the shadows of her voice. "I'm gonna come right out and say it. You know I'm the Ward Music Director."

Uh-oh. I know what's coming. And Tabitha's not going to be happy about it.

"Do you need me to sing tomorrow?" Tabitha asked. The forced cheerfulness in her voice barely masking the dread.

"Oh, no!" Maddie replied. "It's not that. I know you would, even on short notice. And you'd be wonderful. That huge voice of yours, coming out of your little body? Filling the whole chapel? You're amazing! But, no." Maddie paused.

Josh finished taping down the sides of the diaper, then picked up the baby. Josh turned his head just in time to hear Maddie Smith say, "Carrie Anders is sick. I've got no one else. I wouldn't ask, but—"

Tabitha's countenance fell. "Oh, Maddie! I'm awful! And I can only play three songs. Four, including 'Silent Night,' but it's too early for that one. It'd be the same three hymns as last time. And I can't play the organ."

Tabitha can also play "Ye Elders of Israel," but that'd be opening a whole different can of worms. And some bad memories.

Maddie smiled. "The piano will be just fine. Just like last time."

"But that was just last month!" Tabitha was obviously struggling mightily to keep the panic out of her voice, and she was losing the battle. "I'm so slow! I mess up."

"You'll be fine. And you know I wouldn't ask if didn't have to. I know it's not your *thing*." There it was again, that Southern drawl.

Tabitha exhaled, noisily flapping her lips as she did so. "Okay."

"I knew you would! When I talked to Torrance about it, he said, 'That Sister Kilmore never turns down a calling or an assignment.' That's quite a compliment, coming from him." She leaned in and whispered loudly. "He gets lots of folks who turn down callings." She leaned back and said, "But never you two. Never. And I know he appreciates you both." She patted Tabitha's knee. "And I do too."

Tabitha smiled and placed her hand on Maddie's shoulder. "I won't say I'm happy to help—I *suck* at playing the piano—but anything the Lord asks."

"I know. You're a treasure." Maddie got to her feet. "I really have to go. Tabitha, you've taken a load off my mind. It's too late to change the program for tomorrow, but I'll change the numbers on the board, and Torrance will announce it over the pulpit. You'll do just fine. I know you will. Thanks!"

Josh handed the baby to Tabitha. "I'll walk you to your car. It's dark and—"

"No." Maddie Smith waved a dismissive hand. "That's all right. It's not like I'm gonna get kidnapped or murdered or something. This is *Provo*, for cryin' out loud."

"Please," Josh said. "I must insist."

"Please, Maddie," Tabitha said. "Let Josh see you to your car. I'll feel better about it."

Maddie frowned. "Not you too. You're as bad as that fellow who was here—the one with the scar and the Hawaiian-sounding name. Torrance told me to be extra careful tonight too. He wouldn't-a let me come by myself, but I just ran out the door anyway. But that's me. I try to not listen to a thing that man says." She winked. "Secret of a happy marriage. I'll be fine."

And with that, she was out the door. Josh followed her, but not down the stairs. He stood on the landing, watching her.

Maddie waved at him as she got into her car. "Good night!"

Josh waved back, but he continued to watch until Maddie Smith had driven safely out of the parking lot. And still he stood there, watching the shadows, watching for a hooded figure wearing a demonic clown mask.

You should listen to your husband, Sister Smith, at least about this.

Terror.

Paralyzing, heart-pounding, finger-cramping terror.

Few things struck fear into Tabitha's heart like the horror of playing the piano in church.

That—and, of course, tap-dancing.

And the Devourer.

Tabitha sat on the piano bench in the chapel about a half hour before sacrament meeting was to start at noon. She stared at the huge, intimidating musical instrument before her. It wasn't simply a piano. It was the grand variety of the treacherous device with its myriad of strings waiting to be struck by fingers far more talented than hers.

I'm going to suck. Absolutely suck.

Just like last time.

She opened the hymn book to "Come, Come, Ye Saints," positioned her foot on the pedal, and poised her fingers over the piano keys. She struck the first chord and somehow, miraculously, hit all the right notes—without any extraneous ones. She allowed herself a small grin.

It wasn't until the fourth chord that she hit her first wrong note. The next chord, she struck two. After that, it seemed as if she could do nothing right. F-sharp became F-natural when it wasn't supposed to be, major chords became erroneously minor, and soon most of the chords could only be called "chords" in the most charitable sense of the word.

By the time Tabitha had stumbled through the first verse, her hands were trembling, and she was fighting back tears.

Maddie's depending on me!

Who am I kidding? The whole congregation's depending on me.

She felt a gentle hand on her shoulder.

She twisted around on the bench to see who was behind her, who was there to state the obvious.

Josh gazed down upon her, his mouth twisted into a mischievous grin. He held Joseph in the crook of one arm. "Elton John had better watch his back."

Tabitha scowled. "Shut up. You're not helping."

He brushed her cheek softly with his finger, setting her tingling with the Power. "Sorry. I was just teasing."

"I wish Maddie hadn't asked me. Why couldn't she ask Brother Watanabe? He can play. He's good!"

"That's putting it mildly. But you know why Maddie asked you."

And she did know why. Hiro Watanabe was an excellent piano player, a professional musician. But he never accompanied the singing in church. He'd play a piano solo, and he'd play it masterfully. But he had never once consented to just play the hymns during congregational singing.

Josh kissed the top of her head. "Brother Watanabe thinks it's beneath him. And Maddie knew you would say yes."

"But I suck!" Tabitha brushed away an angry tear.

"You'll do fine." He caressed her cheek again, pulling more of the Power, sending a warm tingle through her. "And even if you do mess up… Okay, when you mess up, remember, when the Lord asked for someone to go and do, you went and did. Like Nephi. Like Moses. Like Gideon. I'll bet you Mary was terrified, but she said, 'Behold the handmaid of the Lord.' You don't have to be the best. You just have to be willing to serve."

She pressed her cheek against his fingers. "I love you. You know that?"

"I love you too. And I'm proud of you. You're so talented and so smart. And darn near perfect. In fact, I think there are only two things that're keeping you from being translated."

She sighed and grinned. "Two things? Let me guess. I totally suck at the piano, and I can't dance to save my life."

He chuckled. "Okay. Three things. But you're a good dancer. Good enough."

"Okay. I'll bite." She turned and tilted her head to look up at him, breaking physical contact and cutting off the Power. "What's the third thing?"

His mischievous grin had become positively wicked. "Your lousy taste in men."

She snapped her teeth at him, nearly chomping on his fingers. Then she grinned. "I have to practice."

He chuckled. "You sure do!"

She turned her head and glared at the piano. She muttered, "For all the good it'll do."

"Joseph and I'll go change the numbers on the hymn board."

Tabitha paused with her fingers hovering over the keyboard. "Change the numbers?" She turned on the bench to face the hymn board, the small wooden plaque with its four rows of movable number cards displaying the hymn numbers for the congregation. "Maddie said she was going to change them."

Josh shrugged. "I guess she's running late." He shifted their son so the baby could face forward. "Come on, big guy. Let's go help Mommy with the numbers. See? This is a one. That's a three. We'll need both of those."

Tabitha sighed and turned back to the dreaded grand piano and its sinister array of white and black keys. "'I will go and do as the Lord commands.'" She lined up her fingers and once more began to play, growling as she plunked out a particularly sour note.

At five minutes before the start of sacrament meeting, Tabitha began to play "Abide with Me" as the prelude music. She played clunkily and slowly enough to make the hymn sound like an out-of-tune funeral dirge. As the clock ticked inexorably toward the starting time, she looked around in panic for Maddie, but Tabitha couldn't spy the bishop's wife anywhere. Bishop Smith wasn't even in his usual seat on the stand yet, between his two counselors, Brother DeMolay and Brother Watkins.

Who's gonna lead the music? She trusted Maddie to go slow when conducting, to keep time with Tabitha's tortuous pace.

Her frantic eyes sought out Josh, who was sitting in the third row with Joseph, next to J.L., Mikey, and their girls.

Josh met her gaze.

Tabitha nodded her head toward the empty choir seats behind the chorister's music stand.

Josh must've seen the panic in her eyes. He nodded, turned to J.L., said something, and then rose. He made his way up to the stand, carrying Joseph, his scriptures, and the diaper bag. As he passed Tabitha, he leaned down and whispered, "Don't worry. I'll go slow." He kissed her quickly, pulling a momentary tingle of the Power through her lips.

He then sat with Joseph behind the music stand. He pulled a hymnbook from under the seat, then opened it and flipped to the proper page. He gave her a wink, and then began to wave his hand slowly, practicing the peculiar four-four-then-three-four-then-four-four-then-three-four timing of "Come, Come, Ye Saints." Like most returned missionaries, Josh knew the rudiments of leading music, but this particular hymn was a bit challenging.

Brother DeMolay rose and stepped to the pulpit. "Good afternoon, Brothers and Sisters. Welcome to sacrament meeting. Bishop Smith has asked to be excused and has asked that I conduct in his place. We would like to thank Brother and Sister Kilmore for providing our music this afternoon."

Tabitha listened for the sound of collective groaning from the congregation, but to her shock, she heard none.

"Contrary to what is printed in your programs," Brother DeMolay continued, "our opening hymn will be Number Thirteen, 'Come, Come, Ye Saints,' after which, Brother Jesse Montrose"—he paused, apparently looking at J.L., and J.L. nodded—"will offer our opening prayer."

Tabitha played the introduction to the opening hymn, with relatively few mistakes, and Josh stood behind the music stand, Joseph in one arm, and the other arm raised to give the upbeat.

Somehow with Josh leading the music, Tabitha felt more confident than she had only a minute before. He gave her a wink and a smile, and flipped his hand upward, signaling the start of the hymn.

Tabitha struck her first chord, and it was, to her great astonishment, and most likely to the astonishment of the entire ward, perfect.

The sacrament was finished, and Tabitha was seated next to Josh, in the choir seats. Most of the pressure was off. The closing hymn was at least thirty minutes away, and "Abide with Me," though it had three flats in the key signature, was at least meant to be played more slowly. Joseph was mercifully asleep in his carry-cradle. Tabitha took Josh's hand. The Power flowed in a pleasant trickle that wasn't in the least bit distracting. It was just normal and comforting. She whispered, "Thank you for coming to my rescue."

He kissed the crown of her head and whispered, "You did great."

"There you go, lying in church again." She grinned at him.

"I'm not lying. I'm sitting. Same as you. And you really did fine."

"Didn't suck too much, huh?"

"Not too much." He squeezed her hand and the Power surged. "Hey, look!" He pointed his chin toward the back of the chapel.

Bishop Smith strode quickly up the aisle. Instead of a Sunday suit, he wore a white T-shirt, blue jeans, and high-top tennis shoes. At the sight of him, some of the congregation gasped. Brother DeMolay, who stood at the pulpit and was announcing the rest of the program, stopped speaking abruptly. But it was the bishop's eyes that drew Tabitha's attention as he hurried forward.

Bishop Smith was staring intently at her. Tabitha had seen her bishop and doctor weep while speaking or testifying at the pulpit. She'd seen his eyes streaked with red. She'd seen them narrowed with concern. But she had never before seen those kind and gentle eyes wide with terror.

Bishop Smith made straight for Tabitha and Josh. He took all three steps up to the stand in a single bound, scrambled around the piano, and threw himself at Tabitha's feet. A collective gasp rose from the congregation. "Please!" he whispered loudly, clearly out of breath. "Come with me!" He turned his tear-streaked face to Josh. "Both of you! Please. Now!"

Stifling her fear, Tabitha got to her feet, followed immediately by her husband. Josh grabbed the carry-cradle with Joseph inside. Tabitha grabbed both their sets of scriptures and the diaper bag in one hand. She and Josh instinctively joined hands, and she felt the Power flowing.

"Lead the way," Josh whispered.

The bishop was already on his feet. He wheeled and hurried toward the side door, right at the base of the stand. He held the door for them as they exited. As the door closed, he put his hands together as if praying.

"What's going on?" Josh asked.

"Please!" the bishop said. "I-I don't know what you can do, but I know you're keeping a secret—a big secret."

A chill like a claw of ice seized Tabitha's gut and twisted. Josh squeezed her hand hard, making her wince. *He knows.*

"What's wrong, Bishop?" she asked, fighting down the bile that had suddenly risen in her throat.

Bishop Smith wrung his dark hands. "I-I-I didn't know what to do! I called the police, but they said it's too soon. Twenty-four hours, they said. So, I've been praying all night, all morning. I haven't stopped! But then the Spirit says, clear as day— He says, 'Go to Tabitha and Joshua Kilmore. They can help.'" He shook his head, putting a hand to his mouth. "I came right over. P-Please help me!"

"Help you?" Josh asked. "How?"

The older man's lips quivered. He seemed as if he couldn't catch his breath. "M-Maddie! She's gone! She's been taken!"

Torrance Smith stared at the Hate Chest—that's what *he* called it. The wooden box, about the size and shape of an old military footlocker, that he'd finally convinced Maddie to put away at New Year's. The Hate Chest sat in the corner of the garage, seeming to stare at him. *Something iron,* he thought. *Something that belongs to Maddie and is made of iron. Not steel. Can't be steel, they said. Iron.*

He didn't want to show the horrid thing to the Kilmores. He didn't want them to see that dark side of Maddie's personality. He didn't want them to know about the biggest bone of contention in their marriage.

He squatted and reached for the box. It was heavy, he knew. So heavy, like the ancient hatred it embodied. Grasping the handles on either side, he braced to heft it. Torrance nearly toppled over backward when the box practically leapt off the concrete floor.

Panic and terror rocked him as he stumbled, attempting to keep his balance. It couldn't be empty!

But then he heard the rattling inside. Hope surged up in him like the flare of a match struck in a dark room.

He carried the too-light box out of the garage and into the kitchen, where Josh, Tabitha, and their infant son waited. The baby was asleep in his carry-cradle on the floor.

Torrance set the Hate Chest on the linoleum floor. He knelt in front of the box, reaching for the lock.

But the combination lock was missing.

"Where's the lock?" he wondered aloud. He pointed at the latch at the top and front of the box where the lock should have been. "Maddie keeps this locked." He stared at it, blinking stupidly.

"Was it the lock itself?" Tabitha asked. "Was that the iron?"

He looked up at her in confusion. "What?" Then understanding burst upon him like a shaft of sunlight piercing through storm clouds. "No." He flipped the latch up, then yanked the lid open. Inside, he found a single iron manacle—a leg iron—attached to a chain. The scent of motor oil and rust assailed his nostrils. The preserving oil gleamed dully on the horrid iron instrument.

"Where's the rest?" he asked aloud.

"The rest?" Josh asked.

"There used to be more. A-a-a set of leg irons. Manacles. More chains. Slave things. From Maddie's ancestors."

"Does that belong to Maddie?" Tabitha asked, kneeling beside the box.

"Yes," Torrance replied. "Now, please! Can you help find her?"

Tabitha looked as if she might be sick. "I can try."

"Bishop," Josh said, kneeling behind Tabitha, "where are your kids?"

"What? My kids?" Torrance shook his head. "W-with my mother. At her house in Lehi. She came and picked them up this morning. Why?"

"They're not here." Josh put his hands on Tabitha's shoulders. "Good. Bishop, we're trusting you. With our lives."

"Whatever you're going to do, just do it!"

"Bishop," Tabitha said, her eyes at once wide with fear and moist with pleading. "Please, don't freak out. Okay?"

"Freak out?"

Tabitha turned her frightened eyes on the ugly iron thing in the chest—a reminder of the hatred of a bygone age. Tentatively, she reached toward the leg-iron. Then her hand recoiled. She stared into the chest, her breath coming in short, rapid succession.

"It's okay," Josh said, his voice gentle, though his eyes carried the same fear as his wife's. "You can do it, Sweetheart."

Tabitha nodded. "For Maddie. And for her children. *Your* children." She thrust her hand into the chest and grasped the leg-iron.

Tabitha's body froze, rigid, all her muscles tensed and clenching.

Torrance cried in alarm. "She's seizing!" He reached for her.

"No!" Josh said, shaking his head. "It's okay. This is what she does."

"I'm your doctor, Josh. I know what a seizure looks like!"

"Please," Josh said, a tear spilling from one eye. "Don't touch her. She's okay. Really, she is."

"What's she doing?"

"She's seeing through Maddie's eyes. Accessing her memories."

"Maddie's eyes? Her memories?"

Josh nodded. "Yeah. Usually, traumatic ones."

"H-how long? How long does it take?"

Josh shook his head. "It depends. Not long, usu—"

The iron dropped from Tabitha's hand, clattering on the bottom of the chest. She gasped. "No!" She choked down a sob. "He's got her!"

"Who?" Torrance cried. "Who's got her?"

Tabitha gritted her teeth for a moment. Then a cry ripped from her lips. "The Devourer!"

142

Terror shot up Torrance's spine, shooting daggers of ice into his brain. "Devourer?"

Josh pulled Tabitha into his arms. He reached for one of her hands and she clutched his. As soon as her hand touched his, she shuddered and exhaled.

"I've got you, Sweetheart," Josh said. Then he looked at Torrance. "When did Maddie go missing?"

"Last night. Must've been after she went to see you."

"Yes," Tabitha said, nodding. "She swerved." She shivered as if she were freezing. "To avoid another car. Hit the curb. Hard. She got out to check her tire. Make sure she hadn't popped it. She was kneeling. She was angry with herself. Worried that you'd be angry. You told her not to go out." Tabitha wiped at her tears. "He must've come up behind. He— He put a hand over her mouth. Stuck a needle in her neck. He *took* her."

"Needle? In her neck? Injected her? With what? Who? Who took her? What'd you call him? The Devourer?"

Tabitha nodded. "I'm sorry, bishop. He's a serial killer."

Torrance felt the air freeze in his lungs. "S-serial killer? Is Maddie... dead?" His voice dropped to a whisper on the last word, afraid of Tabitha's answer.

Tabitha shook her head quickly. "I don't know. Let me try again." She wriggled out of Josh's arms.

Josh took her by the shoulders again.

Tabitha's face hardened in an expression of fierce determination. A whimper of fear escaped her.

BAM! BAM! BAM! BAM!

Cabinet doors all around the kitchen opened and slammed. Repeatedly.

Torrance cried out. "What the—"

"S-sorry!" Tabitha was panting, wiping at angry tears. Her eyes darted about. "Th-that was me."

"What d'you mean? That was you?"

"S-sorry. It happens sometimes when I'm angry or scared. And r-right now, I'm both."

"I don't understand. What is this?" *Magic? Witchcraft?*

She shook her head, choking down a sob. "Later." She glanced quickly toward the carry-cradle, but the baby didn't seem to have been awakened by the slamming cupboards. Then she glared at the iron inside the chest. With a snarl, she snatched up the fallen iron.

She seized up once more.

Abruptly she dropped the leg iron. She shook her head. "That's not it."

"What do you mean, that's not it? Where's Maddie?"

Tabitha gave him a vehement shake of her head. "That memory, it was just an argument. You were fighting. About the manacles. There used to be more of them. L-like that one." She pointed into the Hate Chest, keeping her hand well clear of it.

"Yes." He nodded. "They're missing. I don't know what she did with them."

"*He* has them," she said with absolute certainty. "I don't know how he got them, but he has them."

"Who has them? This devourer person?"

Tabitha nodded.

"Bishop, who else has seen these things?" Josh asked.

"Why?"

"Trust me," Josh said. "It's important."

"Okay. Maddie used to show them to everybody. All her friends. Her graduate professors. Her theatre friends. Anybody who's been to our house."

Tabitha stared at him in apparent shock. "Maddie is into theatre?"

Torrance nodded quickly. "Her degree. Like you." He shook his head. "Doesn't matter now. She had the darn things on display. She was proud of them. Showed them to everyone and their dog. Made folks uncomfortable. Made me uncomfortable. I only convinced her to put them away this year—at New Year's—New Year's resolution, you see. Before you moved into the ward. But please! Never mind about all that! Where's Maddie?"

Tabitha nodded, her tight-lipped expression stoic. "Let me try again." She thrust her hand into the box and gripped the leg iron once more, bracing her body for the tremors that seized her again.

The seconds ticked by, stretching into minutes.

As he watched Tabitha, Torrance's mind raced. *What is this? Some kind of psychic thing? Magic?*

Witchcraft? Real, actual witchcraft? Right under my nose?

I knew she was keeping secrets, but…

"What's taking so long?" Torrance's words came out as a wail of terror.

"Been too long." Josh let go of one of Tabitha's shoulders and ripped the manacle out of her clenched fingers. He dropped it back into the box.

Tabitha gasped. She blinked and then swallowed. "She's alive. He's got her, but she's alive." She began to laugh through fresh tears. "She's alive!"

Torrance suddenly found breathing to be difficult. "Sh-she's alive?"

Tabitha nodded. "Yes. This was different. It was as if… it was *live*. Happening right now. The present."

"Maddie's alive?" *Maddie's alive!* Torrance clung to the phrase as if it were his only lifeline. "Where is she?"

Tabitha nodded. Then she turned her face to her husband. "She's in the pit. It's dark. He hasn't come back. Not since she woke up."

"The pit?" The lifeline had been ripped from his grasp. "What's that? Where is it?"

Josh shook his head. "We don't know. A friend of ours—a cop—he's been trying to find it. We think it's on a farm somewhere."

Torrance's eyes were wide with terror.

"I could smell the animals," Tabitha said. "Maddie's scared. But she's alive."

"But where is she?"

"Hey!" Josh said. "The last victim with the rental car. It was southwest of town."

"Yeah?" Tabitha narrowed her eyes. "What if he found her when he was on his way back? Back from consum—" She glanced guiltily at Torrance. "On the way back from the last one?"

Josh nodded. "That's what I was thinking. We could look out that way. Bishop, are there any farms southwest of town?"

Torrance shrugged and shook his head. "I guess so. I don't know."

Tabitha glanced at him. To his eye, it appeared as if she were burdened down with guilt and secrets. Then she focused on Josh. "We could go looking out that direction."

Josh nodded slowly. "Are you sure, Sweetheart? In broad daylight?"

Torrance groaned in frustration. "Look where? What're you suggesting? We just drive *south and west*? Do you know how big 'southwest' is? There are so many little roads to follow. You could drive for days and not find anything."

Tabitha took a deep breath. "We're not going to drive."

"What do you mean? How do we find Maddie?"

Josh shook his head. "Not we, Bishop. Just Tabitha and me."

Tabitha took Josh's hand. She and Josh stared intently at each other, sharing a silent decision. "Bishop, we need you to watch the baby."

She and Josh stood.

Josh dug in his pockets, then handed a keyring to Torrance. "There's breastmilk in the fridge at our place. He can eat mashed-up bananas too. We're out, but if you have any. His car seat is in the car."

Torrance stared at the keys in his hand. "Where are you going?"

"Bishop," Tabitha said, getting his attention. "We'll explain later. Please don't freak out."

She and Josh turned toward the back door, holding hands. They were always holding hands, always touching. As if they couldn't bear to be separated. As if, when they were not touching, they were somehow… *less*.

Torrance followed them out the door. "Where are you going?" he repeated.

They halted right outside, in the backyard. Josh gulped. "Bishop, you're right. We'd probably never find her. Not from the ground."

Tabitha's eyes were hard, even as tears ran down her cheeks. "This isn't magic. It isn't witchcraft. It's not evil. It's just… me and Josh."

"What are you talking about?"

"Pray for us," Josh said. "Pray for Maddie. And have faith."

Tabitha looked at her husband. She lifted Josh's hand to her lips, and he nodded. With that, Tabitha and Josh shot into the air.

Torrance stumbled backward. He fell to the lawn. And uttered a phrase that was most unbecoming for any man of God.

But he didn't take his eyes off the Kilmores.

Holding hands, Tabitha and Josh flew upward, toward the lowering October overcast. In seconds, they were just two dark specks against the clouds. If Torrance didn't know better, they could be a pair of birds—a pair of birds touching wings.

He watched them fly away. To the southwest.

Torrance couldn't seem to catch his breath. His heart pounded in his chest, the blood thundered in his ears. The world began to spin around him.

Hyperventilating. Breathe.

He took a few slower breaths. The world stopped spinning.

Not magic. Not witchcraft. Not evil.

"Please find her!" he shouted after them.

He got to his knees and bowed his head. "Heavenly Father! Please lead Josh and Tabitha to Maddie. Please bring her home."

He paused, trembling, as terror and doubt washed over him. He was a doctor, a man of science. A man of faith. A bishop.

Not witchcraft.

"Please. Please help them. Guide them. And help me to understand. I don't understand the things I've seen. But please, bring Maddie home. Safe. Alive. I did as Thou didst command. I went to them. I just don't understand what's going on. It isn't the priesthood. It's something else. Is it from Thee? If it is used for good, it must be. Please help thou mine unbelief. Never mind. I don't need to understand. Please just tell me it's not evil."

Warmth washed over him, like warm honey poured over his head, enveloping him, speaking peace to his soul. It didn't erase his fear, not quite, but it erased his doubt.

Not witchcraft. Just Tabitha and Josh. A gift from God.

He looked to the western sky. He could no longer see the Kilmores.

"Please, Heavenly Father, guide them to Maddie. Bring her home."

"Glory, glory, hallelujah!"

He softly sang along with the Mormon Tabernacle Choir as the music filled his car. "Glory, glory, halle—"

What the hell are they doing in there?

He could see the yellow Volkswagen parked in front of the prey's house.

It's Tabitha. She knows. She knows about the prey.

He laughed softly. *Of course, she knows. She's Tabitha.*

She's special.

Perfect.

My Treasure.

He sat in his car, watching the house, watching the yellow Bug.

But she doesn't know where I'm keeping the prey.

People will be looking for this one, though. Too visible. Too well known.

Shouldn't have taken her.

No. God gave her to me. Put her right in my path.

Bitch almost hit my car.

I could've been killed!

And if I'd been killed, who would there be to feed on them? Who would make the world right?

Consume her tonight. Feed the husk to Ozzie and Harriet and the brood.

He licked his lips. *Some of the piglets are ripe for butchering. Make for some good, tasty eating.*

Like consuming my women twice.

Maybe I'll give some pork chops to Tabitha.

"Oh, yes," he said aloud. "She'll eat them. She'll eat the residue of their delicious souls." He smiled and sighed happily at the thought. "Just like in the play."

Tasty. The anticipation sent a shiver up his spine.

His heart pounded, and his breathing quickened. "Yes. Sweet Tabitha. I will love you. Love you with my body. With my soul. And you will love me with yours."

He chuckled. "Heart and soul! I fell in love with you, heart and soul!" he sang, clashing with the majestic strains of the Mormon Tabernacle Choir. "Madly!"

He laughed then. "Madly. Madly. Madly."

You and I, Tabitha. You and I.

As it always should have been. Not that damned interloper you call a husband. He's not worthy of you. He never was.

"I will take you unto myself, my love. And then I will take you *into* myself. All the souls in me will be in you as well. Just like Renfield."

But the play's not real. Oh, no.

This. This *is real.*

But the play's important to her. It means everything to her.

Must let her finish the play first.

But the pigs!

I see it now. I have been fattening up the pigs. Fattening them with woman-souls.

So that you *could consume them, my sweet Tabitha. And you will consume them.*

And then I will consume you.

"And then we will be—"

The words froze on his lips, and his heart seemed to stop, as his eyes beheld the impossible. Two figures, rising, shooting upward, into the air, clasping hands. One tall. One short, with long hair and a full-length skirt.

Tabitha! Flying!

With Josh.

Flying? How?

And then he observed the direction in which they flew—southwest.

"No!"

He jammed the gearshift into drive and lurched away from the curb. The engine roared, and the tires squealed, the smoke of burnt rubber rising up behind him. For a moment, even the Mormon Tabernacle Choir was drowned out as he drove south. He'd turn west when he got to Springville.

A dog darted into the street, in front of him. He swerved, almost losing control of his vehicle. But he sped on, cursing the dog and himself even louder.

Get into a stupid accident, and they'll get there before me!

Flying! Like a couple of bats straight out of hell. How is that possible? Flying? How?

They'll get there first.

Damn you, Josh! She's not yours! She's mine!

Mine! Mine! Mine!

God promised her to me*!*

They'll get there first! They'll find the prey. The Pit. Ozzie and Harriet. The piglets. They'll find it all!

No soul-laden pork chops.

"Bitch!" He pounded the steering wheel. "You'll ruin everything! It was all for *you*! All for you!"

But they don't know where they're going. Do they?

The car! That flippin' rental car. Shouldn't have left it there. South of town. On that dirt road west of Springville.

But...

Hope blossomed in his chest. "They don't know where it is! Southwest. Southwest! That's all they know!"

All those little dirt roads. They don't know where to look. It'll take them forever.

Flying! Like a couple of bats out of hell.

He giggled as he drove. The giggle grew into a chuckle, and the chuckle exploded into a full-throated, belly-shaking laugh. "They don't know where to look!"

But I do.

As he roared down the road, he hit a button on the dash of his car. The Mormon Tabernacle Choir abruptly ceased singing, as a cassette tape popped out. Across the front of the white plastic cassette were emblazoned the words "Mormon Tabernacle Choir." He opened the box on the console between the two front seats. He carefully placed the Sabbath-appropriate cassette into an open slot within the box, then selected music more appropriate to his mood: Meatloaf.

He grinned savagely as he jammed the tape into the dashboard player.

The song started just before the final chorus. He cranked up the volume 'til the blaring music hurt his ears. He screamed along with the music.

"Oh, like a bat out of hell!" *I'm gonna get there first!*

"Oh, like a bat out of hell!"

Tabitha sniffed the air wafting from the barn below them. She made a sour face and shook her head. "This one doesn't smell right either. The place we're looking for *really* stinks."

"Okay," Josh said. "I thought those dairy cows at the last place smelled bad enough. Maybe it's not cows were looking for. Maybe some other kind of animal."

We're not looking for animals. We're looking for Maddie. But Tabitha knew what Josh meant. That animal stench was seared into her brain. She was certain she'd know it when she smelled it.

The Power surged through Tabitha as Josh took them higher into the lowering sky. As they'd searched, flying frantically from farm to farm, the dark clouds had descended. The air had gotten colder too—not that they were bothered by the temperature with the Power warming them.

Josh pointed to the west, toward Utah Lake. "There's another one." They flew, accelerating toward yet another isolated farm.

Tabitha continued to pray, as she had been ever since they'd flown off on their quixotic, needle-in-a-haystack quest. "Please, Heavenly Father. Please lead us to Maddie. Show us the—"

"Bollocks!"

Tabitha glanced at her husband, but then she too recognized the source of his distress. A snowflake struck her nose. Another hit her cheek. In moments, the air was full of swirling, white flakes.

"We're running out of time," Josh said.

Another snowflake hit Tabitha's eyelash. She snapped her eyes closed. "Please, Heavenly Father! Guide us!"

A tingling warmth, completely unrelated to the Power, spread through her. She squeezed Josh's hand.

"Yeah," was all he said.

He feels it too.

Josh's free hand snapped up, and he pointed at a cluster of three buildings, none of which could be termed a barn. "There! Two o'clock!"

Tabitha looked where he was indicating. She saw what looked like a two-story wooden house, a large tin Quonset hut, and a small, low shed with a fenced enclosure around it. The warm assurance of the Spirit intensified. "That's it!"

Her stomach lurched upward as they dropped precipitously toward the structures, as if they were riding a roller coaster, shooting down an invisible track. *Like Space Mountain. Disneyland. Our honeymoon.*

Focus! On Maddie!

"Does it smell right?" Josh asked.

"I don't know. But it feels right."

Then the stench hit her—an almost overpowering reek of urine and feces—assaulting her nose. She gagged on the bile that suddenly rose in her throat. "Oh, *gross!*"

"Yeah," Josh said, wrinkling his nose. "Is that it?"

The putrescence from her visions. "Oh, yeah." Mentally, she braced her stomach for another unseen-roller-coaster fall. "Quick."

They alighted outside the animal pen, the snow swirling and gusting around them in tiny, short-lived whirlwinds. The fence was constructed of stout wooden rails, with only small gaps. *Meant to keep something big and strong inside. Horses? No, the shed's too low for horses.* Tabitha had little experience with farm animals, but she knew horse droppings didn't reek like the horrific stench filling her nostrils.

The ground around the enclosure appeared to be dried mud—composed chiefly of excrement—on which the snow had barely begun to stick. No animals were visible inside the pen, but something stirred inside the open shed. Then, with a series of grunts and squeals, an enormous pig trotted out. The animal was nearly as tall as Tabitha. A second, slightly smaller, but still massive, swine also emerged from the shed. The second beast was obviously female, judging from its dangling teats. Five piglets followed, squealing loudly. One of the piglets was obviously smaller than the others. The pink animals were spattered with the brown, pungent mud. They trotted up to the fence, eagerly snuffling.

Tabitha put her free hand to her nose. *How can they stand the stench? Living in their own filth?*

The sow sniffed at Tabitha and then Josh. But when neither human offered any food, the beast began rooting in the foul muck. In moments, it lifted its snout, chewing on something it had found.

The object was brown with the mud, but the shape was unmistakable.

A human foot.

"Maddie!" Tabitha cried. Bile rose in her throat.

The Power surged, and the bit of human remains was ripped from the porcine jaws. The foot floated until it came to rest outside the pen.

The sow let out an angry, almost human shriek. It charged the fence, causing both Tabitha and Josh to step back. The beast jabbed its snout through the rails, but not in front of the severed foot.

It's trying to get to us.

The enormous sow squealed, bellowing in its rage.

"It's not Maddie's," Josh said.

Tabitha's head snapped away from the furious pig. She gazed down at the cadaverous foot. She felt a small surge in the Power as Josh used it to strip away the mud, revealing the dead flesh.

Tabitha was surprised to find that the foot wasn't red. She had expected it to be crimson. The toenails displayed the remnants of pink nail polish.

No blood. No blood left in it. "It's pale."

Josh squatted down, but he still held her hand. He still held the Power. He didn't touch the gruesome thing, he merely gazed at it. "Even in this condition, it'd be brown—or at least darker—if it were hers. It's not Maddie's."

"No." Relief washed over Tabitha, temporarily overcoming the urge to empty her stomach. "It's not Maddie." Then the bile in her stomach drowned her relief. "It's Janessa Koenig." *Maybe all that's left of her.*

Josh stood. He also appeared to be battling the urge to vomit. His Adam's apple bobbed erratically up and down. "But that means Maddie's still here."

"Maddie!" Tabitha shouted, heedless of the danger. "Where are you? Maddie! Maddie Smith!"

Josh tugged her hand. "Let's check out the house."

Tabitha shook her head. "No. She's in the pit. Probably no pit in the house. The pit smelled of motor oil." She pointed at the Quonset hut. "In there."

Still ashen-faced, Josh nodded. "Okay."

They turned their backs on the ghoulish swine.

Josh quickly flew them to the front of the hut. They alighted in front of a pair of large metal doors. The entrance was large enough to drive a truck through. A heavy padlock sealed the doors together.

"Bollocks," Josh muttered. "This is breaking and entering. Are you sure she's in there?"

Tabitha hesitated just a moment, waiting for spiritual confirmation.

And then it came—a gentle, reassuring warmth. "Yes," she said.

"Yeah. Me too. She's in there."

The Power spiked. The lock ripped apart, the pieces dropping to the snow-covered ground. The doors swung open.

Through swirling flakes of white, Tabitha stared into the gloomy, tin hut, shaped like one half of a pipe, cut longways down the middle. Shelves stood against the curved wall on the left. Near the other side, an ancient truck stood amid several old-fashioned, military-surplus-type five-gallon gas cans. But Tabitha focused on the large, wooden rectangle in the center of the floor—a massive trapdoor with a heavy chain attached. The chain ran from an iron ring secured to the trapdoor up to a pulley suspended from the curved ceiling and back down to a winch. At the far end of the trapdoor, a wooden ladder rested on the concrete floor.

Tabitha had seen that ladder before. She'd seen the Devourer descending it before killing his victims. Fear twisted her gut.

The pit. We found it. She swallowed hard. "Open it up."

Josh nodded. "Give me a second. Gotta figure this out. If I don't do this right, it could fall in on her."

"Help!" Maddie Smith's voice was no more than a harsh croak. She'd been screaming for hours. "Please help me."

When Maddie had drifted back to consciousness, she had found herself in a blackness so complete, she could see nothing. She couldn't hear anything either, except for her own breathing, her own hoarse screaming, the drumming of her heart, and—when she moved—the clanking of the chain running from the padlocked collar at her neck. The collar wasn't hers. It wasn't one of the relics in her Box of Remembrance. But the collar had the same feel—cold iron pressing into flesh like the degradation, the hopelessness of her ancestors' bondage.

She could hear nothing else. And she could see nothing at all.

But she could *smell*. The cloying scent of roses, motor oil, the odors of human waste mixed with chemicals coming from the toilet she'd discovered and been forced to use.

And she could *feel*—the mattress and sheets beneath her and the unyielding metal collar at her neck.

She could feel the cold too, despite the thick comforter she'd found and wrapped around herself.

She bowed her head and prayed. Again.

Please, Heavenly Father! Deliver me from bondage! Before he comes back.

She didn't know who he was. Somehow, never having seen him made her abductor all the more terrifying. He was a shadow in her mind—a shadow with the burning, crimson eyes of a demon and the teeth and claws of a monstrous beast. She could imagine the many horrible things he might do to her before he killed her. And he *would* kill her. Maddie was certain of that.

Please watch over Torrance and the children. When I'm… When I'm gone. Please help me. Send Thine angels to—

Light! Blinding. Searing into her eyes.

She blinked, through her tears, gripped by terror as the ceiling above her opened like the lid of a massive box. Like the lid of her Box of Remembrance.

"No!" she croaked. "Help! Someone! Help me!"

Two figures, black silhouettes against the light, appeared at the edge.

"Maddie!" said a female voice.

She knew that voice! "T-Tabitha?"

"Sister Smith!" cried a male voice. "Thank God!"

She felt a sharp tug at her neck and heard a metallic snap. The lock at her neck flew apart as if powerful, unseen hands had ripped it to pieces. The iron collar opened. The chain dropped to the mattress.

Free! I'm free!

She unwrapped herself from the comforter and began to get to her feet. Suddenly she was floating as if by magic, up, out of her dark prison.

Flying!

Even as Maddie hovered in the air, Tabitha reached for her hand. "We've got you," Tabitha said. "You're safe now."

The instant Tabitha clasped Maddie's hand, Maddie felt a tingling warmth surge through her. It flowed from her and into Tabitha.

And it felt good.

"Don't freak out," Tabitha said, giving Maddie a kindly smile. "It's just… the Power. I'll explain it all later."

"P-power? Wha—"

"Seriously," Josh said, "don't freak out."

Then the three of them were flying. Maddie gasped. She clutched Tabitha's arm with her free hand, clinging for her life. They zoomed out of the building, through a wide doorway, and into a blizzard.

Snow was all around her, above her, below her. The wind howled as they flew. But Maddie was not cold. She was warm—as if she were wrapped from head to toe in an electric blanket. Only she felt as if she herself were the blanket.

"Can you see where you're going?" Tabitha shouted above the gale.

"No," Josh replied, shouting to be heard. "I'm going to have to fly low. Lower than I want to. Try to find some kind of landmark. I can't even tell how high we are—unless we get into the clouds. And even then… We'll just head"—he pointed ahead—"that-away. I think that's north. Hopefully, we'll find the city. Or maybe, a road."

Maddie could see almost nothing of the ground below her. The world was a white blur. *This is impossible! We're flying.* "Torrance? The kids?"

"They're okay. Scared. Frantic about you, but okay."

Maddie choked on a sob. "Thank You, Jesus!" she cried, slipping back into the familiar prayer language of her Baptist youth. "Thank—"

Snowflakes flew into her mouth. She spluttered. *It's just snow. Just snow. Flying into my mouth. I'm flying!* The energy flowing through her was pleasurable. *Is this what Heaven feels like?* "Am I dreaming?"

Tabitha hesitated for just a moment before answering. She shook her head and gave Maddie a sad smile. "No. This is real. Very real."

"Are you angels?"

Tabitha laughed.

So did Josh. "Not even close!"

"We're just…" Tabitha began. "Just trust me. This is just something Josh and I can do. Together. But now's not the time to explain things."

Josh shouted against the wind, "Let's just get you home!"

"You're safe now," Tabitha said. "That's all that matters. And the bishop, Torrance, is waiting for you."

Torrance is waiting for me. Thank You, God. "But this? I don't understand what this is. It feels so…" *Sweet. Good.* "Is it magic?"

"Not exactly," Tabitha said. "But we'd appreciate it if you didn't tell anybody. It's secret. You know, sorta sacred. To us."

"Does Torrance know? A-about this?"

Tabitha visibly sighed. "He does now."

"Oh." *I'm flying!* "My babies? Are they safe?"

Tabitha squeezed her hand. "Yeah. They're at your mother-in-law's house. That's what the bishop said."

Without warning, they lurched downward. Maddie yelped in terror.

Tabitha cried out too.

"Sorry," Josh said. "I see something." He pointed. "Look! It's the temple!"

Maddie couldn't see the white walls or roof of the temple itself, but she could see the spire thrusting up into the maelstrom like a golden lighthouse in a sea of white.

"We're a lot further north than I thought," Josh shouted. "And east. We're almost to the mountains."

Tabitha trembled as if with excitement. "Thank heavens! At least we know where we are!"

Maddie realized with a start that the trembling wasn't caused by excitement. *They're scared? They can fly, but they're flying* blind. *In a blizzard.*

They wheeled about in the air, their backs to the House of the Lord. They descended until Maddie could see a snow-blanketed street below them.

"That's Nine-Hundred East!" Tabitha cried. "We can follow that. For a while, at least."

Josh nodded. "Yeah, we'll follow the streets. Follow them home."

Home! "You sure my babies are safe?"

"Yes." And then Tabitha groaned, looking distressed. "Not now!"

"What is it?" Josh asked.

"What's wrong?" Fear ripped through Maddie. *We're gonna crash! Crash into an airplane. Or a mountain. Or—*

"I'm leaking." Tabitha shook her head. "It's all your talk of babies and… Well, we took off looking for you before I got a chance to feed Joseph. I sure hope he's okay."

"Your baby? Where is he?"

"We left him with the bishop," Josh said. "I'm pretty sure that's Center Street coming up. I'm going to turn west."

The three of them wheeled to the right and floated quickly above Center Street.

"You left Torrance alone with a baby?" In spite of everything she'd been through, Maddie choked back a laugh. She was afraid that once she started laughing, she wouldn't be able to stop. *Don't think about it. Just get me home. Pretend it's okay. Everything's normal. Normal.*

Don't laugh. Don't cry.

I was kidnapped.

154

I'm flying.

Chained up.

Yessir! Normal as could be.

She bit down another laugh. An insane laugh. "H-honey, that man may be a doctor, but he's all thumbs when it comes to changing a diaper. He——" Hot tears fell from her eyes and into the air below them. "No! If I ever see him again, I will *never* say another negative word about him. Never." She lifted her eyes to heaven. "I promise, Heavenly Father, I will never criticize him again. I promise." *Don't make promises you can't keep, Laticia Madison Brown Smith.* "I'm gonna try my darndest, okay? Torrance is a good man." *And I'm going to burn that darn box.*

"Yes, he is." Tabitha said. "He prayed and listened to the Spirit. He sought us out, asked us to help."

"Because he knows what you can do?" *This magic? This strange, amazing, delicious thing?*

Tabitha shook her head. "He didn't know. The Spirit told him to come to us. And he did."

Maddie felt a surge of warmth that had nothing to do with the tingling energy flowing from her into Tabitha's hand. *I love that man!* "Hurry. Please, hurry!"

Josh shouted. "I can't go any faster. I can barely see where we're going as it is. I don't want to get lost again."

Maddie shivered, but not with the cold. "How come I'm warm? I should be freezing." She'd heard of people who felt warm right before they fell asleep in a snowstorm, fell asleep and never woke up. *Please, God! Don't let me die. Let me see Torrance again. And my sweet children!*

"That's the Power," Tabitha said. Being closer to Maddie, Tabitha raised her voice as if she was standing on a stage. "My Power. Your Power. It's keeping us warm."

My power? I don't have any power. "What about Josh's Power?"

"Nope," Tabitha said. "It's just you and me. Mostly me. But some of it's coming from you. But I can't do anything without Josh. He controls it. He wields it."

"Like the priesthood?"

"No. Not the priesthood. Not many men can channel a woman's Power. Josh is special. But he can't do anything without me either. We do this *together*."

Maddie spotted the lights of a familiar convenience store. A violent shudder tore through her. "That's the Seven-Eleven! That's where he— that man took me. He stuck a needle in my neck. I couldn't scream. Just passed out. Then I woke up in that—that hole. With a collar. And a chain." She shivered again.

"I know," Tabitha said.

"You know? Of course, you know. You found me. How'd you find me?"

They wheeled to the left, heading south.

Tabitha grimaced and she looked guilty. "That's something else I can do."

Something else? More than this? "Do you know who he is? The man who…"

Tabitha shook her head. "No. I've never seen his face."

"But you've seen him?"

155

"Once." Tabitha shook her head, and tears streamed down her cheeks. "But he was wearing a mask."

"I never saw him." All the terror came washing back. "He—he came up from behind. And—and..."

"It's okay. You're safe now. You're almost home."

Safe? I'm floating through the air in the middle of a blizzard.

And he's *still out there.*

"She's gone! Gone!" he keened, kneeling at the edge of the Pit, staring down, yanking at his hair with both hands, strands coming loose and falling into the Pit.

The prey was gone.

Behind him, the storm raged, blowing snow into the Quonset hut, into the Pit, onto all his loving preparations for Tabitha.

He'd barely made it there, hampered as he was by the snow, even in four-wheel drive. Getting back wasn't going to be any easier. But at the moment, none of that mattered.

He was too late.

"You've ruined everything, you stupid bitch!"

No! Not Tabitha. She's not a bitch. She's my Prize. My Treasure.

But she did this. She and Josh.

"No, no, no, no, no!" he howled. *They flew out here. How can they fly?*

They found it. How?

"What am I going to do?" He raised his face to the swirling white of heaven. "What am I going to do? Answer me!"

"Burn it." The voice—or was it *voices*?—was barely a whisper in the darkest recesses of his mind. But he heard it clearly. "Burn it all."

Who said that?

He leapt to his feet, nearly tottering into the Pit. But he caught himself. Barely. *Mustn't fall. No! Mustn't fall. If I fall, I'd never get out.*

Then they'd find me. They'd stop me. And then what would become of my sacred mission?

"Burn it all."

His head snapped around as he searched for the voice—the voices.

But he could see no one.

"Burn it down quickly, before you're trapped here. Before they find you. Before they find *us*."

And then he understood.

It's them. My women! My woman-souls. They're whispering to me. Guiding me. Because they love me.

"I love you too!" he said aloud. "I love you all."

"We love you too. Now, burn it."

"Yes! Yes, my dears. Of course."

He got quickly to his feet, but carefully that time, so that he wouldn't fall into the Pit. "Lead me. Guide me," he sang. "Walk *inside* me." He went to one of the metal gas cans, putting on gloves as he did so. *Never leave fingerprints. That's my motto!* It was a motto he had observed faithfully in that place, except, of course, when he devoured his prey. Then he needed to be barehanded. He needed to touch the iron with his flesh, just as the prey did. To commune with the prey. To feed on her delicious fear. To consume her precious soul.

The gas can—like all the others—was painted olive-drab, with the letters "US" stenciled in white on the front. He'd kept the gas cans full. Perhaps, at the back of his mind, he'd always known this day would come. He twisted off the lid.

He went to the edge of the Pit, and while circling deliberately around it, doused the mattress, the table with its vase of roses, the chairs, the chemical toilet, the comforter. The thick comforter had been cast aside, discarded, as if the prey hadn't even appreciated it! He emptied the gas can and tossed it into the Pit. It landed on the mattress, the bed he'd intended to share with Tabitha.

I'll find another place, Tabitha, my love, my Treasure.

In fact, I know the right place.

He chuckled. "This is the place!" *Or was it, "This is the right place?" I always get those two mixed up.* He grinned. *Brother Brigham will forgive me. I'm continuing his work, after all.*

Or at least the work he should have done.

He strode quickly to one of the storage shelves lining the wall. From among the various tools and bits of hardware, he grabbed the metal case labeled, "Property of the Utah Department of Fish and Wildlife," and below that, "CARFENTANIL." And below the name of the sedative was the skull-and-crossbones, the universal symbol for poison. *Can't forget this!* He carried the case outside and stashed it inside his trunk, right beside the masks, the hooded jacket, and the box of syringes. And, of course, the manacles and chains he'd removed from the Pit days earlier.

He froze. "Forgot the flippin' collar!"

But he couldn't go back into the Pit now, not with all the gas everywhere. He smiled, baring his teeth. "Still have one shackle!" He could use that. He *needed* that.

No collar? No problem. Still have something iron to bind her, to allow me to feed from her.

Soon, sweet Tabitha. Soon, my love, my Prize.

He returned to the Quonset hut and began splashing gasoline all around the tin building with its half-pipe walls and roof. He didn't splash any of the gas *on* the walls or roof, just on anything that would burn—everything except the remaining gas cans and a large pair of rubber over-boots. The flames would obliterate any evidence of his presence. Every hair, every fiber of clothing, every stray fingerprint. The process took several more cans. He carried two more gas cans out into the storm, into the small farmhouse.

He removed an old, dust-covered vinyl tablecloth from the house, which he folded, fighting with the wind. He laid it on the snow, a short distance away from the buildings. He scooped more snow onto the vinyl to keep it from blowing away in the howling storm. Then he returned to the farmhouse and began distributing gas in strategic locations.

When he had finished preparing the house, he returned to the Quonset hut. He slipped on the pair of oversized rubber boots, to protect his best Sunday shoes. Then he picked up the last two gas cans. These final cans he carried to the pigpen. The pink-nail-polish-adorned toe of the human foot poking out of the snow caught his eye. He kicked the foot into the pen. "Ozzie!" he called. "Harriet! Dinner!"

The pigs came running.

Ozzie, huge-bodied and tiny-eyed, spied the foot and snatched it up before an angry Harriet could get to it. Then the great hog retreated to the shelter of the shed. The sow followed its mate, screaming in aggrieved rage. The piglets followed their parents.

All except one.

He reached over the fence and snatched up the smallest piglet, the runt of the litter. He carried the squealing, squirming beast a few paces away, close, but not too close, to the tablecloth. Then he knelt, pinning the earsplitting animal to the snow. He pulled a folding knife from his pocket, opened the blade using his teeth, and then plunged the knife through the thick hide of the piglet's neck. Quickly and neatly, he slit the throat of the young animal. He was careful, of course, to not get any blood on his clothes.

Mustn't come back all bloody! Cleanliness is next to godliness, or haven't you heard, piggy?

He let go of the dying animal, ignoring the large crimson patch on the white snow, the gurgling sounds, and the piglet's thrashing, which, of course, would all end soon enough. He wiped the blade on the unstained, virgin snow. Then he strode to the enclosure. He opened the pen, then latched it behind himself. He kept the blade pointed in front of him.

Just in case.

I mean, it's not like you didn't kill and eat the guy who used to live here or anything, huh, piggies? You killed and ate Ol' Lou, didn't you?

I mean, I'm grateful, Ozzie and Harriet. If it wasn't for you, I'd have had to kill him myself. And you know I don't like killing.

Killing men, anyway.

Just as he was about to close the shed door, Harriet poked her snout at him. She snuffled, then retreated.

What a terrible mother you are, Harriet. You don't even care that I just slaughtered your little baby, even if it was the runt.

You're a bitch. Like the prey you've pigged out on.

He chuckled. *Pigged out on!*

I'm gonna pig out on your baby! And all the precious husks it's consumed. Just like Renfield.

He shut the shed doors, locking Ozzie, Harriet, and their surviving brood inside.

"This little piggy went to market. This little piggy stayed home. This little piggy had human flesh. Every little piggy had some. And I'm taking one little piggy—wee-wee-wee…" He stopped and laughed softly. "No! Not wee-wee-wee. Gurgle-gurgle-gurgle, all the way home!"

I crack me up.

He poured gasoline onto the walls of the shed and onto the railings of the pen. Then he went to the leeward side of the shed, where he was sheltered from the wind, if not the falling snow. The pigs had begun to scream, frightened by the unfamiliar, piercing reek of the gasoline.

It's as if they know what's coming.

Well, of course, they do. Pigs are smart!

He lit a match, ignited the shed wall, and leapt back to avoid the sudden flames.

He then returned to the Quonset hut. He removed the over-boots and tossed them into the Pit. He set fire to the Quonset hut, tossing a lit match into the Pit after the boots, and then to the farmhouse.

The pigs' screams coming from the burning shed had taken on an almost human quality. He smiled and nodded wisely.

Of course, you sound human. Just think of all those lovely, lovely remnants of woman-souls you've consumed.

"You've feasted well. And now you're going to be barbecued pork."

He dragged the carcass of the piglet away from the gore-soaked snow, then he wrapped the body in the tablecloth. *You ate some too, didn't you, piggy? I know I haven't fed you anything else. Even if you just got it from Harriet's milk.* He carried the dead piglet to his car and stashed the vinyl-shrouded carcass in the trunk.

He turned and took just a moment to admire his handiwork. The wind whipped the flames, twisting them into three long, red-and-yellow plumes, bent almost parallel to the ground. The wind shredded the black smoke into ghostly tatters.

Better get going. Soon I'll have wasted the whole damned Sabbath. Isn't this supposed to be a day of flippin' rest?

He made sure the four-wheel drive was still engaged. *Gonna need that to get home. Get back to the main road before this dirt track turns to mud.*

As he drove away from the farm for the last time, he passed a small, wooden sign which tilted at a severe angle. He had often marveled that the sign was still hanging on. Of course, the snow-caked placard could not be read, but he knew what it said.

LOUSIANA LOU'S
By appointment only
WARNING:
Trespassers will be EATEN!

Soon the decrepit sign would be all that was left standing of Ol' Lou's farmstead with its illegal product.

A congregation—*isn't that the collective noun? Or is it a* bask? *I'll have to look it up. Not that Ol' Lou ever used the proper collective noun to describe his animals.*

"Bye, Lou. Thanks for letting me borrow the place." His mouth widened into a savage grin. "Not that you care anymore. Nothing's left of you except a mire of pig crap."

Okay. So, one problem solved, thanks to my beloved woman-souls.

"We love you," whispered the voices. "We love you forever."

"Thank you, my dears. Together, we shall be immortal." *Once I have my Prize. Once I have Tabitha.*

But now I have to prepare a new place—a place where Tabitha and I can love and become one. But she can fly. *How is that possible?*

"Tabitha," whispered the souls in his mind. "She's special."

Yes, she is. So special. But flying?

"That was Josh," the voices said. "Tabitha can't do it without Josh."

Josh. Of course.

He laughed. It was all so clear.

All I have to do is eliminate the unworthy husband, and then Tabitha will be mine. Might have to get rid of the damned baby too. Or use him.

"Yes! That's the ticket!"

He grinned as he remembered the words of the psalmist. "Children are an heritage of the Lord."

The fire just wouldn't start. Angry tears coursed down Maddie's cheeks as she knelt in front of the Smiths' fireplace and lit her final match. "Please work," she whispered. "Please." She held the tiny firebrand to the latest batch of wadded newspaper in the fireplace. The newspaper rested atop the ashes of several previous batches of burnt paper. And just as with the other attempts, the paper flared up, but was consumed far too quickly. However, the smashed wooden remnants of Maddie's Box of Remembrance stubbornly refused to catch fire.

Tabitha had watched in helpless frustration as Maddie had struggled, first to smash the chest, which she insisted she had to do all by herself, and then to reduce the broken wood to ash. The leg-iron with its chain—the only remaining slavery artifact from the chest—had been tossed into the fireplace as well.

Josh held Tabitha's hand as the two of them sat on the sofa in the Smith's living room. Joseph lay on his back atop his blanket on the floor, enthusiastically gnawing on his teething ring.

"Why won't it burn?" Maddie wailed as she knelt in front of the recalcitrant wood.

"Because it's oak, honey." The bishop's tone was gentle, but weary. "The wood's just too hard, too dense. And we don't have any kindling. I'm sorry, Maddie."

"What good is it to have a darn fireplace without any darn wood that'll burn?" Maddie pounded a fist against her thigh. "I just want it gone! I want it all gone!"

"You smashed it up," the bishop said. "That was a big step. That was brave, honey."

Maddie put her hands to her neck. "I had a *collar* around my neck, Torrance. A collar! Like a slave. That man *owned* me!"

"You're free, Sister Smith," Josh said. "You're safe now. You survived." He held Tabitha's hand, but even the trickle of the Power gave Tabitha no solace.

Maddie survived, but she was also traumatized.

And I know exactly how she felt—because I was her.

Maddie turned her red-streaked, brown eyes to Tabitha. "Can you help me?" Then she looked at Josh. "Please? Can you make it burn?"

Josh shook his head. "It's not up to me." He squeezed Tabitha's hand. "It's up to Tabitha. It's *her* Power. I don't use it without her permission."

"Please," Maddie whispered, turning her pleading eyes back to Tabitha. "Help me."

Tabitha gave Maddie a weary but kindly smile. "Sure." She shivered with the horrible, borrowed memory of the iron around her neck. *Better hurry up, before Folau gets here.* She'd called the detective as soon as they'd gotten Maddie safely home. She turned to Josh. "Take care of that *thing* first." She didn't have to name it. Josh knew exactly what she meant.

"With pleasure." Josh's voice was cold and hard. Like iron.

Tabitha felt the Power surge.

The leg iron and its attached chain rose from the fireplace, floating above the stone hearth. Newspaper ash drifted down from the iron, falling like gray snowflakes.

Maddie gasped. She scrambled away from the fireplace and the suspended iron. She crawled quickly to her husband's side as he sat in an overstuffed easy chair. She knelt and grasped his hand. She and the bishop watched the floating objects with awe and fear.

Josh nodded. "Stay back."

A corner of the pastel-blue blanket lifted by itself, shielding Joseph's face from what was about to happen.

The Power coursed—tingling exquisite pleasure—from Tabitha and into Josh. The leg iron and the chain twisted into a tight ball. Then with a metallic groan, the ball seemed to collapse into itself, chain links and manacle fusing into one solid mass. Then the iron began to glow—first a dull red, then yellow, then almost white. Heat radiated through the room. The pungent reek of smelting iron filled Tabitha's nostrils.

Uttering wordless cries, Maddie and her husband shrank away from the heat and the light.

"Don't worry," Josh said. "Two birds with one stone—that's all."

The white-hot iron mass floated back into the fireplace, into the midst of the wood.

With a sudden roar, the broken remnants of the chest burst into flames. The fire shot up the flue, roaring to meet the howling wind outside.

The metal fireplace screen that Maddie had set aside during her futile efforts to start the fire floated and then settled in front of the fireplace.

"Oh my!" the bishop said. "I've seen you fly."

Maddie nodded, breathing rapidly. "And I've flown with you."

Bishop Smith shook his head. "But I've never seen what you can do. And you're sure it's not witchcraft? You just melted iron! Do you have any idea how much *energy* that takes?"

"Technically," Tabitha said, her heart thundering with Power-fueled joy, even as the Power rapidly dropped off, "it didn't melt. It was just really hot."

"But you *could've* melted it?" the bishop asked, his eyes wide.

Josh nodded. "We've never tried, but yeah, I'm sure we could. We were nowhere near Tabitha's limit." *Nowhere near the threshold.* Josh shrugged. "I'm not sure she even *has* a limit."

"Incredible," Maddie breathed. "You could…"

"You could level this house," the bishop said.

Tabitha nodded. "Yeah, but"—she gave the bishop a sheepish grin—"we're not going to. We don't use it to hurt people. Not if we don't have to." *But Magnus used my Power. To kill my friends.*

And I broke both my father's arms. My biological *father. Not my daddy.*

"What about the monster who took me?" Maddie said. "The man who killed all those other women? Would you kill *him* if you had the chance?"

A tear spilled from Tabitha's eye. "I wish I had. I had a chance once."

Josh squeezed her hand. "No, you didn't. You didn't have that chance. We weren't holding the Power at the time. We weren't *together*. You saved that girl. And you did it without the Power."

All I did was scream. Tabitha's tears fell freely. "I'm just glad we found you in time, Maddie. I'm just glad you came to us, Bishop. If you hadn't…"

Maddie closed her eyes and shuddered. "I'd be dead."

Not until tonight. He never devours his victims in the light.

"What"—Bishop Smith cleared his throat—"What *can't* you do?"

Tabitha chuckled softly. "Well, I can't tap dance to save my life."

Both Maddie's and the bishop's jaws dropped as they gaped at her.

"Seriously," Tabitha said, "I'd almost sell my soul"—she held up a hand—"just kidding about the selling-my-soul part, Bishop… if somehow I could dance worth a darn."

Laughter exploded from Maddie. "Tap dance?"

Bishop Smith shook his head. "Of all the—" Then he burst into laughter as well.

Soon they were all laughing, including Joseph, although the baby's laughter had a nervous timbre to it.

As the cathartic merriment began to quiet down, the bishop said, "In all seriousness"—he laughed again—"I mean it. Seriously, with all you can do, how come you're so, well, poor? I mean, you've never come to the Church for food assistance, but I know for a fact you're as poor as church mice. I bet, most of the time, you don't even have two nickels to rub together."

Josh grinned. "Been looking at our tithing receipts, Bishop?"

Tabitha elbowed her husband. "Not funny."

"What?" Josh asked innocently. "I did that stint as a ward financial clerk." He shrugged. "You're not supposed to notice, but sometimes you just do."

The bishop looked suddenly very uncomfortable. "It happens." He shrugged. "But seriously? Why don't you use your powers to—I don't know—find gold or something? You could do that, couldn't you?"

Tabitha blinked at him. "I, uh… We don't know how to do that. And besides…"

Help me out here, Josh!

As if hearing her thoughts, Josh said, "If we could find gold or diamonds, wouldn't it be on somebody else's land? We're not going to just *take* it. That would be stealing.

We couldn't do that anymore than we could rob a bank. Or shoplift a bag of diapers."

The bishop shook his head quickly and held up a calming hand. "I'm sorry. I didn't mean to imply that you would. It's just this is all so…"

"Freaky?" Tabitha volunteered.

The bishop nodded. "Yeah. That's a good word. And it's all so *new*."

Josh shrugged. "It's new to us too. Sorta. I mean, we're still learning."

"Can you heal the sick?" the bishop asked.

Josh shook his head, but Tabitha said, "We can stop bleeding."

Josh gave her a questioning look, but Tabitha shook her head. *Later*, she mouthed.

Josh nodded. "Oh, yeah. We could do that. But that's probably it. First aid stuff. *Healing* is something for the priesthood." He quickly added, "And doctors."

"Are there others?" the bishop asked. "Others like you?"

"Yeah, but"—Tabitha squirmed—"it's not like we're recruiting. We don't talk about it, but I *trust* you, Bishop. And you too, Maddie."

Josh scratched the back of his head and grimaced. "And it's not like we have much of a choice. Not anymore. Not with you two, at least."

"I'm sorry," said the bishop. "And if you don't want to talk about it…" He shook his head. "I'm sorry."

Tabitha shook her head as well. "I'm *not* sorry. I'm glad we could help."

"Have you always been like this?" the bishop asked. "Since you were born?"

"Uh-uh." Tabitha shook her head. "I only found out about the Power when I was a senior in high school. I—" A sudden lump in her throat made it hard for her to say more. She looked at Josh, pleading with her eyes.

He nodded, the corners of his mouth curving into a slight smile. "I only found out when I met her. The first time I shook her hand." He squeezed her hand, and his smile widened. "Ooh. That was something! But as far as we know, for women, it develops sometime after puberty—even though she's completely unaware of it. For men, the ones who can channel"—he grinned sheepishly and shrugged—"the ones like me, we don't know. It seems to be genetic. Our son hasn't shown any signs. Not yet."

"It's extremely rare in men," Tabitha said. She smiled at her husband. "Josh is one in a million." *So's Daddy. Two in a million, I guess. Runs in the family.*

"And Tabitha," Josh said, "is the most Powerful witch in the—" His eyes grew wide with horror. "I mean—"

"That's just our word for it," Tabitha added hastily. "It doesn't mean anything. It's not witchcraft. Honestly, it's not."

"I see," said the bishop, though his expression didn't reflect his words. He stared at Josh. "And I suppose that makes you—what? A warlock?"

"It's just a stupid word," Josh muttered in protest.

"Bishop," Tabitha said, "we don't conjure the Devil or dance naked under the moon or anything."

"It's the Power of Woman," Josh said. "It's as normal and natural as a woman's potential to create life, to nurse a baby, to comfort the sick. To be… a woman. It comes from God." He lowered his voice. "It has to."

"A-and what Josh can do," Tabitha said, "is just a talent. A rare and special talent." Tabitha's heart raced as her gaze flickered from the bishop to Maddie and back again.

"Torrance," Maddie said, "they saved my life."

The bishop wiped away a sudden tear. "I know, doggonit! And the Holy Ghost directed me to seek them out." He shook his head. "And after you two left, after you flew away, I prayed. I prayed, and the Spirit *assured* me that this was of God." His eyes looked heavenward. "Forgive me my doubt. Forgive 'mine unbelief.'"

He turned his eyes back to Tabitha and Josh. "And forgive me my ingratitude." Once more, his eyes were kind and caring—the eyes of a bishop. "Thank you for saving my Maddie."

"Yes," Maddie said, "thank you is just not enough. Not near enough, but thank you."

The bishop cleared his throat. "But now, I have to mention the *other* elephant in the room."

Tabitha felt Josh tense. She squeezed his hand and said, "Are you going to ask for our temple recommends? We're keeping our covenants. This doesn't change that."

"Temple?" Bishop Smith blinked at them. "What? No! It's not that. Not that at all. But it *is* serious."

"What?" Josh asked.

The bishop leaned forward, his expression hardening. He spoke slowly, "Why didn't you warn us about this Devourer? This serial killer?"

"Warn you?" Tabitha's voice came out as a frightened squeak.

"If we had known," the bishop said, "Maddie would not have been out alone at night. She wouldn't have been taken."

Maddie looked up at her husband. "Torrance, I—"

"This is serious, honey." The bishop patted his wife's hand. "And as ungrateful as it sounds, this is not just about you. Not just about us." He focused on Josh. "What about all the other women and girls in the ward? In the stake? In the whole doggone town? What about them?"

Tabitha felt the Power building up. She squeezed Josh's hand. "No."

"No, what?" snapped the bishop.

What were you going to do, Josh?

"Sorry, Sweetheart," Josh muttered, and Tabitha felt the Power settling down to a low trickle again. "We couldn't tell you. It wasn't our call."

"What do you mean by that?" Bishop Smith's eyes narrowed as he stared at Josh. "Not your call?"

Tabitha licked suddenly dry lips. "We're working with the police. Or rather, *I* am. I've been seeing visions from iron objects that belonged to the other victims. Some of the other victims."

The bishop nodded slowly. "That detective you called after you brought Maddie home? This is whom you're assisting?"

Tabitha nodded. "Yes. He should be here anytime."

Maddie glanced at the telephone. "It's been over an hour. Why isn't he here yet?"

"The snowstorm, honey," the bishop said. "The blizzard outside."

Maddie nodded. Then she chuckled nervously. "I'm guessing he can't just fly over here. He can't, can he? Not without a woman, right?" Her eyes fixed on Tabitha's. "A powerful woman, right? Like you?" She looked over at Josh. "Could you fly with just me? Alone?" Then she shook herself, looking away, obviously embarrassed. "Not that I'm asking. Seriously, I'm not."

Josh shook his head, his cheeks flushing. "No. Tabitha is the only woman I've met with that much of the Power. And I don't think the detective can channel. If he could, he'd have reacted to Tabitha. She's that strong." He grinned at Tabitha. "Like an electric shock—only nice."

The bishop cleared his throat. "So, you're saying that you haven't told anyone, because the police won't let you?"

Tabitha nodded. "Yeah. Mostly, these were just missing persons reports. And there haven't been any bodies"—she shuddered in revulsion as she thought of the pigs and the foot—"except one. And until I helped the police out with a vision, they didn't know for sure that anyone had been killed. Or they couldn't prove it." She growled in frustration. "They still can't prove it. But"—she pointed at Maddie—"you can finally give them proof of a kidnapping, at least. They'll find the farm and"—*Janessa's foot*—"the evidence will be there. There'll be fingerprints, DNA, *something* to lead them to the Devourer. Maddie's story will get out, and the newspapers and Channel Five—"

"No!" Maddie shook her head vehemently. "I'll talk to the police, but I *won't* talk to the dang press. If they haven't covered it by now… I am not going to expose you two." She wiped away a tear. "Not after what you did for me. It's none of their dang business how I got out of there."

"Well," said the bishop, "I'm going to send out word through the visiting and home teachers for all the women and girls to not go out alone after dark. I'm going to do that much."

Josh nodded. "Yeah. That sounds like a good idea."

Tabitha bit her lower lip. "What *are* you going to tell the police?"

Maddie sat up straighter on the shag carpet, stiffening her spine. She lifted her chin as if her dignity had been affronted. "I'm going to tell the truth." Then she grinned. "Just not all of it." She turned her face toward her husband. "Don't worry, Torrance. I won't lie." She shrugged and smiled innocently. "I wouldn't even *think* of it."

Her husband sighed, rolling his eyes. "Maddie, what are you going to say?"

Maddie waved a dismissive hand. "I'll tell them everything, right up to the point where I was rescued. And then I'll simply tell them that a couple of angels"—and suddenly she was choking—"rescued m-me and brought me home."

Tabitha choked back tears of her own.

"Thank you," Josh said, his voice husky.

Maddie smiled through her tears. "Well, it's the truth."

Danny Folau will suspect it was us. No, he'll be certain *it was us.*

The doorbell rang, and all four of them jumped.

The bishop patted his wife's hand. "I'll get it." He stood, and for the first time, since their return, Tabitha noticed that the bishop's sweater sagged deeply on one side. One of the pockets bulged.

Bishop Smith reached into that pocket and pulled out a rather large, long-barreled revolver. One corner of his mouth twitched into a half smile. "Just in case." He smiled warmly at his wife. "Honey, please take the chair."

He left the room, pistol in hand.

Maddie shrugged as she rose from the carpet. "He keeps it here. We've had a couple of break-ins. Addicts looking for drugs." She rolled her eyes. "Like he'd keep drugs in the house." She sat in the easy chair and turned her worried gaze toward where her husband had gone.

An awkward and pregnant silence fell over them. Tabitha heard male voices and recognized the voice of Danny Folau.

Soon, Bishop Smith returned. Tabitha noted that his sweater pocket was bulging and sagging once more.

Folau followed the bishop into the living room, the scowl on his face stretching his pale scar into an almost straight line. As soon as he entered the darkened room, his eyes locked with Tabitha's. He gave her a curt nod, and then the ghost of a smile lifted his scarred face.

For a second, Tabitha returned his subtle smile. His eyes softened as he gazed at her.

And for the first time, Tabitha was certain her daddy had been right. *He's in love with me.*

The memory of her moments of seeing Danny Folau through the eyes and heart of his dead wife flooded Tabitha's mind. Tenderness welled up inside her. *What am I doing?*

She averted her eyes and felt her cheeks redden. *No! I am not your Julie!* She glanced back at the detective and observed that Folau was glaring at Josh. Folau's countenance hardened once more, and his scar twitched.

Josh drew a little more of the Power. "What took you so long, Detective?"

Folau averted his eyes, looking toward the large, curtained picture window, as if he were gazing at something outside. "I went out to the crime-scene."

Tabitha gaped at him. "The farm? The pit?"

"How'd you find it?" Josh asked. "Our description was vague."

The scar twitched. "Yeah. I noticed you didn't mention any roads. Just west of Springville, you said." His lips drew tight, and his eyes narrowed. "How'd you find it?"

Tabitha thought it curious that the detective had not pulled his pad and pen from his jacket. *He knows.*

"If we told you," Josh said, "you wouldn't be able to put it in your report."

Folau's eyes flickered to Maddie. "Okay. If that's how you want to play it, we'll leave it at that. Anonymous tip." His gaze returned to Josh, and he narrowed his eyes. "For now." He grimaced, and his scar twitched. "Anyway, there's not much left of the place. Or there won't be soon."

167

"What do you mean?" Tabitha and Josh asked together.

Folau focused on Josh. "I don't suppose you set fire to the place?"

Josh jerked. "Set fire?"

Tabitha gaped at the detective. "Why would we do that?"

Folau shrugged. "To destroy evidence."

"We didn't—" Tabitha began, but Josh cut her off.

"We didn't set fire to anything," Josh growled. "And you know it. We want this guy caught. Same as you."

Folau nodded. "I believe you." He grimaced. "Sorry. That wasn't fair."

No, it wasn't. Stop acting like we're the enemy, Danny!

Stop calling him Danny!

Folau! Folau!

"But all the same," Folau continued, "the place is an inferno. That's how I found it. Even in this storm, I spotted the flames. I radioed dispatch to contact the fire department, but by the time they get there, especially in this storm… Won't be much left."

He was there! The Devourer was there!

Tabitha and Josh exchanged a wide-eyed look.

We must have just missed him. Or was he there, hiding? Watching us?

A tremor of fear ripped through Tabitha, and then a flash of anger. *We could have caught him! We could have—*

"When the fire's out," Folau said, "we'll sift through the rubble, but I doubt we'll find much. The perp made sure of that."

Folau scrutinized Tabitha and Josh for another long moment, and then turned his attention to Maddie, and immediately his face softened as he smiled at her. "Mrs. Smith?"

Maddie rose to her feet. She looked shaken, but she offered the detective her hand. "That's right. Maddie. Maddie Smith."

Folau shook her hand. "I'm terribly sorry for your ordeal, ma'am."

Maddie smiled. "I'm safe now." Her eyes were still red, but neither her expression nor her voice betrayed the slightest hint of the trauma she'd suffered. "Apparently, I got out of there just in time."

Maddie used to be an actress? She must've been pretty good.

Folau's grin widened, showing white teeth that seemed to gleam in the darkened living room. He inclined his head toward Tabitha and Josh. "Thanks to these two."

Maddie's smile never faltered. "I was rescued by angels from Heaven."

"Huh." Folau's smile faltered, and his scar seemed to writhe. "Angels? Ma'am, can we talk somewhere private?"

Maddie shrugged. "Certainly." Then her expression hardened. "I just want you to catch the man who did this. Before he hurts anyone else."

Folau's smile returned. "Then we want the same thing. Like I said, could we talk privately, ma'am?"

The bishop inclined his head back toward the front door. "You can use my office.

My wife will show you the way."

"Follow me, Detective," said Maddie. She turned to go, but hesitated when the detective didn't move.

Folau stared intently at Josh. Then the detective shifted his gaze, locking eyes with Tabitha. One corner of his mouth lifted in a half-grin. "I noticed that yellow Bug of yours is buried in snow. It's been here since the storm began. So, the car didn't go anywhere."

Folau had used the generic word "go," but Tabitha was absolutely certain Folau was thinking of another method of locomotion.

"And," Folau continued, "I noticed there were no other vehicle tracks in the snow outside. Other than my four-wheel drive."

"Are you coming, Detective," Maddie asked, smiling sweetly.

Folau nodded, his eyes never leaving Tabitha's. "In a moment, ma'am. So, these angels, Mrs. Smith? When they rescued you, I don't suppose they just flew in, did they?"

A loud gasp startled Tabitha. For a moment, she was afraid that the betraying sound of surprise might have come from her. But it hadn't.

And mercifully, Folau had at last broken eye-contact.

All eyes turned to the source of the sound—Bishop Smith.

Folau's half-grin became a full-blown smile, wolfish and full of white, gleaming teeth. He turned to face the bishop. "Dr. Smith, you saw these angels too, didn't you? You saw them flying."

Bishop Smith said nothing, but his eyes flickered from Tabitha to Josh, pleading for succor.

"Never mind, Dr. Smith," Folau said. "I'm pretty sure I have my answer." He turned his attention back to Tabitha. "It's not every day you get to talk to an honest-to-goodness angel."

Folau gestured toward Maddie, deferentially inclining his head. "Mrs. Smith, if you'd lead the way?"

"I thought you two kissed and made up, so to speak," Tabitha whispered to her husband as they waited in the Smiths' living room. The last remnants of the smashed oak-chest fire were dying down to embers. The iron ball, no longer glowing, lay hidden under a mound of ash. Bishop Smith sat in his easy chair, his hands clasped tight in his lap. His eyes were shut tight, and his head was bowed. His lips moved silently as he prayed.

Joseph lay on his pastel blanket, snoring in the soft, endearing manner of infant sleep.

"Me and Folau?" Josh raised an eyebrow, reminding Tabitha of Mr. Spock on Josh's beloved *Star Trek*.

"Yeah," she said.

Josh grimaced. "I thought we'd come to a truce, at least. But he seems hostile today. Smug, even."

"Smug." Tabitha nodded. "That's a good word for it." *He knows.* The terrifying certainty gnawed at her.

"It's because he knows everything," Josh whispered, eerily echoing Tabitha's thought. "Or he thinks he does."

"He knows it was us. He knows we rescued Maddie."

Josh nodded slowly, then shook his head. "It's worse than that. He knows we *flew* out there."

Tabitha exhaled a weary sigh. *Not a big leap from a flying Volkswagen to flying Kilmores.*

An image formed in her mind—of her and Josh swinging on a circus trapeze. *The Amazing Flying Kilmores!*

Josh shook his head slowly. "I think the thing that irritates me the most about him—about Folau—is that he's always trying to prove he's got one over on us. Well, on *me*." He squeezed her hand. "That and his obvious feelings for you."

Tabitha opened her mouth to object, but she knew Josh had it right. *If Daddy and*

Josh hadn't pointed it out, hadn't told me Folau had feelings for me—even unconscious ones—I might not have seen it. But now, the way Danny looks at me…

Stop calling him that!

"It's the way he looks at you," Josh whispered. "Then, when he looks at *me,* talks to *me,* it's as plain as the scar on his face—he thinks I'm not good enough for you."

Once again, Tabitha opened her mouth to object, but then she whispered, "Maybe, you're right."

The corners of his lips curled into a mischievous grin. "That I'm not good enough for you?"

She gave his arm a playful punch. "You know what I mean!"

"Ouch!" His grin widened. "Better stop hitting me in front of the bishop. He'll think I'm a battered husband."

"Just you wait 'til I get you home, mister!" She narrowed her eyes at him, but she didn't even try to suppress her grin.

His eyebrows bounced. "Can't wait!"

Their eyes locked, and he lowered his face toward hers. But before their lips could meet, Joseph cried out and squirmed on his blanket. Then he stopped.

Both Tabitha and Josh froze, not daring even to breathe.

Maybe he'll go back to sleep.

Joseph let out a wail.

"So much for that," Josh said. He bent and patted the baby's bottom. "Yep. Soaked. I got this."

He let go of Tabitha's hand.

And the Power abruptly cut off.

Tabitha sighed wistfully at the loss, but she smiled with deep affection at her husband as he knelt on the carpet and began pulling supplies from the diaper bag in practiced, efficient movements. *Just like always.* "You know, Sweetheart, I *can* change a diaper. I do it all the time when you're not around." *But you* are *quick!*

By the time she'd finished speaking, Josh was already fastening the new diaper. He shrugged. "I can't feed him. The least I can do is dispose of the toxic waste at the other end." He taped the diaper closed. "There you are, big guy!" Josh closed up the soaked diaper, put it into a plastic bread bag, and stowed it in the diaper bag. *No sense in stinking up their house.*

The "big guy" in the clean, dry diaper squirmed, reaching for his daddy.

Josh picked his son up and sat back on the couch. He set the child on his knee and bounced him. "Bongo-bongo-bongo-bongo-*butt*!"

Joseph shrieked happily, showing his two bottom teeth.

The phone rang.

The bishop's head snapped up, and his eyes widened. He reached over to a small, round table on which sat a lamp and the ringing telephone with multiple square, plastic buttons at the bottom for multiple lines, the kind of phone found in a business office. The second button was flashing. The bishop punched the lit button, then lifted the handset to his ear, holding the spiral cord in his other hand.

"This is Dr. Smith." He nodded. "Oh, J.L.! It's you. Good. I was just about to call you." He paused, listening. "I need you to activate the ward phone tree." A pause. "Yes, priesthood *and* Relief Society." He glanced at Tabitha and Josh. "I want you to spread the word. We have a danger in…" He paused. "Yes, everything is fine, thank heavens." He paused again. "No, we're all fine here. Now listen, J.L. We have a serial killer in our midst." He shook his head. "Please, J.L., just let me finish." He nodded. "Yes, that's what I said—a serial killer. And he's targeting women and girls. They— the women and girls—yes, young women too—must *not* go out alone, especially at night." Another pause. "No, I'm not trying to cause a panic. I'm trying to save lives!" He shook his head, covering his eyes with one hand. "I'm sorry. I shouldn't've raised my voice. This has been a tough— Yes, Maddie and the kids are okay." He nodded. "Just please spread the word." Another pause. "All I know is he wears a hooded jacket and a mask. Different masks. Full-face masks. Skull. Frankenstein. Werewolf." He looked at Tabitha.

"A clown," Tabitha said. "A clown with sharp teeth. That's all I know about."

The bishop nodded. "A clown with sharp teeth." He gazed at Tabitha, his eyes narrowing. He pursed his lips. "Maybe others—other masks." He nodded. "Yes. Please, let's get the word out to everyone in the ward, okay? Tell the brethren to go in person if they can't get folks on the phone. Even in the snow. Today. It's urgent." Another pause. "No. I haven't seen anything about it on the news. Please, just get the word out." He glanced at Tabitha again. "That's right. You *are* their home teacher." Another pause. "No, that's okay. I can tell them myself. Okay. Thank you. Yes. Goodbye."

He hung up the phone. "Brother Montrose wanted to talk to you—tell you about the serial killer. Since you're right here."

Tabitha blinked. "J.L. knows we're here?"

The bishop nodded. "He recognized your voice. And you *did* follow me out of the chapel after my dramatic entrance. He saw that. Everybody saw that."

And the bishop knows there's something awkward *between J.L. and me.*

"Okay," Josh said. "People are going to ask questions about that."

Bishop Smith waved a dismissive hand. "Brother Kilmore, I'm a bishop *and* a doctor. I know how to keep a confidence. Even under pressure."

Tabitha glanced in the direction that Maddie and Folau had gone. "And Maddie?"

"Don't you worry about Maddie," said the bishop. "My dear wife always does exactly what she says she's going to do. Always." He chuckled softly. "Even when I, uh, *counsel* her otherwise."

"And when"—Maddie strode into the room, followed by Folau—"have I ever disregarded your counsel, my dear husband?"

Judging from her confident, hip-swaying stride, cheery voice, and broad smile, Maddie did not look like a woman who had been drugged, abducted, and imprisoned in a lightless dungeon, nor flown through the air. She looked confident, minus the slight tremor in her hands.

The bishop leapt from his chair, stepped aside, and silently offered the seat to his wife.

She gave him a gracious nod and a million-dollar smile. "Thank you, honey." She sat, regal as a queen, while the bishop knelt beside the easy chair like a fawning servant. "You know"—she inclined her head in Folau's direction—"I told the fine detective here about the angels who rescued me. I told him about the miracle. I don't think he believes me." She turned her head toward Folau. "Don't you believe in miracles, Brother Folau?"

Folau froze, staring at her open-mouthed.

I don't think he likes being called Brother. Not on duty.

Folau shook himself. His expression hardened, and his scar seemed to turn pale against his light-brown skin. "Right now, it's Detective, ma'am."

"Oh," Maddie said, "I thought you were a Mormon, like the rest of us."

He nodded. "I am, but right now, I'm investigating a series of kidnappings and murders. I'm a cop, and I find that folks around here seem to think they can pull the wool over my eyes or get special treatment by appealing to my faith."

"I assure you, *Detective*," Maddie said, narrowing her eyes, her smile gone—"I was rescued by angels. Exactly as I told you."

"Ma'am—" Folau began.

But Maddie dismissed his objection with a wave of her hand. "Oh, don't you dare bother threatening me with obstruction again." She bared her teeth ferociously, but that ferocity was belied by the tears in her eyes. "I'm the victim here, remember?"

She's losing it. I can't blame her.

"I'm trying to save other potential victims. As well as get justice for those who weren't so, shall I say, *blessed* as you." Folau snapped his head to Tabitha. "I'd like to speak with your angels." He gestured toward the bishop's office. "Mrs. Kilmore? If you please?"

And what if I don't please? However, Tabitha stood. Josh stood as well, holding the baby.

Folau's just doing his job.

As Tabitha bent to grab the diaper bag, the detective said, "In private." He pointed at Tabitha. "And just you first."

Josh shook his head vehemently. "Not a chance."

Holding the diaper bag and the baby blanket, Tabitha took Josh's free hand. She felt the Power flowing. She stood as tall as her short stature would allow. "You know the rules, Detective. If you want our cooperation, it's both of us, or not at all."

"You are material witnesses." Folau glared at Josh—but didn't look at Tabitha. "You were *there*." He paused, letting his words sink in. "I need to take your statements. Separate and alone."

"Now just a dang minute!" Josh snapped.

"I can take your statements here, one at a time, or I can—"

This is getting out of control. "You know, Detective"—she met Folau's glare as he turned his attention back to her—"Daddy gave me some good advice when he was here. Advice about *you*."

Folau's eyes went wide. "About me?"

Tabitha nodded. "He told me to never be alone with you. Never."

Folau's mouth hung open. "Mike said that? Mike Kilmore?"

Tabitha nodded. "Now, do you want our statement? Our *joint* statement? Or not?"

"I could have an officer present. Then we wouldn't be alone." The detective stared hard at her. Then his eyes softened. "Nevermind." He nodded to Josh. "This way, please."

Tabitha and Josh, holding hands—with Josh carrying the baby—followed Folau out of the living room. Tabitha turned her head and gazed back at the bishop and his wife.

Maddie was on the floor curled into the arms of Bishop Smith. She buried her face into his shoulder, shaking gently while she wept quietly.

"Look." Folau sighed. "I'm sorry." He sat in a high-backed leather chair behind a mahogany desk in Bishop Smith's private office. In spite of his conciliatory words, Tabitha noted that the detective had taken the room's "seat of power."

Tabitha and Josh sat on the leather sofa on the other side of the desk. Tabitha nursed Joseph under his blanket. Though she and Josh were no longer holding hands, Josh held onto the Power.

Just in case.

"Sorry?" Tabitha raised an eyebrow. "For what? For treating my husband like crap? For treating the two of us as if we're suspects?"

Josh said nothing, and though Tabitha was not looking at her husband, she was certain he was grinning.

Folau grimaced and nodded. "Yeah. All that. And you two are not suspects." He sighed. "But I know you're not telling me everything. And, well, it *irks* me. And I let it get the best of me. But on the one hand, I know you're special." He looked at her, then quickly glanced at Josh. "Both of you. And I know you're protecting yourselves, protecting your secrets."

"But I also know you were *there*. You can give me details that've been destroyed by the fire." He leaned forward. "I need those details. But as for what I put in my report... Mrs. Smith's account of angels works just as well as you two swooping in and saving her." His scar twitched. "I know that's pretty much what happened." He tapped the pen on the desk a few times. "So, let's just set that aside. For now. Please, just tell me what you saw."

Josh and Tabitha exchanged a glance, and Tabitha nodded.

Josh nodded as well, then turned his focus to Folau. "We know how he's disposing of the bodies."

Tabitha shuddered, causing Joseph to jerk. "How he *was* disposing of the bodies," she corrected. The baby resumed feeding.

Josh grimaced in disgust.

Folau waited, saying nothing.

"Pigs," Josh said.

Folau scribbled on his notepad, but gave no other reaction.

He's not surprised? "It was horrible! We found a foot. A human foot. I—I think it was Janessa's."

Folau nodded again, making another note. He looked up, waiting for them to continue.

"Hold on," Josh said. "Doesn't that gross you out or anything? Doesn't that surprise you?"

The detective shrugged. "Pigs'll eat anything. My grandma used to tell us stories of pigs eating folks back on Tonga."

The memory of the pigs and Janessa's foot—and Folau's indifference—suddenly had Tabitha swallowing down bile.

Folau nonchalantly twirled the pen in his hand as if he were discussing a scoreless soccer game. "And in this particular case, it wouldn't surprise me at all. You see, the owner of that farm, an old fella by the name of Louis Marchand, a.k.a. 'Lousiana Lou,' disappeared a couple years back. He was old enough that people just assumed he died of a heart attack, or just plain old age. But, you see, his body was never found." Folau waved a hand, as if dismissing a rather obvious, unspoken question. "Wasn't my case. Out of my jurisdiction. It was treated as a missing person case. Didn't go anywhere. But the neighbors assumed it was the pigs or the gators that ate him."

"Gators?" Tabitha's voice came out as a horrified squeak.

Folau nodded. "Yeah. Ol' Lousiana Lou raised caimans. They're a type of alligator." He frowned. "Or crocodile. I can't remember which. Anyway, these were the small variety—dwarf caimans, I think. He kept them in that pit you described. Sold 'em to collectors. And—what's the word? Oh, yeah! Epicureans. You know, rich folks who like to eat rare and illegal things? And this was illegal as all get out. But Ol' Lou was kind of a local legend. My uncle took me to see the gators once when I was a kid. You had to pay to get in." He shuddered. "Scariest flippin' things I'd ever seen on four legs. He used to take one of the larger ones out on a leash and walk it."

Folau bit his lip and tapped the pencil on the table. Suddenly he gasped. "That's where he got the collar! I bet ya, it was from that dang gator he used to parade around for customers."

Tabitha shivered. If she hadn't been nursing her son, she would have jerked a hand to her own neck.

Folau nodded. "Yeah. That makes sense. Anyway, when Ol' Lou stopped coming into town to buy groceries—and stopped taking appointments to show off his gators— one of his neighbors went to check on the old guy, reported him missing. The sheriff's department came out and investigated. But they couldn't find hide nor hair of Lousiana Lou, just a lot of hungry caimans. So, they called Animal Control. But when Animal Control got there, all the gators had been killed. Shot. I guess a neighbor assumed the caimans had killed Ol' Lousiana Lou. So, Animal Control disposed of the carcasses. I thought they'd taken care of the pigs as well." He shrugged again. "I guess not. So, no"—he shook his head—"corpse-devouring hogs don't surprise me. Not one bit."

*He talks about it so casually. Like man-eating—No!—*woman-*eating pigs are normal, nothing.* Tabitha closed her eyes, fighting a fresh wave of horror and nausea. But closing her eyes only made things worse. In her mind, she saw Janessa's foot and the furious sow. Tabitha opened her eyes and tried to concentrate on the baby at her breast. And on not throwing up.

She felt the flow of the Power increase, soothing. Her churning stomach quieted. *Thank you, Sweetheart.* She smiled at her husband, and he gave her a knowing wink.

When she looked back at Folau, the scarred detective was grinning. And something about that grin unsettled Tabitha.

Again.

"What I need," Folau said, "is to get inside this guy's head. Think like he thinks." He leaned forward. "Before today," Folau continued, "you've only seen things through the eyes of his victims. But now, you've seen his lair."

Lair. The word sent a shudder through Tabitha. *The cave of the beast, the vampire's tomb.*

Josh shook his head. "But the pit is gone. You said it's been destroyed."

Folau nodded. "Yeah, and he'll have to set up shop someplace new. That might buy us some time. Or it might make him more desperate. So, I don't care about you two flying around like the Dynamic Duo." He chuckled and shook his head. "But Batman and Robin can't fly, can they? Not like you two."

Tabitha's stomach threatened to empty itself. "We haven't done anything wrong." Then she gasped. *That's as good as an admission.*

She felt the Power building. "No," she whispered, half-turning to Josh. *Whatever you're thinking, don't do it.*

"No," Folau said, "you're the good guys here." He looked directly at her. His expression softened. "You're just being you." Folau shrugged. "And you're right. I can't put that stuff in my report anyway. No superhero stuff. No magic or whatever it is. No *you.*" He paused, and then slowly his eyes grew large, as he had realized the implications of his words.

That sounded way too personal.

Folau looked down, tapping his pen on the desk in a fast and nervous beat. "Sorry." He huffed. "I keep saying that, don't I?" He looked up once more and smiled, but that smile seemed genuine. It held nothing of the smugness he'd shown earlier. "So, whaddaya say we nail this creep? Tell me what you saw."

He gave the shackle a mighty tug. But no matter how hard he pulled, the manacle and chain held fast.

Good!

He wasn't surprised—this was the *first* shackle. The original.

Reverently, he laid the manacle on the floor. Then he followed the cold chain to where it was padlocked around an ancient and stout lead pipe that ran from the tiled floor to the ceiling of the storage room. He examined the pipe carefully. He saw no dust or marks except where the hard iron had scraped against the softer lead. He saw no sign that the pipe had moved at all during his testing of the chain.

He smiled happily. *That should hold her.* "Can't have you flying away, now can I, my Prize?"

"She won't fly away," the voices whispered, lovingly caressing his mind. "Not when she comes to know you as we do. Not when she knows what you can offer her. Immortality. Eternal life. Perfection. Exaltation."

"She can fly." His sigh was filled with all the love in his soul. "She's magnificent! An angel."

"Yes, she is. The best of us. The ultimate woman. But she cannot fly alone. She can only fly with *him.*"

"When she is one with me, with *us*, she will no longer need to fly." His expression hardened. "She will no longer need him."

"He is not worthy of her."

He shook his head. "Nobody is. Except me. God has appointed me, *chosen* me."

"We love you."

"And I love all of you."

He sighed wearily and sat on the new mattress. It wasn't as nice or expensive as the mattress he'd been forced to burn, but it would do. It would have to.

It's not like I can go out and buy a new one right now—not with the whole world searching for me.

No, mattress-shopping was definitely not something he could afford to do anymore. Money wasn't the issue. Nothing was too good for Tabitha, but he suspected that any lone male purchasing a queen-size mattress would be regarded with suspicion. As would anyone purchasing any full-head vinyl monster masks.

He stretched out on the bare mattress. *Still need to get sheets, a blanket, pillows, pillowcases...* He wasn't about to bring those from home. *If I can't give her the best mattress, I can at least provide her with the best bed coverings.*

Even if it will only be for one night.

He'd come to understand that. He and Tabitha would have but one night of passion. One brief night of love before he consumed her, before he took her into himself. Before they become one. Before he became complete.

"'Nevertheless neither is the man without the woman, neither the woman without the man, in the Lord,'" he quoted from the scripture.

But when we are united...

Apotheosis. Isn't that the word? Becoming a god?

That is what we shall become, my love. God.

"We shall all become one," whispered the voices. "We shall abide in you forever. Our name is Legion."

He frowned at the name. *Legion. That was the name of the devils, the host of demons Jesus cast out of a lunatic and into a herd of swine.* "I don't like that name."

"We are Legion. We are the Many. You are the One. The Many dwell inside the One."

"Yes." He nodded his head. "I see now. Legion. Yes."

Ever since that day at the Pit, the day of the freak blizzard—the day his rightful prey had been stolen from him—he'd been hearing the voices. Whenever he took off the mask, that was. Not the vinyl masks he wore when he took and consumed his prey—no, the *real* mask. The mask he wore when he walked openly among mundane humanity. The invisible mask that made him look just like them.

When he wore that mask, he was not himself, simply an actor, playing the part of a mortal. And he was a *great* actor. He was so good at pretending to be one of them, that oftentimes—when he wore the mask—he forgot who he truly was.

"And now, my loves," he said. "My Legion." Yes, he liked that name after all. "Legion, Legion, Legion!" He rolled it around on his tongue, reveling in the feel of it, the sound of it. The taste of it.

"We love you."

He turned his head and surveyed the fruit of his evening's labors.

It wasn't as good as he'd done in the Pit. Just a scrounged mattress on the floor, a plastic bucket with a roll of toilet paper—he knew he couldn't be caught buying another chemical toilet—and an old milk crate. He would need the crate. Where else would he put the roses?

"At least we'll have roses when the time comes."

It's not the honeymoon suite I planned, sweet Tabitha. But it will do.

He closed his eyes and smiled. "We will have roses."

Soon, my love. After the play. After your triumph.
Then we will be one. After a single night.
Exhaustion took him, and he dreamed.

"I gotta go potty!" he wailed, his little hands squeezing his crotch.
Nancy, fat and ugly and short—short, but still towering over his little four-year-old body—blocked the bathroom door. He tried to push past her, around and then between her stocky legs, but Nancy shoved him back.
She sneered at him. "I gotta go potty!" she taunted back. "I gotta go potty!" She paused, grinning toothily. "Say, please."
"P-please, Nancy! I gotta go potty!"
She laughed at him. "Don't say, 'potty.' Say, 'Please, Nancy, may I go to the toilet?'"
"Please, Nancy, I gotta go t-toilet!" He darted forward again, only to be shoved back once more. "Please!"
Nancy shook her head slowly, deliberately. "Uh-uh. Not what I said. I said, 'Please, Nancy, may I go to the toilet?' Say it right."
"P-please, Nancy, may I go... t-t-toilet?"
She grinned, but her smile wasn't nice. It was her mean smile—mean and ugly— the one she never showed his mommy. "You wanna go to the t-t-toilet?"
He was dancing from foot to foot. "PLEASE!"
She bent down, lowering her pudgy face until her nose was almost touching his. She was still smiling that mean smile, that Big-Bad-Wolf smile. Then she opened her mouth, sucked in a big breath, and screamed.
He screamed in response, peeing his pants.
Warm, wet shame soaked his crotch, his hands, and ran down his legs into his socks and shoes.
"Look at what you did!" Nancy's shrill voice rang through his home—the home where he should've been safe, where he was supposed to be safe. Nancy's voice chased the screams away, into the dark corners. She was smiling that Big-Bad-Wolf smile again. "Little baby just pissed himself!" Her smile disappeared, to be replaced by anger, by rage. "You are in so much trouble, little baby! Just wait 'til your mommy gets home!"
"Sorry!" he wailed, tears streaming down his hot cheeks. "I don't wan' a spankin'! Sorry!"
"Look at the mess you made, little baby. It's all over the floor! You're pathetic!"
"I'm not a baby!" He put his wet hands to his leaking eyes, rubbing at his tears. But the wetness on his hands made his eyes sting. "I'm not a baby. I'm a big boy."
She laughed again. That mean laugh. "Big boys don't piss their pants. I'm gonna put a diaper on you, little baby."
"No! No diaper!" He sobbed. His eyes burned. "No diaper!"
She put both hands on the sides of his wet pants and yanked them down—pants and underwear. Then she stood straight again, looming over him. "You're not a big

boy." She pointed with one fat, accusing finger at his bare, wet crotch. "Just look at that little thing. It's so tiny! You're a baby. A disgusting, little baby boy. Boys are disgusting. You're *disgusting." She laughed. "If you ever piss your pants again, you little baby, I'll get some scissors and cut that pathetic little thing off. You want me to cut your wee-wee off, huh, little baby?"*

"No!" He covered his crotch once more.

She mimicked opening and closing a pair of imaginary scissors. "Snip, snip. And it's gone!" She cackled like the Wicked Witch of the West.

Then she bent once more, putting her face right over his. She opened her mouth, and she screamed.

"No!" he cried. Tears streamed from his tight-shut eyes. "I hate you. I hate…"
And then the dream shifted.

It was her.
Nancy.
She was older, slimmer. But she was still short. Short and ugly and mean.
She was still Nancy.
There she was, laughing and shrieking, walking through his haunted house.
Technically, the house was not his, but he worked there. He played the Hunchback—the makeup and wig making his face grotesque and misshapen, just as the padding on one shoulder distorted his body. The dim lighting coming up from the floor cast unnatural, sinister shadows on his face. Simulated instruments of torture decorated the walls of the room, making his lair seem a dungeon, a prison cell with a single exit. An iron manacle about his wrist and the great chain attached to it were fastened to a ring on the floor, holding him down as he writhed and howled.

He worked nights in the haunted house that October. His job was to scare people.
And he loved his job.

He thrilled at the prospect of frightening people. Especially women.

Every time he was able to elicit a scream from a female—at least from those who'd reached puberty—that fear would wash over him like a wave of unadulterated, almost sensual pleasure. He loved that sensation. He reveled in it.

He even hungered for it.

The fear from some women was stronger, more delicious than from others. He had discovered no reason for it, no pattern, but it was true.

When he terrified a strong *one, the bliss was beyond incredible. He could never get enough of female terror.*

But then Nancy *had come into his haunted house. Nancy—the sadistic babysitter from the lowest depths of hell. Nancy—the childhood horror that still haunted his nightmares. Nancy, who had voluntarily entered his lair. She had volunteered to be scared. No, she had* paid good money *to be scared.*

And oh, would he scare her.
He'd scare the piss out of her.

His act was simple and repetitive. When someone entered his "dungeon," he would scream and howl and yank at his chain and manacle. But then he would quiet down. He would hold his hands out to the patrons and utter one word. "Help," or perhaps, "Mercy."

Invariably, after some hesitation, one or more of the patrons would take a cautious, trembling step toward him—one step, perhaps two.

Once the fools approached close enough, he would howl, yank on the chain—once, twice, three times.

And then the chain would break.

He would lurch to his feet, his hands clawing for them, and they would scream and run away.

He would then reset, crouching on the floor and reattaching his chain. He would resume his moaning and wait for a fresh set of victims.

At least, that's what he would normally *do. But this was* Nancy. *And Nancy* deserved special *treatment.*

She wasn't alone, of course. No one wanted to be terrified alone. Horror was so much more fun when shared with someone else. So, Nancy was not alone. Another woman, about the same age and every bit as repulsive as Nancy, clung to her arm. As if Nancy would protect her.

As if Nancy would ever protect anybody.

The other woman's eyes shone from the shadows, wide with terror. "C-come on, Nancy! Let's go! I wanna go!"

But Nancy pointed at him—the pudgy finger of scorn, mocking him. Again. "The Hunchback of Notre Dame? How pathetic is that? Come on, Patty. You're not scared of this creepy little boy, are you?"

His moaning increased in volume and pitch, rising and undulating to an inhuman howl—a howl fueled by his loathing and his rage.

The other woman—Patty—shrieked, drawing back.

He rattled his chain, tugging on it, being careful to not break it too soon. He quieted and held out his hands. "Help!"

But Nancy merely laughed at him. "Pathetic!"

"Come on, Nancy!" Patty wailed. "Let's go! P-please?"

He extended his hands. "Mercy."

Nancy laughed again. "Mercy? What are we supposed to do? Give you a bone?"

He howled then, his screams joining with Patty's in a mad duet.

He yanked on his chain. Once, twice—

Patty screamed again. Even Nancy's beady eyes were huge with terror. He yanked at his chain a third time. The chain broke. He lurched to his feet. Patty turned and fled the dungeon.

But Nancy remained. She took a step back, retreating from him, putting up a hand to cover her gaping mouth, the other hand was extended to ward him off.

His shriek filled the room, echoing off the walls. He staggered toward her, holding his humped shoulder higher, maneuvering himself between Nancy and the chamber's single exit.

Her wide eyes darted about as she frantically searched for escape.

He could feel the terror coming off her in waves—sweet, warm, delicious terror. He laughed, low in his throat. "Mercy."

"Let me go!"

The sweet strength of her fear crashed against him—a tidal wave of warm honey. "Merssssy." He drew the word out in a hissing stage whisper.

"N-n-not funny!"

He grinned, showing blacked-out gaps between white teeth. "Call for help."

"Help." Her voice came out as a squeak. "H-help me!"

He shook his head and licked his lips. "No help is coming."

She took a quick step, first to one side and then the other, trying to dodge past him, to get to freedom. But he blocked her escape. He blocked the door. "What'ssss the matter, Nansssy? Need to go potty?"

She gasped. "H-how do you know my—"

"Sssssay, pleasssse, Nansssssy."

"P-p-please!" She cowered away from him.

He straightened, ignoring his fake hump. He towered over her. Short, fat, ugly bitch. *"Don't you recognize me, Nansssy?"*

Her wide eyes grew even larger. "You!"

He howled, laughing in triumph. She does! She knows me!

"B-Billy? Is that you? Randy?"

Billy? Randy? Who the heck are they? *"Not Billy or Randy. How many others? How many other defenssselessss little boysss did you terrorize?"*

"I'm s-s-sorry!"

"Need to go potty, Nansssy?"

She whimpered, shivering, and he had the great satisfaction of seeing her pants darken at the crotch. The vindicating stench of urine filled his nostrils. But nothing was as sweet as her terror. Her delicious scream rent the air. Her hands went to her crotch, covering her shame.

He laughed, shaking his head and pointing an accusing finger. "Look at what you did, Nansssy. Little baby just pissssed herssself. Lookssss like you need a diaper."

"No!" Then she lunged to her right, attempting to escape.

He caught her, seizing her wrist.

She shrieked. She twisted, trying to pull away, but he held her fast. She clawed at his hand. Her hand seized the chain dangling from his wrist.

For a moment, he thought she might strike at him with the heavy iron. But instead, she froze, the knuckles of her hand white as she gripped the chain. Like lightning, her terror shot into him.

The sweetness jolted him, almost driving him to his knees. The pleasure surged into him, coming through the manacle at his wrist. Her screams fell upon his ears, thrilling him. But it was the terror *that filled him, that completed him.*

He could feel her—all the horror, all the pettiness, all the emptiness in her soul. All her evil. All of Nancy. She flowed into him.

It was scrumptious. It was electric. It shattered his reality, exploding within him like a supernova of savage joy, making the night seem as bright as noon.

"Yesss!" More! I want more!

He wrapped the chain around her wrist.

Her wide eyes locked with his. "No!" Her scream was weaker than before. She was weaker and he was stronger.

She was his. He could feel her heart beating, feel the raggedness of her rapid breathing.

Killing her. But he didn't care if he did, all he wanted was more.

The light in her eyes faded. Her heart ceased it's thundering. Her breathing stopped.

She slumped to the floor, a broken doll. A lifeless, soulless husk.

The delicious, searing ecstasy faded into nothingness.

She's gone.

No. Not gone. *He could feel her still. Inside him. Part of him.*

He stood, bending over her—a jackal gloating over his rightful prey. He shivered—aftershocks of the joy mingling with tremors of loss.

He had taken her, consumed her.

I killed her. I. Killed. Nancy.

She deserved it. Vengeance. Righteous vengeance.

He chuckled, long and low. "Vengeance is mine, sayeth the Lord."

Voices!

Others were coming. They would find her. They would find him standing over her.

He quickly unwrapped the chain from her wrist, ripped it from her limp fingers. "Help!" *he cried.* "She collapsed!"

The scent of urine filled his nostrils—acrid, sweet perfume, the remnant of her fear. He stifled a laugh. Scared the piss right out of her.

As footsteps approached, he cried again, "Help! I think she's had a heart attack!"

More footsteps. Some of them were women. He could feel their terror, taste it. Sweet. So sweet.

He felt the hunger then. Deep in his belly, in the depths of his soul. In his soul. Where Nancy dwelt.

More. I need more. I must have more!

But he had to be careful. Take his time.

There would be others like Nancy. Other women, women who deserved his vengeance. Divine vengeance.

God had given Nancy to him. God would give him others to feed his hunger.

He knelt beside the corpse. "In here!" he cried.

He smiled then, but only on the inside. No one must see his smile. No one must see his true self. No one could see what he had become.

A perfect expression of horror and grief twisted his features, concealing his joy. It was as if an invisible mask had slid over his features, covered his soul and Nancy's. A

183

mask to hide the truth of who he had become, the truth of his divine mission.

He awoke smiling. He rolled onto his side. He laid a hand on the manacle—the precious iron. The *first* iron. The holy iron. He caressed it reverently. "Nancy."

And he heard Nancy's voice—the voice of one and many. "Legion," she said, they said. "You are the One."

"I am the One." He smiled. "And you are Legion. For you are many." And he felt them all—his Legion—inside him. He felt their love envelope him like a blanket of warm, electric honey.

He sighed happily. "Soon, my Prize. Soon, sweet Tabitha."

He lifted the manacle that would shortly grace Tabitha's wrist or ankle, and he kissed the iron. "Soon, my love, we shall be one."

"I thought you were going on active duty in May." J.L. eyed Josh quizzically, one eyebrow lifted. "Aren't you gonna graduate and get commissioned in the Air Force?" J.L. lounged on the Kilmores' sofa. At Josh's request, J.L. had agreed to stop by on his way home from work. "I thought you were going to pilot training. Gonna go fly jets."

Josh, having just changed the baby's very messy diaper, stood at the changing table, and fastened the snaps on the legs of his son's pajamas. "Yeah, but Tabitha has an opportunity. A great opportunity. She's going to join Dr. Thorpe's Shakespeare company for the summer as the lead actress. I'm just going to delay my entry into active duty for a few months."

"And you want to come work for me for the summer?" J.L. ran his fingers through his hair, then scratched his head. "I thought you'd've had enough of mopping floors and scrubbing toilets to last a lifetime."

Josh picked up his son and sat on the opposite end of the sofa. He grinned. "Speak for yourself."

J.L. chuckled, then shook his head. "Hey, I *manage* the company. I don't clean commodes anymore. Besides, sitting on my butt, telling custodians what to do with themselves pays a whole lot better."

Josh forced a chuckle of his own, but he wasn't really in a laughing mood. *Too much is riding on this. Tabitha's happiness is riding on this.* "So, do you have a spot for me?"

J.L. lowered his eyes and grimaced. "I don't know, man. I've never had a real-live, honest-to-goodness Air Force lieutenant working for me."

"*Second* lieutenant," Josh corrected. "Bottom of the officer totem pole, so to speak. I promise to not get too uppity."

J.L. scratched his head again. "Well, I did pick up the contract for the old Academy building a couple weeks ago—you know where Tabitha's doing the play?"

Josh felt hope rising in him. *Please, Heavenly Father. Let this happen!* He grinned. "I'm familiar with the place."

"It's a real dump. Perfect for the play—spooky as heck—but it needs a ton of work. Can you run a buffer? You know, polish floors?"

Josh's heart sank. "Never done it. But I bet I can figure it out."

J.L. scowled. He twitched his lips thoughtfully. "I suppose, if you're gonna fly jets, you can figure out how to pilot a floor-buffer." He winked. "'Sides, I have a terrible time finding enough students—or former students—who stick around to work over the summer." He extended a hand. "Welcome to the team."

Josh wiped his free hand on his jeans, then shook the proffered hand. "Thanks!" *It's gonna work out! Tabitha will be so happy.* A little voice in the back of his head poked at his doubts. *But, Josh, old man, are you sure you want to keep Tabitha around here? Around Folau and Thorpe? Around J.L.?*

He shook his head, shaking those thoughts free. *It's what Tabitha wants. Not to be around them, but to keep on acting. To do some serious, professional acting.*

Besides I trust Tabitha.

"Tabitha's at rehearsal, right?" J.L. grinned and shook his head. "Of course, she is. The show opens Friday, right? Even in stodgy old Provo, you gotta rehearse the Monday before opening night. Even on Family Home Evening."

Josh nodded. "Yeah. Friday night." The baby was fidgeting, rubbing his eyes. *Uh-oh. He's getting sleepy and hungry. He's not going to make it 'til we go pick up Mommy.* "Just in time for Halloween."

"How come you're not working tonight? Mikey said you gave her the night off from babysitting."

"I worked an extra shift on Friday night. Swapped with someone." *I would've taken the extra shift and worked tonight as well if I could've.* "It meant a couple extra hours, and right now, we can use the money." *Every blasted penny.*

J.L. gestured toward the electric typewriter on the dining table. "I thought Tabitha was typing research papers to help make ends meet."

Josh shrugged. "Yeah. Well. She got stiffed on a big project. Creep refused to pay her, even though she did exactly what he asked. He still took the paper. I bet he turned it in too." *Jerk.*

"That sucks. What're you going to do about it?"

"Me?" *What does he expect me to do? Beat the guy up?* "Basically, it's his word against hers. Which, I'll admit, really gets me steamed. But Tabitha has forbidden me to say anything to the guy." *Or do anything.*

"Forbidden?" J.L. looked shocked. "Who wears the pants in this family? If it was me, and somebody treated Mikey that way—"

"Man, just don't go there." *I wouldn't mind making air-spiders crawl all over the jerk. Or suspend him upside down in the middle of the air.* "Tabitha and I don't operate that way. We talked about it, and there's nothing we can do." *Nothing we would do, at least.* "And besides, it's not the first time somebody has cheated her."

J.L. shook his head. "Man, if it was me—"

Josh fought to keep anger out of his voice. "But it's not you. And Tabitha isn't Mikey." *Even if you wish she were.*

186

"You got that right."

What do you mean by that? Josh looked at J.L., but J.L. seemed to be lost in his own thoughts.

The baby began to fuss, and Josh sighed. "Can you hold him for a minute? I need to warm up some of the breastmilk from the fridge."

"Sure!" J.L. grinned widely. He took the baby from Josh and held the child in his lap. "I can handle a baby. Especially now that you've taken care of all the major grossness."

"Thanks." Josh headed off to the kitchen. He ran the hot water at the sink and got a pan ready. He pulled a plastic baby bottle from the fridge. That left a three-quarters-empty bottle of ketchup, a nearly full package of bologna, and half of a half-gallon of milk—cow's milk—as the only remaining occupants of the refrigerator. Josh's stomach growled. There was a third of a loaf of bread on the counter. In the cupboards was a nearly empty box of frosted flakes and four cans of ravioli—all that was left of the case Uncle Mike and Tabitha's mom had bought for them during their visit—but that was it. No baby food, not even the bananas Joseph loved. That was all the food they had until payday, until Friday. Josh had put his last four dollars and thirty-two cents into the VW's gas tank that evening and was praying earnestly that it would last. He didn't see how the gas could stretch that far.

At least there was a chance Joseph would get by on diapers. *I hope.*

Josh had allowed himself a small handful of dry frosted flakes for breakfast and half a bologna sandwich—with extra ketchup—for lunch, but that was all he'd eaten that day.

He'd made sure Tabitha had a bowl of cereal, a sandwich for lunch, and a full can of ravioli for dinner before rehearsal. She was, after all, eating for two. He'd promised her that he'd have another sandwich for dinner, but that was one promise he fully intended to break.

The two of them had been through some lean times before, but this was probably the worst. *If only that creep had paid up.*

But he didn't *pay up, did he? And the way he was bad-mouthing Tabitha...* That angered Josh more than the jerk's refusal to pay for the exacting, quality work Tabitha had done. But Josh had promised his wife he'd leave the guy alone. *And I will.*

Dang it.

As it was, Josh desperately wanted to buy Tabitha a single rose for her opening night. But that was two bucks and eight cents he just didn't have. He had searched under the cushions of the couch at least a dozen times, but had found no more loose change. He would get paid on Friday—opening night—but between classes that day and getting his paycheck cashed, he wasn't certain he'd be able to pick up a rose in time for the play.

And I'm not *going to miss her show. That would hurt her a heck of a lot more than not having a stupid rose.*

Josh waited for the water to get hot. Tabitha had pumped just before Josh had driven her to rehearsal, so the bottle wasn't terribly cold. "Hey, man," he said, raising his voice slightly, "thanks for the job. It means the world to Tabitha—this opportunity, I mean."

From the living room, J.L. said, "Glad I can help. Anything for you two, you know." He paused. "You *three*." J.L. raised the pitch of his voice. "Aren't you just a cute little guy? Your mommy's little angel. Oh, yes, you are!" His voice resumed its more adult tone. "He takes after his mom, you know."

Josh laughed, placing the bottle in the hot water. "Man, I sure hope so! Although, the way he's growing, I'd bet good money he's gonna be as tall as me. Maybe taller." *If I were a betting man. And if I actually had money to bet. Or any money at all.*

"It wasn't that long ago our little Marie was still in diapers," J.L. said. "Potty training, man! That's what you have to look forward to! Stacy was easy. Marie? She was a holy terror. Tantrums like you wouldn't believe." J.L. laughed. "Listen to us! A couple of old, whipped guys, talking about diapers and toilet training. How very *domesticated* of us!"

Josh chuckled. "Quick! Let's discuss something manly! Hey, how about them Jazz, huh?" He twirled the bottle around in the hot water.

"I never took you for a basketball fan. You a Jazz fan?"

Josh shrugged, even though he knew J.L. couldn't see it. "Nope. Not much of a sports guy at all."

"Really? As tall as you are?" J.L. paused. "Come to think of it, though, I've never seen you playing church basketball."

Josh pulled the bottle from the hot water, shook it, then sprinkled a few drops of milk on the inside of his forearm. *'Bout right.* He could hear Joseph beginning to fuss in earnest and with all his infantile vigor.

Just in time.

Josh dried the bottle with a hand towel, then headed back into the living room. "Bollocks." He grinned. "Like you ever showed up for church B-ball."

J.L. chuckled and handed the crying baby to Josh. "He's all yours, man."

Josh had barely settled on the sofa, with Joseph sucking greedily on the bottle, when a loud knock came at the door.

Joseph jerked, whimpered a little, then went back to drinking.

"I'll get it," J.L. said, jumping up. He strode quickly to the door and opened it. "Hello."

Josh gazed past J.L. and saw Folau framed in the open doorway. "Come in, Brother Folau." Josh withheld "Detective," unsure how to proceed with J.L. in the room.

J.L. stepped aside, making room for Folau to enter.

The detective glanced at J.L., but said nothing by way of greeting. He also did not enter the apartment. The detective jerked a thumb to his right. "Somebody left a box out here for you. At least, I assume it's for you."

Josh blinked. "A box?"

J.L. stuck his head out the door. "Hey, yeah! There *is* a box! I'll get it."

Folau stepped aside, and J.L. disappeared through the doorway.

Josh eyed the detective with annoyance. *Why didn't you just pick it up and bring it in yourself, Folau?*

Maybe it's a cop thing. Who knows?

Josh stood and carried Joseph to his playpen. He laid the baby inside and got Joseph settled with his bottle.

Then Josh turned back toward the door.

J.L. held a large cardboard box. The box was open at the top. And out of the box protruded a large package of spaghetti noodles, a loaf of bread, and a bag of Pampers. J.L. was grinning like the Cheshire Cat. "Hey, where do you want this?"

Somebody left us a care package? "Uh, put it on the table. Next to the typewriter." *Who would know how bad things are? We haven't told anyone we were desperate.*

J.L. deposited the box on the table. "You've got some good stuff here! Diapers, spaghetti, spaghetti sauce, cheese, milk, hamburger, eggs, bread, peanut butter, jam, butter. Hey! Real butter! Even some sausage."

Sausage? Josh felt his mouth watering at the prospect of a full belly, let alone a belly filled with the savory goodness of fresh-cooked sausage.

"Excuse me," interrupted Folau. "We haven't been introduced."

J.L. stopped his enthusiastic rummaging through the box. He turned to face the detective, still holding a package wrapped in white paper—presumably the sausage.

Folau extended his hand. "I'm Daniel Folau. I'm a friend of Josh's."

J.L. shook hands. "I'm J.L." He paused. "J.L. Montrose."

Folau raised an eyebrow and grinned. "J.L.?"

J.L. shrugged. "Jesse Levi. But nobody calls me that, 'cept my mother. Not even my wife calls me Jesse."

Folau nodded. "J.L. it is then. Pleased to meet you, J.L. Montrose."

Never seen Folau be so friendly before. He's acting practically human.

"Likewise," J.L. said. "Any friend of Josh and Tabitha's . . ."

"So, how long have you known Josh and Tabitha?"

J.L. shrugged. "A couple years. Ever since they moved into the ward." He grinned. "Tabitha and I were in a play together. *Fiddler on the Roof.* I was Perchik, and she was Hodel."

Folau grinned. "Played opposite each other, huh? Lovebirds?"

"Yeah." J.L.'s grin widened for a second, before faltering. He shrugged. "She's a great actress."

Folau's grin remained, but there was an intensity to his gaze as he looked at J.L. "Yeah, she's pretty special."

And Josh suddenly realized, Folau was interrogating him. *Treating J.L. as a suspect. I guess he has to treat everyone as a suspect.*

Abruptly, Folau turned to Josh. "Hey, I need to talk to you in private. Got a minute?"

J.L. glanced from Josh to Folau and back again. Then he nodded. "I gotta head out anyway. Can't keep Mikey and the girls waiting for dinner. It's enchilada night!" He turned to Josh and handed him the white package. The paper had "PORK SAUSAGE, MILD, 1 LB." hand-printed in black marker. "This feels like it's thawing—you know, half-frozen. You'll have to cook it up soon. Can't refreeze meat, you know!" He turned to Folau. "Nice to meet you, uh, Daniel, was it?"

Folau's smile seemed genuine enough. "Nice to meet you too, J.L."

"Later, gator!" Then J.L. was out the door, closing it behind him.

"He's right, you know," Folau said. "Shouldn't refreeze meat. Especially pork."

Josh nodded and put the sausage in the fridge. His stomach growled loudly. "Can I offer you something, Detective? Some milk, maybe? Water?"

"No, I'm fine." Then, seemingly as an afterthought, Folau added. "Thanks, though."

"I'm gonna have some milk." Josh pulled the half-empty half-gallon from the refrigerator, unscrewed the lid, and gulped down the remaining contents. He smacked his lips and then grinned. *Okay, stomach, you can shut up now.*

He turned back around, only to find Folau holding the new full gallon of milk and some plastic-wrapped mozzarella. Folau handed both to Josh and said, "Better get these in the fridge too."

Josh couldn't resist a smile. "I'm not used to you being so nice."

Folau shrugged and handed him a carton of eggs and the store-wrapped 5-lb. chub of ground beef. "I'm a heck of a nice guy, once you get to know me." He grinned. "A heck of a nice guy. I think that hamburger is fresh. You can probably freeze that." Then he chuckled. "Sorry. I live alone. I'm used to doing all the shopping myself." Folau's face sobered and his pale scar twitched.

Since your wife died. "I understand. When Tabitha's doing a show, I do most of the shopping, too." He put the eggs and the beef in the refrigerator. "I'll split this up and freeze some of it later."

"Here's the butter," Folau said, handing it to him. "The rest doesn't need to be kept cold." He turned back to the box. "Some canned applesauce, peaches. Hey, here's some vitamins—says, 'For nursing mothers.' Somebody really likes you. Or at least likes your wife."

At the mention of the post-natal vitamins, which they had run out of two days before, Josh felt a tear threatening. He forced a soft laugh. "Everybody likes Tabitha." *Including you, Folau.*

Josh half expected Folau to say something in agreement, but instead the detective said, "There's something else here," his tone suddenly sober. "You better come take a look."

Josh hastened over to the table. The food items had been placed beside the box on the table. But Folau was staring into the box.

Inside, lay an envelope—legal-sized, plain, and unlabeled. Josh reached in and retrieved the envelope. He turned it over. The envelope was sealed. He tore it open.

He gasped as he saw what had been concealed inside—money.

With trembling fingers, Josh pulled out the money. He counted out ten twenty-dollar bills. *Two-hundred bucks!* "Who?" *Who could afford this much?*

Folau picked up the discarded envelope and examined it. "No note."

Josh could no longer hold back tears. "Two-hundred dollars! Who could've..." He gazed questioningly up at Folau.

The detective quickly shook his head. "Don't look at me! It wasn't me." Then he looked away, and Josh had the distinct impression that Folau wished he *had* been their benefactor. Or at least, *Tabitha's* benefactor.

Josh counted the money once more. He laughed then. *I'm gonna buy Tabitha a whole dozen roses!*

Folau glanced at him, then glanced away. "I had no idea you folks were struggling. I wish…" He shook himself. "I bet I know who did this."

Josh set the money down on the table. "Who?"

Folau's scar twitched. "Judging by the vitamins and the cash, my prime suspect would be your bishop, the doctor."

"Bishop Smith?"

"Yeah. Him and his wife."

Bishop and Maddie Smith. Josh swallowed. "Makes sense, I suppose." He wiped his eyes, scrubbing away the tears. "Whoever it was, it's an answer to prayer." *A lot of prayers.*

"Yeah, sounds like it." Folau's voice was thick with emotion. He cleared his throat. "But I stopped by for a reason." He pulled up a chair and sat.

Josh glanced at the playpen and his son. The bottle had fallen out of Joseph's limp hands. "Just a second."

Josh quietly crossed the room. He picked up the empty bottle and set it on the changing table. He retrieved a burp rag from a shelf under the table, then bent and carefully picked up his slumbering child. He laid Joseph against his shoulder and gently patted the baby's back.

As Josh walked slowly to the table, he said softly, "If I don't burp him, he'll probably puke."

Folau nodded.

Just as Josh was about to sit at the table with his infant son, Joseph belched.

And didn't wake up.

A miracle! Josh wiped the minimal spit-up from the baby's lips, then mouthed, "Be right back."

Moving with catlike steps, Josh carried his son to the playpen and carefully laid the boy on his stomach. He then, exercising equal stealth, silently returned to the table.

Folau was gazing at the playpen with uncharacteristically soft eyes. "He's a beautiful baby." He was silent for a moment, then said, "He takes after his mother."

Josh resisted a sudden urge to roll his eyes. *Not you too!* "Yes, he does. Thank heavens."

Folau chuckled softly. He turned back to Josh. "You're a lucky man, Kilmore." The scarred detective's eyes were moist. "A very lucky man."

Josh nodded. "Don't I know it." *You didn't just lose your wife, Folau. You also lost your child.*

Folau cleared his throat softly, then rubbed at his eyes, surreptitiously wiped away threatening tears. "I came by to tell you what we learned from the crime scene, from the farm. I know your wife is busy with the play, so I thought I'd talk to you, and you can fill her in."

191

Josh nodded. "I thought you weren't supposed to share details."

Folau shook his head. "Look, we're way past that. We're in this together, the three of us. Besides, with what the two of you can do…" He let the unspoken words linger in the air, then he waved his hand dismissively. "I know you've got to keep your *talents* secret. And I'm trying to respect that as much as I can, but I've still got a job to do. I'm trying to catch this guy, to stop him. And you two are important resources—I mean, important allies in this case."

"Okay. I appreciate your discretion. Tabitha appreciates it too." *Even if you did just refer to us as resources.* Josh put his hands on his knees and leaned forward conspiratorially. "So, what you got?"

Folau reached into his jacket pocket and retrieved his notepad. He flipped it open and thumbed through the pages. "We know what he's using to drug his victims." He looked at his pad, then read slowly, "Carfentanil." He looked up. "It's a synthetic opioid—like heroin, only five-thousand times more potent."

"Wow."

Folau nodded. "It suppresses breathing. It's bad stuff. It's used to sedate large animals. Cougars, bobcats. Elephants. There was a break-in at a ranger station a couple years back. The"—he glanced at his pad again—"carfentanil was stolen. Utah Department of Fish and Wildlife investigators assumed it was stolen to be sold on the street." He shrugged. "I guess not. It's not a well-known street-drug, at least not in Utah. I found one report of a carfentanil overdose early last year, not long after the break-in at the ranger station. The O-D victim showed no signs of prior drug use. My guess is it was a botched abduction. Our perp gave the vic too much, and she died."

Josh shuddered.

"And you were right about the pigs. We found human remains in their stomachs and bits of human remains in the mire of the pigpen."

Suddenly, the milk in Josh's belly felt as if it were curdling. He swallowed down the bile. "Okay."

"We also found evidence that, before the perp set the fire, he slaughtered one of the pigs. A piglet, judging from the relatively small amount of blood. The piglet carcass itself wasn't found, unless the perp slaughtered it and threw it back in with the rest of the pigs before burning them alive."

"Burned alive?" As horrified as Josh was at the idea of pigs devouring human flesh, he was further sickened at the thought of those animals dying in flames.

"Yup. But I think he took one of the piglets with him. After slaughtering it, of course."

"Why?"

"Why kill the piglet? Why take it with him?"

Josh nodded. "Yeah."

Folau scratched his head. "No clue." He grimaced. "I think I know what drives this guy, at least partially. But I'm no closer to figuring out who he is. I haven't noticed a ritualistic pattern to anything the killer does. I'm not saying there isn't a religious aspect to it. There could be, but—"

"Religious aspect?"

Folau nodded. "Serial killers are motivated by a lot of things. In this guy's case, there's definitely a sexual component. All his victims are female."

Josh shuddered. "But he hasn't molested or-or-or raped any of them."

"Doesn't matter. It's still sexual. The torture, the terror, the dominance, even the killing is like the ultimate sexual thrill to this guy. Probably abused by a female when he was a kid—his mother, a big sister, a grandmother, maybe. Could've been the creepy old lady next door or a teacher. Any female authority figure works." Folau shook his head. "That's probably a big part of it, but it's not all." He waved a finger in the air. "It's the masks. The scary masks. This is about frightening his victims. It's like he feeds off their fear."

"You mean like he's really feeding off their fear?"

"Before I met you two, I would've said no. Not just no, but heck no. But now?" Folau shrugged. "With what you two can do? With what your wife can do with the readings? I don't know what to think anymore. But I do think that he thinks he is. Feeding off the fear, I mean."

"Tabitha says it could be their souls. He's consuming their souls. At least that's what it feels like. To her."

Folau shook his head. "That's impossible." Then more softly, he added, "I hope it's impossible."

"God wouldn't allow it." Josh said it, but he was surprised at the lack of conviction in his own words. *The Devourer can't take their souls. He just can't!*

Folau shook himself, as if ridding himself of dark thoughts the way a dog shakes away water. "Anyway, there's the sexual component. And your wife's probably right. He *thinks* he's consuming their souls. And that's what makes me think—despite the lack of religious ritual—that there's a religious aspect too. I think… I think this guy believes he's on a holy mission from God."

"Seriously? A mission to kill women?"

Folau shook his head again. "Naw. If it was just to kill them, he could do that with the drug, or with a knife, or his hands, or a firearm. No. This is…" Folau clenched his hands. "Monsters like this guy have all kinds of reasons for doing what they do. Some just feel compelled, you know? They know it's wrong, but they do it anyway. They can't stop themselves. But some *justify* the evil that they do. They've convinced themselves it's *righteous* somehow."

Righteous? "That's sick."

Folau rolled his eyes and straightened, his hands no longer clenched. "Tell me about it." Then he sighed. "So, that's the why. Or part of it, at least. But that doesn't tell me who. If this guy was abused as a kid, there may be no record of it—not that I haven't looked at child abuse case files. He may not even be from around here. He might not even remember the abuse, not consciously, anyway. So, that's not getting me any closer to identifying him. But"—he pointed his finger at nothing in particular— "since he destroyed his own *lair*—for lack of a better word—he's going to reconstruct it somewhere else. He's going to need to reconstruct it. I've been checking with

193

mattress stores and camping supply outlets. He's gonna need a mattress and a portable chemical toilet at the very least."

"Why?" But Josh knew why. He just needed Folau to say it, to give voice to Josh's greatest fear.

Folau fixed him with his gaze. "You know why. Tabitha. *She's* his goal."

Josh looked away, but he nodded. "Yeah."

"Think about it. He didn't care about the comfort of his victims before. He added the mattress and so on, he added the roses after Tabitha confronted him. He's fixated on Tabitha. He's got some fantasy about her. He thinks he has some kind of romantic connection with her."

Josh swallowed. "Tabitha said she was certain he knows her, knows who she is."

Folau nodded. "Yeah. Good thing you were with her that night, at the Academy."

A tremor ripped through Josh. "I didn't do much. I didn't protect her. Mostly I just slipped and almost fell on my butt."

Folau fixed him with his eyes. "No, you didn't save her. But that's not what I meant. It means now I know you're not him."

Not him? Josh felt as if Folau had gut-punched him. "You thought…"

Folau shrugged. "I'm a cop. It's my job to suspect *everybody*. Especially a weirdo who can make a VW fly. Or can fly through the air with his psychic wife and rescue a kidnap victim from a serial killer in the middle of a freak blizzard." His eyes softened. "But now I know you're not the guy."

And how do I know you're *not the guy?*

Folau suddenly looked uncomfortable. "And you may not have *saved* her that night, but just your presence probably scared him away. So, in a way, you *did* save her. Just by being there for her. I'm glad she's got you. She's…" He let his voice trail off.

She's special. That's what you were going to say.

Abruptly, Folau extended a hand. "You're a good man, Kilmore." He grinned. "Even if you are a weirdo."

Josh chuckled softly as he took the detective's hand. "High praise, coming from you. Don't worry. I won't let it go to my head."

Folau's grin widened, twisting his long scar. "Good idea." Then he pointed to the fridge. "Seriously, you should fry up that sausage soon. Pork doesn't keep once it thaws. Only don't eat it all yourself."

"Wouldn't dream of it." No, he wouldn't eat it all himself, but Josh's mouth watered as he thought of sausage and scrambled eggs. And toast with jam and butter! He felt as if he'd been fasting for days.

"I gotta go," Folau said. "If you find out anything, just call dispatch. They'll patch you through to me." Folau glanced at the playpen. "I'll let myself out."

As the detective closed the door behind himself, Josh got up and turned to the fridge. He retrieved the white-wrapped sausage and unwrapped it. *Just fry it up. Maybe take a taste. Just a taste.*

But, doggonit! If I'm gonna feast on sausage and eggs and toast and butter and jam, I'm gonna wait 'til Tabitha gets home. We'll feast together.

He turned on a stove burner and set a frying pan atop it. Then he dumped the sausage into the pan. He chopped at the gooey mass of meat and fat and spices with a spatula. Then he quickly stepped into the living room to check on his son.

By the time he returned, the tantalizing aroma and inviting sizzle of the cooking sausage greeted him. *Man, that smells good!*

He continued to chop at the pork, creating small chunks.

Bishop and Maddie! Makes sense. Who else would think of the vitamins but Tabitha's doctor? And the cash! It couldn't have come at a better time. Josh offered up a silent, but heartfelt prayer of thanks. *It's almost enough to make me forget there's a serial killer out there. At least for a moment.*

That last thought made him think of Folau. Josh couldn't decide whether to like the man or not. *Could he be the killer?*

He's in love with Tabitha. Like the Devourer.

"No. Can't blame him for loving Tabitha," he said aloud. "Not one bit."

As long as he stays away from her, and he has. He's keeping his distance. Came to see me alone tonight.

He thought over the detective's revelations.

Five-thousand times stronger than heroin! Folau said there were no religious rituals involved. Maybe the Devourer killed that piglet as part of some kind of sacrifice.

Josh spied a small chunk of sausage that appeared to be fully cooked. He fished it out with the spatula, then set it on the counter to cool.

Just a taste.

His mouth watered as he picked up the bit of sausage between thumb and forefinger.

The pigs ate those poor women. Ate them. *Then he burned the pigs alive.*

But he kept one piglet back. Maybe he was planning on eating it himself?

Maybe he's like Renfield, eating flies and spiders to consume their lives, their souls. Maybe he was going to eat the pigs and—

Suddenly, he flung the bit of sausage into the sink.

Even though it had not touched his lips or tongue, Josh spat into the sink. He spat again and again. And then he emptied the meager contents of his stomach.

On the stove, sausage continued to sizzle.

He'd done it! He'd snuck the sausage into the box, hiding it along with the rest of the food. The stupid, unworthy husband would never suspect a thing. Tabitha would never suspect a thing.

Soon Tabitha will be eating it. She will be consuming a small portion of my Woman-souls. Like Renfield. Like me. We are truly becoming one!

"She will never partake of your holy offering," whispered the voices.

"What?" he cried aloud. "Of course, she will. My plan is perfect!"

"Oh, no, Beloved. He has destroyed your precious offering. He has ground it up and sent it down the garbage disposal. All of it."

"Lies!" he snapped. "You can't know that. You are here with me. Inside me!"

"We are inside you, we are everywhere. Here with you. Inside that apartment. All around the world. We watched him for you. We watched to make certain your plan, your glorious plan worked, that he would prepare it for her, for Tabitha. But he did not. He destroyed it. He destroyed your offering."

"No!" he screamed. "No! No!"

"We have seen it, Beloved."

He put his head in his hands and wept. "I'll kill him! I'll kill that worthless bastard!"

"The child," whispered the voice. "The child is Tabitha's. But it is also *his*. You must also kill the child. Slaughter it like a piglet, Beloved."

"I will," he growled. "I'll slit its throat and grind it up and cook it and shove it down his jaws until he chokes on it!" He could see it all in his mind's eye. He could smell the sizzling flesh. He could see Josh's eyes, wide and dimming, as the life faded from them. He wove his hands through the darkness, miming the actions. *Destroy them! Destroy them both!*

He shook his head violently. "No. I need the child. I must remember my Prize! My Treasure."

"But the child, Beloved—the product of their imperfect, unholy union."

"No. I need the baby. I will use the baby to make her see." He grinned and licked his teeth. "To make her choose me."

"Ah, yes, Beloved. You are so clever. So very, clever. We love you."

He could feel them inside him—his Woman-souls. He could feel them all around him, caressing his mind, his flesh with invisible fingers. So many of them. They were everywhere. They could see anything, hear anything.

That meant *he* was everywhere at once, too. He could see everything, hear everything through them. He was omniscient. *A god.* "I am Legion," he said. "We are Legion, for we are many, and we are one."

He calmed himself, and the mask slid into place.

"That was quick," Folau said over the phone, his voice distorted by the radio-to-phone patch. "Let me guess. It was that sausage."

Josh briefly pulled the phone away from his ear and stared at it as he sat on the bed. He put the handset back to his ear. "How'd you know?"

"It was the only thing in that box that didn't come from a store. Other than the money, of course."

"Why didn't you... I almost ate some of it!" Josh felt like he could be sick again, even though nothing—except acid—remained in his stomach.

"It didn't occur to me," the detective said. "Not 'til after I left. Something was nagging at me. I just didn't know what it was. Dang it, I'm a detective! I'm supposed to notice anomalies, things that seem out of place."

"It's okay," Josh said. "Not your fault. It's his. He's the one doing this."

"Did you save it?"

"No. Sent it down the garbage disposal."

"The garbage—" Josh could hear Folau take a deep calming breath. "All of it?"

"I saved the wrapper."

"Thank heavens for that! Good man! Okay, don't touch it anymore. Wait 'til I get there. It'll have *your* prints on it for sure. And your friend's, that J.L. guy who was at your apartment when I arrived. Now if the wrapper has your bishop's or his wife's prints, then it's worthless. That means it just came from their freezer. But if not, if it doesn't have either of their prints—"

"Then it might have the Devourer's!" *We can finally stop him!*

"It may be nothing, but it may just be a huge break in this dang case!"

Exhausted and exhilarated as she always was after rehearsal, Tabitha plopped down in her seat in the front audience row of the Academy building theatre. She set one end of the heavy broomstick—the bristled end—on the floor in front of her and clasped the shaft in her left hand. She set her purse in her lap—and felt the comforting weight of the Glock inside. Then she let out a huge, sigh of satisfaction. The night's rehearsal had gone well. Very well.

So well, it's almost scary, she thought. *I should be more nervous. Nervous about the show. I have so many other things to be worried about, I guess. The Devourer is still out there. And I know Josh isn't getting enough to eat.* She pursed her lips. *I know he skipped that second sandwich.* Her stomach growled at her. *I shouldn't be hungry. Not when Josh isn't eating.*

She resisted the urge to mentally curse the graduate student who'd refused to pay her for typing his stupid, boring paper. It couldn't have come at a worse time.

She needed to nurse. She hoped Joseph would wake up enough to eat when she got home.

Eli Thorpe—tall, thin, and stately—caught her eye as he approached.

When rehearsals had first begun more than a month before, Tabitha had taken care to sit next to Sarah or Caroline—the only other women in the show—after each rehearsal for the reading of the director's notes. But as the weeks had passed, Caroline and Bjorn (who were both young and single) had more often than not wound up sitting together. They weren't dating yet—and heaven knew there was hardly time for any kind of life at this stage of rehearsals—but she suspected that Caroline and Bjorn would soon be a couple.

She no longer actively avoided Dr. Thorpe during the nightly notes. She had grown accustomed to him seeking her out and sitting next to her. And to be perfectly honest, she found that she enjoyed his company. Even though he was still a bit creepy. As long as his hands remained safely in his own lap, and as long as he didn't pat her shoulder, she was more than willing to sit and discuss the play. Strangely, as the show had progressed, and the two of them had spent more time together, the older man had come to respect her personal space more than he ever had on campus.

She smiled at Eli as he took his customary seat next to her. As they awaited Trevor's arrival at the edge of the stage—where, with notepad in hand, the director would read his notes about their performance that night—Eli bent his head to whisper in her ear. "I haven't seen Josh yet. I hope he's on his way." He smiled his thin-lipped, bloodless smile. "Cordelia." His smile broadened, showing yellow teeth. "Cordelia *and* the Fool."

Tabitha blushed and not entirely with embarrassment. "It's not a done deal, you know. Josh still has to line up a summer job." *I hope J.L. has a spot for him. I wonder how that went?*

Eli nodded once. "I am certain he will. Clever young man, your husband."

She nodded. "I hope he finds something." *I hope J.L. comes through. Especially after that jerk ripped me off. I had his instructions in writing! It's not my fault he changed the stupid margins afterwards. I don't get how any decent person can justify—*

"And of course, there will also be—" Eli cut off as he saw the look on her face. "Tabitha, is something wrong."

She shook herself. "No. It was a rough weekend."

"Is there anything I can help with? Anything at all?" The concern in his voice and face touched her heart. He reached a thin hand toward her as if to put it on her shoulder, then abruptly pulled back. "How can I help?"

She gave him a smile she hoped conveyed the gratitude in her heart and none of the discomfort. "It's okay. It's nothing." When he opened his mouth to protest, she hurried on. "What other plays are you—are *we*—going to be doing, besides *King Lear*."

He smiled again. "Most likely, *The Taming of the Shrew* and *Hamlet*. One more, but I haven't made my choice yet. You will, of course, be playing Katharina and Ophelia. Fear not. I, myself, will *not* be playing Petruchio or 'Hamlet.' Although, I do think I shall play the Ghost in *Hamlet*."

Typecasting yourself, Eli? She smiled. "You'll make a great Ghost."

He winked. "One thing is certain—I can *look* the part."

She stifled a giggle.

He covered his mouth, hiding his own quiet laughter. Suddenly, his mirth vanished altogether. "You must promise me one thing, however, if we are to work together professionally."

She raised an eyebrow. "Oh? And what, pray tell, would that be?"

"You must, someday, tell me the full tale of the witch's broom."

Tabitha flushed again. Most people in her theatre life quietly accepted the antique broom as her good luck charm. Tabitha Moonshadow Kilmore's personal quirk. She grinned. "I promise." *Just not the full tale.*

"I assume it is more than a simple, if rather large, good luck talisman. May I also assume you know how to use it?"

Instantly, Tabitha was on edge. *Does he think it's magical?* She forced a grin. "I can't"—she chuckled—"fly around on it, if that's what you mean." *Not without Josh's help. Does he know about that? Could he possibly—*

He chuckled. "Certainly not. Don't be silly. Real witches don't fly on brooms."

Real witches? He can't mean—

"I meant," he said, "as a weapon. It's quite heavy, and—"

Tabitha almost laughed with relief. Instead, she nodded. "Yes. I'm no martial artist, but I know how to use it."

He nodded. "Good. With that vile murderer on the loose, you can't be too careful! What did the Daily Herald call him? Something sensational. Oh, yes. The Night Hunter."

Tabitha swallowed. *The Devourer.*

"I will, of course, stay with you until your husband arrives. See you safely away." He quickly added. "And Sarah and Caroline, of course."

Of course. "I really appreciate it." *I really do.*

"But I fear an old man such as myself is poor protection." He sat up a little straighter. "Although I do have some fight in me still. I may look wiry, but I am stronger than I appear."

In her mind, Tabitha pictured the penultimate scene where Thorpe as Dracula seizes Renfield's head in his thin hands and squeezes. She pictured the vampire's demonic rage as he is about to crush the madwoman's skull with his bare hands. Eli's strength had surprised her. He had never gripped her that hard before tonight.

She put her own clawed hands to her head, seizing it in murderous imitation of that violent scene. Her mouth and eyes went wide as she played out the terror of that moment. "No, Master!" she said in her Renfield voice. Then she winked at him. "Strong! Don't I know it!"

A bit of color appeared in the professor's otherwise cadaverous cheeks. "I was a bit . . . intense tonight. Forgive me."

"No. You were—what's the word you always use?—magnificent." She looked him straight in the eye, even if she did have to crane her neck a bit. "Don't. Change. A. Thing."

"Did I frighten you?" Amusement flickered in his eyes. "Actually frighten you?"

She grinned. "Definitely!"

His toothy smile broadened. "Good." He drew the word out, as if he truly were a vampire savoring the blood of a particularly delicious victim. "Excellent." He turned his face toward the stage where Trevor had finally appeared.

The balding director sat on the edge of the stage and opened his notebook. "Okay, folks." He gazed out upon the cast. "Very good tonight. Very good. But"—he thumbed through several pages of handwritten notes—"it can always be better." He pointed at Zechariah. "Van Helsing, overall, the Dutch accent was a bit thick tonight. Actually, I liked it, but your diction must be better. More crisp." Trevor enunciated the word, almost spitting out the final letter. He pointed to Bjorn. "Harker, your first scene with Seward…"

Tabitha's eyes flickered back to Eli. She glanced at the older man's hands. Strong hands. Thin, but strong.

She closed her eyes for a moment, searching the memories she'd seen through the victims' eyes. She tried to remember the Devourer's hands. They were strong too. She'd seen them only once.

Were they thin? Like Eli's? She couldn't remember. *Maybe.*

She thought of the hand that had covered Maddie Smith's mouth. *Strong. So terribly, terrifyingly strong.*

But had it felt bony? *Maybe.*

A shiver tore through her, and the broom shook in her hand.

Don't be late, Josh!

"How long do you think that box had been sitting there? Outside our door?" Tabitha resisted the urge to put her hand on the back of her husband's neck. As much as she wanted, as much as she needed to feel the comfort of the Power flowing at that moment, she didn't want to distract Josh while he was driving. She glanced back at Joseph, just to reassure herself that her son was still there, asleep.

Josh shrugged, even as he shifted the Bug's gears. "I don't know. Sometime after J.L. arrived, and sometime before Folau arrived." He paused. "Or perhaps one of them brought it."

A tremor of fear caused her to shudder. "Not J.L. or Da—" *Stop calling him that!* "Or Folau. Surely not one of them." *But the Devourer is someone who knows me. He has to be.*

Eli? He was a bit late to rehearsal. And that's just not like him. I didn't hear his explanation, but—No! I refuse to believe it. Not Eli.

"We have to consider it," Josh said. Then he growled. "I'm getting to be as bad as Folau now! Suspecting everybody. What a flippin' way to live!"

But Daddy suspects everybody too. He has to. "Okay, but how about this? What if the person who dropped it off—assuming the person who dropped off the box and the person who left the sausage are two different people—"

"And that's actually a pretty big assumption."

She nodded. "Yeah. But I hope. I want to believe someone was just being nice to us."

"Probably the Smiths, Bishop and Maddie. That's what Folau thinks."

She smiled. "Oh, I hope it was them!" She rolled her eyes and shook her head in irritation. "I hope it was *they.*" *Stupid, dang English language!* "Anyway, they probably didn't want to get caught. They saw the lights on and just dumped it off. Maybe? I hope?"

"Yep. Probably. And the same thing with the Devourer, assuming it was him."

Assuming it was he, Tabitha corrected in her head. But she said nothing. *It can't be one of them.*

"Oops. Sorry." Josh glanced at her and grimaced. "Assuming it was he." Then he grinned. "See? You're a good influence on me!"

She forced a weak smile. "How long was J.L. there?"

Josh narrowed his eyes thoughtfully. "About a half hour, I guess. Maybe a little less. I, uh, took a little bit to work up to it. But he said yes! Oh yeah, I forgot to tell you about that! So, basically, it's all set. I talked to the commandant today and—"

"Are you sure about this? You really don't have to."

He reached over to her and took her hand. The Power flowed. Comforting. Warm. Sweet. "I love you. I want you to be happy."

"I love you too. And I *am* happy. I chose you. I chose the life of an Air Force officer's wife. I have no regrets."

He glanced at her, smiling. "Not even one regret?"

She smiled back at him. "Not a single one. But what you're giving up for me is—"

"Has Dr. Thorpe said anything?"

Tabitha couldn't help but laugh. Softly. "Are you kidding? He already knew! You were sure right about Major Kimball figuring out just who Eli was talking about. I'm not sure if Eli called the major or the other way around, but Eli was positively *crowing* about it when he arrived tonight." *Late.* She tented her hands together, tapping her fingertips repeatedly against each other. She lowered her voice, imitating the professor's. "'I have you now, my treasure!'" She rolled her eyes. "Dracula!" she said. "Am I right?"

Josh's hand trembled in hers.

"What?" she asked. "What is it?"

He grimaced. "I don't know. Sometimes, he just gives me the creeps. You know what I mean?"

Tabitha was about to dismiss her husband's words with, *He's just a great actor,* but a shudder went through her as well, as if Josh's quiver had been contagious. "Yeah. I get that too, sometimes." *He is a tremendous actor, though. Perhaps the best I've ever known.* "He's going to play Lear."

Josh nodded, sticking out his bottom lip. "He'll be good in that role."

Tabitha brightened. "And I get to play Cordelia! *And* the Fool."

"So, he's interpreting the Fool as actually being Cordelia in disguise?"

Tabitha grinned at him. "Look at you! Mr. Shakespeare-Literate!"

He shrugged, and there was a pleasant, momentary surge in the Power. "If it's important to my wife!"

She squeezed his hand. "I love you." Suddenly, her voice was thick. "Thank you."

"And besides, since I've got all this competition lately."

"What competition?" She had almost shouted it. Then she glanced nervously at her son.

"Every single one of them knows more about Shakespeare than I do . . . Thorpe, J.L., even Folau…"

"Stop it!"

"I figured I'd better bone up a little." He gave her a sly grin. "At least about *King Lear.*"

"Really? When did you find the time?"

"Ah, my lovely, sexy witch, a little thing called CliffsNotes in the Harold B. Lee Library."

She giggled. "In other words—"

"Yep! In other words, I cheated! Just like Admiral James T. Kirk."

They both laughed—each with a glance at the sleeping baby in the backseat.

However, Tabitha abruptly sobered. "How long until we know? About the fingerprints?"

"Well, like I said, Folau explained we'd better not get our hopes up just yet."

"Okay."

"Another detective got there not long after Folau came back. She and Folau dusted the box and all the stuff it came with for fingerprints. Even the money. She dusted the butcher paper from the sausage, too. Folau said they're going to get prints from J.L., Maddie, and Bishop Smith to compare and eliminate."

"What about *your* fingerprints?"

Josh chuckled. "Well, I'm the only one with prints actually on file. Because of my security clearance paperwork. So, they've already got mine. The others shouldn't be in the system, unless one of them has a criminal record or something. Was Bishop Smith ever in the military?"

Tabitha shrugged. "Not that I know of. Maybe." *He never mentioned anything about the military in a talk or anything.*

"Anyway," Josh continued, "*if* they find any usable prints on the butcher paper and *if* those prints don't match any of us, then they'll check with other government agencies, like the FBI and so on. They might get a hit." He shrugged. "And they might not."

"And maybe the sausage was just something from the Smith's food storage—completely innocent."

Josh shook his head. Then he shook it again. "I don't think so. Neither does Folau. But he'll ask the Smiths tomorrow if they put it in the box, to be sure. And that might be the end of that."

"I feel bad for them, you know," Tabitha said. "For the Smiths."

"Yeah. Me too. They did something nice. Something *really* nice, and now it's come back to bite them."

"That's not what I meant."

Josh gave her a quizzical glance. "What then?"

"I mean, they did this anonymously. They wanted to keep it that way. Now we know, and *they* are going to know that we know."

Josh nodded, then released her hand—and the Power—as he slowed for a stoplight and down-shifted the gears. "They'll feel awkward. It'll take some of the joy out of what they've done."

Tabitha sighed. "So, how long did Folau say it'll take?"

"At least a few days. It's not like on TV. And the killer may have used gloves. This whole thing could be a bust."

Tabitha frowned at that.

"Folau also said he's going to check butcher shops. The kind that handle whole animals."

Tabitha shuddered. *That poor, little piglet. It must've been so scared.* "Okay. Maybe he'll get lucky there." *I just want this to be over.*

So gross! The Devourer wanted me to eat that pork. He wanted me to eat the souls of his victims. He knows who I am. He knows where I live.

He's coming for me. But he won't get me. Not as long as Josh and I are together. If we could only figure out who the Devourer is.

"They're gone, right? Folau and the fingerprint woman?"

"Yeah. I felt like I was rushing them, but there was no way I was going to make you wait, no way I'd leave you alone."

"I'd have been okay. Trevor, Bjorn, and Eli would've all stuck around 'til you got there. And I have my broom and my gun. And my blasts."

He shook his head. "I would've left Folau at the apartment and told him to lock up if I had to. Or kicked him and the other detective out." He paused. "How was rehearsal? You guys going to be ready?"

Tabitha sighed. "You know, I think we are. It's been great to work with so many good people. I got to see my makeup tonight. I look so creepy! Costumes are done. Props are done. They even got that silly bat flying outside Lucy's window to look pretty convincing. Sets will be done by tomorrow night, at least. The paint will still be wet on some of the flats, but that's okay. Even the lighting's all set. Tech rehearsal is tomorrow. Then two dress rehearsals Wednesday and Thursday."

He took her hand again, starting the Power flowing once more. "And you open Friday. Can't wait. You're gonna knock 'em dead! Scare the pants off them."

"Yeah." *If the Devourer doesn't get me first.* "Knock 'em dead."

The ringing phone ripped Tabitha from sleep. She rolled over in bed, clawing desperately for the telephone in the darkness. *Don't wake the baby! Don't wake the baby!*

Josh was out of bed too, scrambling around the foot of the mattress, attempting to get to the ringing phone. "Bollocks!" he hissed. "Bollocks! Bollocks!"

After the third jarringly shrill ring, Tabitha finally managed to lift the handset off the hook. She glanced at the luminescent hands of the alarm clock—not quite 3:00 a.m. She put the handset to her ear just as Joseph in the outer room let loose with a scream sure to freeze the blood of any parent.

"I'll get him," Josh said as he yanked open the door to the living room.

"H-hello?" Tabitha said into the phone. Then she heard the wailing on the other end of the line—the heart-wrenching sobbing of a small child.

"Auntie T-Tabitha?" said a little girl's voice.

Tabitha recognized the voice instantly—Stacy Montrose, Mikey and J.L.'s oldest daughter—barely five years old. Terror ripped through Tabitha like a serrated blade of ice. "Stacy?"

"Auntie Tabitha!" the girl howled, forcing Tabitha to pull the phone back from her ear.

"What's wrong, sweetie?" Tabitha asked as the light from the living room burst through the doorway. Tabitha fought to calm her own breathing as her heart threatened to jump out of her throat. "Stacy, sweetie, what's wrong?"

Joseph's screams quieted, and Tabitha could hear Josh making soothing noises to their infant son.

"Mommy won't wake up!" Stacy wailed. "I tried and tried and tried. But she won't w-wake up!" The girl sobbed. "I'm scared!"

Josh entered from the living room, gently bouncing the baby as he held the boy against his chest. Josh's eyes were wide with concern. He flipped on the bedroom light. He mouthed, "Who is it?"

Tabitha said, "Stacy, where's your daddy?"

"Daddy won't wake up! He's in the kitchen. He's on the floor. He won't wake up!"

"Okay, sweetie." She locked eyes with her husband and cupped her hand over the phone's receiver. "Mikey and J.L. are unconscious. Passed out, maybe. Stacy's—" Tabitha uncapped the phone. "Stacy, where's Marie? Where's your little sister?"

"Marie's scared too!"

Tabitha suddenly became aware of the three-year-old howling in the background through the phone. "Okay, Stacy, sweetie. I know you're scared."

Josh laid the baby on the bed, then hurriedly pulled on his jeans and a t-shirt.

Joseph began to cry again.

Tabitha covered the phone. "I'm coming too."

Josh opened his mouth to protest, then shut it again with a nod. "Hurry."

"Stacy, listen to me," Tabitha said as she bolted out of bed. "I'm coming over—me and Uncle Josh." She closed her eyes as if attempting to shut out the increasingly loud wailing of her own baby. "Where are you, sweetie? What room?"

"Mommy and daddy's room. I'm scared! I'm so scared!"

"I'm going to call the police, sweetie. They'll come too. And Bishop Smith. But until I get there, you take Marie, and you go into Mommy and Daddy's bathroom and shut the door. Lock it. Do you know how to lock the door?"

"I'm not supposed to lock the door!" the child cried. "I don' wanna be in trouble."

Josh handed Tabitha one of her long skirts, a t-shirt, and a bra. Tabitha nodded to him in acknowledgement. "Listen, Stacy, you won't be in trouble. Just take Marie and lock the door and don't open it for anybody. Except me or Uncle Josh. Or Bishop Smith. Okay? Can you do that, Stacy? I need you to be a big girl and take your little sister into the bathroom and lock the door. Then I want you to hide in the bathtub behind the shower curtain. And try hard, try very hard to be quiet. Like little mice. Can you do that."

Stacy snuffled. "Okay."

"Good girl! What a good, brave, big girl you are. Now hang up and take Marie and hide. And lock the door."

"Okay. Bye-bye."

The phone clicked, and the line went dead, followed by the drone of the dial tone.

Tabitha handed the handset to Josh and took her son in her arms. "Call the bishop. He's only a block away." *He's a doctor.* "He can be there faster than the police or the ambulance."

Josh nodded. "Bishop first. Then nine-one-one. Got it!"

As Tabitha threw on her clothes, Josh grabbed the ward directory and looked up the bishop's number. Then he dialed the phone.

Tabitha gently bounced her screaming child. "I'll get my gun. And then, we're flying over there. I don't care if the whole world sees us."

Armed with a Glock, a diaper bag, and a smiling, happily gurgling baby, Tabitha and Josh touched down in front of the Montrose's home. Tabitha held ready her emergency key for Mikey and J.L.'s house, but she needn't have bothered.

And that was terrifying.

The front door stood wide open, gaping like the dark maw of some house-shaped beast, ready to swallow up intruders. Inside, all was black. And silent as a tomb.

The sound of pounding feet to their left, made both Tabitha and Josh jump. Still holding hands, they wheeled to face the danger, the Power surging as it rushed from Tabitha into Josh.

Bishop Smith dashed toward them, a black valise in his hand, panting like a racehorse. "Where—"

Josh held up a hand and the bishop halted a few paces away.

Tabitha put a finger to her lips, then she pointed to herself, then Josh, and then toward the door. Then she pointed at the bishop and held up her hand in a halting gesture. *We're going in first.*

Bishop Smith hesitated and then nodded.

Tabitha handed her son over to the bishop. She also handed the man her gun. She pointed to the safety switch. "Here's the safety," she whispered. She dropped the diaper bag at the older man's feet.

Bishop Smith nodded again as he held the baby with one hand and the semiautomatic in the other. Then Tabitha and Josh turned as one and silently strode into the dark house.

The flow of the Power was so strong, so sweet, it bordered on painful. *Almost at the threshold!* And Tabitha realized two things—they were prepared for almost anything, and Josh himself must be terrified if he was channeling that much of the Power without actually using it.

Tabitha took the lead. She knew the house well, silently guiding Josh through the blackness. As they entered the living room, Tabitha, flipped on the light switch. She hissed softly and shielded her eyes against the sudden glare. Josh used the Power to move curtains and furniture aside to be sure the room was clear of danger.

They saw no one.

They moved from the living room to the kitchen. A plastic bowl and a spilt box of Cheerio's lay on Mikey's normally immaculate kitchen floor. And so did J.L. He was sprawled and unmoving on the linoleum, clad in nothing but his underwear and a pair of checkered gray pajama pants. Beside him lay the shattered remnants of a syringe.

The Devourer! He was here! Maybe he still is.

For one brief moment, Tabitha almost went to J.L., to see if he was still breathing. But that wasn't the plan. That wasn't what she and Josh had agreed upon during their short flight over. Josh had said, "Secure the scene, eliminate any threat, make sure the girls are safe. Then we can attend to the adults."

The backdoor was latched. Locked from the inside. No intruder would be coming from that direction.

Tabitha was suddenly struck by her own calm.

Why aren't I scared? I should be peeing my—

Focus! Find the girls!

They moved on, leaving J.L. alone, his fate unknown. They opened each door and flipped on the lights as they progressed down the hall. Josh used the Power to open each closet and lift each bed, looking for anyone hiding, and still they saw no one. They skipped the attic, but Tabitha well knew that the overhead door squeaked loudly whenever it was pulled down. They'd hear anyone attempting to descend from there.

They had saved the master bedroom for last.

Mikey lay face-up on the bed, still in her nightgown, her blank eyes staring at the ceiling, her mouth agape. She had not flinched when the lights had come on.

Josh opened the closet with the Power, rifled through the hanging clothes, and lifted the bed with Mikey still on it. No one was concealed in the closet or beneath the bed. Josh settled the bed back to the floor.

Mikey had not moved. Not at all.

She could be dead. They could both be dead.

Tabitha led Josh to the master bathroom door. She called softly, "Stacy? Marie? It's Auntie Tabitha. You can open the door now."

Silence.

Tabitha shuddered. *No! Not the girls!* "Stacy? Marie?"

The lock clicked, and then the door opened a crack. A single wide eye appeared below the door latch. "Auntie Tabitha?"

"Auntie Tabah!" cried a second childish voice.

The door flew open, and two sobbing little girls threw themselves at her.

Tabitha let go of Josh's hand—though the Power continued to flow—and scooped Mikey's daughters into her arms. "I've got you. You're safe!"

"I got up to get a drink," Stacy sobbed. "Daddy's on the floor! He won't wake up!"

Marie screamed. "Mommy, wake up! Wake up, Mommy! Pwease, Mommy!"

Josh left the room, calling out for the bishop.

"Make Mommy wake up, Auntie Tabitha!" Stacy wailed. "Please! Please, Auntie Tabitha!"

Bishop Smith stormed into the room without Joseph in his arms.

"Bishop!" Tabitha cried.

But Josh was on the doctor's heels, with Joseph held tight and safe.

Doctor Smith stood at the bedside. He placed two fingers at Mikey's neck.

"Mommy!" wailed both little girls.

"Your mommy's gonna be okay," the bishop said. "She's got a pulse." He bent, lowering his ear until it hovered right above Mikey's pale lips.

Tabitha realized with a start that she had never, ever seen Mikey without lipstick. Or makeup. *Makeup? Who cares about her makeup?*

"Breathing's shallow, slow," said the doctor as he dug in his black bag. He pulled out a syringe and a small, glass bottle. He uncapped the needle and stuck it into the inverted bottle. "Naloxone. Counteracts that opiate you told me about." He withdrew the needle, keeping it pointing up. He pushed lightly on the plunger while tapping the syringe until fluid leaked out of the needle's tip.

The doctor jabbed the needle into Mikey's shoulder and depressed the plunger. "Come on, Mikey. Come on." His calm voice belied the intensity of his stare.

Mikey gasped and her eyelids fluttered.

"Mommy!" cried the two little girls together. They wriggled out of Tabitha's arms and scrambled onto the bed.

Dr. Smith nodded, but to Tabitha it seemed as if his head were sagging in relief. "Stay with her." He recapped the needle and grabbed his bag. "I'll see to J.L." He hurried out of the room.

Tabitha turned to Josh. She so wanted to hold her baby, to keep him safe, but at that moment Mikey and Stacy and Marie needed her. "Go with him, Josh. Hold onto it." *Hold onto the Power. Keep our son safe.*

Josh nodded and followed the doctor, carrying Joseph, while the Power continued to flow.

Mikey tried to sit up, but her daughters flung themselves against her, pushing her back down. "Mommy! Mommy!" they cried.

Mikey screamed.

The Power fluctuated, almost cutting off. *Hold onto it, Josh!* Tabitha was at her friend's side in an instant. Tabitha grasped Mikey's trembling hand.

"The clown!" Mikey's wide, terrified eyes darted around the room. "He's here!"

The Devourer was here. "It's okay," Tabitha said. "You're safe." She glanced around the shadows, looking for a hooded shape.

Stacy and Marie were screaming again, pulling back from their mother, reaching in terror for Tabitha.

"Stacy! Marie!" Mikey sobbed. "I'm sorry! I didn't mean to— Come to Mommy."

"It's okay," Tabitha said. "Your Mommy's okay." She squeezed Mikey's hand. "He's gone. You're safe."

The little girls had reattached themselves to their mother. Both were crying and saying, "Mommy, are you okay?"

Still lying on the bed, Mikey held her daughters tight. "Mommy's okay. My babies! My sweet little girls! Are you okay?"

Stacy nodded. "I was so brave. Auntie Tabitha said take Marie and hide in the bathroom. Your bathroom, Mommy." Then she sobbed. "I locked the door! I'm s-sorry. Auntie Tabitha told me to!"

Mikey kissed Stacy's cheek. "You did the right thing, sweetie. You did the right thing." She kissed Marie's cheek as well. "You both did. You were both so brave." She looked up at Tabitha. "He—he didn't…"

Tabitha shook her head. "No. They're fine. Scared. But fine."

"J.L.!" Mikey struggled to sit up.

Tabitha tugged on Mikey's arm. "He's…" *You don't know. You don't know if J.L.'s okay.* "I'll go check."

"No! Don't leave—" Mikey shuddered and let go of Tabitha's hand. "Go! Go!"

Bishop Smith appeared in the doorway. "J.L.'s going to be just fine. He's breathing and sitting up. Josh is with him." He smiled at her, his white teeth gleaming in the darkness. He sat on the edge of the bed and took Mikey's pale hand in his dark one. He felt her pulse with the other hand. "How are you feeling?"

"I'm fine," Mikey said. "A little dizzy." Then her eyes fixed on Tabitha. "What are you doing here? Josh is here? What are you doing here?" Something was *off* about the way Mikey looked at her. Mikey's eyes were narrowed.

Is she suspicious? Jealous? "Stacy called me."

"I called Auntie Tabitha, Mommy!" Stacy said, beaming. "On the phone. Like you showed me. I was so brave."

Mikey nodded and kissed her daughter again. "Yes, you were. You were so brave."

"I was bwave too, Mommy!" Marie said. "Stacy say, 'No cwying.' An' I didn't cwy."

"Listen, Mikey," the bishop said. "In about thirty minutes or so, that injection I gave you will begin to wear off. You'll start to get very sleepy again. I'll stay here, or Maddie will. Because, when you fall asleep, someone needs to make sure you keep on *breathing*. I'll give you both follow-up injections as needed. You should be fine tomorrow."

"What about J.L.?" Mikey asked, obviously fighting down her panic, protecting her children. "Is J.L...." Her voice trailed off as if she couldn't bear to speak the words.

The doctor smiled again. "I told you—J.L. will be fine, too. He got lucky. It looks like he only got a partial dose. He fought the attacker. When he's up to walking, I'll get him in here." He patted her hand. "Now, if you'll excuse me, I'll go back and check on him again." He winked. "It looks like you're in good hands here."

Mikey nodded. "Thank you." Her body convulsed in a brief, but violent shudder. "I'm okay. Just take care of J.L." After the doctor left the room, Mikey managed a weak smile for her daughters. "And now, my brave girls, you need to go back to bed." She glanced at Tabitha.

"Tuck in, Mommy!" Marie looked as if she were about to burst into tears again. "Tuck in. Pwease?"

Mikey shook her head and smiled. "Auntie Tabitha will tuck you in. And then she'll come right back." Mikey's voice was calm, even as her eyes pleaded with Tabitha.

"Of course, I will." Tabitha stood and extended her hands to Stacy and Marie. "Come on, girls."

Tabitha took both children by the hand and led them from the bedroom. As the three of them moved down the hallway, Tabitha tried to catch a glimpse of what was going on in the kitchen. *I hope Joseph's alright. We had no choice but to bring him.* She listened for the sound of her own baby's crying, but she heard only J.L.'s voice.

"...behind. Stuck me. In the neck. Clown mask. Freaky. Hit him. Right in the face. Hope I broke his flippin'—"

"Daddy!" squealed two little voices. Two little hands jerked out of Tabitha's.

"Daddy!" they both squealed as they ran into the kitchen.

Tabitha gathered her skirt and scampered after Stacy and Marie.

When she entered the kitchen, she saw J.L. sitting on the floor, his back braced against a cabinet. He held his daughters and wept. "Stacy! Marie! My sweet girls!"

Bishop Smith knelt beside J.L. He held the end of a stethoscope aloft since he'd been interrupted by the arrival of the little.

Josh stood, holding Joseph. Josh's eyes flitted from entrance to entrance as if he were looking for danger. The Power still flowed.

The baby was looking around. As soon as his eyes lit on Tabitha, he reached for her. Josh's eyes locked on her a moment later. He wore a questioning expression, and Tabitha understood his unspoken question.

She nodded, Josh worked his way around to her and transferred the baby to her arms. Tabitha's eyes filled with tears as she held her son. *You're safe, Joseph. I'm sorry. We should never have flown with you. If anything had gone wrong…No! It was the only way to get here in time.*

Josh leaned down and whispered, "It's in the diaper bag. Safety's on."

Tabitha nodded and took the diaper bag from him, the bag uncharacteristically heavy with the added weight of the Glock. "What about you?"

He gave her a quick smile, and the Power surged. "I got you, babe."

"I was bwave, Daddy!" Marie declared with childish pride. "I didn't cwy at all! Stacy cwied. I saw." She shook her little head, her golden curls swirling.

"You did too cry!" Stacy said. "She was crying, Daddy. She was!"

J.L. laughed. "It's okay. It's okay to cry. You were scared. It's okay. It's okay to be scared. But you were brave, too. Both of you." He kissed each of them on the tops of their heads. "I'm sure you were. I love you so much! Is Mommy okay?"

Stacy nodded enthusiastically. "Mommy's okay. Bishop gave her a shot! An' she woked up." The child frowned. "I don't like shots."

J.L. stretched his neck and rotated his head as if recalling his own assault. "I don't like shots either. They hurt, don't they?"

"Uh-huh." Stacy nodded. "Shots hurt. Mommy was crying. I think the shot hurt her."

Marie shook her head. "I don' like shots!" Tears spilled from her eyes.

J.L. chuckled. "But this one made Mommy all better, didn't it?"

Marie wiped at a suddenly snotty nose. "Mommy all better now."

J.L. looked at Tabitha and then at the bishop. "Mikey's really okay? He didn't, you know, *hurt* her, did he?" The word carried with it horrible, dreaded implications.

He didn't rape her. The Devourer hasn't done that. But he's never attacked his victims inside a house before, either. "She's okay. She wants to see you."

"Sure." J.L. nodded. "Girls, let me up."

Stacy and Marie detached themselves from him, running immediately to Tabitha for safety. They attached themselves to her skirt.

J.L. began to get up, but the doctor put a restraining hand on his shoulder.

Dr. Smith smiled at him. "Give yourself a few minutes. I'll get you in there as soon as—"

The wail of a police siren shredded the night.

The bishop frowned and shook his head. "About dang time."

"Police?" J.L. asked. "You called the police?"

"I called them," Tabitha said.

J.L. nodded. "Oh, yeah. Course, you did." He took a few deep breaths, then shook his head, an expression of wonder on his face. "It's like I forgot how to breathe. Wow."

Still holding Joseph, Tabitha took Marie by the hand. "Come on, girls. Let's get you back to bed. Just like your mommy said."

The siren was getting louder. Another, more distant siren could be heard.

J.L. smiled at his daughters. "Nigh-night, girls. I love you."

"Nigh-night, Daddy," Stacy said.

Marie waved. "Nigh-Nigh."

Tabitha led them away, toward the girls' room. As she went, she heard Josh say, "I'll wait for the cops outside."

She felt a slight increase of the Power, but she took no pleasure in it. She was worried about her husband.

Heavenly Father, I know we called the police. I know we want them to be here, but please don't let Josh get hurt. Please, please, don't let Josh get hurt.

Don't let the police mistake him for the Devourer.

Don't let them shoot him.

The Power surged, and she added, *Don't let Josh hurt* them.

After some internal debate, Josh had decided to hold his hands over his head. *Might look like I'm surrendering, but at least it won't look like I'm a threat. Even if I could be.*

He stood on the front lawn, his hands held high as the first squad car approached, sirens blaring and red-and-blue lights flashing. He could hear a second police vehicle getting close as well.

The siren cut off abruptly as the black-and-white car stopped in front of J.L. and Mikey's house. A uniformed police officer quickly exited his vehicle and crouched behind it, gun levelled at Josh. "Provo Police!" the cop shouted. "Keep your hands where I can see them!"

"I am." Josh kept his voice calm, but spoke loudly and clearly. "I was the one who called you." He focused on the sidearm, ready to force the barrel away with the Power. "We're all safe inside."

"On your knees!" the policeman commanded.

Bollocks! Better just do as he says. He knelt, never lowering his hands, and never taking his eyes off the weapon.

A second police car screeched to a halt in front of the house, and a second officer climbed out of his vehicle. In moments, Josh had two guns aimed at his chest.

Bollocks! This is not good.

"Are you okay, sir?" said the newcomer. In contrast to the inquiry after Josh's well-being, the second cop kept his gun aimed at Josh's heart.

I could stop one of them, but probably not both. Not before one of them shoots. "I'd be a lot better if you weren't about to shoot me."

"Put your hands on your head," said the second officer. "Interlace your fingers."

I'm one of the good guys, dang it! But Josh complied. His palms were sweating, his heart racing. "We have injured people inside, little kids, and my baby. I'm the one who called you," he repeated, as the first officer approached, gun still pointed at him.

The second cop holstered his weapon and produced a set of handcuffs. "Don't move."

A third vehicle, with a small red-and-blue flashing light perched above the driver-side window, stopped in front of the house. Josh recognized the car. A man in jeans and a sweatshirt emerged. He carried a sidearm and a flashlight, and Josh had never been so glad to see him. "Folau! Can you tell them I'm not the bad guy?"

The scarred detective shined his flashlight in Josh's eyes. "Kilmore?"

"That's me."

"It's okay, guys," Folau said. "I know this guy. Stand down."

Both officers stopped where they were. Weapons were lowered, and the officer with handcuffs took a step back.

"Kilmore," Folau said, "is the house secure?"

Josh nodded. "Yeah. We checked everywhere." He paused. "Except the attic. You should check there."

"Detective Folau," said the first cop, "he said there are injured people inside. Do I call an ambulance?"

Josh said, "We have a doctor inside. Everyone's okay. The intruder injected them on the neck. But Dr. Smith took care of them. They're okay. They're awake, at least. The kids are okay." He paused, a sheepish grin on his face. "Uh, can I get up now?"

"Is Tabitha here with you?"

Something about the detective's question, something in the man's tone, caught Josh's attention. "Yeah, and so is my son."

Folau looked at him askance. "You brought your baby?" Then he nodded. "Of course, you did." Folau holstered his weapon and then offered Josh his hand. "What else could you do in the middle of the night?"

Josh took the hand, and Folau helped Josh to his feet. "Secure the house," he said to the uniformed cops. "Check the attic for sure. There are kids inside. Try not to scare them."

"Yes, Detective," said both officers at once. They approached the open door from opposite sides, weapons drawn. "Provo Police!"

Folau rubbed at his jaw as he eyed Josh. "You think this was our guy?"

Josh nodded. "Yeah. Clown mask. Syringes."

"Syringes? Plural?"

"Two of them, I think. He broke one when he drugged J.L.—you know, the husband? So, he must've had another one to drug Mikey. You've met Mikey, right?"

Folau nodded, grimaced, and rubbed his jaw. "I know Mikey. She was there when Tabitha did her first reading for me. She's okay, right?"

Tabitha or Mikey? "Mikey's okay. He didn't take her."

Folau shook his head and grunted. "Yeah. That doesn't fit. Why enter the house and not take the victim?"

The second officer to arrive on scene exited the front door. "All clear, Detective. Two adult males, two adult females, three children inside, one infant. We checked the attic." He grinned. "And we didn't scare the kids."

"Good work, Drake. Have Jenkins take up station in the backyard. I want you in the front. Tell dispatch to get another detective over here with a fingerprint kit."

"You got it." Officer Drake reentered the house.

Folau went up to the front door, with Josh following, and shined his flashlight around the doorframe. "No sign of forced entry."

Josh nodded. "Yeah. J.L. thinks he must've left the door unlocked."

Folau scowled. "Maybe. Hm." He shook his head. "Just doesn't fit the M.O. Good thing your wife is here."

"Why?"

"Because she can do a reading. She's the only one who has a chance of telling me if this is our guy or just a copycat."

Josh swallowed hard. "Makes sense. She'll do it, but she's not going to like it. And Mikey won't be happy either."

"Mikey wants to catch this guy, right?"

Josh shrugged. "Yeah. I guess you're right."

Folau nodded, rubbed his jaw again, and hissed.

"What's wrong?"

Folau shook his head angrily. "I don't know. Everything. Something's not right here." He growled. "And on top of all that, when the flippin' radio woke me up, I fell out of the dang bed. Clonked my jaw good on the nightstand. *Real* good."

Josh's eyes snapped to the detective's jaw, at the scar. And in the light streaming through the doorway, Josh could see the red discoloration of a large, fresh bruise forming around the base of the pale, jagged scar.

J.L.'s words reared up in his mind—

Hit him. Right in the face. Hope I broke his flippin'—

Folau growled, then he chuckled. "'Bout broke my dang jaw."

Tabitha stared at the cast-iron skillet in Folau's hand. To her, the dark cooking pan reminded her of a black cobra, hood flared, fangs bared, and ready to strike or spit venom in her face.

Tabitha, Josh, and Folau, with Joseph asleep on his blanket on the floor, sat in Mikey and J.L.'s living room. Tabitha and Josh were on the sofa. Josh had his arm firmly and protectively around Tabitha's shoulders. Folau sat in a chair borrowed from the dining room. He held out the dreaded iron object.

I'm sorry, Mikey, Tabitha thought.

Mikey had sobbed when she'd given permission for Tabitha to attempt the vision. J.L. was with Mikey at that point, sitting beside her on their bed, holding her as she wept. J.L. obviously hadn't understood what Folau was asking for, or why.

But Mikey had. Mikey had known exactly what was coming. She had hesitated for a moment, then she'd told the detective where to find the skillet. Mikey had hidden it away so Tabitha wouldn't be able to find or touch it. Not even accidentally.

Mikey had given her permission, reluctantly, to do the reading. Tabitha was about to access Mikey's memories and her privacy.

I'm so sorry.

Tabitha braced herself mentally and physically. She glanced once more at the darkening bruise on Folau's scarred cheek. She tried to not focus on the possibilities the bruise implied. She and Josh had briefly and quietly discussed those implications well out of Folau's earshot.

Danny is not the Devourer. He's not. Can you be so sure? How did he get here so quickly?

She extended her hands for the skillet. "Okay, do it."

Folau put the iron into her hands and the world dissolved to memory.

She drew the brush through the golden waves of her hair as she sat in front of the vanity mirror. The loose curls still had some bounce to them, but not as much as she'd like. She pursed her lips in consternation. "I need a new perm," she said, "and a trim. I'll call tomorrow and make an appointment."

Lying on the bed, still fully clothed, and reading his scriptures, J.L. groaned. "Another perm? Can it wait at least until after Tabitha's show?"

She tried not to roll her eyes at the mention of her best friend. "That'll be almost two more weeks. I'm not sure my hair will last that long."

In the mirror, she could see him shaking his head and scowling. He snapped his Quadruple Combination closed and pressed his head back into the pillow. "It's gonna stink! I hate that dang ammonia smell. And during the show. It'll be so distracting."

She blinked her eyes rapidly. I will not cry. I will not cry! At least she'd washed her face for bed. At least her mascara wouldn't run.

J.L. sighed and got out of bed. He came over and stood behind her. Gently, he took the brush from her and began brushing her hair.

Warmth spread through her, along with a surge of affection. "That feels nice. Thank you." She smiled up at him.

He smiled as well, but he didn't meet her eyes—his gaze was focused on her hair. The brush strokes went all the way down to the ends of her tresses, a good six inches below her shoulders. "Why don't you just let it grow out long?"

She arched a well-plucked eyebrow. "How long do you want it to get? I thought you liked the Farrah Fawcett look."

He shrugged as he continued to stroke the brush through her hair. "I don't know. Just longer. And maybe straighter."

She stiffened. "Maybe I should dye it raven black too, huh?" Angry tears spilled from her eyes. "Would that make me acceptable?"

He dropped the hairbrush on the vanity. "Don't you even start." He stomped toward the door. "I gotta go to the office for a bit. Take the end-of-shift reports. Don't bother waiting up."

He didn't slam the bedroom door—not exactly—and yet there was anger in the sound as he closed it.

She folded her arms across the vanity, bowed her head, and sobbed.

Tabitha dropped the heavy skillet to the floor. She turned and buried her face in Josh's shoulder, now sobbing herself.

Why didn't I pull out of that one? I'm sorry, Mikey!

Josh pulled her close, enveloping her in his strength. One of his hands found hers. The Power flowed, comforting her, filling her with warmth.

"I'm sorry," he whispered.

"What did you see?" Folau asked, picking up the fallen pan. "Was it—"

Tabitha shook her head and turned her face toward him. "Nothing. It was private." *I'm so sorry, Mikey! I'm so sorry! For everything.*

Folau handed her a Kleenex, and Tabitha wiped at her eyes and then at her nose. "Are you sure? If it'll help the investigation—"

"She said it was private," Josh snapped. "Leave it alone."

Tabitha stuffed the used tissue in her skirt pocket. Turned back toward the detective. *You are not the Devourer. You can't be.*

Wordlessly, she extended her hands for the skillet once more. Folau nodded. He placed the horrible iron in her hands again.

Her eyes snapped open to darkness.

Above her loomed the face of madness. A lunatic clown face surrounded by a hood. Sharp white teeth had been painted over the mouth of the mask.

She tried to move, to scramble away, but her muscles wouldn't obey her.

She opened her mouth to scream, but a gloved hand clamped down on it, smothering her. A strong, acrid scent assailed her nostrils.

"Bitch!" screeched the clown, though the vinyl face didn't move. The voice was high-pitched. "Pathetic bitch! Not strong enough! Why the hell aren't you strong enough?"

Another gloved hand appeared, bearing a hypodermic syringe. The needle glinted in the dim light coming through the bedroom window.

She tried to get a hand up, to defend herself. No! Stop!

She felt the jab of the needle in her neck.

And with that sharp pain, she was able to move, to squirm, but she couldn't breathe. She couldn't pull air into her lungs.

The insane clown face, all whites and reds and blues, bent closer to hers. "You're worthless! Worthless bitch! Not even a damn morsel!"

Heavenly Father! Don't let him hurt my babies. Please! Stacy and—

The darkness consumed her.

Tabitha dropped the skillet to the floor. "My babies! Don't hurt my babies!" Sobs wracked her body.

Josh held her tight as she trembled. He also clasped her hand. The Power flowed through her.

"I've got you," he cooed. "The baby's okay. Still asleep."

Tabitha shook her head. "Mikey's babies. Stacy and Marie."

"They're safe too," Josh said. "We're all safe."

"What did you see?" Folau said.

Tabitha eyed the detective, her eyes flickering to his scar. And to the bruise. "It's him. The Devourer." She met Folau's eyes. "He was here. No copycat. It was the same mask. With the teeth." *But did you know that already?*

Are you *the Devourer?*

Folau's lips were drawn in a tight, thin line. He nodded. "Okay." Then he shook his head. "It just doesn't fit."

Tabitha opened her mouth to protest, but he raised a hand.

"No, I believe you," he said. "But if he's entering homes now… And he left his victim behind. Assaulted the husband first. But… he left her behind. He's deviating, escalating, building up to something. Something big." He shook his head. "But he left

217

her behind. Why? What am I missing?"

You can't be the Devourer.

The lady doth protest too much, methinks.

No! Danny is not the killer!

Stop it! Stop calling him Danny! *He's Folau! Folau!*

But he's not the killer. He's not.

Tabitha swallowed. "He called her worthless. Said she wasn't even a-a-a morsel."

Josh twitched. "Like she wasn't *strong* enough?"

Tabitha locked eyes with her husband. *Strong enough? As in, with the Power? You said Mikey wasn't strong. Not strong at all in the Power.*

"She wasn't afraid?" Folau asked. "This guy feeds on fear, right? A woman's fear?"

"Maybe it's not fear." Tabitha had said it slowly, considering each word. *Not fear. He's feeding on the Power. And if he takes it all from a woman...*

A frown creased Folau's face, causing his scar to twitch. "What are you talking about? What is it?"

The Power.

But as much as you know... or suspect, *Folau, I'm not going to talk to you about the Power.*

But then another detail popped into her head. "Ammonia!"

"What?" asked both Josh and Folau at once.

"Ammonia!" she repeated. "His gloves stank. Like ammonia."

Folau blinked. "His gloves smelled like ammonia?"

Tabitha nodded. "Yeah. Other things too. Leather, maybe? Oh, I don't know what else. But I definitely smelled ammonia."

Folau cursed softly.

"What does that mean?" Josh asked. "Ammonia?"

Folau cursed again. "Ammonia." He growled and shook his head. "It doesn't fit the profile! You don't switch from serial killer to mass—" He fixed Tabitha with an intense stare. "Tabitha, do you know what fertilizer smells like?"

It was Tabitha's turn to blink in confusion. "Fertilizer? You mean, like manure?" She shuddered as she thought of the horrid, flesh-eating pigs. "It didn't smell like that exactly." *But it did too, sort of.*

Folau shook his head. "No, I mean, like in a farm supply or hardware store. You know, commercial fertilizer?"

Tabitha shook her head. "I don't think so."

"Why?" asked Josh.

Folau turned his intense stare on Josh. "Ammonium nitrate. Commercial fertilizer. Smells like ammonia. It takes a lot of the stuff, but if you combine it with diesel and provide a spark, it explodes."

The blood froze in Tabitha's veins. "Explodes?"

Folau's jaw clenched. "Big time. He *is* building up to something big. Something *really* big. I think he's making a bomb."

Folau was waiting for him.

Josh was hurrying out of the Marriott Center parking lot when he spied the detective. Josh had just completed his AFROTC Lab—a class which, on that day and for the last few weeks, had consisted of practicing for a "pass-in-review." This basically amounted to a lot of marching and, in Josh's case, commanding other cadets in that marching. Josh was hurrying to get to his next class, and stopping to talk to Folau meant he'd be late. If Josh walked into class late while wearing a military uniform, it would draw extra attention. It reflected badly, not just on himself, but on the Air Force as a whole.

What are you doing here, Folau? Can't it wait?

The detective wasn't hard to miss. Folau's avocado-colored sedan was the solitary vehicle in the otherwise empty parking lot. Folau slouched against his car at the southwest corner of the parking lot. The car had been strategically placed so every cadet returning to campus would have to walk past it.

While the other cadets parted around the K-car like the Red Sea, Josh walked right up to Folau.

The bruise on Folau's scarred cheek had bloomed and darkened. It consisted of a variety of nasty-looking hues, from green to purple to black, with the pale scar slicing up from the center. The detective smirked. "Looking sharp out there."

Josh couldn't tell if the man was mocking him or not. He didn't really care. "You know, you're not supposed to park here. It's reserved for the Air Force."

Folau shrugged. "It's not federal property. And I'm pretty sure I could pull rank on you, cadet."

Josh set his book bag on the ground. "Pull rank, huh?" He pointed to Folau's cheek. "That looks pretty bad."

Folau reached up and gingerly prodded the bruise with his finger. "Nasty, isn't it?" The pale scar twitched. "I know what you're thinking."

That you're the Devourer, Folau? A part of me wants you to be. A part of me I really don't like.

"You think I'm the killer, don't you?"

Josh said nothing.

Folau growled softly. "You said Montrose told you he hit the perp in the face. He told me the same thing when I interviewed him."

Josh's eyes flickered to the bruise and the scar, then back to the detective's eyes. "Well, you were there awfully quick last night."

"I only live—" Folau scowled, then shook his head. "Aw, to tell you the truth, I don't blame you. I'd suspect me too."

That's not an admission. But is it a diversion?

"So," Josh said, cautiously drawing out the one-syllable word, "where does that leave us right now?"

"Think about it for just a second, will you?" The annoyance in the detective's voice was evident. "Your friend is right-handed, right?"

Josh nodded. "Yeah. So?" But Josh knew where Folau was going. *Just like Tabitha said last night when she defended you.*

"Odds are he'd have struck his assailant on the left side of the face." Folau pointed to his discolored cheek. "Right side, see?"

"Yeah. Okay." Josh cocked an eyebrow and sighed. "And just when I thought I had you." *Don't be a jerk, Josh, old man. I'm just trying to protect my wife!*

"Besides," said Folau, "I got an alibi." He gave Josh a smirk. "But that's what every perp says, right?"

"Let me guess. You were in bed with your girlfriend all night. She'll swear to it, right?"

Folau's head jerked as if he'd been struck.

Josh groaned. "Aw, crap. Look, man. That was awful. I'm sorry." He rubbed his temples. "Last night with no sleep. I'm sorry. No excuse."

Folau rubbed at his own temples—or perhaps at his eyes. "It was a rough night. For everybody."

"Especially Mikey and J.L. And their little girls."

"Yeah, it was. Just for the record, I don't have a girlfriend. There hasn't been anybody since my wife. Since Julie." He cleared his throat. "And even if I did have a girlfriend, I wouldn't betray Julie by breaking my own temple covenants." A tear threatened at the corner of his eye.

"Man, I'm really sorry." *Doesn't mean you're not the killer.* "That was a lousy thing of me to say." For one moment, Josh considered giving the man a hug, but he quickly dismissed the impulse.

Folau nodded and turned his face away, hiding his bruise. "Apology accepted. We're all on edge. Things are getting worse. But to alleviate at least some of your suspicions, I have an alibi--not for the home invasion and the assaults, but for the fertilizer, at least."

That got Josh's attention. "You know something?"

Folau turned his face back to Josh. "Uh-huh. A couple things. We got a report of a break-in at an agriculture supply warehouse last night. The perp was caught on tape, on the security footage. He was wearing a hood and a clown mask." Folau waved a hand in dismissal. "Before you ask, I was working late, going over the fingerprint report on that care package you received. So, at the time of the break-in, I was working."

A sudden wave of nausea threatened as Josh remembered the tainted pork. "Do you"—he swallowed down bile—"know who it was?"

Folau grimaced and shook his head. "Naw. That's more bad news. Only usable prints on the paper were mine, yours, and Mr. Montrose's, and I saw you both handle it with my own eyes. We also know the meat didn't come from Dr. or Mrs. Smith—their prints were all over the rest of the stuff, but not on the butcher paper. They denied adding the sausage. So, it was definitely planted by our guy. Only he must've used gloves."

"Bollocks!" *So much for that.*

"My sentiments exactly." Folau scowled. "So that's a dead end. But the security tape caught him. Couldn't see the vehicle—just him. Carrying big bags of fertilizer."

"So, what does that tell us?"

"Not much about him. It just confirms that he took the stuff. The mask says it was him. Unless he has an accomplice. Not likely, but we've still got to consider the possibility." He sighed. "An accomplice doesn't fit the profile. Then again, neither does a flippin' home invasion. Or attacking the husband. Or leaving the vic behind. Or making a dang bomb. Serial killers aren't usually mass murderers, too." He shook his head. "Can you imagine if there were two of this guy? Man-oh-man-oh-man! Anyway, I thought you ought to know." He paused, and his eyes flickered to Josh's and then away. "You'll, uh, tell Tabitha, right?"

Josh nodded. "Yeah." *That's it, Folau. Keep your distance. Even if you're not the killer, I still don't want you hanging around my wife. Not when you're in love with her.*

Folau gave his chin a thoughtful scratch. "I noticed you two got there awful quick. I actually live closer than you. Different ward and stake, but closer."

Josh forced himself to unclench his jaw. "The little girl called us. And we called the police. That's what brought you there."

Folau nodded. He tilted his head to the side and looked at Josh. "But I noticed there was no yellow Volkswagen out front."

Bollocks.

"And?"

Folau straightened his head and shrugged. "Just observing. That's my job, you know—observe. Gather clues. Piece together conclusions." One corner of his mouth lifted in the hint of a smile. "What I wouldn't give to see the two of you flying."

I bet. "Any luck on finding the fertilizer? The bomb?"

Folau chuckled softly. "Nice change of subject." Then he grimaced and shook his head. "Nope. Not yet."

"How much of the stuff was stolen?"

Folau frowned. "Forty fifty-pound sacks. Two-thousand pounds. A ton. Which also tells us the thief has access to a truck of some kind. Anyway, it's enough to bring down any building in town, even the Kimball Tower on campus. If you put it in the right place, that is. Down in the basement, near the center or the central supports."

Josh couldn't suppress a shudder. "Wow."

"I mean, I'm no demolitions expert. But with that much, you wouldn't have to be. Just have to make sure you don't blow yourself up in the process. But even an amateur could take down an entire building."

"Horseshoes and nuclear weapons."

Folau scowled at him. "What's that?"

Josh shook his head. "Old joke. Dumb joke. 'Close only counts in horseshoes and nuclear weapons.'"

"Wow, man. That's dark."

This coming from a guy who might be a serial killer? "Yeah."

Josh picked up his book bag. "Look, I gotta get to Russian class."

Folau raised an eyebrow. "Russian? Learn the language before you blow them all to kingdom come?"

Are you the guy planning to blow someone to kingdom come? "Just want to understand them. I hope and pray it never comes to that—to actually using the bomb, that is."

Folau shrugged. "Never saw the point in making a bomb you don't intend to use. Our guy sure as heck is going to use his bomb." He growled, shaking his head. "Even if it doesn't fit the dang profile."

"I gotta go." Josh began to walk around Folau's green Chrysler K-car.

"Hey, uh, do me a favor, will you?"

Josh turned back. "How can I help?"

Folau met his eyes. The detective's eyes looked haunted—and not just from sleep-deprivation. "You'll tell her about . . . my alibi. Tell her it wasn't me." He swallowed. "Please?"

Josh hesitated for just a moment. Then he nodded. "You bet. For what it's worth, Tabitha and I discussed it at length . . . after we . . . left the Montrose's house. In spite of that"—Josh gestured at the detective's bruise.—"she, *we,* don't think it's you." *Mostly not.*

A tear spilled from Folau's eye. He nodded, and his scar with the bruise twitched. "Thanks. Hey, uh, can I give you a ride? To class? Or somewhere close?"

Josh smiled. "Yeah. That'd be great. It is at the other end of campus."

As he scurried to the passenger side of the car, Josh prayed.

Please, Heavenly Father, help us catch the killer. I think this man is a good man. I hope he's a good man. But help me to know for sure.

But if he is the killer, please let me know. Help me keep Tabitha safe.

Is Folau the Devourer?

Josh tried to listen for an answer, but none came.

"Tabitha?"

Tabitha recognized the voice of Dr. Engelhard. Tabitha stopped as she'd been scuttling toward the southern exit of the Harris Fine Arts Center. She turned and smiled. "Dr. Daisy!"

The slightly heavy and terminally cheerful theatre professor hurried to catch up to her. Dr. Daisy waved. "I'm so glad I caught you! I meant to talk to you after class this morning, but I got cornered by another student."

As the professor, her breathing slightly labored, halted in front of her, Tabitha realized the woman must have been chasing her all the way from the other end of the building, probably ascending two flights of stairs to boot. "What's up?"

Dr. Daisy opened her mouth to speak, then shut it. She sighed. "Are you okay? You seem a little *off* today."

Tabitha blinked at her. *Off? Yeah. Exhausted. Drained.* "Sure, I guess. Just tired. I didn't get much sleep last night."

Dr. Daisy gave her a smile that radiated sympathy as she put a hand on Tabitha's shoulder. "That cute baby keeping you up at night?"

Tabitha resisted the temptation to roll her eyes. *If only that were the problem.* "No. I was attending to a friend in need."

"In the middle of the night?"

Tabitha hesitated, and then nodded. "Yeah."

"Oh, you poor thing." Then the woman gasped. She withdrew her hand from Tabitha's shoulder. She looked at Tabitha curiously, her lips pursing in concern. "It wasn't. No, of course not."

"What? Wasn't what?"

Dr. Daisy shook her head and waved a dismissive hand. "Nothing. I was being silly."

Tabitha shook her head. "Silly? I don't—"

"It's just what they've been talking about on the news—this serial killer out there. I'm scared."

Tabitha swallowed before replying. "Yeah. We're all scared."

"Besides, if he'd already got you, you wouldn't be here, right?" The professor giggled nervously. "To talk to now, right? But we're safe during the day, right? And at home. We're safe at home. Just don't go out alone." In spite of her words, the normally ebullient lady appeared to be genuinely frightened, and that was an emotion Tabitha had never seen in her favorite professor, at least off-stage.

Tabitha wanted to say something reassuring, but after the events of the previous night, she just couldn't. She shook her head. "There was another attack last night."

Daisy Engelhard put a hand to her lips, covering a mouth suddenly wide in shock. "No!"

"No one was killed," Tabitha added quickly. "But my friend and her husband were both attacked last night in their home. That's where I was. Helping them."

The color drained from Dr. Daisy's face. She glanced around as if hooded and masked killers might be hiding anywhere in the building. "Your friend?"

Tabitha nodded.

"But she's okay? She wasn't hurt? She called you?"

"Actually, her five-year-old daughter did. Called me, that is. I babysit for them and—"

"A child called you?"

"Yeah."

"Was she hurt? The little girl? Was she hurt?"

"No. No. They're okay. They're all okay. Just scared. Really scared." Tabitha took Dr. Daisy by the hand and drew her aside, toward a wall. It wouldn't be exactly private, but at least they wouldn't be in the middle of the cavernous building. "Nobody was hurt. Not bad, at least. My friend and her husband were drugged, but the killer left them alive."

"Oh, thank heavens!"

Tabitha nodded. "They were lucky." *He said Mikey was worthless. Not even a morsel.*

But at least she's alive.

"And that's where you were last night?"

"Yeah. After the fact, it was a really long night." Tabitha stifled a yawn.

The professor threw her arms around Tabitha, holding her tight. "You poor thing!" She pulled out of the bear hug and held Tabitha at arms-length. "I would tell you to go home and get some rest, but I know you've got the show. You open tomorrow!"

Tabitha's nod was interrupted by another huge yawn. "Excuse me!"

"You must really be worn out. I keep saying that." She chuckled. "I'm coming Saturday night." Then she quickly added, "With my husband, of course. I won't be alone."

None of us are safe. Not even in our own homes. Not even if we're not alone. "Okay, but be careful. Lock your doors."

Dr. Daisy nodded. "I do. I will. You be careful, too. Never be alone. Especially after rehearsal tonight. Not 'til they catch this monster. Promise me?"

Tabitha nodded. "I promise." *The Devourer's coming for me. I know he is.* "I'm never alone after rehearsal. A couple of the men in the production always walk us ladies to our cars. Including Dr. Thorpe."

The professor's eyes went wide with shock. "Dr. Thorpe!"

Tabitha nodded and gave the woman a puzzled frown. "Yeah. He's in the show. You know he is. He's Dracula."

Dr. Daisy glanced around, again as if looking for dark figures in masks and hoods. "Didn't you hear? Oh, I thought for sure you knew. It's all over the department."

Tabitha blinked at her in confusion. "Knew what?"

After another glance around, Dr. Daisy leaned toward her and whispered, "Eli Thorpe was in the emergency room early this morning."

It was Tabitha's turn to cover her mouth. "No! Is he okay?"

Dr. Daisy nodded, but her expression told a different tale. "He was attacked last night. Mugged."

Tabitha grabbed for the woman's hand. "Is he okay?"

"I think so. They released him a little while ago, and he came straight to work. He may've gotten beat up, but if I know Eli—and I do—he probably gave as good as he got. He may look older than sin and as boney as a skeleton, but Eli's tough. And a lot stronger than he looks. Other than a few bruises, I'm sure he'll be okay. Did you know he fences? Of course, you do. Any decent Shakespearean actor knows how to fence. Anyway, he's got quite a shiner, though. A huge black eye. Lucky it's not swollen shut. Says he'll be okay." She lowered the pitch of her voice, imitating the gaunt, older man. "The show must go on!"

A tremor ripped through Tabitha. "Which eye is it?"

Dr. Daisy blinked. "Which eye?"

"Which eye?" Tabitha repeated, fighting to keep her voice calm. "The black eye. Right or left?"

"Left. Left eye." Dr. Daisy seemed flummoxed. "What difference does that make?"

Maybe no difference at all. Or maybe all the difference in the world.

Blasted knees! Gonna be the death of me someday.

Rufus Praeger's arthritis was especially bad that morning.

Stormed Omaha Beach in the Big One. Didn't get a scratch. Not a scratch. But now, my dang knees.

"Ya know what ya done wrong, Rufus?" he asked aloud to his reflection in the church's glass door. "Ya went an' got old. That's what ya done."

He chuckled softly as he selected a key from the oversized keyring dangling from his belt loop. "Ya got old, soldier."

There are old soldiers and there are bold soldiers. But there are no old, bold soldiers. Ain't that what Sergeant Jimenez used to say?

He unlocked one of the two glass doors. "Well, I was bold, but now I'm old." He shook his head and chuckled again. "Sorry, Sarge."

For a brief moment, he thought of the fourteen men in his unit who had not survived that D-Day landing. In his mind, he called up the young faces of George Harris and Walt Zemanski, who'd been on either side of him when a Nazi machine gun had mowed them down, miraculously sparing him. "Sorry, boys. It ain't fair. I got to go home, and you guys didn't."

At least ya died for somethin'. Me? What've I ever done, huh?

He opened the door, then turned and depressed the bar and twisted the knob that would leave the door unlocked. Rufus knew the Relief Society ladies weren't scheduled to show up for another thirty minutes or so, but that didn't preclude that perky Sister Morales from being there early. She was always early.

He smiled again as he thought of her. She always had a smile for him.

Ah, if I was forty years younger and she wasn't married, of course.

When Rufus had returned from the Second World War, he'd discovered that his girl, Ida Mae Gallagher, had married that no-good 4-F coward, Billy Sorenson. *Well, she had to get married, now didn't she? With a baby on the way and all.* Rufus had thought he'd never get over the betrayal—though he'd still prayed she'd be happy, wherever she and 4-F Billy ended up. He'd also thought he'd be alone all his life. And then he'd met Rose. They'd been happy—so happy. But Rose had died in childbirth two years after they'd been married in the Salt Lake Temple. The baby, a boy Rufus had named Hank, had survived only a few hours after he was born.

Then Rufus had been alone. Again. He'd been alone ever since.

Stop relivin' the bygones, ya old coot! Ya got responsibilities today! Indeed, he did have responsibilities. He had to make sure the Relief Society room was all set up for the ladies' Friday morning Jazzercize class and the nursery for their kids. He'd set up and then he'd go. *Them ladies don't want no old codger hangin' around, watchin' 'em dancin' in their leotards. No, sir.* He'd go, and then come back when they were done.

What the Sam Hill?

He wrinkled his nose. The scent wasn't strong, but old Rufus had been a church janitor for more than two decades. He knew ammonia when he smelled it.

There was another odor mixed with the acrid stench of ammonia. Something elusively familiar. Rufus was certain he should know that other pungent smell, and though he couldn't identify it, he was absolutely certain of one thing—whatever it was, it had no business being inside a church.

At first, Rufus tried to follow his nose, but the faint stench was everywhere. He moved quickly through the hallway, turning on lights as he went, moving his head from side to side, sniffing at each wooden door. But each door smelled pretty much the same.

When he reached the janitorial closet, he checked the doorknob—still locked. He unlocked it, turned on the light, and stepped inside. He did a quick scan of the cleaning supplies. Two one-gallon jugs of ammonia still sat on the shelf—one unopened, and the other three-quarters full. He shook his head in consternation. "Don't look like any's missin'." He did a quick inventory of the other cleaning supplies. "All here."

But the scent of ammonia was unmistakable, even if he couldn't identify that other smell.

He left the janitorial closet and continued his search around the building. He checked the pair of glass doors at the back end of the church. They were both locked. Rufus knew darn well, if you tugged real hard at the left one, it'd pop open. Half the kids in the stake knew that. Many times, he'd caught kids playing basketball in the cultural hall when they weren't supposed to be.

On impulse, he backtracked and checked the cultural hall, which also served as basketball court, dance hall, theatre, and overflow for Sunday services, but the odor wasn't as strong in there. The cultural hall was empty too, but Rufus called out, "Anyone in here?"

It wasn't that he expected to find anyone, but that smell—especially the tantalizingly familiar, but as yet unidentified component—made Rufus feel wrong. That sense of wrongness made the small hairs rise on the back of his neck.

He shook himself, gritting his teeth angrily. "Stop it, ya old fool," he muttered. "Ya took on the Nazis at Normandy and the Battle of the Bulge, didn't ya? Don't let a little spilt ammonia spook ya. Probably just some kids trying to get high."

He lifted his voice. "Hey, you little idiots!" *Assumin' there's anyone in here. Probably long gone by now.* "Ammonia's poison! You'll just get yourselves sick! Or worse!"

He listened, moving closer to the stage. He heard nothing. He saw no one. He took the side door to the stage and climbed the few stairs. Still no one. The stench was no stronger up there.

He left the stage and the cultural hall and headed back out into the hallway. The smell was definitely strong here, and it was getting stronger.

Need to find it and clean it up. Can't have the sisters breathin' them fumes.

He headed to the Relief Society room, where the ladies would be doing their exercise class. It was the third largest room in the building, right behind the cultural hall and the chapel-proper.

The instant he opened the wooden door, the smell was stronger. It wasn't overwhelming, but it was definitely stronger in that room than in the hall.

Rufus flipped on the light and entered. The wooden door shut itself behind him—just as it was designed to do—with a click that seemed unnervingly loud in that empty space. The room was deserted, except for a wooden table with a small podium atop it, an upright piano and piano bench, and the small army of folding chairs that stood flattened and stacked against the walls. An array of storage closets lined the only unobstructed wall. He approached the nearest closet and halted.

Here! Definitely coming from here.

The closet door was not locked. "All s'posed to be locked, dad-blast it."

He yanked open the door. The stench nearly bowled him over.

"What the Sam Hill?"

At first, Rufus couldn't make sense of what his eyes were telling him. Just inside the door, instead of the usual assortment of decorations, tablecloths, Styrofoam plates, and what-have-you, he saw two large, canvas bags, the size of the rock salt bags he used to de-ice the outside walkways in winter. The bags had been crammed into the closet, one on top of the other. Only these bags didn't contain rock salt.

The horrid smell was definitely coming from the bags. Rufus squinted at the label on the side of one bag.

FERTILIZER

"What the Sam Hill is this doin' here?" he asked aloud.

Something flashed atop the bags. Something red. A clock. It was one of those new-fangled digital jobs, flashing the time over and over. But it wasn't the right time. It was counting down.

19:10, 19:09, 19:08, 19:07...

He recognized the other smell—the scent that had no business inside a church.

"Gas!" The blood froze in his veins as the realization hit him. "Bomb!"

He heard the door click behind him, again.

Rufus spun around and saw a nightmare. A monster. A clown with teeth like a shark in a dark hood.

A fist crashed into his jaw. Rufus saw stars. He staggered back, clutching at his face. Another blow struck him in the face, and Rufus crumpled to the carpeted floor.

He saw the hooded figure towering over him. It raised a foot, and the foot stomped down. Rufus felt the sickening crunch as his knee shattered. He howled in agony. Then his other knee suffered the same fate. The bones in his right hand, brittle with old age, were crushed by the next stomp. The foot raised again and came down on Rufus's left hand.

And the world exploded into white agony.

Rufus awoke to throbbing, searing pain. His jaw pulsed with agony.

His knees and hands were on fire. He tried to open his mouth to howl, but his jaw wouldn't move right. All that came out was a loud moan.

Something was wrong with his eyes, too. He couldn't see right. He tried to bring his hands to his face, but his mangled hands wouldn't obey him. He blinked. It was as if he were looking out of dark holes.

Clown. Mask. Can't see right.

Then he understood. *I'm wearing the mask.*

He turned his head. Even lying on his back, the world around him spun in a whirlwind of agony and vertigo. Through one eyehole of the mask, his eye focused on the red, glowing digits of the clock atop the bomb.

2:17, 2:16, 2:15…

Rufus rolled onto his belly, his ruined bones howling in protest. He began crawling toward the door, using only his elbows.

The door was shut.

Frantically, desperately, he cast about in his mind for a way to open the door, to escape the bomb. His crushed hands were worthless.

If he could only force himself onto his shattered knees, he might be able to use his teeth to turn the knob.

Please, God! Don't let me die like this!

The door opened.

Sister Morales stood framed in the open doorway. She stared down at him, her mouth agape, her eyes wide in horror.

Thank you, God!

He tried to say, "Help me," but with his broken jaw, all he managed was "Hell—"

The woman stood in the doorway, frozen.

Suddenly, Rufus knew with terrible certainty that if she stayed or if she tried to help him, she would die too. Even if she did manage to get him to the other side of the door and closed it behind them, the explosion would shred both their bodies with shards of wood. She couldn't save him.

Not her too! Please, God. Not that! Run! Run!

But she didn't move, like a deer in headlights as a heedless semi barreled toward it.

Save her!

So, Rufus did the only thing he could, using the only thing that was left to him.

He howled. He howled as loud and long as he could, channeling all his agony and all his terror into the horrible sound.

Run! Please run!

Sister Morales jumped. She screamed. Rufus filled his lungs and howled again. She turned and ran.

The door swung shut once more, blocking any hope for Rufus's escape. But that didn't matter.

Saved her.

He rolled over, whimpering with the pain. He raised his head. His eye—the one not blocked by the mask—fixed on the timer as it counted down the final seconds of his mortal life.

0:17, 0:16, 0:15...

Please, God! Let her get clear. Don't let me die for nothin'.

Through a fog of pain, in his mind, he heard a voice—clear and strong and infinitely kind, as if the Speaker knelt beside him. "Fear not, Rufus. She is safe. Well done. And now, Rufus, it is time for you to come home. Rose and Hank are waiting for you."

0:02, 0:01...

Inside the mask and in spite of his shattered jaw, Rufus smiled.

0:00

A tiny spark, an instant of flame, and Rufus Praeger began his journey home.

"Are you sure you want to do this?" Josh glanced at Tabitha as he shut off the engine and set the parking brake. He unbuckled his seat beat, but had not yet opened the door of the yellow Bug. The three of them—Tabitha, Josh, and Joseph—were parked in front of Mikey and J.L.'s home.

Joseph gurgled from his car seat in the back. The baby hadn't started fussing yet, but he might at any moment—especially since the car was no longer moving.

Tabitha hesitated before answering her husband. *No,* she thought, *I am most definitely not sure I want to do this.* "I have to. None of this is Mikey's fault."

Josh gently took her hand. The Power flowed—just a trickle, just enough to strengthen her, to comfort her. He gave her a sad, sympathetic smile. "It's not your fault either. You didn't do anything wrong."

Why does it feel *like it is my fault? At least partially?* She closed her eyes, suppressing the urge to roll them. "Then whose fault is it?" *Not J.L.'s. He can't help the way he feels.*

"As much as I hate to say it"—he hesitated, as if truly reluctant, but still determined to say something he knew might hurt—"if anyone is to blame, it's J.L."

"That's not fair. He can't help the way he feels."

Josh chuckled softly. "I'm the first one to admit that you are irresistible."

"Not helping," she muttered.

The Power surged a little.

"Sorry." Then he smiled. "No, not really all that sorry. You are wonderful, sweetheart. But"—he squeezed her hand to cut off her protest—"even if he can't help the way that he feels, he's the only one who chooses how he acts. He has to move past it. Mikey's a wonderful woman. She's the one he's sealed to. For eternity. She's not you." He lifted her hand and kissed it, sending more tingles of the Power through her. "No one compares to you."

"Stop it." *But honestly, you could say that all day, and I could never get enough. Especially right now.* "I'm glad you love me, but—"

"I do. With all my heart. I'm the luckiest, most blessed man on the planet, but J.L.'s pretty lucky too. Mikey's quite a catch. Not my type, but…"

That time, Tabitha did roll her eyes. "Not your type? Tall, blonde, busty, leggy Surfer Barbie, Betty Crocker, and Farah Fawcett—all rolled into one? I've seen your blood, mister. It's as red as every other American male."

He lifted her hand and kissed it once more. "That's all fine and good, but you know darn well I prefer shorter women with long, black hair. At least one in particular. In spite of you wearing those wonderful full-length skirts all the time, I've seen your legs and the rest of you. Mikey's got nothing on you."

"Okay, seriously—stop it." But she didn't even try to suppress a smile. "And the fact that I'm a witch has nothing to do with it? The fact that you can channel my Power, Mr. Warlock?"

He grinned from ear to ear. "That helps, of course. A little bit." The Power surged to a truly delicious level. "But you forget, I fell madly in love with you long before you ever told me about the Power." His eyebrows bounced, and his grin broadened even more. "Madly. I fell for you the first day I met you—at Uncle Mike and your mom's wedding, even before I knew your name."

Tabitha turned her head and gazed lovingly up at him. "For me, it was the moment you asked me if I loved old, scary movies."

He leaned over and kissed her tenderly. She closed her eyes, basking in the glow of his love and the Power. Then she broke the kiss and sighed.

"I need to do this." She glanced at her watch. "And quickly! I don't have that much time to spare before I have to be there before call. I've got to get into costume, makeup—"

"Opening night!"

She nodded. "Opening night!"

"I'll get the baby."

She shook her head. "No. I need to do this alone." She shrugged, then looked back at her child with a smile. "Not exactly alone. I'll have my cute little man along. You'll protect Mommy, won't you?"

Joseph gurgled and reached for her.

"Okay," Josh said, "but I'll be waiting by the car. Outside the car." He paused. "Uh, with your permission? Just in case?"

She blinked at him, not comprehending. *Permission? To wait by the*—"Oh, yeah." She nodded. "Yes. Hold onto the Power."

He nodded as well and let go of her hand. The Power continued to flow.

In less than a minute, armed only with her son, the diaper bag, and the knowledge that Josh was still holding onto the Power, Tabitha rang Mikey's doorbell.

Not my fault. Not Mikey's fault. She shivered. *Not really J.L.'s fault either.*

She heard footsteps inside, approaching.

But it wasn't Mikey who opened the door.

J.L. stood, framed in the doorway. A broad smile lit his face. "Hey, you!"

Tabitha managed an awkward smile in return. "Hi. Uh"—she tried to look past him into the house—"is Mikey here?"

J.L. nodded. "Of course!" He stepped aside, gallantly holding the door open for her with one hand. "Come on in." He reached for the carry-cradle with the other hand.

Tabitha surrendered her son to J.L. and stepped past him and into the house.

"Mikey!" J.L. called toward the kitchen. He set the carry-cradle down on the living room floor.

Tabitha glanced around the living room. *Immaculate. As always.*

Almost always.

Mikey emerged from the kitchen, wiping her perfectly manicured hands on her apron. The inviting, homey scent of roast pork followed after her.

Mikey's smile was bright and welcoming.

And too perfect—not merely pretty with perfect teeth—but bordering on sculpted. Frozen. Forced.

"Hi!" she said. "All ready for the big night?"

Tabitha lifted her shoulders in an exaggerated shrug and let out a deep sigh. "As ready as I'll ever be."

J.L. chuckled. "That means you'll be fabulous! Can't wait to see it. I'm coming tonight, you know."

Tabitha grinned nervously. "Okay. I hope we don't disappoint." *J.L.'s coming? Of course, he is.*

She glanced at Mikey and her too-perfect smile.

"So," J.L. said, beaming, "did you hear?"

Tabitha gave him a curious look. "Hear what?"

J.L. bounced on his heels, like a little boy with a big secret he just had to tell or burst. "He's dead!"

Tabitha blinked. "Who? Who's dead?"

"Ding-dong, the witch is dead!" J.L. sang.

Tabitha jerked. "The witch?" *Me?*

"No, you turkey!" J.L. said. "The killer! The Night Hunter! It was on the news!" He pointed at the turned-off color television set. "He blew himself up!"

It's over? It's really over? "Blew himself up? How do they know? If he blew—"

"There was a witness," Mikey said.

J.L. nodded. "Yeah! He was wearing a mask. A werewolf mask. Just like we were told."

Mikey's smile faltered. "It wasn't that awful clown mask." She shivered at the memory.

Annoyance flashed across J.L.'s face for a moment as if he didn't appreciate Mikey interrupting his story again, but his grin quickly returned. "Yeah. It was at a chapel out in Springville."

Blew himself up? "Why, uh, why would he blow himself up?"

"Not on purpose!" J.L. continued. "I don't know. He screwed up. Maybe he had a timer and didn't set it right or something."

"The reporter on Channel 5 said—" Mikey began, but J.L. cut her off with a small wave of his hand.

The look of annoyance had returned. "Yeah, on KSL, they said something about a timer." J.L. grinned. "But it's over! He's dead!"

"We're safe," Mikey said. She rolled her shoulders suddenly as if shivering. "We're all safe."

The room seemed to spin around Tabitha. *Dead?* "How can they be sure it was him?"

"The witness!" J.L. said. "Saw him before he went boom. He tried to grab her or something. Not sure. Anyway, thought you'd like to know. It's over! It's flippin' over!" He pointed toward the door. "Gotta go. Need to make sure my custodians are all on-shift tonight." His smile broadened, rivalling that of the Cheshire Cat. "Before the show-o-o-o!" He grabbed his jacket from the coat closet. "Anyway, gotta go. Break a leg!"

Tabitha smiled, still trying to take in the news. *Dead? He's really dead? Thank you, Heavenly Father. I thank thee!*

She felt as if her knees might give way. She felt as if she needed to drop to her knees right there.

I thank thee!

"Hurry back, honey," Mikey said. "Dinner's almost ready."

J.L. gave his wife a quick peck on the lips. "Back in just a little bit." He hurried out the door, singing, "Who's afraid of the Big Bad Wolf?" leaving Tabitha and Mikey alone with the kids.

Joseph let out a squeal that threatened to quickly become a scream.

Tabitha knelt and removed her baby from the carry-cradle.

When she stood, holding her son to her chest, she saw a tear leaking from Mikey's eye.

Tabitha swallowed hard. She swallowed again, but the sudden lump in her throat simply would not go down. "Mikey, I…"

Mikey crossed her arms under her breasts as if she were holding in her guts. "When you didn't come over last night when you took Joseph to Maddie…" She dabbed at her tears. "I thought, I thought…"

She thinks I'm upset with her? "Uh, Maddie volunteered. Said you'd been through enough. She wanted to give you a break. She said she called you."

"I know that!" Mikey snapped. She wiped at her tears again. "You know." She looked directly at Tabitha. "Don't you?" The words had both an accusatory and a desolate tone. Mikey lowered her eyes. "I knew you would. I knew you'd see *that*."

Joseph squirmed. He looked at Mikey, worry on his little face, and he reached for her.

"Mikey," Tabitha said, clutching her son to her like a shield. "I'm so sorry. I should have pulled out of that one. I should have."

"But you didn't."

Tabitha shook her head. "No. I didn't."

Mikey nodded, wiping away another tear. "Not your fault." She shook her head.

"Not your fault. I'm the one who's, who's not…"

Joseph began to cry, and he still reached for Mikey.

Mikey dabbed at her own tears. "Oh, let me have him. Come here, you cutie!"

Tabitha gave her child over to Mikey.

Mikey held the baby to her, bouncing him gently and smiling at him through her tears. "It's okay, little guy. Auntie Mikey's okay."

Joseph grinned at her.

Mikey's smile didn't waver, but she said. "I'm the one who's not enough. For him. Not good enough."

"You?" Tabitha stared at her friend with wide eyes. "Not enough? You're? You make me sick—you know that?"

Mikey's gaze shot to her, but she said nothing.

"You're so darn perfect!" Tabitha kept the volume of her voice low to keep from upsetting Joseph as much as to keep herself from losing complete control. "Look at yourself! You're every man's dream girl—you and your perfect face, your perfect hair, your perfect figure. Your house is always immaculate. Your kids are always well-behaved. You sew your own clothes, and you still look like a fashion model! A movie star. You're an excellent cook." Tabitha pointed a finger at her friend. "Don't you dare try to deny it! I can barely warm up canned ravioli and make a PB-n-J, but your food is gourmet. I bet you mill your own wheat, butcher your own meat, and grind your own hamburger. What more could any man want?"

Mikey's eyes bored into hers. "You." The word sounded like an epithet.

Tabitha met her friend's gaze. "He doesn't want me."

Mikey's expression hardened. "Oh, yes, he does. You saw it. You saw everything."

"I saw a fight. An argument. All couples fight."

"Not all couples fight about other women. About you. He wants you." She averted her gaze. The hardness melted from her face. "Not me. You."

Tabitha shook her head. "He doesn't want me. He doesn't know me. Not the real me. He wants . . . Hodel. A girl in a play. He wants… I didn't, I wouldn't! It was just acting. Off-stage, I didn't even—" She wrung her hands. "Mikey, I'm sorry!"

Mikey nodded, but she didn't meet Tabitha's gaze. "I know. I know you didn't encourage it. Would never encourage it. I've seen the way you are with Josh. You two are perfect for each other. You fit." She finally looked at Tabitha once more. "And I've seen the way you are around J.L." A sad smile played at the corners of her mouth. "You're so uncomfortable around him. So awkward." She lifted an eyebrow. "Just for the record, I don't butcher my own meat." She grinned, and shrugged. "Unlike some people I could name, I can dance a decent waltz and cha-cha." She stuck out her tongue. "So there." Then Mikey laughed, followed by Joseph.

The tension drained out of the room, like spoiled milk down a drain.

Tabitha grinned. Cautiously. "So, am I forgiven?"

Mikey shook her head slowly. "I don't know. I've seen you dance. If having two left feet is a sin, I don't think you could be forgiven." She winked and lifted a welcoming arm. "Come here."

Tabitha stepped toward Mikey and into her friend's one-armed embrace. She put her arms around Mikey and Joseph, careful to avoid skin-to-skin contact with Mikey. She could still feel the Power tingling through her, held remotely by Josh. As weak in the Power as Mikey might be, Tabitha didn't want her friend to feel it, or to question what that sensation might be. She held her friend, clung to her, both women weeping.

Mikey drew a shuddering sigh. "You know, J.L. may be an idiot. But he's *my* idiot. And this will pass. It's not your fault."

"It's not yours either. You know that, right?" She looked up at her friend's face.

Mikey nodded slowly. "Yeah." After a long moment, Mikey whispered, "Do you think he's really dead?"

Tabitha shuddered. "I hope so. I really hope so." She pulled out of the embrace. "I—" The Power surged within her. Three times in a row. Almost as if Josh were trying to get her attention.

She glanced at her watch. "Oh, crap. I gotta go!"

Mikey nodded. "Break a leg, okay?" She gave Tabitha a wicked grin. "In fact, while you're at it, break both of them."

The breath caught in Tabitha's throat.

Mikey shook her head. "Just kidding. You should see yourself. Now, go knock 'em dead. Make little Joseph proud!"

"Thanks!" Tabitha kissed her son's cheek. "Be good for Auntie Mikey, okay, handsome?"

In answer, Joseph gurgled, burped, and spit up on Mikey's apron.

Tabitha shook her head. "I said, be good, Joseph! Not off to a great start."

Mikey chuckled. "Go on. Get out of here."

"Thanks." Tabitha headed for the door.

Josh was standing at the car, holding the passenger door open for Tabitha as she scurried toward him. "We gotta hurry," he said.

"Sorry." She gathered her long skirt and slipped into the seat. "Got your signal." She glanced into the backseat to assure herself that White Lettie's broom was there. Then she fastened her seatbelt.

"Wasn't sure you'd get the message." He shut the door and scrambled around to the driver-side of the already running Volkswagen. "I didn't want to go in there and interrupt." He buckled his seatbelt. "How'd it go?" He stomped on the clutch, put the car in gear, and pulled away from the curb.

Tabitha shrugged. "A lot better than I expected."

"Good." He paused. "J.L. told me about the explosion. About the Devourer. If it was really him."

"You think maybe it wasn't?"

"I hope it was. I hope it's over." He reached over and squeezed her knee. "I hope you're safe." He hesitated and looked as if he wanted to say more.

"But?"

He grimaced and shook his head. "It's just something Folau said. Yesterday. He said that there might be an accomplice." He glanced at her, then focused on the road.

"He said it was unlikely, but, bollocks!" He thumped the steering wheel with a fist. "I just want you to be safe! Why'd he have to put that idea in my head? He said it was unlikely. Bollocks!"

The Power cut off, as if a switch had been flipped. They both gasped at the sudden absence.

"I lost it," he said. "Sorry."

She put her hand on his arm, no skin-to-skin contact, no reconnection with the Power, just a gesture of comfort. "It's okay, sweetheart. For now. You did really well." She smiled at him, and he glanced at her just long enough to see that smile and return it. She sighed. "Man, I love you!"

"I love you, too." His smile vanished. "J.L.'s an idiot."

Tabitha nodded slowly, then she shook her head. "Poor Mikey."

"Not just that."

She gave him a quizzical look. "What?"

He shook his head, clearly annoyed. "He's mad at Folau."

Mad at Folau? "What for?"

"Apparently, Folau was on the news, urging caution, saying women should still be on their guard. I suppose J.L. just wants it to be over."

"Me too. But why be mad at Folau? He's just doing his job. He has to be cautious, make sure the Devourer's really dead."

Josh shrugged. "Think about it this way, maybe J.L. feels like he failed to protect his wife, to protect his family."

"That's not fair. He did the best he could. At least he managed to hit the guy."

"You're right. It's not fair. But you're not a man." He grinned. "A fact for which I am eternally grateful, by the way." The grin vanished. "A man protects his wife, his children, and J.L. failed in that. Things aren't great in his marriage right now. Another way he's being a complete idiot. In the middle of all that, the killer breaks into his home, overpowers him, attacks his wife, and tells her she's somehow inadequate, that she isn't worth the killer's time. In some twisted way, that comes back on J.L. That makes him feel like he's less of a man. Maybe he just doesn't like Folau suggesting that the real killer might still be out there. Makes him feel even more like a failure. Do you get what I'm saying?"

"I think so." She shook her head and chuckled. "You men with your stupid, fragile egos."

"Yeah, men! Stupid men." He smirked. "Sure glad I'm not one of 'em."

She rolled her eyes. "Not one of which? Men? Or *stupid* men?"

He shrugged, grinning wickedly. "Take your pick."

Tabitha laughed, then quickly sobered. "Do you really think he's dead? The Devourer? Could it really be over?"

His expression hardened. "For the moment, it doesn't matter. Folau's right." He muttered something under his breath that Tabitha didn't quite catch. "For now, we continue to take precautions."

She nodded. She patted her purse with the Glock inside. Then she put her hand atop his.

Immediately, she felt him draw the Power. "Hold onto it until we get there, until I get inside." She gave him a sly grin. "If you can."

He nodded. "But not while you're performing. I remember, no distractions." He lifted her hand and kissed it, pulling a delightful surge of the Power through where his lips touched the back of her hand.

She sighed, adopting a Southern accent. "Except for the handsome warlock in the audience. Oh, my!" She fanned herself dramatically with her free hand. "I feel an attack of the vapors comin' on." She put the hand to her forehead. "I fear I may swoon!"

Josh grinned. "You're gonna knock 'em dead, Scarlet O'Hara."

"This seat taken?"

Josh looked up from his theatre seat in the dead center of the fifth row. Folau's scarred face beamed down at him. Josh didn't exactly relish the idea of sharing Tabitha's first performance with the detective.

Maybe if Folau sits with me, J.L. won't want to. And right now, I do not *want to sit with J.L.* "I was saving it for you."

Folau lifted an eyebrow. "Oh, really? Good thing this isn't a court of law, and you're not under oath."

Josh patted the seat. "Naw. You're welcome to it." He shrugged. "I'd welcome the company."

"Cool." Folau sat. "You two are really into this stuff—horror movies and stuff like that?"

Josh shrugged and then nodded. "Different strokes and all that. You don't like scary movies or plays, Detective?"

Folau shook his head. "Not really. I've seen enough of the evil people can do to each other in real life. This fake stuff is... I bet she's gonna be great."

Josh grinned. "Yeah, she's the best."

He spied Bishop and Maddie Smith as they took seats in the same row, leaving a gap of several seats between themselves and Josh. The bishop carried a black leather bag.

Still carrying your medical bag, Doc? Just in case? Didn't you get the word? The killer's dead. Right?

Josh waved. Maddie waved back and Bishop Smith nodded, grinning widely.

Folau pointed at the roses in Josh's lap. "Nice. A whole dozen?"

Josh chuckled. "Yeah." He shrugged. "Wouldn't've been able to afford them if it weren't for that care package." He suppressed a shudder. *With that dang sausage.*

"I'm sure she'll love 'em." His eyes took on a faraway look, and the corners of his mouth lifted in a wistful smile. "My Julie loved roses." Then his mouth drooped.

A sudden, uncomfortable silence descended between them.

I sure wish I hadn't made that awful crack about a girlfriend the other day. Josh cleared his throat. "So, uh, what do we know? Is he dead?"

Folau glanced around as if checking to make sure they wouldn't be overheard. He leaned toward Josh and lowered his voice. "Maybe. Man, I sure hope so. But it could take a while before we know for sure. Of course, if there are no more abductions and murders, that's a sign right there. In the meantime, here's what we do know." He pulled his notepad from his jacket pocket. "At this point, we think there was only the one casualty in the explosion." He checked his notepad. "One Rufus Jedediah Praeger. Sixty-six years old. White male. Church custodian. Widower. No children. World War Two vet. We only know his identity because a witness said she saw him just before the explosion. She said he was wearing a werewolf mask, but she identified him by his clothes, and by the fact that Mr. Praeger was scheduled to be in the building at that time. He was setting up for some Relief Society exercise class. Or he was supposed to be."

"Hold on," Josh said, turning to him. "Sixty-six? Are you sure? Wouldn't that be, like, too old to do all the things this guy has done?"

Folau shrugged. "If this was our guy, sixty-six isn't that old. And if insanity is involved, let's just say, madmen can be pretty dang strong. So, might still be our guy. Certainly doesn't rule him out."

"Okay. What else?"

"He screamed at her—at the witness. No words—just screamed. Like in your wife's visions. So that fits. What doesn't fit? The explosion itself. Wasn't big enough. Not near big enough. Not for two-thousand pounds of ammonium-nitrate. But maybe this was just a trial run. A trial run that backfired on him."

"Trial run? But if he's dead?"

Folau's scar twitched. "If he's dead? Well, we still can't rule out an accomplice."

"Right. But you said—"

"Not likely. I know, but I'm not ready to let my guard down based just on that assumption. Are you? You willing to bet your wife's life on 'not likely?'"

"No." Josh shook his head, his jaw clenching.

Folau nodded. "Good man." He stuffed the notepad back into his jacket pocket.

"But what do you really think?" Josh asked. "What does your fabled gut tell you?"

The detective shrugged. "I'm cautiously optimistic. Emphasis on 'cautiously.'"

"Okay." *Please, Heavenly Father, let it be over!*

"Hey!" said a familiar voice from the right.

Both men's heads snapped to the right.

J.L. was making his way toward them, one row back. He waved, grinning widely. Josh waved back with the roses.

When J.L. was no more than three seats away, he halted, and his grin vanished. Hope flared anew in Josh. *He sees Folau.*

Folau stood, turned, and faced J.L. "Mr. Montrose. Glad to see you up and about. How's your wife doing?" He extended a hand to J.L.

J.L.'s grin returned, though it wasn't as wide as before. He crossed the remaining distance and shook the detective's hand. "She's doing great. Not here. She's babysitting Josh's kid." He shrugged. "And this show is too scary for our daughters." He pointed at the seat on Josh's right. "Expecting anybody?"

So much for that. But Josh managed a smile. "Just you."

"Great!" J.L. put a hand on the back of the seat and lifted his leg as if to climb over. He hesitated, looked around, and then said, "Actually, I think I'll sit right behind you guys." He plopped down into the seat directly behind Folau. "I'm so flippin' excited to see this one! Josh, you've seen some of the rehearsals, right? How is she as Renfield?" Josh opened his mouth to reply, but J.L. charged ahead. "Tabitha's gonna be great!" He leaned to the right and tapped Folau's shoulder. "I told her about the audition. We were in *Fiddler on the Roof* together. Opposite each other. We were Hodel and Perchik together. She's one heck of an actress!"

The enthusiasm in J.L.'s tone and the gushing praise for Tabitha would have made Josh feel good if they'd come from anyone else. But it had the opposite effect.

She's my wife. How the heck did I end up sitting with two guys who've got the hots for my wife?

Be nice. Folau's keeping his distance. And J.L. hasn't done anything. Yet.

"And the killer's dead," J.L. said. He leaned forward and mimed an explosion with his hands. "Boom!" He chuckled and nodded enthusiastically. "Couldn't have happened to a nicer guy." He chuckled again. "Boom! Yep! It's a good day! She's gonna be brilliant! Great casting decision—Tabitha as Renfield. The blood is the life! The blood is the life!" He frowned. "How long 'til the show starts?" J.L. glanced at his watch. "Twenty-five minutes? Too flippin' long!"

Josh's irritation was getting the better of him. *Don't know how much more of J.L. I can take right now.* To avoid looking at the man, Josh looked instead at Folau.

The detective met Josh's eye. Folau appeared to be just as annoyed at J.L.'s antics as Josh was. Folau's scar twitched as he whispered, "Amen to that."

"Does it hurt?" Tabitha winced as she watched Eli Thorpe applying pale greasepaint to his dark bruise as the two of them shared one of the makeup tables. "That looks really nasty." It wasn't the first time she'd seen the injury, of course, but it certainly looked worse than it had the day before. Blacks and purples surrounded the professor's left eye, but the pale greasepaint covered the darkened skin perfectly. For all the discoloration, however, the wrinkled flesh did not appear particularly swollen.

Thorpe chuckled. "Not so bad. A bit tender, of course." He waved the greasepaint stick, which resembled a very wide, pale lipstick, in the air. "And applying the base hurts a little, but I've kept ice on my eye as often as I could for the last two days. In the end, it doesn't matter. The show must go on!"

Tabitha couldn't help smiling. "Thank heavens." *Just yesterday, I thought you might be the Devourer.*

Sorry, Eli. Let my fears run wild.

Sweet old guy. Old. Too old to be the Devourer.

It's gonna be fun working with him all summer.

Eli resumed concealing his bruise with greasepaint. "I don't suppose you were able to watch the TV news this evening. Did you listen to the radio on the way over?"

"No, but we've heard about the explosion."

The professor nodded. "What do you think? Is the killer dead?"

Tabitha sighed. She almost put her face in her hands before remembering to avoid smudging her own makeup. "I sure hope so! I think so." *I want to believe it.*

"Strange, don't you think," Eli continued," that he would use an explosive? I mean, it wasn't part of his *modus operandi*, as they say." He hastened to add, "At least as far as I've heard on the news."

"The police think he might've been escalating, working up to something big."

Eli turned his face and looked at her. He scowled. "I didn't hear that on the news."

Tabitha was suddenly aware of the other faces, the other cast members pausing in the applications of their own makeup, staring at her and the gaunt professor.

"Where did you hear that?" asked Sarah Abercrombie, the actress playing Lucy.

Oh, crud! Can't tell them I'm working with Folau. "I, uh, my friends. Two of my friends were attacked." At the collective gasps from the assembled cast, Tabitha quickly waved both hands. "They both survived! They're okay. But, well, I, uh, overheard things. From the police." *Don't say anything about the bomb!* "That's what this kind of monster does, isn't it? He keeps . . . escalating. Getting worse. More violent."

"But we're safe now, right?" asked Caroline.

Bjorn put his arm around Caroline. "It's over. You're safe."

Caroline snuggled closer to Bjorn Carpenter. She sighed. "Safe."

Those two will be engaged before the show is done.

"Let's hope so," intoned Eli. "But, just to be safe, until we know for certain, I would consider it an honor if you ladies would continue to allow myself and the other men to escort you to your vehicles after each performance."

"Yeah!" Bjorn had spoken quickly, as if he'd wished he'd said it first.

Sarah bit her lower lip. "Thank you." Her eyes swept over all the men who'd watched over them recently, keeping them safe. "All of you. I'm so—so grateful. ,"she dabbed quickly at a tear before it could smudge her stage makeup She smiled, shaking her head and then dabbing at another tear. "You have no idea."

Tabitha nodded her head. "Me too. We're all so grateful."

A nervous chuckle escaped Caroline. "Even if the danger's over."

Please, Heavenly Father—is it really over?

She tried to listen for the comforting, assuring voice of the Spirit, but no answer came. She was unsure if it was because it wasn't over, or because she wasn't calm enough to listen for the answer. She would ask again later, after the show.

Gradually, one by one, people went back to applying their makeup. Caroline aged her face, while Eli made himself pale and ageless, with blood red lips, deep-set eyes, and hollow cheeks. Tabitha heightened her eyebrows, lined her eyes heavily, making herself look as deranged and disturbed as possible. She made one eye appear significantly larger than the other by adding far more eyeliner around the eye. She also heightened and darkened the corresponding eyebrow. She added a downward curve to her lips on that side. The effect was to make her face appear unbalanced like Renfield's mind.

She looked at the results in the mirror and then turned to Eli Thorpe who was powdering his own face, to set his makeup. "How do I look?" she asked.

Looking at her in the mirror, Eli's jaw dropped, then his look of surprise slowly morphed into a grin. "Magnificent. Truly deranged. I like it!" He chuckled, and there was a sinister, Dracula quality to his soft laugh. "You are going to frighten everyone. Creep. Them. Out."

She gave him a maniacal grin. "Perfect." She quickly powdered her own makeup.

Alice Rigby, the young stage manager, poked her head into the room as she stood on the bottom step of the stairs leading up to the stage. "Twenty minutes to curtain, folks!" she announced.

Tabitha rubbed her hands briskly through her long, black hair, thoroughly mussing it, adding to her already disheveled appearance. She gave her reflection an approving nod, then pulled off the towel that had protected her costume from the makeup process. Setting the towel on the table, she stood. "See you upstairs!"

Eli Thorpe rose to his feet as well. "Break a leg, everyone. Let's have a great show!"

Tabitha strode to the wall and retrieved her sturdy broom from where it stood, propped near the stairwell. The iron-cored broomstick felt solid and heavy in her hands—comforting and reassuring, lending her strength. She patted the pocket of her skirt, feeling the iron washer through the fabric. Both White Lettie and her mom, two women who had profoundly shaped her life, were with her in spirit. *Knock 'em dead. Creep 'em out.* She smiled as she gathered her black, full-length skirt with her free hand and started up the stairs.

When she reached the first landing, she turned and saw Eli Thorpe ascending close behind her, tall and dignified as a Transylvanian nobleman. He grinned up at her with his cadaverous face, made all the more ghoulish by his expertly applied makeup. *Man! He's scary.*

This is going to be so cool!

She turned, and the broom—her good luck charm—caught against the handrailing. Tabitha stepped on the hem of her skirt. She stumbled, whirled, falling toward the stairs behind her.

She let go of both the broom and her skirt, clawing in vain at the air.

The next moment, she was weightless, falling. Two strong arms caught her, arresting her fall.

"Got you!" said a strong baritone voice.

Tabitha looked up into the face of Eli Thorpe.

He held her, one arm under her back, the other under her knees like a groom carrying a bride across the threshold. He climbed the last step and set her on her feet on the landing.

242

"You— You saved me!" was all she managed to say as she gripped his upper arms. His muscles were firm and shockingly strong.

He smiled at her. "Yes, I suppose. It was nothing, my dear."

Tabitha barely suppressed a gasp at the phrase. "My dear." *Magnus.*

Suddenly, embarrassment and remorse blanketed Eli's features. "I'm sorry. I promised to not call you that." He pulled away. "I'm so sorry." He swallowed. "I'm sorry, Tabitha."

"No." She shook her head. "It's okay. Really. You saved me. Probably saved my life. Thank you."

His smile returned as he shrugged. "It was the least I could do." He sighed. "Besides, I can't lose you now." His eyes softened, and he looked on her with an unsettling tenderness, made even more disturbing and incongruous by the vampiric makeup. "My Cordelia. My treasure."

The tenderness vanished as his jaw dropped, and his eyes widened. Then his jaw snapped shut as he seemed to collect himself, his mask of professionalism dropping back into place. "Best be getting upstairs." He bent and retrieved Tabitha's broom. As he set the heavy stick into Tabitha's trembling hand, he said, "Your talisman, dear lady. Careful now." He turned and gestured up the stairs. "After you, Miss Renfield."

But Tabitha stood, rooted to the stair landing, her palms sweating. A shudder ripped through her spine.

The Devourer's dead. He's dead. Dead! Please, Heavenly Father, let him be dead!

She managed a quick smile and muttered, "Break a leg." Then she scurried up the stairs, her broomstick gripped tight in her sweat-slick hand.

Fear. Sweet, delicious fear filled the theatre. It saturated the air. It vibrated in his soul. It all centered around Tabitha. The terror rose and fell like waves crashing upon him, filling him, drowning him in honey. Almost feeding him. Almost, but not quite. Like a starving man drooling over the scent of a freshly baked apple pie—a sumptuous, nourishing pie that is just out of reach.

So hungry.

Every moment Tabitha was upon the stage as Renfield, every word she uttered, every insane look.

"The blood is the Life!" She cackled.

The horror swelled, thundering, crashing upon him. But he could not consume it. Could not draw it in. None of it came from her. She drew it from others. Vampires they knew. Vampires were *passé*. But they had never seen her Renfield. She was new. She was unknown. Terrifying.

Of course. Of course, it would be Tabitha. Magnificent. My Prize. My Treasure.

"Yes, Beloved," whispered the voices of his Legion. "She is magnificent. She will complete us. Complete you."

Exalt me!

If he had been free to do so, he would have gazed lovingly upon her, but he could not. Love, adoration—these could not be visible on his face—not at that moment. Not where others could see. Not even where she could see. Not yet.

"Take her, Beloved. Take her now." The voices spoke as one, as many, layer upon layer, each united, each distinct.

He could no longer remember their names. Not a single one of them, because they were a part of him now. They were no longer individuals as they had once been. Now, they existed only as a part of him.

"Take her now."

Not yet. She must have her triumph.

"Now, while they believe you are dead."

Not all believe.

"No, Beloved. Not all."

When I put on the mask, I'm not even sure I believe. Not when I wear the mask. Not when I pretend to be mundane.

"Many believe. We know. We are everywhere. In their secret places. In their whispers. We hear them. We are Legion."

Does she believe?

"She doubts, Beloved. She doubts. But she desires to believe the deception. She needs to believe."

What about the husband? The worthless, wretched, unworthy husband?

"He also doubts. But he also doubts his doubts."

Inwardly, he smiled. *Then he will be off his guard. He will fail.*

"Take her now, Beloved. Take her. Consume her. Devour her! Make her one with us! One with us!" Legion's several voices fractured, shattered apart—no longer a united chorus, but an angry, ravening mob—echoing and re-echoing through his brain. "Now-now-now-now-now!"

Soon! Very soon.

"Yes, Beloved." The voices coalesced once more into a single choir singing harmony in the tabernacle of the damned. "Soon."

Yes. Tonight.

Tabitha laughed, low and unhinged. "The Master comes!"

Something's wrong.

The dread had settled on Josh like a great, black crow, sitting on his shoulder. Ever since the first intermission, after Act One of the play. He'd been able to push the sense of unease to the back of his mind, watching his wife.

Tabitha had been spectacular. The entire cast had been great. The sets were delightfully creepy. Even the decrepitness of the old theatre added to the haunted atmosphere.

During his missionary service in Scotland, Josh had once known a beggar who kept a trained crow. The man had been called Old Gordie. He would sit on the bridge over the River Ness, and Archie, the crow, would caw and coo at the passersby as he bobbed his black head and capered back and forth on Old Gordie's shoulder—a shoulder stained white by Archie's waste. Occasionally, Archie would utter a single word, mimicking human speech with a startling clarity—"Bollocks!" And when Archie would utter his word, people would laugh and point and put a few coins in Old Gordie's hat. The old man shared all he had with the crow. And if Archie, in his birdie judgement, determined that Old Gordie wasn't feeding him fast enough or sharing as much as he should, Archie would nip at the old man's ear until Old Gordie rewarded his bad behavior.

Nip, nip. That's how Josh felt, as if a carrion bird were nipping at his ear, demanding his attention.

"Bollocks," Josh muttered as the curtain closed after Act Two. *What is it? What's wrong?* "Bollocks."

Nip, nip.

"Be right back," J.L. said, from his seat behind him. "That Sprite went right through me." J.L. patted Josh and Folau on the shoulders and rose. Then he headed for the aisle. Luckily for J.L., the seats between himself and the aisle were unoccupied.

The fact that any seats were unoccupied bothered Josh. He wanted a full house for Tabitha. And for the rest of the cast and crew, of course.

Folau inclined his head toward Josh. "She's scary. Scary good. Steals the show every time she's onstage."

Josh nodded, barely registering the detective's praise. "She's great." *What is it?* Josh glanced at his watch. *Tabitha's okay. Maybe it's Joseph. Naw. Just jumpy.* "Gonna go call the babysitter." He stood. "Excuse me."

"Sure." Folau stood as well and stepped back so Josh could get past him. "Be quick. You only have ten minutes."

"Thanks," Josh murmured. "Hold these for me?" He handed the roses to Folau without waiting for a response. Then he hurried out of the theatre and into the hallway. The old building had two old-fashioned, wood-paneled phonebooths near the restrooms, and Josh headed that way.

Both were occupied. Below the wooden door, Josh could see a set of shoes in each. A pair of men's dress shoes in one and a pair of ladies' heels in the other.

Hurry up. Please.

Nip, nip.

He sighed with relief when, fortunately, one of the phonebooths opened, and a smartly dressed, middle-aged lady slowly emerged.

Josh forced himself to not tap his foot in his mounting impatience. As soon as the booth was unoccupied, he entered, fishing a quarter out of his pocket. He lifted the receiver and put the quarter into the coin slot. He listened for the dial tone and then dialed Mikey's number on the rotary phone.

Rather than a ring, he received only the frustrating, repeated buzzing of a busy signal. Josh hung up. His quarter dropped into the coin retrieval slot. He fished the coin out and tried once more.

Busy.

He tried three additional times, but encountered the same result with each attempt. He checked his watch. "Bollocks!"

Who's she talking to?

He remembered the other occupied phonebooth. *Probably J.L. Could've been his shoes. What do his shoes look like? Maybe he's calling home.*

Nip-nip-nip.

It's nothing. Just nerves.

"Bollocks!" With a sigh of resignation, he hurried back into the theatre. By the time he got there, the house lights were already dimmed to half, signaling for the audience to retake their seats.

As soon as Josh got back to his seat, Folau handed him back the roses.

The scarred detective grinned. "Take the flowers quick. I don't want anybody getting any funny ideas. Just because I gave you roses, don't think it means—" The detective's grin faded. "Everything okay?" Folau glanced around the theatre as if searching the shadows. "Where's Mr. Montrose?"

Josh glanced back, noticing that J.L.'s seat was empty. "I think he's calling his wife."

Folau turned his head toward the exit. He nodded. "Here he comes."

J.L. smiled as he hurried down the aisle. He got into his seat.

"Where've you been?" Josh asked, a touch more testily than he'd intended.

"Just calling Mikey." J.L. seemed almost out of breath.

Knew it. "How's she doing?" *Is my son okay?*

J.L. shrugged. "She's Mikey. That means everything is perfect. Sometimes, I think I take that woman for granted."

Amen to that. Mikey will have things well in hand.

The house lights went out, leaving only the obligatory green "EXIT" signs lit, their eerie glow all that stood between the audience and the darkness.

Folau hissed, "It's starting!"

The curtain opened on the final act of the play.

But that night, when Renfield strode onto the stage for her part in the curtain call, the entire audience was standing, cheering enthusiastically.

No one cheered louder than Josh—though J.L. was giving him a run for his money. Josh waved briefly at Tabitha, then resumed his clapping.

When Dracula took his bow, flourishing his cape dramatically. The applause surged briefly, but there could be no doubt in anyone's mind as to who was the true star that night. Tabitha had completely stolen the show.

The applause had not abated by the time the curtain finally closed.

Josh sighed happily and sat down, cradling his precious roses. *I can't wait to give her these!*

Folau sat as well. "She's magnificent. You're a lucky man." His smile was wide and genuine. "A very lucky man."

Josh couldn't help but return the smile. "Yeah, I am. Thanks."

J.L. leaned forward. "You don't deserve her."

Josh's head swiveled back toward J.L. So did Folau's. J.L.'s hand as it plunged toward Folau's neck. Josh didn't see the hand that went for his own neck, but he felt the sting of the needle. Then he felt J.L.'s hand over his mouth.

He couldn't cry out. He couldn't breathe. His precious roses dropped from his hand.

Dimly, he was aware of Folau thrashing next to him.

As the darkness took Josh, he heard J.L. whisper, "Now and forever, she's mine!"

"He's still not breathing!" Maddie's voice trembled with panic and terror as she knelt over Folau's unconscious body. "Torrance! He's not—"

Torrance Smith nodded quickly, but kept his voice calm, reassuring. "It's okay, honey. Just keep breathing for him. Just like I trained you." Keeping Josh's head tilted back, Torrance placed his mouth over Josh Kilmore's mouth, pinched Josh's nose, and blew, forcing air into the unconscious man's lungs. Twice more he breathed for Josh. Torrance put two fingers against Josh's jugular vein. *Still got a pulse.*

Not dead yet. Not today, Death! Not today!

Torrance had dragged both Josh and Detective Folau to the theatre aisle, after he'd given each man an injection of Naloxone from the medical bag he'd brought with him. He'd been carrying the bag everywhere since Maddie's abduction and safe return. But even with the injection, followed by a second dose each, neither man had resumed breathing on his own. And so, Torrance and Maddie had been administering mouth-to-mouth resuscitation. They forced air into each unconscious man's lungs every five seconds, twelve times per minute. And the minutes ticked away.

Naloxone should've worked by now.

A crowd had gathered around them, murmuring, some of them weeping. A constant barrage of "Are they okay?" and "What happened?" and similar questions peppered him from all sides.

Torrance ignored them as he fought to save Josh—as he battled Death.

He must've given them a lethal dose.

"The phones!" cried a man from the back of the mob. "The lines are cut!"

Torrance cursed under his breath. He spared another angry glance at the shattered ruins of the detective's radio lying in front of the seat J.L. had occupied. "Get outside!" he commanded. "Flag down a—"

"The doors! Locked!" a woman wailed nearby. "Chained shut! We're trapped!"

A scream. "Trapped!"

More screaming.

Something struck Torrance in the back almost knocking the wind from him, a foot or a knee as the stampede scrambled around and over him. The mob fled toward the locked doors.

Torrance grunted in pain, even as he tried to shield Josh's body with his own. He heard Maddie cry out. His head snapped toward her.

"No!" She flung up a hand to reassure him, but tears dripped from her eyes. "I'm okay. I'm okay." She bent her head and breathed into Folau's mouth again.

Torrance did the same for Josh.

Come on, Josh! Breathe!

He forced air into Josh's lungs again.

Not today, Death!

Rage frothed up inside him.

Not today, J.L.!

The screams were fading. "Trapped! Help us!"

"Torrance!" Maddie cried. "If we're trapped—"

"Don't think about it!" Torrance breathed into Josh's mouth. "We can't save them all. Just save him. Just save the one you can! Leave the rest to God. Just keep fighting!"

Torrance glanced at his wife who was working furiously to save the detective.

Please, Heavenly Father! Save him! Please!

From the theatre doors, someone wailed, "We're trapped!"

Save us all.

A baby screamed.

And with a mother's absolute certainty, Tabitha recognized the cry of her own child. "Joseph?" Gripping her broomstick like a weapon in one hand, and clinging to the handrail, Tabitha descended blindly into the stygian depths of the basement of the old Academy building. She'd found a light switch, but the switch hadn't worked.

Blackness enveloped her, swallowing her.

The rest of the show's cast had gone to the hallway in front of the theatre to greet the audience, but *en route*, Tabitha, who'd been at the back of the troupe, had heard the scream. She'd turned back.

Joseph can't be here! He can't. He's safe with Mikey at her house.

As soon as she reached the basement, the stench hit her: gasoline.

And Tabitha knew exactly what that odor—so wrong inside the confines of a building—meant.

Bomb! He's here! The Devourer's here, and he's got my baby.

She stepped into the dark hallway and groped along the wall for another light switch.

An infant screamed.

"Joseph!" Tabitha lifted her long skirt and lurched forward into the blackness, following the echoing cries, groping her way with one hand on the wall. The screaming surrounded her, stole the breath from her lungs, and robbed the strength from her wobbling legs. In the darkness, she lost all sense of distance. The hallway seemed to stretch forever.

A door opened ahead, on the left side of the hall. Light streamed into the corridor, and a figure stepped into the light. The figure was holding a screaming, struggling baby.

"Joseph!" Tabitha screeched.

The figure held up a hand. "Tabitha!"

J.L.?

"It's okay," he said, lowering his hand and gently cradling Tabitha's son. "I found him! He's okay."

Tabitha halted, panting hard. "J.L.?" *Found him?*

J.L. nodded, half his face illuminated by the light from the doorway, half his face cast in shadow.

"What are you doing down here? Why's Joseph—"

"The killer! The clown." J.L. began bouncing the child, and Joseph stopped screaming. "He took Mikey! Took the girls and Joseph. Brought them here. Locked them up!"

Fear ripped through Tabitha. She shivered. Her hand was suddenly slick with perspiration, and the broomstick felt as if it would slide out of her grip. She pulled her hand from the wall and put that hand on the weapon as well. "Where's Mikey? Stacy and Marie?"

J.L. seemed to be trembling too. He gasped, his whole body shuddering. He turned, pointing with a shaking finger back into the room from which he'd come. "In there. Mikey's hurt. Help me! Tabitha, please!"

"Help you?" She hurried forward. "J.L.! Give me my baby!"

Before she could reach him, J.L. turned. "In here." He strode into the room and out of sight, taking Tabitha's child with him.

"J.L.!" She chased after them.

As she dashed into the doorway, the light smote her eyes. She threw up a hand to shield them and winced in pain. "J.L.? Mikey?"

She cast her eyes about, squinting against the searing light. But she couldn't make sense of what she saw.

A low bed, covered with blankets and pillows. No, not a bed, a mattress on the floor. Roses in a vase on a crate. A plastic bucket. A roll of toilet paper. An iron chain fastened to a large, vertical pipe.

And a manacle.

"J.L.?"

Movement to her left.

As she whirled to face him, the broomstick was snatched from her sweat-slick hand and cast aside. She was shoved violently toward the mattress. Joseph screamed.

Tabitha landed hard, the air exploding from her lungs. She rolled over, fighting for breath.

J.L. stood framed in the doorway. He held Joseph at arm's length, dangling the baby by one small leg.

Joseph howled, red-faced and squirming.

J.L. grinned like a wolf with a cornered a rabbit.

"No!" Tabitha cried as she began to scramble to her feet.

J.L. laughed and shook his head. "Stay right there." His grin widened. "Or I'll drop him on his soft, little head."

Tabitha froze. "No! P-please." Fear made her voice tremble.

The expression on J.L.'s face was near paroxysm of mad joy. "Yes! So sweet!"

Fear? I'm feeding him. Devourer.

I need anger. Rage to—

She struggled to control her terror and her anger. She didn't want to hurt her son on accident. She needed to dampen her rage.

J.L. moaned with delight. "So strong. So sweet. My prize." He panted like a man who'd just completed a marathon. "My treasure." His breathy voice caressed the word.

"Please, J.L. Give me my baby. Don't hurt him. Please don't—"

J.L. frowned. "Put it on. The shackle. Put it on." He snarled. "Or I'll bash his brains in." He shook the baby.

Joseph screamed all the louder.

"Okay." Tabitha put up a placating hand. "I'll d-do it. Just don't hurt my baby. Please."

J.L. shifted his grip on the child. In a heartbeat he was cradling Joseph in his arms. "No, no, no," he said in a soothing tone, "that wouldn't be nice—crushing his skull like that." He smiled at the baby, who had abruptly ceased his howling. "Maybe I'll just snap your spine. How about that, you little cutie? Maybe I'll just rip your arms and legs off? Huh?" He cooed at the child. "Ooh, you should've been mine. You know that? You should've been mine. Mine and your mommy's."

He turned his smile on Tabitha.

She was horrified at how beatific the smile was. There was not the slightest gleam of madness in those eyes.

"Put it on." His voice was soft, his smile broad. He licked his lips, like a small boy anticipating an especially sweet dessert. "Now."

"J.L., listen to me." She swallowed hard. *Don't be afraid. Fear feeds him. If I put on the iron, if I reason with him. Try.* "When I touch iron, I"—she searched for something he could understand—"I black out." She forced a tiny smile. "I won't be any use to you. I won't be afraid, and—"

He smiled, shaking his head. "Of use to me? I'm not going to use you. I would never use you." Suddenly he appeared to be confused. "I would never use you. I love you, Tabitha. With all my heart and all my soul. Soon I will love you with my body too."

"J.L., I—"

"Don't say it." He scowled, and his eyes burned with sudden anger. "Don't say you love me too. I'm not an idiot!" He jabbed a finger toward the shackle. "Now, put it on!"

A fresh wave of panic threatened to overwhelm her, to drown her. "I can't! Once I touch it, I'll—"

Suddenly, Joseph was dangling by his leg again and screaming.

"Okay!" Tabitha held up her hand again. "I-I-I'll do it. I'll do it." *Once I touch it, I'll be in a vision. I'll be helpless.* "If I pass out—"

"You're a wonderful actress. But if you fake a faint, I'll know. Fake a faint, and he dies." He shook the screaming baby by the leg. "Now!"

Tabitha scrambled for the leg iron. She grasped it.

Dizziness, weakness hit her like a blow from a baseball bat. But the world did not dissolve.

No vision?

It was ever owned by a woman!

I won't have the Power while I wear this! I can still fight him though. I can still protect my son. Somehow.

But how? Heavenly Father! Help me!

She fastened the iron about her bare ankle, just above her shoe.

No lock. I can just take it off when he's not looking! A spark of hope flared in her as she covered the empty slot for the lock, hiding it with her hand.

Something small bounced onto the mattress—a heavy combination lock.

"Lock it." J.L.'s toothy, predatory grin had returned. "Now."

The spark of hope died. Tabitha put the lock on the manacle and clicked it into place.

J.L. stepped closer until he was just barely within arm's reach. "Take him."

With trembling hands, Tabitha received her son. She clutched him to her bosom. She looked down into the tear-streaked face of her only child. "It's okay, Joseph. Mommy's got you."

J.L. stepped back. He smiled, eerily tender. "There you go. Now feed him. You must be desperate to. I've got to do a few things. So, you'll have a few minutes. But just a few minutes, okay?"

He pulled a thin object from his pocket. It caught the light and glinted.

A capped syringe.

"Don't make me use this." He shook his head. "Not on you. I don't want to hurt you." He cocked his head. "I could use it on him." He pointed with the syringe at Joseph. "Enough in here to kill him. That'd shut him up. Yes, indeed, it would."

Tabitha clutched her son, shielding him with her arms. "No. Please. Don't hurt him. Please, J.L. I'll—"

"So, feed him. Shut him up. Can't have him crying while we make love." His face twisted in a savage snarl. "I hate it when kids cry in the middle of sex."

Tabitha tried not to look at J.L. She tried to keep her eyes on her son. But she could still see the monster.

"I'll be back soon." J.L. winked. "Keep the bed warm."

As he turned to go, Tabitha asked, "Where's Josh? Is Josh, okay?" *Please let Josh be safe!*

J.L. turned back to her. He gave her a courtly bow as if he were a knight honoring his lady. But his eyes never left hers. He bared his teeth in a wide grin. "Don't worry about Josh, my love. I killed him. That annoying detective, too."

Tabitha clamped her jaws, sealed her quivering lips, stifling a howl of anguish and loss. But she couldn't stop the tears that spilled freely from her eyes. *Josh! No!*

"You're free now." J.L. straightened. "No barriers between us." He winked. "Be right back!"

He sauntered out of the room.

A sob erupted from Tabitha. "Josh!"

Joseph was crying again.

"I told you to shut him up!" J.L.'s voice echoed from the hallway.

I have to save Joseph. Somehow. Feed him. Soothe him.

"It's okay, Joseph." Tabitha unbuttoned her blouse. "Mommy's here. Mommy will protect you."

Tabitha sobbed quietly as she nursed and comforted her tiny son. As she mourned her husband.

Madness surrounded Trevor Anderson.

"Trapped!"

"Help!"

Everyone seemed to be screaming. They pounded at the doors. Men threw themselves at the exit doors, but the push handles of each were bound on the inside by thick chains. Shove as they might, none of the doors had given way. The windows, at least on the ground floor, were all blocked by heavy, wrought-iron bars.

Everyone could smell the gasoline. The odor was faint, but it was also terrifying.

Trevor had tried to calm them down. As director of the play, he felt as if everyone in the old Academy building was his personal responsibility. But his calm words, even his commanding shouts had not quieted the screaming.

"Please!" he cried as he stood near the door. "Everyone, please! Someone's going to get trampled!"

"Out of my way!" The bellowing voice came from behind the howling mob. "Move!"

Miraculously, the churning mass of panicked humanity parted, like the Red Sea before Moses. Only, it wasn't Moses. It was Dracula.

Eli Thorpe, still in full costume, his crimson-lined black cape billowing behind him, charged toward the door.

In his hands, he carried an axe.

"Trevor," Eli said. "If you please?"

Trevor nodded and backed away from the door with its massive chain.

Eli smiled toothily. In his vampire makeup, that smile was unsettling. "Thank you, Trevor. Now, if you'd please keep everyone back?"

"Yeah. Sure." Trevor raised both hands, and in his best director's voice, which hardly shook at all and commanded the crowd. "Okay, everyone! Move back. Give the man some room. He'll have us all out of here soon!" He eyed the axe, one of those scattered at intervals throughout the old building, kept in metal cases with glass windows labeled, "BREAK GLASS IN CASE OF FIRE." It seemed so small compared to the thick chains. "Eli," he whispered. "Are you sure this is going to work?"

Eli swung the axe. Sparks flew as steel met steel. Eli snarled as he hefted the axe above his head. Again, he struck. Again, the sparks flew, but the chain held fast.

"You'll set off the gas!" cried a woman. "We'll all burn!"

"Please," Trevor said. "Let the man work."

"He'll kill us all!" cried another woman.

Eli growled as he swung his axe again. "Everyone's a critic." He smote the chain once more. "Break, curse you!" He swung again. "Just!" And again. "Flippin'!" And again. "Break!"

The chain stubbornly refused to obey him.

Mikey Montrose awoke to absolute darkness and to bone-rattling cold.

She was on her back, shivering as the hard, frozen floor beneath her leached the warmth from her body.

Where am I? She sat up. *The girls! Joseph! Where are they?*

Her head spun madly in the blackness. She fell back down, striking her head on the floor with a soft thump. She grunted in pain.

Mikey rolled over and pushed herself onto her hands and knees, keeping her head bowed. Her head spun less. She was able to hold that position as she waited for her head to quit whirling, breathing steadily through her nose and out her mouth.

The clown. He's still alive.

Drugged me, again.

On all fours, panting, she struggled to control her terror even as she fought against the vertigo. *Stacy! Marie! They're alone. And Joseph!*

Are they still alive? Where am I?

Heavenly Father, protect my girls! And Joseph.

Her head bumped into a wall. She turned away from the wall and kept going. Soon she hit another wall.

Small room. A closet, maybe?

Find the kids!

"Stacy?" she whispered. "Marie?"

"M-Mommy?" Stacy's voice, hollow and echoing in the enclosed space.

"Stacy?"

Mikey heard snuffling. "Stacy!" Mikey crawled toward the sound, brushing her shoulder against one wall.

"Mommy," Stacy said, "I'm c-cold."

"I'm coming, honey! Mommy's coming." *Stacy's alive!*

"I'm scared. Mommy, I'm scared. It's dark."

As she crawled, Mikey swept the floor in front her with a hand. "Keep talking, Stacy. Mommy's—" Her hand struck something soft. Mikey halted, knelt, and felt with both hands.

A tiny body. With soft hair.

"Stacy?" *Too small. Marie?*

"Mommy?" Stacy's voice again, from further ahead.

Over there! Stacy's over there. "Coming, honey." *Marie!* She felt the soft features of the child's face with trembling fingers. *Marie!* She gathered the tiny girl into her arms.

She's so cold!

Mikey fought down a sob. *Please don't be dead!* She clutched Marie to her chest. Marie stirred. "Mommy?"

The sob burst from Mikey. "Marie!" *She's alive! Alive!*

Thank you, God! Thank you!

"It's Mommy!" Mikey cradled her small daughter. "Mommy's here!"

"Mommy?" Stacy again.

"I'm coming, sweetie!" Still on her knees and holding Marie to her chest with one arm, Mikey inched toward Stacy. "I'm coming." *Still alive!* She swept the darkness before her with her free hand.

Her hand brushed against another wall. She'd reached the other end of the room. She lowered her hand and touched soft curls.

"Mommy!" Stacy cried.

"Stacy!" She wrapped an arm around the five-year-old. "I've got you!"

"Mommy!" both girls cried.

Mikey held her daughters close, and she wept. She kissed them both. Multiple times. "Mommy's here. Mommy's got you."

"Mommy?" Stacy asked. "Where are we? I'm scared."

Mikey nodded. "I know you are, sweetie." *I'm scared, too.* "But I need you to be brave. Be brave while Mommy figures out what to do. Honey, is Joseph here too?"

Mikey felt the girl shake her head. "I don't think so. He's not crying."

If Joseph was drugged too, he might be here. "Okay, honey. We need to check around."

Marie squirmed, then put her arms around Mikey's neck. "Mommy, I'm scared. It's dark."

"I know, honey." She forced a smile, even though she knew her daughters couldn't see it. *Maybe they'll hear the smile in my voice.* "Be brave for Mommy. We have to find Joseph." She released her precious daughters. "Come on, girls. Crawl with Mommy. We're going to find Joseph."

"Crawl?" Marie asked. "Like babies?"

"Uh-huh," Mikey replied. "Like babies. We don't want to step on Joseph in the dark, now do we? Can you do that for Mommy?"

THE WITCH AND THE DEVOURER OF SOULS

"Okay," said Stacy.

"I can crawl like a baby!" Marie said.

"Good girls," Mikey said. "Such good, brave girls." She swallowed. "We'll be brave girls together."

Together, they crawled down the narrow room, searching for Joseph. But the baby was not to be found.

She pictured Joseph screaming alone in her empty house.

Heavenly Father, protect Joseph. Please. Please, save us.

She hadn't found the baby, but she had found a door. Mikey stood, tried the doorknob. *Locked.* She pulled hard.

But the door wouldn't budge.

She slammed her shoulder against it. It rattled in its frame, but held steady. She slammed again, using all her one-hundred and twenty pounds. No luck.

She pounded on the door. "Help! Help us!"

There was no answer.

Stacy and Marie were crying again, clinging to her legs.

"It's okay, girls. Mommy will get you out of here. I will. Then we'll find Joseph and Daddy. We'll find Daddy." Mikey nodded, firm in her belief that if she found J.L. he would help her save their girls.

"No!" Stacy cried, squeezing her leg, startling Mikey. "Daddy gave me a shot. I don't want daddy."

Mikey froze. "Sh-shot? Your daddy gave—"

Marie nodded. "Me, too! A shot in my shoulder. It hurt! It hurt a lot!"

J.L.? J.L.?

The darkness seemed to weigh her down, squeezing her, crushing her, driving the breath from her lungs, turning her knees to jelly. "No, honey. It was the *clown*. The clown. He gave Mommy a shot, too." *Not J.L.! It can't be. J.L., it can't be.*

"Daddy gave me a shot!" Stacy said. "He said, 'I love you.' Then he gave me a shot. He said, it make me sleepy."

Marie nodded against Mikey's leg. "Daddy say, 'Over soon.'"

"Uh-huh," Stacy said. "Daddy said, 'We're all gonna go to heaven.' Me and Marie and Joseph and Daddy and Auntie Tabitha." She shook her head. "But not you, Mommy. He said, 'Not Mommy. Mommy's going to hell.' Why, Mommy? Why did Daddy say that? Was you a bad girl?"

Mikey felt the blood drain from her head. *Not bad. Worthless.*

A worthless bitch. That's what the clown said.

The clown. The killer. My husband. They're the same person.

Grief and rage ripped through her, as if her heart were being torn out of her chest by some savage beast and devoured in front of her. She pounded both fists against the door.

All those women. He killed them. Why? Why would he do that?

He's going to kill us all. Stacy. Marie. Me. Joseph.

And Tabitha. He wants Tabitha.

256

"Listen, girls. I need you to listen to Mommy. Mommy's going to find a way out of here."

I will. I will save my girls. I will save Joseph. I am not worthless.

She bared her teeth in a silent snarl, a she-bear protecting her cubs.

Please, Heavenly Father, give me strength.

Mikey took both her daughters by the hand. She guided them through the darkness to the wall opposite the door. "Stay here, girls. Put both hands on the wall. Stay here, okay?"

"Okay," they replied. They let go of her hands. Marie snuffled.

Mikey ran her hands over each girl to make sure they were holding onto the wall. "Good girls. That's right. Stay right here."

Then she turned back to the unseen door.

In the darkness, she bared her teeth once more. *With Thy help, with Thy strength, I can save my daughters.*

Please, God, give me the strength to break this door.

Mikey turned her shoulder, and with a roar worthy of a lioness, crashed into the door.

Almost there!

He laughed softly as he resisted the urge to whistle and sing.

Oh, how he wanted to caper and leap about! *No! Not without my Prize. Not without Tabitha.*

When we are one, my love, at last, you'll be able to dance. Really dance.

Just like we did on stage—only better. So much better.

We will dance together for all eternity.

There were women up there, terrified for their lives. He could hear the shouts from up above.

"So sweet!" He shivered in ecstasy. "Thank You, God."

The clanging of steel striking iron disturbed his joy. A scowl twisted his face. *Trying to break the chains.*

"Did I miss one of those flippin' fire axes?"

He closed the second of the wrought-iron, floor-to-ceiling gates—he'd installed them a few nights before at the base of each stairwell.

He closed the massive padlock in the latch.

That's it. Both staircases.

Nobody's getting in or out of this basement.

He wrinkled his nose. He didn't particularly like the smell of gasoline or in this case, diesel. He hated the reek of ammonia even though nothing cleans a window like ammonia! But given the lack of ventilation in the Academy basement, the stench was getting obnoxious.

He shook his head. *Nope. My own dang fault it's this bad. I just* had *to check on the bomb again, now didn't I? Opened the door and let the stink right out.*

Stink, like Mikey's perms.

A woman's hair should be long and straight. Like Tabi—

"Don't worry, Beloved," his Legion whispered.

He sighed in happy relief, almost slumping against the wrought-iron barrier. "I thought you'd forsaken me."

"No, Beloved." The voices flowed apart and merged and flowed apart once more. A raucous cavalcade of voices. A *legion* of voices. "We will never forsake you. We are with you to the end. To the end, and beyond."

He hugged himself, stroking his shoulders as if he were embracing his Legion, caressing them all. "I love you, my Legion."

"And we love you."

The clanging intruded once more, marring his joy—*their* joy.

He glanced through the iron bars and up the stairs, worry twisting his features. "The chain?"

"The chain holds, Beloved. It is strong. Like you. Stout and strong. Indomitable. They will not escape. They shall make a fitting sacrifice."

He nodded. "Yes. But even if they were to escape, Tabitha . . . Tabitha would still be enough. More than enough."

"Yes, Beloved One. She is magnificent."

He sighed again, nodding happily. "She was certainly magnificent tonight."

"Yes, Beloved. We eagerly anticipate her joining with us."

He listened for the sound of the baby crying. *As long as he's being fed, he won't make a sound. Damn brat.* He glanced at his watch. *She's had enough time, hasn't she?* He wanted to see her breasts—he most certainly did—just not while she was nursing. That was definitely *not* the image he wanted in his brain. He checked his watch again. *Running out of time. I wanted an hour. One hour together. Was that so much to ask?*

But time and tide and ascension to godhood wait for no man.

It'll be enough. It has to be. I can be quick if I must.

He checked his watch again and growled. "Is she done feeding that damn baby yet? Can you check on her?"

"Yes, Beloved. She is—" The voices ceased.

He straightened, shivering, suddenly worried. Suddenly frightened. "What? What is it? Legion? Legion?"

"She has betrayed you."

Tabitha? "What?"

"Go to her, Beloved! Quickly! Stop her!"

He ran, charging through the darkened hallway, toward the light spilling from the room, from the bedchamber, from his carefully prepared love nest.

In spite of the omnipresent reek of ammonia and diesel, a new aroma hit him as soon as he crossed the threshold of the bridal chamber. A foul putrescence. One he hated. One that irritated and disgusted him beyond measure.

He stopped just inside the doorway, staring, mouth agape in horror and revulsion. "What have you done?"

Tabitha stood at the far end of the room. He couldn't see her feet, but the iron chain still ran from under her long, black skirt to the vertical pipe at the back wall.

Still here. Still captive. Still mine.

Tabitha stood behind the mattress—behind their wedding bed. She'd shoved it forward, away from the wall. He would have to cross it to get to her. Tabitha's black eyes blazed with hatred, and her cheeks were streaked with tears. Protectively, she held her son in one arm. In her right hand, she held a clump of something white.

She drew back her arm, and she hurled the clump with all her might. As it flew, it unraveled.

He put up his arms defensively to ward off the object, but it still struck him on the face—wet and squishy. And putrid.

He looked down. A filthy, sodden, disposable diaper lay at his feet.

"What?" He couldn't make sense of anything. He wiped at his face. His fingers came away brown. "Why would you—"

"You murdered Josh, you bastard!" She spat at him. She *literally* spat at him.

No. Not at him. She spat on the bed.

For the first time, his eyes really took in what she'd done to their bridal bed.

The sheets had been ripped to shreds. The comforter had been cast aside, discarded like garbage. The mattress was smeared with brown streaks. The same brown that dirtied his fingers.

"On our *bed*?"

She shook her head contemptuously. "You actually thought I'd just submit to you? To *you*?"

Her words tore at his soul, ripping his heart to pieces. "Tabitha! I—I love you!"

She pointed a scorning finger at the brown-streaked mattress. "That's what I think of your so-called love!"

"But—"

"And don't even think about the quilt." She sneered at him. "I wiped that down too. It's all crap. Crap, J.L." She huffed. "Just. Like. You."

He snarled. He wanted to lunge at her, to tackle her, to *take* her. "You won't submit?" He pulled a capped syringe from his pocket. He yanked the cap off the needle, then held the syringe aloft, his thumb on the plunger. "Not even to save your precious son? You'll spread your legs like any other bitch wh—"

She laughed at him. She threw back her head and howled as she mocked him. "You're going to kill him anyway, aren't you, J.L.? You're going to blow us all to kingdom come. Where's the bomb, J.L.?"

She knows about the bomb?

Of course, she does. She can smell it.

She's Tabitha. So smart. So beautiful.

So strong.

He could still feel it. *The fear. So sweet.*

But not strong enough. Not afraid enough.

Not yet.

She was still glaring at him, waiting.

"Yes, there is a bomb," he said. "But you don't understand. It's the last step. The final step." He waited for her to say something. Anything. But she just scowled at him.

The baby whimpered, nuzzling against her chest. She bounced the baby gently, but her expression of loathing never faltered.

He noticed that the baby was clad only in a diaper. *Where'd she get a new—*He glanced down at the soiled diaper at his feet, even as he rubbed more brown from his face. Then he looked more closely at the child's white-clad bottom.

The sheet? My expensive bedsheet? She made a diaper out of— His lips curled as he growled through clenched teeth. "That was for us! For our wedding night."

She shook her head. "I'm married."

It was his turn to laugh at her. "You're a widow."

"And you're a monster."

His lips trembled as rage flared within him. "I'm a god!"

"You? A god?" She spat at him again. "You're not even a man. Just a creep. A bully who preys on women, because he's bigger than they are."

"No!" *She doesn't understand!* "I love them! And they love me. All the ones I've taken." He patted his chest with his free hand. "They're here. With me. *Within* me. And when we are one, when I have taken you into myself, together, we will leave this world behind. We will become a god. Together. You and me." He wrung his hands. "Don't you see?"

She nodded. "Yeah. I see. I see that you're going to kill us. Kill us all. You murdered my husband. Now, you're going to kill my son. You're going to try. But I'm going to stop you." She shook her head and snarled. "Never. Come. Between. A mother and her child. Never!"

He raised the syringe again and took a step toward her.

"I'm not going to give you what you want." She shook her head. "I'm not *afraid* of you, you big bully."

He halted, uncertain. *She is afraid. Not enough to feed on.*

Why isn't she afraid enough?

She must be afraid! If I'm going to consume her. "I'll kill your damn brat."

"Where's Mikey? Is she here? What about Stacy and Marie? Where are they, J.L.?"

"Mikey?" He sneered. "That worthless bitch? She's here, alright. She and my girls. We'll all ascend to heaven. Together." He shook his head. "But not Mikey. She's going straight to Hell. She's *nothing*." He smiled then, his voice softening. "Not compared to you. My Prize. The greatest, most magnificent woman in all creation." He took another step toward her. His shoe crunched on something. He looked down.

Plastic.

Shards of broken, clear plastic.

Then he saw the roses.

They'd been smashed, along with the vase, as if she'd stomped on them, ground them under the heels of her shoes.

"That's what I think of your roses. They're pathetic. Just like you."

Rage exploded in him. He howled at her, roaring. Joseph screamed. Tabitha barely flinched. She still wore her Renfield makeup, giving her face an unbalanced, lunatic appearance.

"Bitch!" he growled. "Why aren't you afraid?"

"Where's the bomb, J.L.?"

He glanced toward the door behind them. Then back at her.

She bared her teeth, a feral grin. A she-wolf eyeing a rabbit. "Thank you, J.L. That's all I needed to know."

"What?"

Still grinning, she lifted her skirt about a foot, exposing her ankle, the leg iron, the padlock, and the chain. She appeared to be staring intently at her ankle. She was growling like a little dog—a little *bitch* dog.

He chuckled. "You can't do it. Not without that bastard Josh. And not while you're touching iron. I know all about the Power."

She hesitated, looking up at him. Uncertainty filled her eyes.

Fear surged, sweet and thrilling.

"How"—she appeared to swallow—"how do you know?"

Her delicious fear swelled, filling him. Not feeding him. Not yet. He needed to touch the iron, the chain, for that. "You're powerless when you touch the iron, Tabitha. I know. *They* told me."

"Th-they?"

It was his turn to grin, savagely. He was the wolf once more, and she the prey. "My Legion." He felt them. Gathering inside him. They flowed out of him, filling the room.

"We shall show her, Beloved. We shall make her truly afraid. We shall make her know true terror."

Darkness filled the room, swallowing the light. Joseph wailed. Tabitha screamed.

Her terror washed over him, strong and pure and sweet as warm honey. Victory would taste sweet. "Yes!" he cackled, his laughter echoing through the defiled bedchamber.

Thick darkness gathered around Tabitha and her son. Surrounded by voices. Thousands of voices, howling together in a choir of insanity. Screeches, screams, whispered threats and promises.

"We are Legion, for we are many! Howl, woman! Howl and despair, for your doom is come!"

Tabitha did as she was told. She howled in the darkness, accompanied by her son's screams.

"Do you hear them?" J.L. shouted. "My Woman-souls! All those I have taken. All mine. All part of me. Soon, Tabitha, my love, you will be one of them. And we will be together, always!"

The blackness pressed on her chest, filled her lungs. Her breath came in short, tortured gasps. She held her baby in quaking arms, vainly attempting to shield him from the darkness and the monsters in the dark.

Please, God! My baby! Save my baby!

"They love me!" J.L. crowed. "You will love me too!"

"Yes!" cried the demonic voices. "Beloved One! Take her! Take her now!"

"Yes," said J.L. "Before it's too late. Before the bomb. Before I ascend unto Heaven!"

Tabitha felt a sharp tug at her ankle. The cold iron biting into her skin.

She kicked with her free foot, but struck only the black air. She kicked again and again, maintaining her balance only by some miracle. But her efforts made no difference.

The chain tugged again, harder. The leg iron dug deeper into her ankle, tearing her skin open. The warm trickle of blood seeped down her foot.

"Where are you?" J.L. wailed, like a lost child crying for its mother. "Why can't I feel you?" Tabitha steeled herself. She would fight.

"Right here." *Come on! Follow the chain! Come closer. So, I can kick you in your face!*

If only I could see!

He yanked again. "Where is it? Where's the fear?"

She forced a laugh. Then she laughed again, adding a mocking note even as she quaked with terror. "You're pathetic! I'm not afraid of you." *Liar.*

Not now. Rage! I need rage!

He jerked the chain again.

"You are afraid! I can feel it. Taste it. So sweet. But I can't . . ."

You can't touch it. "You must be crawling through p-poop, J.L. That's what happens when you don't change a baby's diaper for hours on end. But you'd know that if you were a real man, a real father. Like"—she fought to keep the tremor from her voice—"Josh."

"Josh is dead. I killed him." J.L.'s voice was cold, flat, and completely devoid of emotion in that moment.

Tabitha suppressed a sob.

"Yes, Beloved," howled the demons. "You killed him. Now take her! Kill her!"

"She's blocking me!" he whined. "How?" He jerked the chain again.

Tabitha clamped her mouth shut to stifle an agonized cry. *Think, Tabitha!* she ordered herself. Tabitha's fingers fluttered over the floor, a scrap of bedsheet meeting her fingers.

Joseph screamed in terror. Tabitha ached for her son, but she ignored his cries stuffing the bedsheet between her skin and the leg iron.

"I hate you!" she growled through clenched teeth. "I *am* blocking you. It's so easy. If you weren't so stupid, you'd figure it out. But you're a moron, and you're afraid. Yes, you, J.L. Afraid of me! You can't even face a woman. You coward!" *Come on! Give me back the light!*

"Kill her!" roared the voices.

"Face me!" Tabitha cried.

"Let me see!" J.L. cried. "Legion! Let there be light!"

Light stabbed into Tabitha's eyes. She cried out, shading her eyes, even as they fixed on J.L., standing up straight.

He knelt before her on the soiled mattress. He grasped the chain with one hand and shielded his own eyes with the other.

"Blood?" He seemed to be staring at her ankle. His eyes traveled to the leg iron and the blood-soaked scrap of bedsheet that she'd stuffed between her ankle, her flesh, and the Power-sapping iron.

Rage! I need rage! "I hate you!"

But she was no longer looking at him. She wasn't looking at her screaming baby, either. Her eyes were focused on the lock holding the manacle.

Don't be afraid. Be mad. "You. Murdered. Josh!"

He reached for her ankle, for the bloody rag that protected her from the iron, protected her from *him.*

"You. Hurt. My. Baby!"

The door slammed, and she jumped. *Yes!*

She hurled all her rage at the lock, and it exploded from her.

BOOM!

The lock vanished, vaporized, along with several inches of the chain, and all of J.L.'s right hand.

Tabitha kicked.

The manacle fell from her leg.

J.L. screamed, holding up his right arm, which terminated just short of his wrist. Blood spurted from the wound.

"Tabitha? Why?" His eyes were wide with horror and pain.

She scrambled away from him, yanking Joseph back into her arms, scrambled to her feet, almost tripping on her long skirt. She held Joseph tight to her chest. He whimpered, but he was no longer screaming. "It's okay, sweetie," she said, soothing and bouncing him gently even as she trembled. "Mommy's got you." She turned toward the door, ready to flee and to get her child to safety.

J.L. howled from behind her. "Legion! Stop her!"

The darkness returned, enveloping her, blinding her. Smothering her.

"No!" Tabitha cried. "Please, God! Help me! Help me!"

And then the darkness was gone. It was as if someone had stuck a straw into the room and sucked the darkness right out.

"Legion?" J.L. cried.

Tabitha spun halfway around, shielding her baby with her own body.

"Legion!" J.L. was on his knees, his hand and his blood-spurting stump raised in supplication. "No! Come back! Don't abandon me!" His eyes were not focused on Tabitha. They darted about the room, searching for the demons. Despair and loss twisted his face.

Tabitha swallowed "They're gone, J.L. You're all alone."

His eyes focused on her. "Tabitha?" Tears streamed down his face, pale from the rapid loss of blood. "Hodel? I love you! I love you! I—"

"Go to hell." She turned and fled the room and into the dark hallway.

She heard laughter then, following her. She glanced back, down the dark hallway.

J.L. stood in the doorway, leaning against the doorpost. His entire face was cast in shadow, as if he were wearing one of his masks. "Midnight. Ten minutes. Then this whole place...goes to hell," he panted heavily. Blood coated the ground below him. He stood in his own blood. "And you with it. We were supposed to ascend—locked together...in love. "

Clutching her son, Tabitha ran toward the stairwell. She spied the iron gate with its huge padlock.

J.L. laughed again. "You're trapped, bitch."

"Not a bitch," she said, focusing her rage on the padlock. "I'm a witch."

The lock exploded with a boom. The gate swung open, her salvation. Her escape was steps away.

"Tabitha!" J.L. cried. "Don't leave me!"

She heard a thud, and she turned to look back. J.L. lay face down in the doorway, in a pool of blood.

"Tabitha!" The voice came from up the stairs.

She spun around, opened her mouth to utter his name, but could not force the word past her quivering lips. *Josh?*

Josh came stumbling down the stairs, gripping the handrail tightly as if his legs were unsteady. "Tabitha!"

"Josh?" The word escaped her lips as a shuddering whisper. "You're alive!"

Then he was there, holding her, clinging to her and their son. As their cheeks brushed, she felt small bursts of the Power, kissing her skin.

"Searching for you," he said. "Heard the blast. Your blast. Knew you were down—"

"Tabitha!" Another voice.

Folau. Stumbling down the stairs. Quickly following on the detective's heels, came Eli Thorpe, still in his costume, clutching a very battered looking axe in his hands.

"Where is he?" Folau demanded. "Where's Montrose?"

"B-back there!" Tabitha jerked her head.

Folau snatched the axe from Eli's hands, then rushed past her, his stride growing stronger with every step.

"Are you alright?" Josh asked. "What about Joseph?"

Alive! She wanted to hold onto him and never let go, to drink him in, to drown in him. But Tabitha pushed back from her husband, shaking her head. "Bomb! Midnight!"

Folau trotted up. "Montrose is dead. Where's the bomb?"

Josh grabbed her hand, drawing the Power from her. "Let's go!" He began to pull her toward the stairs, but Tabitha resisted. "We got everyone else out. It's just us left. Let's—"

"No!" she cried. "Mikey's here! With Stacy and Marie! Somewhere in the building."

"Midnight!" Folau checked his watch in the light from the stairs. "That's eight minutes." His face hardened, and his scar twitched. "I'll find them. You, go. Please, Tabitha. Josh. Now."

Tabitha shook her head. "We have to stop the bomb." She lifted Josh's hand, clutched in hers, and felt the Power surge. "Me and Josh. We're the only ones who can. For Mikey and the girls."

"Stop the bomb?" Eli, pale in his smudged Dracula makeup, stared at her in disbelief. "How?"

"Trust me," Tabitha said. "Trust *us*." She handed her son to the professor. "Save my"—her voice hitched, and tears spilled from her eyes—"my son." She gazed at her son, her beautiful, perfect baby. "Goodbye, handsome." She caressed his cheek with a trembling finger. "Be good for Mommy and Daddy, okay?" She smiled at the baby through her tears.

Joseph reached for her with his chubby little hands, but Tabitha stepped out of the boy's reach.

Josh said, "Get him out of here." He choked on his own tears. "Please, Professor."

Eli nodded. He wrapped Joseph in his vampire cloak, turned, and dashed up the stairs.

Folau was already opening doors, as he moved quickly down the hallway, axe in hand. "I'll find them!" He opened the one opposite where Tabitha and Joseph had been held prisoner.

He stopped, pointing with the axe. "Bomb's in here." His voice held not the slightest note of fear.

Tabitha felt the Power surge. She and Josh flew down the hallway to land right in front of Folau.

The reek of diesel and ammonia was suffocating.

Folau had barely flinched at the sight of them flying, but a grim smile flickered at the corners of his mouth. "Wanted to see that." The smile vanished. "Listen carefully. Gotta be a timer. Probably buried inside. There's probably a pressure switch too." He shook his head. "If you try an' move anything—*anything*—you'll set it off. Enough here to take down the whole building. Kill everyone outside too. For a block around too. Building's been evacuated, but that won't save— Listen, whatever you're gonna do—"

He looked as if he wanted to say more, but after a moment, he simply wheeled away, continuing his frantic, room-by-room search, calling, "Mikey! Stacy! Marie!"

Joseph's outside, but probably not far enough away.

Tabitha gazed up at Josh. "I love you."

He grinned down at her. "I love you, too. Let's try and save the world."

She felt the Power surge.

Hand in hand, Tabitha and Josh stepped into the room.

"Mommy, I'm sorry." Marie put her little arms around Mikey's neck and squeezed.

Mikey sat on the floor, her back slumped against the door of the classroom. The door that had defeated her. She'd managed to crash through the coat closet door—that's what it had turned out to be—but this second door had not budged. It hadn't even cracked.

The door wasn't locked from the inside. Mikey had turned the lock, turned the knob. Something was barring it from the outside. Something that, try as she might, she could not break.

At least there was a dim light in the classroom, filtering in from the small window in the door.

Mikey could smell the gasoline. The stench was much stronger than it had been. She knew what the smell meant.

A bomb. J.L., her husband, had planted a bomb. She choked back a sob. She and her precious daughters were going to die and there was nothing she could do to stop it.

"I'm sorry, Mommy," Marie repeated.

"I'm sorry too, Mommy," Stacy said, as she also wrapped her arms around her mother's neck.

Mikey put an arm around each child and held them close. "Why are you sorry, girls?"

"Because you're so sad," Stacy said.

"I'm brave, Mommy," Marie said.

Mikey nodded. "Yes, you are. So brave. Both of you. My brave girls. I love you so much."

"Mommy," Stacy said. She tugged at Mikey's shirt. "Should we pray?"

Mikey chuckled bitterly. "I've been praying, sweetie. I've been praying so hard."

"Say fam'ly prayers?" Marie asked.

Mikey opened her mouth to protest, but then she nodded. "Of course, sweetie." *We'll die together. Praying.* "Come on." She let go of her children, and got on her knees. "Let's pray together. Hold hands."

She took each of them by the hand, and Stacy held Marie's hand as well. They formed a circle of three—a circle that didn't, and never again would, include J.L.

Mikey bowed her head, but she didn't close her eyes. *I want the last things I see to be the faces of my angels.*

Stacy bowed her head, then lifted it once more. "Pray together, Mommy." Then she shook her head. "But not Daddy."

Mikey nodded. "No, not Daddy. Stacy, you say it. Okay, sweetie?"

Stacy nodded. She scrunched her eyes closed, tightly, as only a child can do. "Heavenly Father, we thank thee for this day. And all our many blessings. Bless us to sleep well tonight. And have nice dreams. But not about Daddy. Bless Daddy to stop being mean."

Mikey bit down a sob.

Stacy paused. "Mommy's sad. And I'm scared. And Marie's scared too."

"Uh-uh," the three-year-old protested.

"It's okay, sweetie," Mikey whispered as she squeezed Marie's little hand. Fresh tears fell from her face. *Help me to be brave, Heavenly Father. I got them this far. With Thy help.*

"Please bless us," Stacy continued, "to be brave. And Mommy not to be sad. And Daddy to not be mean anymore."

I've done all I can. I can't do any more. I need Thy help. Please. I'm not strong enough to break down this door. Why wouldst Thou help me this far and not the rest of the way? What was the point?

"Mommy's a good mommy. The best mommy."

Mikey really did sob that time. *Not good enough. Not good enough for J.L. Not strong enough to save my girls. Never enough.*

"Please bless us. Send an angel to save us. You can send an angel if we ask. Mommy says if we ask in faith, You—"

"—acy? Marie?" The voice was faint and coming from beyond the door.

"In here!" Mikey cried.

She let go of her girls' hands, turned, still on her knees, and pounded on the door with both fists. "In here!"

"Mikey Montrose?" asked the voice. Nearer. Right behind the door.

"Yes!" Mikey cried. "Help us!"

"Stand back!" said the suddenly commanding voice.

Mikey scrambled to her feet, took both her daughters by the hand, and retreated from the door.

WHAM! The door shuddered. Stacy and Marie both screamed.

WHAM!

The door cracked.

WHAM!

The door burst open. Dim light streamed in. A man stood in the doorway, and he held an axe.

"Are your daughters here?" asked the man. "Both of them?" The dim light caught the jagged scar running down the side of his face.

Mikey knew him.

The detective! "Yes!"

The scarred man cast the axe aside. He rushed into the room and scooped up both girls, one in each arm. "Come on! Run!"

She froze.

"Move, lady! Or we're all dead!"

She ran through the door.

"Follow me!" he shouted and led the way toward the stairs. Mikey followed, but even as she ran, she prayed.

Save us! Save my girls!

The detective bounded down stair after stair. Still carrying the little girls, he glanced back at each landing to see if Mikey was following.

Unburdened though she was, she was barely keeping up. "Go!" she cried. "Save them!"

"In this together," he panted as he rushed toward the bottom. "All or noth—"

Mikey heard the crunch accompanied by Folau's loud grunt of pain.

He'd landed badly on the final landing—the main floor. Still, he did not drop his precious burdens.

He took a step forward, growling as he put weight on the injured ankle.

Mikey pulled Marie from him, hugged the girl to her side, and then put her arm around his back. "Lean on me!"

He put his now free arm across her shoulders.

Together, like participants in a life-or-death three-legged race, they lumbered forward.

"Go on!" he growled through clenched teeth. "Take her." He leaned his head toward Stacy. "Get out of here!"

"Nope," she said as they pushed on. "In this together, you said. Come on, Detective. I've got you! We can do this!"

Somewhere, a clock began to strike midnight.

Folau had been wrong about the timer. Dead wrong.

There was indeed a timer, and it was indeed visible, just not from the doorway.

The digital display peeked out from under the topmost bag of fertilizer. Josh could see no wires, but he could see a small box beside the timer, what he assumed was the pressure switch.

If we move anything, we're dead.

Me. Tabitha. Joseph.

And everybody for a block around here.

Josh stared as the red digits counted inexorably down toward zero, toward the end of their lives. Every instinct screamed for him to take Tabitha and fly out of there to protect his wife at all costs. *We could scoop Joseph up on the way and—No! Tabitha's right.*

We have to stop this bomb. We're the only ones who can.

If *we can.*

Mikey, Stacy, and Marie are still in this building. Somewhere.

And Joseph's not far enough away. Eli just took him outside. Eli's out there, waiting with my son. Waiting for us.

He doesn't know he needs to be farther away from the blast zone. A lot farther.

"Folau's gonna do it," Josh said. "He *will* find Mikey and the girls. Get them clear. He'll get Joseph clear too."

Tabitha squeezed his hand. "I'm sure you're right. I... pray you're right."

But even if Folau can save them, it won't save everyone else. All the people outside. All the people who live around here. All the people who don't even know they're in danger.

It won't save Tabitha.

Please, Heavenly Father. Please. Let this work!

It has to work.

It's all we can think of to do.

The timer counted down, inexorably ticking off the remaining seconds of their lives—of Tabitha's precious life. Of Joseph's life.

He tried and failed to swallow the gigantic lump in his throat. *Give me courage. Help me be as brave as my wife.*

00:00:11

00:00:10

"Do it." Tabitha's voice was calm—as calm as if she were discussing what to make for dinner. "Do it now."

"Okay."

00:00:07

He drew on the Power, more than he'd ever drawn before. He drew and he drew and he drew.

"That's it! The threshold!" Tabitha cried as they reached the level where it felt as if they could do anything together. And yet, it didn't feel as if it were enough. "More!" she yelled. "All of it!"

He pulled the Power past the threshold, far, far beyond it.

The Power was so sweet, so intensely sweet, that it was pure agony. Sweetness and pain such as he had never known, as if every atom in his body were aflame with ecstasy.

"I love you!" Tabitha screamed. Or he screamed. Or they both did.

00:00:04

He enveloped the bomb, all thirty-eight of the fifty-pound sacks of diesel-soaked ammonium-nitrate in the Power. He extended the blanket of protection above it, below it, and all around it, imagining the air molecules congealing into a solid, indestructible mass.

00:00:03

He couldn't see the air solidifying, of course, that was all in his head.

00:00:02

And in his head, wielding Tabitha's Power, Josh squeezed the bomb. He squeezed with all his mind. With all his might. With all his soul.

00:00:01

Let it work!

00:00:00

He saw the spark, and then he saw nothing.

"We've got to get back in there!" Thorpe cried, wringing his boney hands. "We've got to go back and save them!"

"Not yet!" Danny Folau growled through clenched teeth. "I told you. Nobody's going in there until I can get the bomb squad down here."

Danny's ankle hurt like absolute, flaming hell. He had to admit it *had* felt better since Dr. Smith had wrapped it in an Ace bandage. But it still screamed at him.

"Can't tell for sure without an x-ray," the doctor said, giving Danny a few more painful prods with his strong, dark fingers, "but I think it's just a bad sprain." Danny winced as he sat on the grass on the other side of University Avenue, across the street from the Academy building, his legs stretched out in front of him. "Thanks, Doc."

The crowd from the theatre lined the sidewalk, staring at the Academy. Light streamed from a single, shattered door in the front of the old building. It was the door that Thorpe had broken open with a fire axe, allowing the audience, cast, and crew to escape. Once the old guy had figured out that the stout chain wasn't going to break, he'd turned the axe on the wood of the door. There had been, of course, a few injuries as the panicked mob had shoved their way to freedom—at least at first. But after the initial terror subsided and the first few minor injuries, people's better natures had won out. There had even been cries of "Women and children first!" and the crowd had responded accordingly.

At least, that was how Maddie Smith had described it.

Danny hadn't been there, of course. He'd come limping out, carrying Stacy Montrose, while being half-carried by Mikey Montrose who was burdened with her younger daughter. The four had burst from the door several seconds after the distant clock finished chiming the midnight hour.

Mikey Montrose knelt at his side, cradling Joseph Kilmore, the baby still wrapped against the cold night air in the black-and-red vampire cape. Both of Mikey's young daughters sat on either side of their mother, clinging to her. Mikey rocked the baby in her arms. She made cooing noises to comfort the boy. She even smiled through the tears streaming freely down her face.

Danny—ever the cop—had been the one to tell her that her husband was dead. She'd taken the news with far more dignity than Danny had expected. He hadn't told her that J.L. Montrose had been the serial killer, but Danny had the distinct impression that she already knew about that. She'd wept non-stop. She'd been doing that ever since they'd gotten her children to safety. Before their escape, she'd been a lioness protecting her cubs, even saving him after he'd come to save her. But she hadn't screamed or wailed or collapsed as he'd seen other women do when informed of the death of a loved one. Danny had been the one to deliver such news on far too many occasions and he'd seen women do far worse than Mikey Montrose. He'd seen strong men do far worse than Mikey. She simply nodded once, hugged her children, and cried silently for all that she had lost.

She's being strong for her children, Danny thought with no small degree of admiration.

Danny rubbed at his neck. As bad as his ankle hurt, he could still feel the sore spot where Montrose had jabbed him with the needle. He'd been dead, or dead enough, but Dr. Smith and his wife had brought him back to the land of the living. Just in time, too.

But now Josh and Tabitha were still in there, still in the building and that fear ate at him.

"Why hasn't it gone off?" Maddie Smith asked, staring at the as-yet-unexploded building. "You said it was set to go off at midnight." She quickly added, "Not that I want it to go off or anything like that." She checked her watch by the light of the streetlamp. "But it's ten past."

Dr. Smith put an arm around his wife. "Just keep praying, sweetheart. Dracula here said Josh and Tabitha stayed behind to take care of the bomb."

"But how?" Thorpe demanded. "How are they supposed to defuse a bomb?" He turned his still-made-up face and his intense gaze—every bit as creepy and commanding as the vampire he portrayed—on Danny. "You said the bomb couldn't be defused. It had a pressure switch or something. You said it was impossible."

"If anyone can do the impossible," Dr. Smith said, "it's those two." He exchanged a quick, knowing look with his wife.

Thorpe bit his lower lip and shook his head. "Maybe the timer's off. Maybe there's still time! Time to save them. Maybe the killer's watch was slow."

Mikey barked a bitter laugh, shaking her head. "Not slow by ten minutes. J.L. may be many things"—she shuddered—"horrible things, but he knows... he *knew* how to tell time."

Dr. Smith nodded, scowling. "J.L. is—*was* punctual to a fault."

"I'm going back in there!" Thorpe said. "Now!"

No! "You take one step in that direction, sir," Danny barked through his pain, "and I'll arrest you. No one goes in there until the bomb squad—"

"A pox on your bomb squad!" Thorpe snapped. "Have you even called them in? I haven't seen you call anybody."

Danny shook his head. "Montrose smashed my radio. I sent one of the civilians to find a phone. I'll flag down a patrol car when—"

"Do we even have a bomb squad?" Maddie gave him a quizzical look. "In Provo?"

Danny rolled his eyes. "In Salt Lake."

"That's it!" Thorpe growled. "I don't care if you *do* arrest me, I'm—"

"That's enough!" Danny lurched to his feet. He hobbled over to stand before the actor. He had to look up to stare the tall man in the eye. "You think I don't want to go back? That it's not killing me to just sit here waiting?" He stabbed a hand toward the Academy. "Those people are my friends! They're special, dang it! But we have a bomb in there. A big bomb. Big enough to level this whole dang block. And we don't know why it hasn't exploded yet. The *only* reason we're not even farther away is because I don't trust this bunch-a flippin' looky-loos to not wander back into the danger zone." Suddenly tears leaked from his eyes. "I can't save them." *I couldn't save Julie. Or our child.* "I can only try to save these people here. To save you, sir. That bomb could still go off at any moment. Any moment. It's my job to keep you safe. It's my job...my job."

He realized he was sobbing, but he didn't care.

"If only I'd been smarter"—he choked around the bitter words—"if only I'd done my job better, I could've caught this guy. I could've stopped him. I *should* have stopped him."

He felt an arm around him, holding him, comforting him. Golden curls pressed into his shoulder. Tears that were not his own soaked through his shirt.

Without thinking, he put both arms around Mikey Montrose. Mikey still held the baby in one arm, but she clung to Danny with her free arm. Danny felt another pair of small arms encircle one of his legs. He looked down to see five-year-old Stacy Montrose. She looked up at him, new tears coursing down the furrows left by older tears on her young face. "It's okay, Brother Policeman. It's okay to cry."

Marie Montrose, the three-year-old, joined them as well, clinging to her mother's leg.

Together, the four of them wept. The only one not crying was the baby.

"Maybe they're hurt," Thorpe said. "Maybe they need help."

Ah, hell. Danny nodded slowly, then faster, more decisively. He pulled reluctantly out of Mikey's comforting embrace, and out of little Stacy's as well. "Okay. I'm going in." He fixed Dracula with a hard stare. "But just me. I won't risk—"

"I'm going with you." Dr. Smith hefted his black medical bag, his tone blocking any debate. "If they're hurt, they'll need a doctor."

"And if they need to be carried out"—Thorpe pointed to Danny's bandaged ankle—"you're in no shape to carry either one of them to safety."

Danny opened his mouth to protest, but the actor said, "Don't make me punch some sense into you, detective. Because I am perfectly capable of knocking you flat on your ass and *then* going in and doing the right thing."

Danny shook his head, grimacing. "You win, sir. Give me a hand, will you?"

Thorpe nodded. "Certainly. Now that you've come to your senses." Thorpe put a supporting arm around Danny's back, and Danny put his arm around Thorpe. "Let's get moving."

"Just a second." Danny turned his face toward the doctor's wife—the only one of Montrose's victims to ever escape captivity—before tonight, before Tabitha. And Mikey Montrose. "Mrs. Smith?"

"Yes?" Maddie's lip trembled, and even as she answered Danny, her eyes were focused on her husband. "Yes, detective?"

"You're in charge here," Danny said. "Keep these people back, okay?"

Maddie Smith nodded without hesitation. "Yes, sir. Now, Torrance"—a tear rolled down the woman's cheek—"you come back to me. You hear me? Torrance, are you listening?"

Torrance Smith smiled. "Yes, Sweetheart. I promise."

You can't promise that.

"You come back too." Mikey stared intently at Danny.

Danny swallowed the sudden lump that had formed in his throat. "Yes, ma'am." *I'll do my best. I'll come back with Tabitha and Josh.*

And with that, the damaged cop, the vampire actor, and the doctor bishop—turned toward the brooding Academy building.

Supported by Thorpe, Danny limped along as fast as he could on his injured ankle. Each step sent daggers of pain stabbing up his leg, but perhaps because of the tall actor supporting him and perhaps because Danny was finally *doing* something, the pain was somehow bearable. He glared at the Academy as if the building itself were somehow complicit in Montrose's crimes.

Montrose barred up all the first-floor windows and no one noticed.

He must've been planning this for a while. Turned the whole place into a deathtrap. Just another janitor. An invisible man.

The bastard.

Danny pictured Montrose lying face-down in a pool of his own blood, his right hand missing.

Tabitha must've done that with her magic.

A savage smile curled his lips.

Burn in hell, Montrose!

He shook his head violently as if to clear it of dark thoughts, and to shake loose the ghosts of the past and present.

Thorpe glanced at him. "Are you alright, detective?"

"Fine." Danny nodded, then pointed toward the Academy door. "Just keep going."

Dr. Smith eyed Danny with concern. "Are you feeling dizzy? Light-headed? Sleepy?"

Danny shook his head again. "Nope. Fit as a fiddle." *Except for my dang ankle.*

"Well," Smith continued, "you let me know. Because that naloxone I gave you will wear off before the carfentanil is done. You'll need another dose. Probably several. It shouldn't wear off this soon, but that was a nasty dose of opiate you got. You're lucky to be alive. You and Josh. We almost lost you both."

We're not out of the woods yet, Danny thought.

"I'm fine. Uh, thanks for saving my life. You and, uh, Mrs. Smith. I should've said something before."

Smith shook his head. "That's my job. Fighting death. Sometimes death wins. Sometimes I win."

A small part of him understood obsession. Tabitha Kilmore was unique, amazing. Beautiful. Brave. Dark eyes. Raven hair.

Her presence reminded Danny of his wife Julie. Not her looks, but the essence of her. The gentle flame, the wild fire of her soul. He thought of Julie and Tabitha often. But tonight, walking into danger—blue eyes and blonde hair occupied his thoughts.

So lost. So vulnerable. So brave. Mikey Montrose was an incredible woman.

A misstep sent a jolt of agony up his leg, driving away thoughts of Mikey Montrose. He grunted, gritting his teeth against the pain.

As the three men entered through the shattered door of the building, they saw no signs of life. Debris littered the flour, mostly purses and theatre programs. A few candy wrappers. The lights were still on, adding to the feeling of abandonment and desolation.

"Which way?" asked Dr. Smith.

"The basement," replied Thorpe, already moving toward the stairs, hauling Danny along with him.

"Tabitha!" Danny called. "Josh!"

Dr. Smith echoed the cry, but when Thorpe joined in, his booming voice filled the building, echoing down the hallway. "Tabitha! Josh!"

The three of them hurried toward the basement stairs.

"Tabitha!" trumpeted the actor. "Josh!"

"Down here!" The cry was faint, coming up from the stairs. "Hurry!"

Buried. Under rubble. Trapped. Mangled. Danny's thoughts were gruesome.

"We're coming!" Thorpe hoisted Danny, lifting his feet off the floor.

Danny yelped at the shock of being borne along like a rag doll, but in spite of carrying Danny, the tall actor was practically running toward the stairs. Danny's feet only occasionally brushed on the floor. Dr. Smith kept close behind them.

As they descended into the basement, darkness swallowed them. The basement hallway was black, except for the light spilling from two open doors.

Just outside the door on the left, Montrose's corpse lay in a pool of blood. From the door on the right, they could hear Tabitha's anguished cry. "He's not breathing!"

Terror seized Danny in a grip tighter than Thorpe's surprisingly strong hand. *Josh! Josh isn't breathing!*

Dr. Smith sprinted ahead, disappearing into the right-hand door.

Thorpe dragged Danny to the door and set him down to rush forward, leaving Danny to hobble into the room last.

There was no rubble or any sign of a detonation.

Tabitha knelt over Josh's face. She clamped her mouth over her husband's mouth, pinched Josh's nose closed, and blew into his lungs. Josh's chest rose, then fell.

Dr. Smith jabbed a syringe into Josh's arm, then he turned his concerned face toward Tabitha. "Let me take over." He reached for Josh's face, preparing to save Josh for a second time that night.

Tabitha swatted his hands away. "No!" She sealed her mouth over Josh's again and blew once more. When her face came up, Danny could see the tears that smeared her madwoman's makeup. "Please, Josh!" she cried. "Please breathe!"

She turned her face toward Josh again, taking a deep breath, ready to force air into Josh's lungs once more. But a shaky breath stopped her.

Josh's chest expanded. He was breathing. On his own.

"Give him some room," said Dr. Smith.

But Tabitha disregarded the doctor. She bent and wrapped her arms around Josh's neck and lifted him until she held his head against her chest. She kissed his forehead. She shook with sobs that sounded as if they'd been pent up forever and had finally escaped. Between sobs, she kept repeating. "Alive! Alive!"

Josh's eyes fluttered open. He took one deep, shuddering breath, and then tilted his head back. He smiled weakly up at his wife. "Hey," he said, his voice a whisper.

Tabitha smiled as well. "Hey, yourself."

"Got you roses. Lost 'em. Sorry."

"I don't care about roses, you goof."

She bent and kissed Josh. She kissed him as if the two of them were the only people in the room. Danny felt a flush of embarrassment. He averted his eyes, but then his gaze alighted on the pile of ash at the center of the room.

Holy crud.

"Shouldn't we get out of here?" Thorpe said. "The bomb could go off."

Danny shook his head slowly. "We don't have to worry about the bomb anymore."

Where the bomb had been—thirty-eight huge sacks of diesel-soaked fertilizer— only a large mound of ash remained. There was no timer, no pressure switch, no wires. Even the smell of diesel and ammonium-nitrate was gone. Only a vague smell of smoke lingered on the air, as if someone had blown out a lit match.

No bomb. Danny could only stare, open-mouthed. *Holy crud. Holy flippin' crud.*

"Did it work?" Josh's voice sounded stronger. "I guess it worked." He let out a weak laugh at Folau's expression. He sat up and wrapped his arms around his wife.

Tabitha's sobs had turned to laughter. "It worked!" She kissed him again. "And you're alive! Alive!"

"It must've been what you did," Dr. Smith said. He had somehow managed to worm two fingers between the lovers and had laid those fingers against Josh's neck, checking Josh's pulse. "It must've, for lack of a better explanation, caused you to metabolize the naloxone very rapidly. That left only the carfentanil in your system." Still kneeling beside the Kilmores, the doctor pointed up at Danny. "Are you feeling sleepy, detective? Having difficulty breathing? You're going to need another shot before this is over. You've been active, too."

Danny shook his head, turning his eyes back to the ash. "I'm fine. For now."

"I don't understand," Thorpe said. "What happened to the bomb?"

"It was Josh," Tabitha said, still clinging to her husband. "He contained the blast.

Put pressure around it and—"

Josh cut her off with another kiss, then he beamed at her. "It was both of us. *We* did it. Together. Took every last scrap of the Power, more than we've ever— *Way* past the threshold."

Dr. Smith coughed pointedly. "You two are not exactly alone here."

Both Josh and Tabitha looked around. Their eyes fixed first on Danny, and then on Thorpe.

Tabitha chuckled nervously and shrugged. "Oops?"

Thorpe shook his head. "I don't understand. Is there a bomb or isn't there? I mean, I'm glad you're alright, Josh. A-and Tabitha too, of course, but I don't . . ."

Tabitha smiled sheepishly at the professor. "Uh, professor? Eli? Can you... keep a secret?"

The tall professor drew himself up even taller and straighter, looking every whit a Transylvanian nobleman. "Dear lady, I am the very soul of discretion." His tone communicated affronted dignity, but his smile was warm and affectionate.

Josh nodded toward Danny and grinned. "And you can trust our good friend, the detective, too."

Good friend? Does he mean it? And it surprised Danny just how much he suddenly *hoped* Josh Kilmore thought of him as a friend.

"Okay," Tabitha said, sighing dramatically. "I guess we'll have to tell you everything."

Josh nodded. "Everything."

In spite of his throbbing ankle, Danny could not suppress a thrill of anticipation. *Finally!*

"But first," Tabitha said as she and Josh rose unsteadily to their feet, "is my son safe?" She gazed pointedly up at Thorpe.

The actor nodded vigorously, even while his vampire-made-up countenance looked decidedly guilty. "He is in the care of Mrs. Montrose." He winced, even as he uttered the murderer's name. "I know you entrusted him to my care, but she insisted. She was able to comfort him as I could not."

"Mikey's okay?" Tabitha asked, turning to face Danny. "Stacy and Marie?" Her dark-eyed stare pierced Danny to his soul. Those eyes were not accusing or even questioning. They held no doubt. Only confidence.

Confidence in *him.*

"They're safe." Danny flushed at her gaze. "I got them out. Most of the way. I , uh, hurt my ankle." He chuckled, grinning. "Mikey half-carried *me* to safety."

Danny couldn't swallow the lump that seemed to have taken up permanent residence in his throat. "She's a strong woman," he croaked. *An incredible woman. A woman Montrose thought was worthless.*

And Montrose was going to kill her. Called her "worthless." Throw her away.

Tabitha wiped at a fresh tear, further smearing her "Renfield" makeup. "Strong." She nodded, then shook her head. "With what she's lost, she'll have to be."

Dr. Smith—who, Danny reminded himself, was also Mikey's bishop—was standing as well. "She's lost everything. Marriage. Husband. Security. We have to let her know she's not alone. Show her that God has not abandoned her." He looked intently at Danny. "And neither will we."

I don't believe she had any part in all this, but I'm still going to have to investigate her—even if it's only to clear her of suspicion.

And that's just gonna add to her suffering.

Sometimes I just hate my job.

"Look," Josh said, "I'm glad everybody's okay, but we still need to see our son. Hold him, ya know?"

"Exactly!" Tabitha tugged visibly at her husband's hand. "Sweetheart, let's get the heck outta here!" She glanced around the basement storage room—the room that had only minutes before held a bomb, a bomb that had become nothing more than ash. She looked at each of them in turn—Danny, Dr. Smith, and Thorpe—and finally at Josh. "The fastest way possible."

Josh looked at her askance. "You mean…"

She shrugged and grinned at him. "We're going to tell them anyway. Make sure you put us down before we exit the building."

"You heard the lady," Josh said with a wide grin.

And with that, the pair of them lifted into the air and shot through the door.

Thorpe gasped in shock and wonder.

And he wasn't the only one. Even Dr. Smith and Danny gasped.

I swear—that's never gonna get old.

"O brave new world," Thorpe intoned in a reverent voice, "that has such people in't!"

Danny recognized the Shakespearean quote. *The Tempest. Nice. Can't remember who said that one. Miranda? Prospero's daughter? Doesn't matter.* He nodded. "Amen."

Moments later, as the three men made their way out of the Academy—after Dr. Smith had performed an extremely quick and cursory examination of Montrose's corpse—Thorpe asked, "You knew about this? About *them*? Both of you?"

"I suspected," Danny said as he limped along, supported by the tall, surprisingly strong professor. "*Strongly* suspected. But"—he shook his head in wonder—"I never saw it with my own eyes."

Dr. Smith, walking beside Danny, shrugged his broad shoulders. "Not my secret to divulge. Not after they saved Maddie."

Thorpe muttered, "Lord, what fools these mortals be."

Midsummer Night's Dream. Puck.

After they exited the building and were crossing the parking lot toward the crowd on the other side of the street, Danny could clearly see Tabitha and Josh racing ahead of them on foot.

He watched as Tabitha and Josh dashed across University Avenue and snatched their son—from Mikey's arms.

Josh had his arms around his wife and child. He lifted them off the ground and twirled, swinging them around. Danny could hear the joyous laughter. And it smote at his heart. He felt a sharp pang of loss over the child—his and Julie's—that he'd never even gotten to hold.

Mrs. Smith dashed forward as the trio crossed the street. She wrapped her arms around the doctor, kissing him in joy and relief, repeating his name over and over.

Thorpe let go of Danny. "Are you okay to stand, detective?"

Danny nodded. "Good to go." He looked around. "Need to flag down a patrol car. Interview witnesses." His ankle throbbed.

Thorpe eyed him dubiously. "Tonight?"

"Yep. Crime scene." He sighed. *Man! I feel tired.* "Long night." Suddenly, he wasn't just tired—he felt dizzy. "Hey, Doc? I think maybe . . ." But thinking was difficult. So was breathing.

Danny staggered. Someone caught him before he crashed to the ground and eased him on to the grass.

Danny could see the doctor coming toward him, syringe in hand. His vision was fuzzy, but as the needle pierced his shoulder, Danny looked up into the face of his savior. His vision cleared and lovely, blue eyes, soft red lips, fair flawless skin, all framed by waves of golden hair stared down at him.

"Don't worry," Mikey said, smiling down at him through her tears. "I've got you."

And Danny slipped into slumber.

35

"You're doing the show anyway? Tonight?"

The incredulity in her mother's voice coming from the phone made Tabitha laugh. It felt good to laugh. "Well as you well know, Mom, the show must go on!"

"The show must go on," Molly repeated.

Tabitha could almost hear her mother shaking her head. "We talked about it as a cast and crew and—"

"But isn't it a crime scene?" Molly asked. "Don't the police have the whole building taped off?"

"The basement is still taped off." *Where J.L. died.* "The first-floor windows and the phonebooths. And the room where Mikey and the girls were held. But Danny got the rest of the building cleared. He even gave me my broom back."

"So, it's *Danny* now, is it?" The disapproval in Molly's tone was mixed with a healthy dose of worry. "I thought Mike warned you to—"

"Don't worry, Mom. After all we've been through, Danny's a friend. A *true* friend. And I'm still following Daddy's advice. I'm never alone with him." Tabitha smiled. "Besides, I think his attention is drawn *elsewhere*."

"Elsewhere?"

"Yeah. I really shouldn't say anything. But someone has been someone else's knight-in-shining-armor."

"Mikey? But she just lost her husband!"

"Yeah." Tabitha shuddered. "Yeah, she did."

"I mean, I know he was a monster."

"But Mikey didn't know that," Tabitha interrupted. "He was a monster. He threatened their daughters. And things have been difficult between them for a while before all this."

"But still, yesterday, she was married. Today…"

"Oh, she's grieving, Mom. It's bad. And why wouldn't it be? And her little girls— they miss their father. They miss their daddy." *Just like when Jerry left us. When I was six. Stacy's not even that old.*

"I bet they do." Molly's voice was soft. Knowing.

Mom knows exactly what I'm thinking. She knows me too well. "And she can't go out anywhere. The press is camped outside her door, hoping for an interview. Or just a glimpse of the serial killer's widow."

"That's awful. Surely they don't think she had anything to do with it?"

Tabitha sighed. "It sells papers. Boosts ratings. Danny says they have every right to do it, as long as they don't cross onto the sidewalk and into Mikey's yard. Something about a 'public easement.' So, they're on the grass strip between the sidewalk and the street. Vultures. Mikey went out to confront them, to tell them to leave her and her daughters alone. But that didn't do any good."

Molly sighed as well. "Of course, it didn't. Poor thing, and those poor children!"

"Danny spoke to the reporters, though. He said that Mikey was not a suspect or even a person-of-interest, as they say, in the case."

"He spoke to the press? What about his ankle?"

"He's wearing a walking cast and using crutches. But he's *there*, Mom. Protecting Mikey. And Stacy and Marie."

"Wow. That's certainly going above and beyond."

"Yeah. Yeah, it is. The doctor said it was just a bad sprain, not a break, but I don't think even that would've kept him away." Tabitha's eyes welled with tears. "He's a good man. I'm glad she's got him, but…"

"But what?"

"Mikey's going to have to move. Away. Out of town. Even if she wanted to stay, to face the horrible things people are saying—she's that brave—she wouldn't put her girls through that. Mom, he was going to kill those sweet little girls! His own daughters!"

"I know, Tabby-Cat. I know."

Tabitha vainly attempted to clear her throat. "She's going to have to sell her house. And it's gonna take a long time. She won't be able to sell it for what it's worth, either. Probably have to take a loss on it."

"Because, who's going to want to buy the house of a serial killer?" Molly finished for her.

"Exactly." The tears spilled from Tabitha's eyes. "Mom, Mikey doesn't deserve any of this!" She glanced nervously in the direction of the living room. Joseph was still asleep in his playpen. Asleep and safe. Tabitha lowered her voice. "She doesn't."

"Of course not, sweetie."

"It sucks. It completely sucks." In her mind, she cursed J.L. for what felt like the thousandth time.

"How's Josh doing? You said *Danny*"—Molly hesitated over the familiar name—"was up and about. Is Josh okay? Did he go to the hospital?"

"No. Bishop Smith sat up with him all night at our place to make sure he kept breathing. Danny went to the hospital to get his cast on and for observation. He has better insurance than we do."

"But Josh is okay?"

Tabitha smiled and shook her head—even though she knew her mother couldn't see it. "He's at work. We can't afford for him to miss a shift." *Even with the bishop and Maddie's gift.*

"Really? At work? Wow." Molly sighed. "Those Kilmore men! Stubborn as Poplar Bluff Mules and just as strong." She paused. "Hi, honey." Molly then stage-whispered into the phone. "Your daddy's here." Speaking louder again, she said, "We were just talking about you, sweetheart!"

Tabitha could hear Mike Kilmore laughing heartily in the background. "Y'all talkin' 'bout stubborn mules again, huh?"

"You know it!" Molly said. "Mike, they're doing the show tonight!"

For a long moment, there was silence on the other end of the line. Then finally, Mike said, loud and firm, "Good. Just the thing for it."

Tabitha smiled. *Daddy gets it.* "Tell him the show is *sold out*. We barely had half the seats filled last night. Tonight, it's sold out. And Trevor—he's the director—says the entire run is probably going to sell out. He's considering extending the show by another week!"

"She says it's sold out," Molly said, obviously not speaking to Tabitha. "Probably the whole show will sell out. And they may extend a week."

"Don't doubt it," Mike said, still speaking loud enough for Tabitha to hear. "Nothin' sells like sex and murder. Well, murder, in this case." Then he quickly added, "They may be coming because of the headline, sweetie-girl, but they'll stay because of the show." He raised the volume of his voice even higher. "Because my daughter's gonna knock 'em dead! Break a leg, sweetie-girl!"

Molly chuckled. "So, Tabby-Cat, is Josh staying home with the baby tonight?"

"Yeah. Though Mikey insisted she wants to keep on watching Joseph. As long as she's in town, at least." She paused. "Josh is going to watch him tonight, though. Mikey will watch him on Monday. That way, at least Josh will get to stay home and hand out candy to all the cute trick-or-treaters tonight. We're celebrating Halloween tonight—Saturday instead of Sunday. Utah, ya know? I mean, I'm glad I get to do the show, but I'm just a little bit jealous. Just a little."

"So, honey," Mike said, sounding as if he was sharing the phone with Molly, "how much does the press know about your involvement?" Mike's folksy Missouri accent was gone. He was all cop.

Tabitha grunted in disgust. "They know I killed him—killed J.L. That much has leaked out. They don't know how I killed him. Just that I was defending myself and my baby." She glanced again toward the living room. *At least they're not parked outside our door.* The parking lot of the apartment complex being private property, the police had chased the reporters off. "And Danny's advised me to not speak to the press. Says he'll find a truthful way of explaining everything." She rolled her eyes. "Heaven knows what that will be."

"So, he knows?" Molly spoke softly, as if fearing the walls would hear. "Everything?"

"Yup. He knows. And so does Eli Thorpe—Dracula—my professor. And the

THE WITCH AND THE DEVOURER OF SOULS

Smiths, of course."

"Loose lips sink ships," Mike muttered, quoting the World War Two slogan. "The more people who know what you can do…"

"It was unavoidable." *Maybe could've kept some of it back, but they deserved to know.* "And I still have to tell Mikey everything."

"Tabby-Cat," Molly said, "are you sure that's a good idea?"

Tabitha laughed bitterly even as she brushed away another tear. "I have to, Mom. No more secrets between Mikey and me. But I'll probably wait 'til tomorrow. At least. I have to tell her how I killed her husband."

"She's sealed to him, isn't she?" Molly asked.

Tabitha swallowed. "Yeah, I suppose she is. But it can't mean anything. Not after what he did. Can it?"

"Well," Mike said. "She's still covered by the covenant she made to God in the temple. She and her girls. But he broke the covenant. She won't be sealed to him. Not in the eternities." He sighed. "But in any case, she won't have any trouble at all getting a temple annulment. She'll be able to marry again, in the temple. For eternity. To a good man next time. The Lord'll take care of your friend and her girls." The folksy charm was back. "Don't y'all worry 'bout that. You just worry about bein' a good friend, and a good mama. How's my grandson?"

Tabitha let out a shuddering breath. "He's wonderful. No worse after last night."

"Not with you to protect him." Mike's accent had vanished again.

"Speaking of babies, how's my little brother or sister doing?"

"Kicking!" Molly laughed. "A lot. Usually right on my bladder. Kicking a lot harder than you did. At least as far as I remember. Maybe this one will be a boy. Anyway, no worries at all. But I can't travel." Her voice sobered. "Or else I'd be there. You know that."

"We both would," Mike added.

"I know." Tabitha smiled. "But I've got Josh and Joseph. And Heavenly Father. And good friends. We'll be fine. You just take care of him. Or her."

She heard Joseph fussing in the next room. "Gotta go. Baby's awake. I love you both!"

Barely giving her mom and dad a chance to say their loves and goodbyes, Tabitha hung up the phone. She hurried into the living room.

Joseph had rolled over and was lying on his back rubbing his eyes furiously. At the sight of her, however, his fussy, sleep-mussed expression morphed into a huge, two-toothed smile. He squealed with delight.

Tabitha bent and scooped up her son, holding him to her chest. She beamed at Joseph. "Hello, handsome! Are you hungry?"

Joseph gurgled happily and reached for her.

The house was packed. The applause was thunderous. Tabitha was riding high as the curtain closed.

But as the cast was hurrying toward the hallway to greet the audience, she gripped Eli by the arm, stopping him.

Can't put it off any longer.

The Count turned toward her. "Yes, sweet lady? Sweet, brave, powerful lady?" His smile, even through the pale vampire makeup, conveyed concern.

This is going to be so hard!

Tabitha managed an awkward smile. "I, uh, didn't want to tell you before the play tonight, but you need to know."

His eyes widened. "Know what? Are you ill? Has something happened?" He rolled his eyes and shivered. "Of course, much has happened. But—"

"I can't do the Shakespeare company this summer," she blurted out. "I'm sorry, Eli, but I can't."

He nodded slowly. "I see. So much has happened. The horror. The trauma."

Tabitha shook her head. "No. That's not it. Josh, he doesn't…"

Eli nodded again. "Josh has changed his mind."

"No! That's not it either. He was going to work for *J.L.* this summer."

Eli blinked. "Oh. Oh, dear. I see. Well, I do understand." His eyes brightened. "Actually," he said, and waggled a boney finger at her. "I happen to know for a fact that the Shakespearean Company has an opening for a stage manager. I also happen to know for a fact that said position will pay as well or better than any part-time custodial job."

It was Tabitha's turn to blink. "Pay? As in you'd pay him?"

The tall professor drew up to his full height. "I'll have you know, dear lady, that this will be a *professional* theatre company. We already have a number of venues booked. And with the publicity of your"—he spun his hand as if looking for the proper word—"adventures, I'm certain that our box-office take will be stupendous—if I may borrow that word from Mr. P. T. Barnum. There will be, of course, a generous salary for you, too. Commensurate with your leading-lady billing, not to mention a share of the profits, which I expect to be magnificent. Did you actually think that I expected you—*you?*—to work *gratis?*" He lifted his nose so high in the air that Tabitha could see straight up his hair-forested nostrils. "The very idea!"

Then he bent his head and winked at her, grinning widely.

She inclined her head and assumed an expression as calm as a glacial lake. "Very well then, sir, since you put it that way!" She threw her arms around him and hugged him as she bounced on her toes. "I accept!"

He gave her an awkward pat on the shoulder. "Wonderful!"

She released him. Then she grabbed his hand and yanked him toward the hallway. "Come on, Count!"

She tilted back her head and let loose with a Renfield laugh that quickly morphed into a howl of joy. "Massssster! The public awaitssss!"

April 21ˢᵗ, 1983

The ghostly light of the waxing gibbous moon shone over Provo. Tabitha knew it was possible that, she and Josh might be silhouetted against that moon if someone looked up at just the right time.

But in the moment, she didn't care.

She snuggled close to her husband, resting her face on his shoulder. They slowly twirled in the cold night air like the lovers they were. The air at that altitude was freezing. Tabitha was aware of the cold, because the wind whipped her long, black hair, streaming it out behind her, then wrapping it around the pair of them as they floated. But she was not cold. She was warm in Josh's arms and warm in the tingle of the Power she shared with her husband.

"You do realize, my lovely witch," Josh said into her swirling hair, speaking loud enough to be heard above the wind, "our whole world is about to change."

Finals were done, and graduation—for both of them was less than two days away. Freedom. Josh's and Tabitha's parents were both due to arrive at Salt Lake International Airport the following afternoon. Tabitha would finally get to meet her new baby brother-slash-cousin, Michael—named after their father. Molly had won that particular argument, although, to hear Mike Kilmore tell it, there hadn't been much of an argument. As Molly was fond of saying, when it came to the Kilmore men, the Moonshadow women tended to get their way.

A few hours after graduation from the university, Josh would be commissioned a second lieutenant in the United States Air Force—not that he'd be going on active duty before August, but not until after the Wasatch Shakespeare Company had finished its inaugural season. He'd be a *bona fide* Air Force officer with a slot at USAF Undergraduate Pilot Training. Tabitha had already begun rehearsals for *King Lear* as Cordelia and The Fool—and was, in true Tabitha-fashion, already off-book. Josh had worked his last shift as a janitor and on Monday, he'd start his new, temporary, job as stage manager for the Shakespeare Company.

Tabitha sighed contentedly. "Tomorrow, everything changes. But tonight? Tonight, we have this." She turned her head and kissed him, feeling the Power flow through her lips into his. She gazed into his eyes. "I love you, my sexy warlock."

"I love you too." He kissed her again. Then he twirled them around—two dancers spinning across a dancefloor of air—even if Tabitha's feet dangled much higher than his.

She laid her head on his shoulder again. "The movie was fun. Not great, but fun."

"Are you kidding me?" He chuckled. "Vincent Price, Peter Cushing, John Carradine, *and* Christopher-flippin'-Lee! All in one movie! That *alone* was worth the price of the ticket. Mark my words—*House of Long Shadows* is going to be a classic!"

Tabitha laughed. "But Desi Arnaz, Jr.? Surely, they could've come up with someone better than that! I mean, he was the main character, for crying out loud. It was hard to take him seriously. But that ending? Now, *that* was fun."

"A classic. All those horror greats in one place. I'm telling you, twenty years from now—"

Tabitha shook her head. "Twenty years from now, Joseph will be on his mission. Do you realize that? You might be getting close to retirement from the Air Force. And I'll be so old, the only roles I'll get will be for grandmothers! Heck, if Joseph gets married soon after, a couple of years later, and I'll be a grandma for real."

Josh kissed the back of her head. "Sexiest grandma ever!"

She turned her head and nipped playfully at his nose. She missed, of course, but then she grinned and kissed the tip.

He laughed and spun them around again. "Maybe, our grandkids'll call you Granny-Tabby-Cat!"

Tabitha laughed aloud. Then she fixed him with a mockingly severe scowl. "Don't you *dare* teach them that!"

He gave her a wicked grin. "I thought you *liked* that nickname. The 'Tabby-Cat' part at least, not the 'Granny' part."

She laid her head on his shoulder again. "Only when my mom says it. She's the only one who gets to use that name." She snapped her face back toward him, giving him a stern look. "You got that, mister?"

He nodded, grinning widely. "Oh, yeah. Got it." Then he chuckled and mouthed, "Granny-Tabby-Cat."

She growled at him, and then sighed again, her expression sobering quickly. "Do you think Joseph's okay? I mean, he's not used to Maddie yet. Not as his babysitter."

"I'm sure he's fine. Maddie's watched him before. Besides, I told Bishop to just give him some Benadryl, and it'd knock him right out."

"You didn't!"

He shrugged, squeezing her hand and the Power surged a bit. It was nothing like it had been the night they'd contained the bomb-blast, but it was sweet. "Of course not. I didn't have to. Bishop's got all kinds of drugs he can use."

Her jaw dropped. "Oh, you! You're—You're awful!"

He winked at her. "That's me, Mr. Awful."

A sly grin spread across her face. "Soon to be *Lieutenant* Awful."

"That's *Second* Lieutenant Awful, ma'am."

She chuckled. "Picky, picky."

"Hey, I met with Eli today. He briefed me on my new duties. Did he tell you his big idea for *Hamlet*?"

She shook her head. "What big idea?"

"When he makes his entrance as The Ghost, he wants you and me to *fly* him onto the stage."

"He said that?" *We should never have told him about the Power.* "I hope you talked him out of it."

Josh shrugged. "I tried, but he claims nobody will know the difference. They'll think it's just wires. Claims he'll tell everybody that I'm 'running the fly'—whatever that means."

Tabitha sighed. "The *fly* is the area over the stage where the lights and wires are. I think I better have a talk with our dear director about his big idea."

Josh chuckled. "Good luck with that. Old Eli is very persistent." Then his playful expression became serious. "So, uh, did you call Mikey today?"

Tabitha nodded. "Yeah. She's all settled in at her aunt's house in Idaho Falls. She and the girls."

He nodded. "That's good, I guess."

She shook her head sadly. "She couldn't stay here." *The only kids at Stacy's birthday party were Maddie's son and, of course, Joseph and Marie. Not one other child from the ward. Not one.* "She couldn't do that to her girls."

"Nope."

"But I have some good news." Her face brightened. "She got an offer on the house finally."

"Finally." His lips twisted in a sour grimace. "How much is she going to *lose* on it?"

"She's not. Full-asking-price. She said she prayed about it and felt prompted to hold out."

"Full price? Really? How?"

Tabitha nodded. "Seems some movie director from Hollywood is going to buy it—don't ask who. I didn't recognize the name."

"Movie director? Hollywood? Why on earth?"

A number of emotions chased each other across Tabitha's face none of them happy. "It seems he wants to use it as a set for horror movies. Slasher films, probably. You know. Planning on billing it as the actual home of a real-life serial killer. It's sad."

He nodded slowly, his expression thoughtful. "Yeah. But at least she got full price. At least she'll have something to live on until . . ." His voice trailed off.

"Until what?"

"Well, I've got some news of my own." He gave her a sheepish grin. "Well, it's not my news."

"But what? Spill it, mister!"

"Well, I heard it straight from the horse's mouth. You might say the *Tongan* horse's mouth." The corner of his mouth lifted in a sly grin.

"Really?" She gaped at him in wonder as hope flared within her.

"Yep! Danny Folau has taken a position with the Idaho Falls Police Department. He's going to be Chief of Detectives. He leaves for Idaho in two weeks."

"Two weeks? Does Mikey know?"

Josh shrugged. "Maybe. I hope so. He told me he's already bought the ring."

She gaped at him. "The ring? Well, that stinker! He tells you, but not me?"

Josh shrugged again. "He wasn't sure you'd approve."

"Not approve? Are you kidding me?"

"Well, it hasn't even been six months since, uh, J.L. died."

Since I killed J.L., you mean, Tabitha thought. *Since Mikey's life was ripped to shreds.*

"Do you think she's ready?"

"Ready?" Tabitha laughed, shaking her head. "She's so besotted with the man—and he with her... Stacy and Marie love him too." She grinned widely. "I guess they'll have to stop calling him Uncle Danny."

He chuckled. "Last I heard, Marie was still calling him 'Brother Policeman.'"

Tabitha laughed out loud at that. "And Stacy is probably still correcting her and saying"—she raised the pitch of her voice and added a nasal tone, imitating the five-year-old—"It's not Brother Policeman, silly! It's Brother *Detective*-man!"

They laughed together, and Josh twirled them around again.

"Everything's about to change." Josh closed his eyes, his nostrils flaring as he sucked in the cold night air.

Tabitha felt him draw more of the Power. A *lot* more.

They gasped together in sudden delight.

"Not everything." Tabitha trembled in her husband's arms—and not with the cold. "Thank heaven."

"Amen to that."

She put her lips to his ear and whispered, "Ready for the next great adventure, Mr. Kilmore? Soon to be Second Lieutenant Kilmore?"

He laughed softly. "With you, sweetheart, every single, flippin' day"—he gave her a lascivious wink—"not to mention every night—is a new and great adventure." And he kissed her, pulling a surge of the Power, tingling deliciously, through her lips, taking her breath away.

When they broke the kiss—when they came up for air—she said breathlessly, "I suggest we go collect our son—*now*—and get home and"—she gave him a gleaming wink of her own—"celebrate."

He grinned back. "Amen to that!"

THE END

Acknowledgements

When I come to the end of a novel such as this, I inevitably experience a strong (and anatomically infeasible) urge to give myself a firm kick in the behind, because I have once again failed to keep a running list of those who have helped me along the way. As a consequence, I end up wracking my brain as I attempt to recall everyone to whom I should express gratitude. I am absolutely certain I end up forgetting someone. Ah, well. Live and learn. (Except I don't ever seem to learn.) But here goes…

Darren Watts graciously provided his expertise on legal matters. Chris Belt is always my go-to guy in matters of law enforcement, and I needed a lot of help in this area. Also, Special Agent Barry C. Burnette Jr. gave me insights into law enforcement in Provo in the early 1980's. Earle Gardner assisted with research on the old Brigham Young Academy building. Eric D. Huntsman, Ph.D., and Cliff Park consulted on ecclesiastical matters. Week after week, Jay Powell has picked up and dropped off my music folders before Tabernacle Choir rehearsals, saving me time and energy for writing. (This may seem like a small thing, but it was huge.) Dr. Stephen Devenport, M.D., and Dr. William D. Voss, D.O., have been invaluable resources on all matters medical. Dr. Willie Lanier, D.V.M., helped immensely with information about veterinary medicine, particularly Carfentanil. Bram Stoker inspired me at the tender age of nine (when I first read "Dracula"). The Horror Huddle—Alicia Morley Dodson, Brandon Bluhm, Crystal Brinkerhoff, and Dan Earl—are simply the best Latter-day Saint horror beta-readers ever to walk the Earth (or be beamed through cyberspace). The members of the Tabernacle Choir and Orchestra at Temple Square and the directors and staff have inspired me in so many ways (although some of those good folks may find this fact a wee bit disturbing). Mable Belt and Cindy Belt have been my frontline of defense when it comes to proofreading and feedback. My beloved Cindy gets a double mention, because she has been my primary sounding board on this project and my greatest inspiration. A profound thank you to all of you for lifting me and carrying me on your shoulders along this grand adventure.

And finally, I have sought divine help as I've labored on this story, and I humbly thank my Father in Heaven for His loving guidance. I gratefully acknowledge His hand in all things.

About the Author

C. David Belt was born in the wilds of Evanston, Wyoming. As a child, he lived and traveled extensively around the Far East. In Thailand, he once fed so many bananas to a monkey, the poor creature swore off bananas for life. He served as a missionary in South Korea and southern California (Korean-speaking), and yes, he loves kimchi. He graduated from Brigham Young University with a BS in Computer Science and a minor in Aerospace Studies, but he managed to bypass all English and writing classes. He served as a B-52 pilot in the US Air Force and as an Air Weapons Controller in the Washington Air National Guard and was deployed to locations so secret, his family still does not know where he risked life and limb (other than in an 192' wingspan aircraft flying 200' off the ground in mountainous terrain).

When he is not writing, he sings in the Tabernacle Choir at Temple Square and works as a software engineer. He collects and researches swords, spears, and axes (oh, my!), and other medieval weapons and armor. He and his wife have six children (and a growing number of grandchildren) and live in Utah with an eclectus parrot named Mork (who likes to jump on the keyboard when David is writing). There is also a cat, but she can't be bothered to take notice of the parrot, and so that is all the mention we shall make of her.

C. David Belt is the author of *The Children of Lilith* trilogy (*The Unwilling, The Penitent, The Prophecy*), *The Sweet Sister, Time's Plague, The Arawn Prophecy, The Whole Armor of God, The Executioner of God, An Enchantress of Ravens,* and *The Witch of White Lady Hollow.* For more information, please visit www.unwillingchild. com.

Printed in Great Britain
by Amazon

48464655R10169